Mer-Cycle

● ● ●

by Piers Anthony

Tafford Publishing, Inc.
Houston

Tafford Publishing, Inc., P. O. Box 271804,
Houston, Texas 77277

ISBN 0-9623712-6-2
Library of Congress Catalog Card Number 91-65498

Printed in the United States of America
Printed on acid-free paper

Mer-Cycle

Contents

1.   Don..1

2.   Gaspar..16

3.   Melanie 29

4.   Eleph...48

5.   Pacifa..58

6.   Mystery...75

7.   Crevasse..88

8.   City..105

9.   Glowcloud.....................................126

10. Decoy..144

11. Ship...162

12. Splendid..175

13. Minos...189

14. Atlantis..205

15. Crisis..220

16. Mission..237

     Author's Note................................261

Chapter 1

•

Don

Proxy 5-12-5-16-8: Attention.
Acknowledging.
Status?
Four locals have been recruited and equipped. They are waiting for the signal to commence.
They are ignorant of their mission?
They believe they have missions, but none know the true one. They have been given a cover story relevant to their interests. By the time they realize that the cover story is irrelevant, they should be ready for the truth.
Contraindications?
One is an agent of a local government.
Why is this allowed?
The recruitment brought the response of this person. It seemed worth trying. That one can be eliminated if necessary. Such involvement might prove to be advantageous.
With the fate of a world at stake?
We do not know what will be most effective. It is no more risky than the exclusion of such persons might be.
It remains a gamble.
Any course is a gamble.
True. Proceed.
Acknowledged. I will start the first one through the phasing tunnel.

•   •   •

Don Kestle pedaled down the road, watching nervously for life. It was early dawn, and the sparrows were twittering in the Australian Pines as they waited for the picnickers, but nothing human was visible.

Now was the time. He shifted down to second, muttering as the chain caught between gear-sprockets and spun without effect. He still wasn't used to this multiple-speed bicycle, and it seemed to be more trouble than it was worth. He fiddled with the lever, and finally it caught.

He bucked the bike over the bank and into the unkempt grass, moving as rapidly as he could. He winced as he saw his thin tires going over formidable spreads of sandspur, though he knew the stuff was harmless to him and his equipment. That was because, as he understood it, he wasn't really here.

Soon he hit the fine white dry sand. He braked, remembering this time to use the hand levers instead of embarrassing himself by pedaling backwards, and dismounted automatically. Actually it was quite possible to ride over the sand, for it could not toss this bike—but anyone who happened to see him doing that might suspect that something was funny. A bicycle tire normally lost traction and support, skewing badly in such a situation.

In a moment the beach opened out to the sea: typical palm-studded Florida coastline. Seagulls were already airborne, raucously calling out. A sign warned NO SWIMMING, for there were treacherous tidal currents here. That was why Don had selected this spot and this time to make his cycling debut; it was least likely to harbor prying eyes. He had been given a place and a time to be there; his exact schedule was his own business.

The tide was out. Don walked his bicycle across the beach until he reached the packed sand near the small breaking waves. Myriad tiny shells formed a long low hump, and he realized that early-rising collectors could appear at any moment. Why hadn't he thought of that before? Yet when else could he enter the water, clothed and on a bicycle, by daylight? He simply had to risk it.

Beyond the shell ridge, the sand was wet and smooth. He looked carefully, both ways, as if crossing a busy intersection. Was he hoping that there would be someone, so that he would have to call it off?

No, he *wanted* to do it, Don reassured himself. In any event, his timing was such that he could not spare the hours an alternate approach would require. He had chosen dawn at this beach, and now he was committed. He had been committed all along. It was just that—well, a bit hard to believe. Here he was, a healthy impetuous fair-complexioned beginning archaeologist with a bicycle—and a remarkable opportunity. What could he do except grasp it, though he hardly comprehended it?

Don remounted and pushed down hard, driving his machine forward into the flexing ocean. The waves surged through the wheels, offering no more resistance than air. He moved on, feeling the liquid against his legs as the force of gentle wind. He didn't really need more power, but he shifted into first anyway, bolstering his confidence. It remained hard to believe that he was doing this.

The bottom dropped, and abruptly he was coasting down into deeper water. Too fast for his taste. Now he did backpedal, futilely. There was no coaster brake on this machine!

The water rose up to his thighs, then his chest, then his neck. Still he coasted down. In another instant it was up across his face, and then it closed over his head. Don did not slow or float; he just kept going in.

He could see beneath, now. There was a rocky formation here, perhaps formed of shell. He would have investigated the local marine terrain more carefully, if only he had had time. But the whole thing had been set up so rapidly that he had barely had time to buy his bike before going through the tunnel. Now here he—

He realized that he was holding his breath. He forced himself to breathe, surprised in spite of himself that he still could do it. He had tested it by plunging his head into a tub of water, but somehow the surging sea water had restored his doubt. He applied his handbrakes.

The bicycle glided to a halt. Don braced it upright by spreading his legs, and rested in place for a moment with his eyes closed. This way he could breathe freely, for he couldn't see the surrounding water.

Don found himself cowering. He knew he was not physically courageous, but this seemed to be an overreaction. In a moment he realized why: it was the noise.

He had somehow imagined that the underwater realm was silent. Instead it was noisier than the land. Some was staccato sound, some was whistling, and some was like the crackling of a hot frying pan. Grunts, clicks, flutters, swishes, honks, rattling chains, cackling hens, childish laughter, jackhammers, growls, knocking, whining, groaning, mouse squeaks—it all merged into a semi-melodious cacophony. He had no idea what was responsible for the assault, but was sure that it couldn't all be inanimate. The nearest commercial enterprise was twenty miles away!

Could fish talk? Probably he would soon find out. It would be no more fantastic than the other recent developments of his life.

He was way under the water, standing and breathing as if it didn't exist. How had he gotten into this?

"Well, it all started about twenty three years ago when I was b-born," he said aloud, and laughed. He was not unduly reflective, but he did stutter a bit under tension. So maybe it wasn't really funny.

Don opened his eyes.

He was down under, all right. He could see clearly for perhaps twenty feet. Beyond that was just bluegreen water-color wash. Above him, eight or ten feet, was the restless surface: little waves cruising toward ruin against the beach. Beneath him was a green meadow of sea grass, sloping irregularly down.

Now that he was stationary, he did not feel the water. He waved his hands, and they met no more resistance than they might have in air. It was warm here: about 88° Fahrenheit according to the indicator clipped to his bicycle. The temperature of sub-tropical coastal water in summer. He would be able to work up a sweat very quickly—unless he chose to descend to the deeper levels where the water got cold. He did not choose to do so, yet. Anyway, he was largely insulated from the water's temperature, as he was from its density. That was all part of the miracle of his situation.

A small fish swam toward him, evidently curious about this weird intruder. Don didn't recognize the type; he was no expert on marine biology. In fact he didn't know much about anything to do with the ocean. It was probably a nondescript trash fish, the kind that survived in these increasingly polluted waters. This one looked harmless, but of course even the deadliest killer shark was not harmful to him now. He was really not in the water, but in an aspect of reality that was just about 99.9% out of phase with what he saw about him. Thus the water had the effective density of air.

In impulse, he grabbed at the fish as it nosed within reach. His hand closed about its body—and passed through the flesh as if it were liquid foam. The bones of his fingers hooked into the bones of its skeleton without actually snagging.

Don snatched his hand away. Equally startled, the fish flexed its body and shot out of range. There had been a kind of contact, but not one that either party cared to repeat. No damage done, but it had been a weird experience.

It was one thing to contemplate a reality interaction of one part in a thousand, intellectually. It was quite another to tangle with a living skeleton.

Well, he had been warned. He couldn't stand around gawking. He had a distance to travel. The coordinate meter mounted beside the temperature gauge said 27°40′—82°45′. He had fifteen hours to reach 27°0′—83°15′ He had been told that a degree was sixty minutes, and a minute just about a mile, depending on location and direction. This sounded to his untrained ear like a mishmash of temperature, time, and distance muddled by an incomprehensible variable. It seemed that he had about thirty miles west to go, and about forty south, assuming that he had not become hopelessly confused. The hypotenuse would be fifty miles, per the three-four-five triangle ratio. Easy to make on a bicycle, since it came to only three and a third miles per hour average speed.

Of course he probably wouldn't be able to go straight. What was his best immediate route?

He didn't want to remain in shallow water, for there would be bathers and boaters and fishermen all along the coast. His depth meter showed two fathoms. That would be twelve feet from bike to surface. Entirely too little, for he must be as visible from above as those ripples were from below. How would a boater react if he peered down and saw a man bicycling blithely along under the water?

But deep water awed him, though he knew that pressure was not a significant factor in this situation. Men could withstand several atmospheres if they were careful, and he had been told that there were no depths in the great Atlantic Ocean capable of putting so much as two atmospheres on him in his phased-out state. He could ignore pressure. All of which somehow failed to ease the pressure on his worried mind. This business just wasn't *natu-*

ral.

He would take a middle course. Say about a hundred feet, or a bit shy of seventeen fathoms. He would stick to that contour until he made his rendezvous.

Don pushed on the left pedal—somehow that was his only comfortable starting position—and moved out. The seagrass reached up with its long green leaves, obscuring his view of the sloping floor. But his wheels passed through the weeds, or the weeds through the wheels, and so did his body. There was only a gentle stroking sensation that affected him with an almost sexual intimacy as plant collided with flesh. The grass might be no denser than the water, but it was solid, not liquid, and that affected the contact.

He didn't like it, this naked probing of his muscle and gut, but there was nothing he could do about it. Except to get out of this cloying patch of feelers.

At nine fathoms the grass did thin out and leave the bottom exposed. It needed light, and the light was dimming. Good enough. But this had a consequence for Don, too. Just below the surface things had looked normal, for the limited distance he could see. Now the color red was gone. It had vanished somewhere between three and four fathoms, he decided; he hadn't been paying proper attention. He had a red bag on his bicycle that now looked orange-brown. The effect was eerie and it alarmed him despite his awareness of its cause.

"S-steady," he told himself. "The water absorbs the red frequencies first. That's all there is to it. Next orange will go, then yellow, then green. Finally it will be completely dark." He found his heart pounding, and knew he had succeeded only in bringing out another fear. He just didn't feel safe in dark water.

He had somehow supposed that the ocean floor would be sandy and even, just like a broad beach. Instead it was a tangled mass of vegetation and shell—and much of the latter was living. Sponges grew everywhere, all colors (except red, now) and shapes and sizes. His wheels could not avoid the myriad starfish and crablike creatures that covered the bottom in places.

But at least he was getting his depth. The indicator showed ten fathoms, then fifteen, then twenty. Down far enough now to make headway toward the rendezvous.

But he had to go deeper, because the contour would have taken him in the wrong direction. He had been naive about that; if he tried to adhere strictly to a given depth, he would be forced to detour ludicrously. The ocean bottom was not even; there were ridges and channels, just as there were on land.

The medley of mysterious sounds had continued, though he had soon tuned most of it out. Now there was something new. A more mechanical throbbing, very strong, pulsing through the water. Growing. Like an approaching ship.

A ship! He was in the harbor channel for the commercial ships using the port of Tampa. No wonder he had gotten his depth so readily.

Don turned around and pedaled madly back the way he had come. He had to get to shallow water before that ship came through, churning the water with its deadly screws. He could be sucked in and cut into shreds.

Then he remembered. He was out of phase with the world; nothing here could touch him. He had little to fear from ships.

Still, he climbed out of the way. A ship was a mighty solid artifact. The hull would be thick metal—perhaps solid enough to interact with his bones and smash him up anyway. After all, the bicycle's wheels interacted with the ocean floor, supporting him nicely. Could he expect less of metal?

The throbbing grew loud, then terrible. There was sound throughout the sea, but the rest of it was natural. Now Don appreciated the viewpoint of the fish, wary of the alien monsters made by man, intruding into the heart of their domain. But then it diminished. The ship had passed, unseen—and he felt deviously humiliated. He had been driven aside, in awe of the thing despite being a man. It was not a fun sensation.

Don resumed his journey. He followed the channel several miles, then pulled off it for a rest break. The coordinate meter said he had traversed only about four minutes of his fifty, and he was tiring already. He was wearing himself down, and he had hardly started. Cross-country underwater biking was hardly the joy that travel on land-pavement was.

Wouldn't it be nice if he had a motorcycle instead of this pedaler. But that was out of the question; he had been told, in that single compacted anonymous briefing, that a motor would not function in the phase. So he had to provide his own power, with a bicycle being the most efficient transportation. He had accepted this because it made sense, though he had never seen his informant.

Something flapped toward him. Don stiffened in place, ready to leap toward the bike. He felt a chill that was certainly not of the water. The thing was *flying*, not swimming! Not like a bird, but like a monstrous butterfly.

It was a small ray, a skate. A flattened fish with broad, undulating, winglike fins. All quite normal, nothing to be alarmed about.

But Don's emotion was not to be placated so simply. A skate was a thing of inherent terror. Once as a child he had been wading in the sea, and a skate had passed between him and the shore. That hadn't frightened him unduly at the time, for he had never seen one before and didn't even realize that it was really alive. But afterwards friends had spun him stories about the long stinging tail, poisonous, that could stun a man so that he drowned. And about the creature's cousins, the great manta rays, big as flying saucers, that could sail up out of the water and smack down from above. "You're lucky you got out in time!" they said, blowing up the episode as boys did, inventing facts to fit.

Don had shrugged it off, not feeling easy about taking credit for a bravery he knew he lacked. But the notion of the skate grew on him, haunting him retrospectively. It entered his dreams: standing knee-deep or even waist-deep in a mighty ocean, the lone small beach far away, seeing the devilfish, being cut off from escape, horrified at the approach of the stinger but afraid to wade out farther into that murky swirling unknown. But the ray came nearer, expanding into immensity, and he had to retreat, and the sand gave way under his feet, pitching him into the abyss, into cold smothering darkness, where nothing could reach him except the terrible stinger, and he woke gasping and crying.

For several nights it haunted him. Then it passed, being no more than a childish fancy he knew was exaggerated. He never had liked ocean water particularly—but since he didn't live near the shore, this was no handicap. For fifteen years the nightmare had lain quiescent, forgotten—until this moment.

Of course the creature couldn't get at him now, any more than it could have in the dream. Not when its body was phased out, with respect to him, to that one thousandth of its actual solidity. Or vice versa. Same thing. Let it pass right through him. Let it feel the brushing of bones.

The skate veered, birdlike—then came back unexpectedly. It was aware of him. Without conscious volition Don was on the bike and pedaling desperately, fleeing a specter that was only partly real. The thing's flesh might be no more than a ghost to him, but that very insubstantiality enhanced the effect. The supernatural had manifested itself.

Adrenaline gave him strength. By the time he convinced himself that the skate was gone, he was miles farther along. He had never been overly bold, but this episode had certainly given his schedule a boost.

Next time, however, he would force himself to break out his camera and take a picture. He couldn't afford to run from every imaginary threat.

He had lost track of the channel. The meter now read eight fathoms. He had moved about three minutes west, and would have to bear mainly south henceforth. But he could use some deeper water, as patches of weed still got in his way.

But deep water was not to be found. Sometimes it was nine or ten fathoms, but then it would shrink to six. He had to shift gears frequently to navigate the minor hills and dales of this benthic terrain, for he was tired. The wind—really the currents of the water—made significant difference. Some spots were hot, others cool, without seeming pattern. Some were darker, too, as if polluted, but this could have been the effect of clouds cutting off the direct sunlight.

Don was tired of this. The novelty had worn off quite quickly. His time in the water had acclimated him; what could there be in the depths more annoying than this? He cut due west again, knowing that there had to be a descent at some point. The entire Gulf of Mexico couldn't remain within ten fathoms.

His legs protested, but he kept on. Miles passed—and gradually it did get deeper. When he hit fifteen fathoms he turned south, for he was now almost precisely north of his target area.

There was still enough glow for him to see by, which was good, because he didn't want to use his precious headlamp unnecessarily. Actually this objection was nonsensical, he realized, because it had a generator that ran from his pedaling power. But he was still having trouble overcoming his lifelong certainties: such as the fact that one could use a flashlight only so long before the battery gave out. Besides, a light might attract larger creatures. He didn't care how insubstantial they might be; he didn't want to meet them.

Don had thought it ridiculous to enter the water fifty miles from his destination, and doubly so to do it alone. What did he know about the ocean? But now he was able to appreciate the rationale. He had a lot of mundane edges to smooth before he could function efficiently in this medium. Better to work it out by himself, and let the others do likewise; then they would all three be broken in and ready to function as a team, minus embarrassments. That was the number he had guessed; each would have a relevant specialty for the mission. Strangers, who would get along, perforce.

Reassured, he stopped for lunch. Actually it was only nine a.m. and he had been under the water about three hours. But it seemed like noon, and he needed a pretext to rest.

There was a radio mounted within the frame of his bicycle. It was not for news or entertainment, but for communication with his companions, once he had some. He didn't see the need for it, as sound crossed over perfectly well. But of course there could be emergencies requiring separation of a mile or two. The radios would not tune in the various bands of civilization, he had been told; they were on a special limited frequency. But they should reach as far as necessary.

Idly, he turned the ON switch. There was no tuning dial or set of station buttons; all he would get from this thing would be an operative hum.

"Hello," a soft feminine voice said.

Surprised, Don didn't answer.

"Hello," she repeated. Still he was silent, having no idea what to say, or whether he should speak.

"I know your set is on," the voice said. "I can hear the sea-noises in the background."

Don switched off. There wasn't supposed to be anybody on the line! Especially not a woman. Who was she, and what did she want?

By the coordinates, he had come barely ten or twelve miles. It was hard to figure, and not important enough to warrant the necessary mental effort. Three or four miles an hour, average. On land, the little distance he had gone, he was sure his rate had been double or triple that. He could have walked as fast, down here. And with less fatigue.

No, that was not true. He had to be honest with himself. He was carrying considerable weight in the form of food and clothing and related supplies. He even had a small tent. Then there was the converter: portable plumbing. And complex miniaturized equipment to keep the humidity constant, or something. His instrumentation was formidable. That coordinate meter was no two-bit toy, either. He had not known that such things existed, and suspected their cost would have been well beyond his means. Regardless of their miniaturization, they weighed a fair amount. His bicycle weighed about forty pounds, and the other things might total a similar amount. Half his own weight, all told. He would have felt it, hiking, and would not have been able to maintain any four miles an hour.

Naturally the bike was sluggish. Even the quintuple gearing could not ameliorate weight and terrain and indecision. Once he found a good, smooth, level stretch without weeds or shells, he could make much better time.

Even so, he was on schedule. Fortunately he was in good physical condition, and recovered quickly from exertion. How good his mental state was he wasn't sure; small things were setting him off unreasonably, and he was hearing female voices on a closed-circuit radio.

He unpacked the concentrates, having trouble finding what he wanted. These were supposed to be packages of things that expanded into edibility when water was added.

He had a bulb of water: a transparent pint-sized container. There was a second pint in reserve. After that he would have to go to recycled fluid, a prospect he didn't relish.

There were a number of things about this business that did not exactly turn him on. But two things had overwhelmed his aversions: the money and the chance to be involved in something significant. The mission, he had been told, would be done within a month, and the pay matched what he would have had from a year with a good job in his specialty. And if he did not agree that it was a mission he was proud to be associated with, that pay would double. The money had been paid in advance, in full; there was no question about that. So he had been willing to take the rest on faith, and to put up with the awkward details. They were, after all, necessary; he could not drink the water of the sea because it was both salty and phased out, and he could not eat the food of it either. He had to be self sufficient, except for the supplies which would be found in depots along the way.

Don inserted the syringe into the appropriate aperture of his food-packet and squeezed. The wrapping inflated. The principle was simple enough; he could have figured it out for himself if he had not been told, and there were instructions on the packets. He kneaded it, feeling the content solidify squishily. He counted off one minute while it set. His meal was ready.

He tore along the seam, exposing a pinkish mass. Cherry flavored glop, guaranteed to contain all the essential nutrients known to be required by man, plus a few good guesses. Vitamins A, B, C; P and Q; X, Y, and Z? It looked like puréed cow brains.

Don brought it cautiously to his nose and sniffed. Worse. Had he done something wrong? This smelled as if he had used urine as the liquid ingredient. He would never make his mark as a chef!

He suppressed his unreasonable revulsion and took a bite. After all, what could go wrong with a prepackaged meal? He chewed.

He spat it out. The stuff was absolutely vile. It tasted like rotten cheese laced with vinegar, and his stomach refused to believe it was wholesome. He deposited the remains in the converter, for even this must not be wasted.

Now he had sanitary needs. The hard labor of travel had disturbed his digestion. Or was it the experience with the foul glop? No, neither; it was the emotional strain of traversing the ocean floor in this remarkable phase state. He had practiced breathing in that tank of water, just after tunneling through, so that he had known it was feasible. But that had hardly prepared him for the psychological impact of pedaling a bicycle under the heaving sea.

He had to admit that this was an interesting adventure, even in its bad aspects. He knew already that he would not be demanding double pay. He had not been told he would *like* every aspect, just that it would be significant, and *that* it was.

He wound up with a plastic bag of substance. He hesitated, then reluctantly deposited it, too, in the converter. This stuff was in phase with him, and there was not much way to replace it; it must not be wasted. The unit would process it all, powered by a spur from his pedaling crank just below, reducing the solids to ash and filling another pint container with potable water.

Water, water, everywhere—how odd that he should be immersed in it, yet have to conserve it rigidly lest he dehydrate. There was a dichotomy about this phaseout that he wasn't clear about. The sea was like air to him, yet it remained the sea to its denizens. Fish could and did swim right through him and his bicycle without falling or gasping for gill-fluid. So it wasn't air at all, merely water at one one-thousandth effective density. *So how was he able to breathe it?* That little matter had not, in the rush, been clarified.

Don was no chemist, but he knew that H_2O did not convert to—what was it? N_4O? No, air wasn't that kind of combination, it was just a mixture of gases. Anyway, the O, for oxygen, in H_2O could not be assimilated for respiration. He knew that much. Water vapor wasn't breathable. Even the fish had to sift their oxygen from the air dissolved in water, not the water itself. Yet even if he could have breathed the water, he would have been getting only one thousandth of the oxygen it contained, or maybe one five-hundredth what he was accustomed to. That was extremely slim pickings.

He was wasting time. He had perhaps forty miles to go yet—a good four or five hours even on a decent surface. Twelve hours at his present rate. Which left him no time at all to rest or sleep. He had to keep moving.

Maybe his contact was expecting him. Was he in radio range? He flicked the radio switch.

"Now don't turn me off," the female voice said, "before I—" But he had already done so.

Now as he rode he tried to analyze his motive. Why did he object to hearing from a woman? So maybe she had somehow tuned in on this private band; that did not make her a criminal. She evidently had some notion where he was. What harm would there be in talking with her?

He got under way and tuned out the scenery. Not that he had paid much attention to it so far. What had he seen, actually? Fish, sponges, a blur of water, the shift of digits on the meters, and the irregular terrain of the sea floor.

Somehow the radio voice seemed one with the scenery. Both needed to be tuned out. Yet he knew that this was nonsensical. The scenery was already over-familiar, but the woman was a stranger. Why wouldn't he talk to her?

He realized that he couldn't blame it on the secrecy of the mission, because he knew no secrets yet, and was not responsible for radio security. It was the fact that she had caught him by surprise, and that she was a sweet-voiced young woman. That voice conjured a mental image of an attractive creature—the kind that paid no attention to a studious loner like him. So he had tuned out immediately, rather than get involved and risk the kind of put-down that would inevitably come. It was a virtually involuntary reflex.

So now he understood it. That didn't change it. He was afraid to talk to her.

He moved, he rested, he moved less, he rested more, he ground on, he tried another meal—and quickly fed it into the converter. It *couldn't* be his imagination! That food was spoiled. Fortunately his appetite was meager.

Don woke from his travel-effort oblivion to see to his dumbfounded joy that he had picked up on his schedule and could afford an hour's break. So he propped his bike, lay down on the strangely solid sand, and sank into a blissful stupor until the alarm went off. The world outside his little sphere became as unreal as it seemed.

Just so long as he didn't miss his rendezvous. He thought of himself as a loner, but that was mainly with respect to women. He had been alone more than enough, in this odd region on this strange mission.

He made it. He was on 83°15′ west longitude already, and bearing down on 27° north latitude. It was a few minutes (time, not distance) before nine in the morning. Nothing was visible, of course. It was dark above, and even with his headlight on he could not see far enough to locate anything much smaller than an active volcano. Water in his vicinity might feel like air, but it still dampened vision in its normal fashion. Except that the lamp restored full color, blessedly. Even if he could have seen for miles, the problem of pinpoint location would be similar to that in a dry-land wilderness. His meter was not that precise.

As his watch showed the moment of scheduled contact, Don stood still and listened. The ever-present noises of the sea crowded in annoyingly. Sound: there was the key. Here in the ocean, sound traveled at quadruple its speed in air, and it carried much better. Light might damp out, and radar, but sound was in its element here. Make a noise in the sea and it would be heard.

Don heard. It was the faint beep-beep of a signal no marine creature made—he hoped. It was Morse Code. And it had an echo: the slower arrival of the impulse through the air of the phase?

When it paused, he answered. He did not know Morse himself, except as a typical pattern of dots and dashes, so he merely sounded three blasts on his whistle. After a moment the same signal was returned.

Contact had been made.

Chapter 2

•

Gaspar

Proxy 5-12-5-16-8: Attention.

Acknowledging.

Status?

The first three recruits have been sent through the phase tunnel and the fourth alerted. The mission is proceeding as designed.

Contraindications?

The first recruit refuses to hold a radio dialogue. This may indicate an intellectual problem that did not manifest itself on the initial screening. He is otherwise normal, and seems to be pursuing the mission in good faith. The second recruit is more assertive, and may override this attitude or incapacity in the first. This foible does not appear to pose a threat to the mission.

There are always peculiarities of local situations. If this is the extent in your case, you are well off. 5-12-5-16-9 has a suicidal recruit.

That world may be lost!

Not necessarily. A suicidal person may be in a position to understand the loss of a world.

And may not care.

True. But what we offer does seem preferable to complete destruction.

•   •   •

"Gaspar Brown, marine geologist," the man said. He was short and fairly muscular, dark-haired and swarthy and looked to be in his mid thirties.

"Don Kestle, archaeologist," Don responded. "Minoan."

The bicycles drew together and the men reached across to shake hands. Don was phenomenally relieved to feel solid flesh again. He found himself liking Gaspar, though he had never met the man before. At this stage he liked anything human. The specters of his loneliness had retreated immeasurably.

"S-so you know about the ocean," Don said, finding nothing better as conversation fodder at the moment. He had never been much for initiating a relationship, and hoped Gaspar was better at it.

"Almost nothing."

"W-what?"

"I know almost nothing about the ocean," Gaspar said, "compared to what remains to be discovered. I can't even identify half these fish noises I'm hearing. They're much louder and clearer and more intricate than normal."

Don smiled weakly. "Oh. Yes."

"That's why I welcome this opportunity to explore," Gaspar continued, warming. "This way we don't disturb the marine creatures, so they don't hide or shut up. Think of it: the entire ocean basin open to us without the problems of clumsy diving suits, nitrogen narcosis, or the bends."

"N-nitrogen—?"

"You know. Rapture of the deep. Nitrogen dissolves in the blood because of the pressure, and this makes the diver drunk. This can kill him faster than alcohol in a driver, because it's himself at risk, not some innocent pedestrian. So he comes up in a hurry, and that nitrogen bubbles out of his blood like the fizz in fresh soda, blocking blood vessels or lodging in joints and doubling him up like—"

"You're right," Don agreed quickly. "Nice not to have to worry."

"Hey, have you eaten yet? I've been so excited just looking around I haven't—"

"W-well, I—" Don was abashed to admit his problem with the food, so he concealed it. "I haven't eaten, no." Gaspar was carrying the conversational ball, and that was a relief. Don was happy to go along, letting his compliance pass for social adequacy. Once he knew a person, it was easier.

"Great." Gaspar hauled out his packages and chose one. "Steak flavor. Let's see whether it's close."

Don dug out a matching flavor from his pack, not commenting. If Gaspar could eat this stuff . . .

They squeezed the bulbs and the packages ballooned. Gaspar opened his first and took a bite. He chewed. "Not bad, considering," he said. "Not close, but not bad. Maybe it would be closer if it didn't have the texture of paste. Better than K-rations, anyway."

Don got a grip on his nerve and opened his own. The same rotten odor wafted out.

"Hey, is your converter leaking?" Gaspar inquired.

"Not that I know of. Why?" As if he didn't know!

"That smell. Something's foul. No offense."

Wordlessly Don held out his package.

Gaspar sniffed, choked, and took it from him. In a moment it was in the converter. "You got a bad one! Didn't you know?"

"They're all like that, I thought. I was afraid—"

"They can't be! These things are sterile. Let me check."

"B-be my guest."

Gaspar checked. "What a mess! I can tell without having to use the water. Did you actually eat that stuff?"

"One bite."

Gaspar laughed readily. "You've got more grit than I have. What a rotten deal! Have some of mine."

Don accepted it gratefully. Gaspar's cherry glop tasted like cherry, and his steak like steak. Texture was something else, but this wasn't worth a quibble at this stage.

"H-how do you think it happened?" Don asked as his hunger abated.

"Oh, accident, I'd say," Gaspar decided. "You know the government. Three left feet at the taxpayer's expense. We'll share mine, and we'll both reload at the first supply depot. No trouble, really."

The man certainly didn't get upset over trifles. But Don wondered what kind of carelessness would be allowed to imperil this unique, secret mission, not to mention his life. For a man had to eat, and they could only assimilate food that had been phased into this state.

"Is it a government operation?" Don asked. "I thought maybe a private enterprise."

Gaspar shrugged. "Could be. I wasn't told. But somebody went to a pretty formidable expense to set us up with some pretty fancy equipment. If it's not the government, it must be a large corporation. This looks like a million dollar operation to me, apart from what they're paying us. But you're right: the big companies get criminally sloppy too. It could be either. Let's hope their quality control is better on the other stuff."

That reminded Don about the female voice on his radio. Had it been mistuned, so that it connected to someone not with this mission? If so, he had been right to cut off contact, though that was not why he had done it. Obviously that person wasn't Gaspar. Did she speak on both their radios, or only his own? Or had he imagined it? Should he ask?

Yes, he should. "D-did you t-turn on your—?"

"Say, look at that!" Gaspar cried.

Don looked around, alarmed. It was a monstrous fish, three times the length of a man, with a snout like the blade of a chain saw.

"Sawfish," Gaspar exclaimed happily. "Isn't she a beauty! I never saw one in these waters before. But then I never rode a bike here before, either. My scuba gear must have scared them away. What a difference that phase makes. Not that I'm any ichthyologist."

"I thought sea-life was your specialty."

"No. The sea *bottom.* I can tell you something about rock formations, saline diffusion, and sedimentary strata, but the fauna I just pick up in passing. I know the sawfish scouts the bottom— see, there she goes, poking around—and sometimes slashes up whole schools of fish with that snout, so as to eat the pieces, but that's about all. Relative of the rays, I believe."

That ugly chill returned. The fish was horizontally flattened, with vaguely winglike fins. It did resemble a skate, from the right angle.

"Y-you know, w-we aren't completely apart," Don said. "The bones—they interact—"

"Oh, do they?" Gaspar asked, as if this were an interesting scientific sidelight. As of course it was, to him. "I suppose they would, being rigid. There has to be some interaction, or we would sink right through the ground, wouldn't we? In fact, I'm surprised we don't; it isn't that solid, normally. Sediment, you know."

The sawfish vanished, and Don was vastly relieved. "You're right! If we intersect the real world by only a thousandth, why don't we find the sand like muck? If anything, it's harder than it should be. My tires don't sink into it at all. And how is it we can see and hear so well? I should think—"

"I'm no nuclear physicist, either. I have no notion how this field operates, if it is a field—but thank God for its existence."

"Maybe it isn't exactly a field," Don said. He was glad to get into something halfway technical, because it was grist for conversation, and he was curious himself. "Why should we have to ride through that tunnel-thing—you did do that?—to enter it, in that case? But if we were shunted into another, well, dimension—"

"Could be." Gaspar considered for a moment. "Maybe one of the others will know. I'm just glad it works."

"Others? I thought this was a party of three."

"Oh? Maybe you're right. I wasn't told, just that there would be more than one. I thought maybe four." Gaspar seemed to side-step any potential disagreement, inoffensively. "Do you happen to know his specialty?"

"Me? That official was so tight-lipped I was lucky to learn more than my own name. And we're not supposed to tell each other our last names, I think."

"Necessary security, I suppose," Gaspar said. "I clean forgot. Well, you just forget mine, and I'll forget yours. Did you get to see anyone?"

"No, it was just an interviewer behind a screen. A voice, really; it could almost have been a recording."

"Same here. I responded to this targeted ad on my computer, and the pay and conditions—I was about ready for a job change anyway. I still don't know what the mission is, but I'm already glad I'm here." He glanced at Don. "How'd you get into this project, anyway? No offense, but archaeology is mostly landside, isn't it? Digging trenches through old mounds, picking up bits of pottery, publishing scholarly reports? There can't be much for you, under the sea."

"That's a pretty simple view of it," Don said, glad to have a question about his specialty. His reticence faded when he was in his area of competence. "But maybe close enough. The fact is, a great many archaeologists have combed through those mounds and collected that pottery, on land. They've reconstructed some fabulous history. If I could only have been with Bibby at Dilmun . . ." He sighed, knowing that the other would not comprehend his regret. No sense in getting into a lecture. "But I came too late. Today the major horizon in archaeology is marine, and the shallow waters have been pretty well exploited, too. No one knows how thoroughly the Mediterranean Sea has been ransacked. So that leaves deep water, and I guess you know better than I do why that's been left alone."

"Pressure," Gaspar said immediately. "One atmosphere for every thirty four feet depth. A few thousand feet down—ugh! But I was asking about *you*. I don't want to seem more nosy than I am; I just think we'd better have some idea why and how we were picked for this mission. Because the sea is formidable, even phased out as we are; make no mistake about that. The depths are a greater challenge than the moon. So it figures that the most qualified personnel would be used."

Don laughed, but it was forced. "I—I'm the *least* qualified archaeologist around. My only claim to fame is that I can read Minoan script, more or less—and there's precious little of that hereabouts."

"I'm not the world's most notable marine geologist, either," Gaspar agreed. "Any major oil company has a dozen that could give me lessons. But what I'm saying is that for this project, they should have used the best, and they could have, if they cared enough, because they evidently do have the money. Instead they placed little ads and hired nonentities like us, and maybe we aren't quite even in our specialties. You're—what was it?"

"Minoan. That's ancient Crete."

"And I specialize in marine impact craters. Want to know what there're none of, here in the Florida shallows? If they had taken us down to the coast of Columbia, as I had hoped—" He shrugged.

"What's there?" Don asked.

"You don't know? No, I suppose that's no more obvious to you than Crete is to me. That's where we believe the big one splashed down: the meteor that so shook up the Earth's system that it wiped out the dinosaurs."

"The extinction of the dinosaurs!" Don exclaimed.

"Right. But the site has about sixty five million years worth of sediment covering it. So it will take an in depth—no pun— investigation to confirm it, assuming we can. But instead of send- ing me there, they sent me here. We'd have to bike across the Puerto Rico Trench to reach it, which is pointless and probably impossible. So either they have some lesser crater in mind for me, or they don't care whether I see a crater at all. I'm out of special- ty, just as you are. See what I mean?"

Don nodded soberly. "Maybe we're expendable."

"Maybe. Oh, I'm not paranoid about it. This phase thing is such a breakthrough that I'd sell my watery soul for the chance, and I think I mean that literally, to explore the ocean floor at any depth, unfettered by cumbersome equipment—that's the raw stuff of dreams. But why *me?* Why *you?*"

"I can't answer that," Don said. "All I can do is say how I'm here. I wasn't the bright boy of my class, but I was in the top quarter, with my main strength in deciphering. The lucrative foundations passed me up, and anyway, I wanted to go into new territory. Make a real breakthrough, somehow. Too ambitious for my own good. The prof knew it, and he made the contact. Swore me to secrecy, told me to buy myself a good bicycle and ride it to the address he gave me—well, that was two days ago, and here I am."

"You're single?"

"All the way single. My father died about five years ago, and my mother always was sickly—no s-sense going into that. I've got no special ties to this world. Maybe that's why the ancient world fascinates me. You, too?"

"Pretty much. Auto accident when I was ten. Since then the sea has seemed more like home than the city. So nobody is going to be in a hurry to trace down our whereabouts. I think I see a pattern developing. We must have had qualifications we didn't realize."

"Must have," Don agreed. "But you know, it's growing on me too. I don't know a thing about the sea, or even about bicycles, but I do know that the major archaeological horizon is right here. Not that I have the least bit of training for it. I guess I just closed my mind to the notion of going to the sea. But now that I'm *in* it—well, if I have to risk my life using a new device, maybe it's worth it. All those ancient hulks waiting to be discovered in deep water—"

"Sorry. No ancient hulk is in the ocean," Gaspar said. "Not the way you're thinking, anyway. Ever hear of the teredo?"

"No."

"Otherwise known as the shipworm, though it isn't a worm at all. It's a little clam that—"

"Oh, *that*. I had forgotten. It eats the wood, so—"

"So pretty soon no ship is left. Modern metal hulks, yes; ancient wood hulks, no."

"What a loss to archaeology," Don said, mortified. "I could wring that clam's neck."

Gaspar smiled. "Of course the ship's contents may survive. Gold lasts forever underwater, and pottery—"

"Pottery! That's wonderful!" Don exclaimed.

For the first time Gaspar showed annoyance. "I'm just telling you what to expect."

"I wasn't being sarcastic. Pottery is a prime tool of archaeology. It breaks and gets thrown away, and so it remains for centuries or millennia, undisturbed, every shard a key to the culture that made it. Who wants broken pottery—except an archaeologist? There is hardly a finer key to the activities of man through the ages."

Gaspar gazed at him incredulously, or so it seemed in the fading light of the headlamps, whose reservoirs were running down now that the bikes were stationary. "It really is true? You *do* collect broken plates and things? You value them more than gold?"

"Yes! Gold is natural; it tells little unless it has been worked. But pottery is inevitably the handiwork of man. Its style is certain indication of a specific time and culture. Show me a few pottery shards and let me check my references, and I can tell you where and when they were made, sometimes within five or ten miles and twenty years. It may take time to do it, but the end is almost certain."

Gaspar raised his hands in mock surrender. "Okay, friend. If we find a wreck, I'll take the gold and you take the broken plates. Fair enough?"

"I'll have the better bargain. You can't keep the gold, by law, unless it's in international waters; but the shards could make me famous."

"You archaeologists may be smarter than you look!"

"I should hope so."

Gaspar smiled. "Let's sack out. We've got a long ride tomorrow, I fear."

"What's the position?"

"The coordinates for the next rendezvous? I thought you had them."

"N-no. Only this one. The same one you had, it seems, so we could meet."

Gaspar tapped his fingers on his coordinate meter. "What a foul-up! They should have given one of us the next set."

Don's eyes were on Gaspar's fingers, because he couldn't meet the man's eyes. "I guess I should have asked. I just assumed—" He paused. Next to the meter was the radio. He had been about to ask Gaspar about that, when they had been interrupted by the sawfish. "Maybe the—did you check your radio?"

Gaspar snapped his fingers. "That must be it. I just came out here, gaping at the sea-floor and fish, never thinking of that." He flicked his switch.

"Leave it on!" the female voice cried immediately.

Startled, Gaspar looked down. Unlike Don, he was not dismayed, and he did not turn it off. "Who are you?"

Don kept silent, relieved to have the other man handle it. Maybe he should have had more confidence in his own judgment about both this and the bad glop, but he couldn't change his nature.

"I'm Melanie. Your next contact. Why haven't you answered before?"

"Sister, I just turned on my set for the first time! What are your coordinates?"

"I'm not going to give you my coordinates if you're going to be like that," she responded angrily.

"M-my fault," Don said. "I—I heard her voice, and thought—no one told me it would be a woman."

Gaspar looked at him, comprehending. Then his mouth quirked. "Give with the numbers, girl," he said firmly to the radio, "or I'll turn you off for the night. Understand?"

She didn't answer. Gaspar reached for the switch.

"Eighty one degrees, fifty minutes west longitude," she said with a rush, as if she had seen him. "Twenty six degrees ten minutes north latitude."

"That's better," Gaspar said, winking at Don. "What's the rendezvous time, Melanie?"

"Twenty four hours from now," she said. "You did make it to the first rendezvous point?"

"Right. We're both here. Just wanted you to know who's in charge. Don, turn yours on so we can all talk."

Don obeyed. Gaspar had covered nicely for Don's prior mismanagement of the radio, and he appreciated it. Why hadn't he realized that the woman could be one of their party? He had simply assumed without evidence that it was to be three males. Maybe he just hadn't wanted to face the prospect of working with a woman, especially a young one. He wished he could do something about his shyness.

"A day," Gaspar said. "Ten miles an hour for twelve hours, cumulative, and we can sleep as much as we want. That's in the vicinity of Naples, Florida, you see."

Don hoisted up his nerve. "Are—are you—have you gone through the tunnel already? You're in phase with us?"

"Yes," she replied. "I'm still on land, but I'll come into the water at the right time to meet you there."

"D-do you have the coordinates for the next one?"

"Yes, for all of them. I'm your coordinate girl. But I'm allowed to tell only one rendezvous point at a time. You just be thankful you've got company. I'm alone. That is, alone in phase. It's weird."

"Wish you were here," Gaspar said generously.

"Did they tell you what the mission is?" Melanie asked him.

"Nope. They told us no more than you. I answered an ad, believe it or not, and they checked my references—which were strictly average, and sent me out to get a bike. Same as you, probably."

"Yes," she agreed.

"I think this secrecy kick is overdone."

"It certainly is," Melanie agreed. "I never even applied, actually. But here I am."

"There must be some rationale," Don said. "I'm archaeological, you're geological, she's—"

"Hysterical," Melanie said.

"The next member is mechanical, I hope," Gaspar said. "Suppose the phase equipment breaks down when we're a mile under? Do you know how to fix it?"

"N-no." Don shuddered. "I wish you h-hadn't brought that up."

"We're going to click out for about five minutes, Melanie," Gaspar said. "Nothing personal. Man business." Before she could protest, he turned his set off, gesturing Don to do the same.

"Your stutter," Gaspar said then. "Does it affect your decision-making ability in a crisis? I wouldn't ask if I didn't suspect that my life may be subject to your ability to act, at some point."

Don could appreciate why Gaspar had an undistinguished employee record. He was too blunt about sensitive issues. "N-no. Only the v-vocal cords. Only under stress."

"No offense. Ask *me* one now."

"Not n-necessary," Don said, embarrassed.

"Well, I'll tell you anyway. My friends—of which I have surprisingly few—all tell me I'm nice but stubborn and sometimes insensitive. The less tenable my position, the worse I am. They say."

Don shrugged in the dark, not knowing the appropriate response.

"So if its something important, don't come out and tell me I'm crazy, because if I am I'll never admit it. Tell me I'm reasonable, jolly me along—then maybe I'll change my mind. That's what they say they do."

"Okay!" Don didn't laugh, because he suspected this was no joke. Gaspar had given him fair warning.

They turned on their radios again. "Okay, Melanie," Gaspar said. "We're turning in now. No point in leaving the sets on; might run 'em down, and anyway, all you'd hear would be snoring."

"Oh," she said, sounding disappointed. "I suppose so. I need to sleep too. I've been hyper about listening for the contact, but now it's done. They *do* run down; you have to keep the bike moving, for the radio, too. Check in the morning, will you? I do get lonely."

Don felt sudden sympathy for her. She sounded like a nice girl, and Gaspar was treating her rather callously. Did he have something against women?

"Good enough," Gaspar said, clicking off again. Don reluctantly followed suit. Now that the ice had been broken, he would have liked to continue talking with Melanie. But of course he would be meeting her tomorrow, and they would be able to talk without the radio. If his nerve did not disappear in the interim.

It was hard to sleep, though he was quite tired. Don had never cycled such a distance before, and the muscles above his knees were tense, and the rest of his body little better off. The tiny ripples against his face that were all he could see or feel of small fish swimming disturbed him by their incongruity and made him gasp involuntarily. The temperature bothered him as well; he was accustomed to a drop at night, but here it still felt about 80°F.

"Are you as insomniac as I am?" Gaspar inquired after a while.

"Dead tired and wide awake," Don agreed. "I'm afraid I'll poop out tomorrow and miss the rendezvous, and that doesn't soothe me much either."

"I was thinking about your inedible food. I said it was an accident, but now it strikes me as a pretty funny mistake. Now I wonder whether there are any other mistakes." He paused, but Don offered no debate. "Tell me if this is paranoid: we both have the same kind of food packs. They should have come from the same batch. Could yours have been deliberately spoiled?"

Don's jaw dropped. He was glad he could not be seen. "That does seem farfetched. What would be the point?"

"To test us, maybe. See just how resourceful we are."

"Why should anyone care? We're just ordinary folk."

"White rats are selected to be absolutely ordinary. That's the point. How would regular folk survive in a really strange, isolated situation?"

"B-but that would be—be inhuman!"

"What do we really know of the motives of our employer?"

"B-but to just assume—"

"So it's paranoid."

"But m-maybe we should keep a good watch out," Don said. He had been shaken by Gaspar's conjecture; it had a horrible kind of sense. If there were dangerous new conditions to test with uncertain equipment, how would a company get volunteers? Maybe exactly this way.

"That's my notion. I don't think it's the case, but there's this ugly bit of doubt in my mind, and I thought I'd discuss it with you in private before we join the lady."

"Th-thanks," Don said without irony.

After that he did drop off to sleep, as if the awful notion had actually eased his mind. Maybe it merely gave his fears something more tangible to chew on.

●   ●   ●

In the dark morning they ate again and moved out. They gradually ascended, but the slope was generally slight and Don found himself moving better than he had. Gaspar's presence seemed to give him strength; perhaps he had been dissipating some of his energy in nervous tension, and now was more relaxed. Or maybe it was that Gaspar seemed to have a knack for picking out the easiest route. That made sense; the man was conversant with the sea, after all.

As the day ended, they were back in the offshore shallows, having traveled a hundred and twenty miles in about ten hours of actual riding time.

Now it was time to rendezvous with Melanie. Don felt his muscles tightening. It had become excruciatingly important to him that she match his nebulous mental image of her. He might be riding hundreds of miles with her. Suppose—?

Gaspar turned on his radio. "You there, Melanie?"

"Yes," she replied immediately. "Are you close?"

"Close and closing," Gaspar said.

The next contact was upon them.

Chapter 3

●

Melanie

Proxy 5-12-5-16-8: Attention.

Acknowledging.

Status?

Situation developing. First recruit has discovered his defective food supplies, and the second recruit conjectures that this was an intentional lapse. They suspect that it is a test of their survival skills. They are now linking with the third recruit.

Each recruit has a liability?

Yes. The third recruit's liability is inherent; I did not need to interfere with her situation.

This seems like a devious way to convert a world.

The direct approach has been known to fail.

Apology, Proxy; it is your show. Proceed as you see fit.

I have no assurance that this approach will work. Only hope. Much depends on the interaction of the recruits, and how they react when they learn the truth.

True.

●　●　●

They zeroed in on Melanie, proceeding from radio range to voice range, until she came into sight. She was a figure in a blouse and skirt, standing with a loaded bicycle.

A skirt, under the sea? But Don realized that his reaction was mistaken; a skirt was as sensible as any other clothing, here in this phased state.

As they came up, he saw that not only was she female, she was quite attractively so. She was not voluptuous, but was very nicely proportioned in a slender way. Her face was framed by curls so perfect they could have been artificial, and was as pretty as he had seen.

All of which meant that it would be almost impossible for him to talk to her. This was exactly the kind of woman who had no business noticing a man like him.

"Well, hello Melanie!" Gaspar said without any difficulty. "I'm Gaspar, and this is Don."

"I recognize you by your voice," she said. She turned her eyes on Don. They were as green as a painting of the sea. "Hello, Don."

He tried. "H-h-hel—" He gave up the effort, chagrined.

She smiled. "Were you the one who kept cutting me off?"

Don nodded, miserable.

"Because you were shy?"

He nodded again.

"That's a relief! It makes me a whole lot less nervous about meeting you. I thought maybe you had a grudge."

"N-no!" Don protested.

"You're like me: single, unemployed, no prospects?"

"Y-yes." She had answered a question he had been too timid to ask, while seeming to ask one. But Don was unable to follow up on the conversational gambit.

"What's the coordinate for the next person?" Gaspar asked when a silence threatened to develop.

"Twenty four degrees north latitude, thirty minutes," she said immediately. "Eighty one degrees, fifty minutes west longitude. Twenty four hours from now."

"Key West," Gaspar said. We'll have to move right along, but we can do it." He looked around. "That's just about due south of here, but it should be easier riding downhill. Why don't we coast out to deep water where it's cooler? That way we'll make some distance, even if it isn't directly toward Key West, and we can sleep when we can't stay awake any more."

Melanie shrugged. "Why not? As long as you know how to find the way. I memorized the coordinates, but I don't have much of a notion what they mean."

Don was glad to agree. His earlier fear of the deeps seemed irrelevant, now that he had company. Gaspar would not have made the suggestion if he had thought there was any danger, and the man did know something about the ocean.

"Of course we're a good distance from the edge of the continental shelf," Gaspar continued as he started moving. Melanie fell in behind him, and Don followed her. It was easier to hear him even at some distance, because of the carrying capacity of the water. "Too far to get any real depth. But we might make it to forty or fifty fathoms. Extra mileage but easier going. Worth it, I'd say."

That reminded Don of something. "Key West—how did you figure that out? Do you have a map?" He was able to speak more readily to Gaspar than to Melanie.

"I know the coordinates of places like that. Same way you know types of pottery, I suppose. Nothing special."

"Oh." Stupid question.

"You know pottery?" Melanie asked.

"Y-yes. I-I'm an a-arch-archaeologist."

"I envy you. I have no training at all. I don't know why they wanted me here."

Ahead, Gaspar turned on his headlight. They followed suit. The trend was down, and it did make the cycling easier, which was a relief. Melanie might be fresh, but Don wasn't. The temperature did seem to be dropping.

She had spoken to him, and Don wanted to answer. But it remained difficult. What could he say about her lack of training?

Gaspar saved him the trouble. "I'm a marine geologist, and he's an archaeologist, but we're both out of our specialties here, so we're essentially amateurs. We thought we were selected for our skills, but that may not be the case. Maybe we just happened to be available. Were you out of work, Melanie?"

"Yes. But I didn't even apply. I just got a phone call telling me that there was a job for me that would be interesting and challenging and paid well. I was suspicious, but it did seem to be an opportunity, and the more I learned about it, the more intriguing it seemed. So here I am."

They rode twenty miles southwest before quitting. Don felt ashamed for looking, but he admired Melanie's form during much of that travel. It was easy to watch her, because she was right ahead of him. He wondered why she had been both out of work and unmarried. She should have been able to get work as a receptionist readily enough, and any man she smiled at would have been interested.

Gaspar called a halt at what he deemed to be a suitable location. Then they broke out the rations, and Melanie learned about Don's bad food and expressed sympathy, and shared hers with him. She was very nice about it, not prompting him to talk.

They took turns separating from the group in order to handle natural functions. This was in one sense pointless, as each person was self contained in this respect, but the protocol of privacy seemed appropriate to accommodate the two sexes.

Then they lay down beside their bicycles for sleep, in a row of three, Melanie in the middle. Don lay awake for a while, appreciating the proximity of the woman though he knew her interest in him was purely that of mission associate. Then he slept, for suddenly the night-period passed.

●   ●   ●

They proceeded to a point seventy five miles west of Key West, moving well. "To avoid the coral reefs," Gaspar explained. "We'd have to cross them, otherwise, to get to the rendezvous, and it's a populated area. No sense scaring the fish there, either. Also, it's cooler and less cluttered here in deeper water."

"You're the geologist," Melanie agreed.

Indeed, he was. Their depth had, in just the past few miles, changed from forty fathoms to two hundred, and the coasting had allowed Don to recover some strength in the legs. He had seen the colors change from orange to green to blue-black, and the headlights were now necessary at any hour. The fish, too, had changed color, whether by the dim "daylight" or the headlamps. First they were multicolored, then two-tone—black above, light below—and finally silvery.

Camouflage, he decided. Near the surface all colors showed,

so color was used to merge with the throng. Farther down only the silhouettes showed from below, so the bottoms were light to fade into the bright surface, and the tops dark to fade into the nether gloom when viewed from above. In the truly dim light, color didn't matter much.

But the crawling crustaceans had become bright in the depth, and he saw no reason for that. Unless they used color to identify themselves to each other, like women with pretty clothing. Maybe they were not easy for fish to eat, so did not have to hide.

"However, we should keep alert," Gaspar said. "There aren't many dangerous things on the Gulf side of Florida, and you can't fall off the shelf. But here below the Keys we'll hit deep water."

"I noticed," she said.

"I mean five hundred to a thousand fathoms—on the order of a mile. We're still fairly high."

"D-dangerous things?" Don managed to inquire.

"Living things can't touch us, of course. But rough terrain might."

They didn't talk any more, because now they were climbing, gradually but steadily. Don shifted down to second, then to first, and that gave him plenty of power. Melanie had only three gears, and was struggling. Gaspar, who had just the one ratio, stopped.

"Tired?" Don called, surprised, for Gaspar had seemed indefatigable despite his lack of gearing. Don had survived only because of those five speeds.

"Broken chain," Gaspar said.

So it was. "Too bad," Don said. "But not calamitous. You have a spare chain, don't you?"

"Do. But I want to save that for an emergency."

"This is an emergency. You can't ride without a chain."

"I'll fix this one."

"But that will take time. Better to use the spare, and fix the other when there's nothing to do."

"No, I'll replace the rivet on this one."

"But you don't have t-tools."

"I have a pen knife and a screwdriver and a bicycle wrench," Gaspar said, taking out these articles and laying them on the ground beside the propped bicycle. "Haven't done this since I was a kid, but it's not complicated."

"B-but it's unnecessary."

Gaspar ignored him and went to work on the chain.

Belatedly Don remembered the warning about stubbornness. He had been arguing instead of thinking, and now he was stuttering, and Gaspar had tuned him out. His first "but" had probably lost his cause, and he wasn't certain his cause was right. Why *not* fix the chain now? They did have time for that, and he needed a rest. The muscles of his legs were stiff again.

He saw that Melanie was being more practical: she was lying beside her bicycle, squeezing in all the rest for her legs she could. Her skirt had slid up around her full thighs. Oh, her limbs looked nice!

Don returned his gaze to Gaspar's bicycle, before he started blushing or stuttering worse. He tried a new approach. "A chain shouldn't break like that. It must have been defective, or—"

"Oh, it can happen. Stone tossed up—"

"*Here?*"

Gaspar laughed. "Got me that time! Stone couldn't do much unless it was phased in. But this is an old bike—I never was one to waste money, even if Uncle Sam or whoever pays the way. Ten dollars, third hand. Got to expect some kinks."

Ten dollars! A junker would have charged that to haul the thing away! Yet it was now loaded with what might be a hundred thousand dollars worth of specialized equipment. "S-so you don't think that anyone—" But it sounded silly as he said it. How could anyone sabotage a third-hand bicycle that hadn't yet been bought? And what would be the point? It was obvious that it could readily be fixed, so that was no real test of the man's survival skills.

He walked his own bike back to where Melanie lay, wishing he had the courage to start a dialogue with her. He turned around so that he would not be peering at her legs when he lay down, though he wished he could do that too.

"I heard," she said, though he had not spoken to her. "What's this about something happening?"

Don managed to get his mouth going well enough to explain about the possibility of sabotage. "But it was just a conjecture," he hastened to say. "Probably p-paranoia."

"I'm into paranoia," she said, surprising him.

"You are? Why?"

"Maybe some time I'll tell you. For now, just take my word:

I'm more diffident about people than you are, for better reason."

"You?" He was incredulous.

"Oh, I shouldn't have said that. Let's change the subject."

"I—I can't find a subject."

She laughed, tiredly. "Then I'll find one. It's nice talking to you, Don. So much better than waiting around for the radio to sound, with a pile of books and packages of ugh-y food."

He chuckled, surprised that he was now able to do that in her presence. She was making him feel more at ease than he had a right to be.

He glanced at Gaspar. The chain was still off, and the man was doing something with the little screwdriver and pliers. It would be a while more before the job was done.

"Y-you were just waiting?"

"For you, yes. Two days. But my life was much the same before that, mostly alone. Books are great company, but I would have enjoyed them more if I'd had live companions. So when I took this job, hoping my life would change, and then for two days it was just more of the same, well, I had to do something."

"I-I can't believe you were alone!"

"I could make you believe, but I don't want to." She rolled to her side and angled her head to face him. "You're really interested, aren't you?"

"Yes."

"I'll try to explain. When I was just waiting for you, I walked down to the beach."

"The beach?"

"In the early morning, when no one was around. I didn't want anyone to see me, because of the phase."

"I know. I came into the water at dawn."

She laughed again. "Here I'm telling you something that's not meant to be understood, and you're understanding."

"I—uh—"

"Don't apologize! It's not meant to be understood, just felt. But you feel it too, don't you?"

"Yes." This conversation was becoming odder and more comfortable. He could lie here forever, talking with her like this, his shyness ebbing.

"I enjoyed the beach," she continued. "It was raining. Just a little cool. There was a stiff wind—I couldn't really feel it, but I saw the sea-oats leaning. I just had to go out and walk along the surf a way. Right near the edge of the water. In my bare feet. Except there wasn't anything to feel, it's just sort of neutral in phase, and I had to walk the bicycle right along. You know—so I could breathe. That's one thing that doesn't wind down when the bike stops moving: the oxygen field. Lucky thing, or we'd never be able to rest or sleep. Batteries, I guess, that recharge for that. I tried to breathe away from the bike, and couldn't. I'm married to the bike, now. We all are."

"Yes."

"So I had to pretend. I had the whole beach to myself with only the gulls for company. They stood on the sand facing the wind. I saw a horseshoe crab, and I tried to pick it up—it was the first horseshoe crab I had ever seen."

"They're not crabs," Gaspar said without looking up from his work. That surprised Don; he had thought the man had tuned them out. "They're related to the scorpions and are the only living members of a large group of extinct animals. They've survived unchanged for two hundred and fifty million years."

"All the more wonderful to behold," Melanie said. "The beach has a powerful internal significance for me that I've never quite been able to understand. This one I experienced was wonderfully dramatic. They all are. I never just have seen a beach. It's a total experience. The sand under my feet, warmth, wind, smells, sound, and motion. The beach just is. And I am there walking along looking for seashells and somehow I feel that I belong there. For the moment. It feels like something I can always come back to. Something almost unchanged in a sea of change."

Like the horseshoe crabs, Don thought. Unchanged since the dinosaurs. Perhaps man, when he gazed upon the beach, remembered his ancestor who fought the extraordinary battle to free himself from the grip of the sea, and this was that battleground.

"My life so easily slips into things and experiences with labels," Melanie said. "But the beach somehow for me always slips the compass of a label and asserts the primacy of existence." She paused. "If that makes sense to you."

All he could say was "Yes." It wasn't just her perspective on the beach, it was the fact that she had presented it to him as a fellow human being, as if he deserved to have this insight. What a wonderful experience!

● ● ●

Gaspar completed his repair, and they resumed riding. The difference between a slight decline and a slight incline was enormous, when they were pedaling it. But they could not go down forever. Don had been pleased at how well he was keeping up, but now he wondered whether there was something wrong with his own bicycle. He pushed and pushed on the pedals, but the machine moved slowly, and he was out of breath doing a bare five or six miles per hour. Melanie was struggling similarly.

Gaspar abruptly stopped again. This time his rear wheel was loose, so that it rubbed against the frame with every revolution. *Thank God!* Don thought guiltily, offering no argument about repairs. He dropped to the ground and let life soak back into his deadened limbs.

Gaspar was tough. If he was tired, it didn't show. Don had never been partial to muscle, but would have settled for several extra pounds of it for this trip.

Melanie dropped beside him, almost touching. Even through his fatigue, he felt the thrill. "Talk to me, Don," she murmured.

This time he was able to perform. "You know, Gaspar and I are both only-survivors in our families. We think that's because our employer selected for singleness. Maybe they don't want people wondering where we are. In case—you know. Uh, you said you're single, but otherwise—is it the same with you?" He had even asked her a direct personal question!

"Almost," she said. "My father died ten years ago. He married late. My mother was thirty five when I was born. I haven't seen her for a couple of years. So it's the same, I guess. I'm uncommitted. But I'd be uncommitted even if I had a massive crowd of relatives."

"You keep saying that," Don protested. "But you're such a lovely young woman—"

She looked at him. "I guess I'd better take the plunge and show you. Get it over with at the outset. That's maybe better than having it happen by chance, as it surely will otherwise."

"Show me what?"

"Look at me, Don." She sat up.

He sat up too, uncertain what she had in mind. He tried to

keep his eyes from the firm inner thighs that her crossed legs showed under the skirt, but that meant he was focusing on her evocative bosom. He finally had to fix on her lovely face.

Melanie put her hands to her head and slid her fingers in under her perfect hair. She tugged—and her hair came off in a mass. It was a wig—and beneath it she was completely bald.

Don simply stared.

"I'm hairless," she said. "All over my body. My eyebrows are glued on, and my eyelashes are fake. It's a genetic defect, they think. No hair follicles." She lifted one arm and pulled her blouse to the side to show her armpit. "I don't shave there. No need to. No hair grows." She glanced down. "Anywhere."

Don was stunned. She had abruptly converted from a beautiful young woman to a bald mannequin. She now looked like an alien creature from a science fiction movie. Her green eyes shone out from the face on the billiard ball head, as if this were a doll in the process of manufacture.

"So now you know," the mouth in the face said.

Don tried to say something positive, but could not speak at all. Her beauty had been destroyed, and she had been made ludicrous. It might as well have been a robot talking to him.

Gaspar righted his bicycle. "Ready to go," he said. "We shouldn't use up the batteries unnecessarily." Then, after a pause: "Oh."

"Oh," Melanie echoed tonelessly.

"I wasn't paying much attention when it counted, it seems," Gaspar said. "Disease? Radiation therapy?"

"Genetic, from birth," she said.

"Why show us?"

"Because Don was starting to like me."

He nodded. "Hair is superficial. We know it. Now all we have to do is believe it."

Melanie put her wig back on, and pressed it carefully into place. It was evident that it had some kind of adhesive, and would not come loose unless subject to fair stress. She resumed her former appearance. But now, to Don's eye, she looked like a bald doll with a hairpiece. She had set out to disabuse him of his notions of her attractiveness, and had succeeded. Evidently she didn't want to be liked ignorantly.

They resumed travel without further comment. The coordinates were 24°20′—82°30′. Forty minutes west of their rendez-vous, ten south. Depth was one hundred fathoms. They must have been traveling well, indeed, downhill, before starting the laborious climb. Don was amazed to realize that they were now beyond their target, and he had never been aware of their passing it. They had time, plenty of time, thank the god of the sea.

They had climbed six hundred feet in the past two miles, and it didn't look steep, but it was grueling on a bicycle. Now he was glad for the continued struggle, because it gave him something other to think about than Melanie's hair. She had figured him exactly: he was getting to like her, because she was pretty and she talked to him. And now his building illusion had been shattered. He should have known that there would be something like this.

Twenty miles and seventy fathoms east and up, with a break for another bicycle malfunction—this time Don's, whose seat had come loose and twisted sideways—the way abruptly became steep. Gaspar, in the lead, dismounted and walked his bike up the slope. Don and Melanie were glad to do the same; it was a relief to change the motion.

Suddenly Don saw a rough wall, almost overhanging. Jagged white outcroppings and brown recesses made this a formidable barrier, and it extended almost up to the surface of the sea.

"This is it," Gaspar said with satisfaction as they drew beside him.

"But how can we pass?" Don asked. "What is it, anyway?"

Gaspar smiled. "Coral reef. Isn't she a beauty!"

Don, not wanting to admit that he had never seen a coral reef before, and had had a mental picture of a rather pretty plastered wall with brightly colored fish hovering near, merely nodded. It looked ugly to him, because he couldn't see how they were going to get across it. There might be a hundred feet of climbing to do, scaling that treacherous cliff—and how were they going to haul up the bicycles?

He glanced at Melanie, who had not spoken since her revelation. Could she be likened to a coral reef? His mental image suddenly disabused by the reality? Unfortunately, it was the reality that counted.

They did not have to scale the reef. Gaspar merely showed the way east, coasting down the bumpy slope to deeper water. This was why they had come this way: to go around the reef instead of

across it. Don was now increasingly thankful for Gaspar's knowledge of the geography of the sea. When they struck reasonably
level sand they picked up speed. They went another ten miles before he called a halt.

"We're within a dozen miles," Gaspar said, breaking out the
rations. "I guess we'd better get inside the reefs, next chance. Rendezvous is only a couple miles out of Key West."

"Get inside the reefs?" Don asked, dismayed. "I thought we already went around them."

"No, only part way. But this is a better place to cross them, I
think."

"Why is the rendezvous so close to civilization?" Don mused.
"Can this next person know even less about the ocean than I do?"

Melanie remained silent, and Gaspar discreetly avoided the
implication. "The reefs are rough—literally. The edges can cut
like knives, and the wounds are slow to heal. It's no place to learn
to swim, or ride. So we'll have to guide him through with kid
gloves. He probably *does* know less than you—now."

A left-footed compliment! "So how *do* we get through?"

"Oh, the reefs are discontinuous. We'll use a channel and get
into shallow water. Have to watch out for boats, though; we'll be
plainly visible in twenty foot depth." He considered briefly. "In
fact, as I recall, there's a lot of two fathom water in the area.
Twelve feet from wave to shell in mean low water, which means
barely six feet over our heads. That's too much visibility."

Don agreed. He would now feel naked with that thin a covering of water. He was tired, and wanted neither to admit it nor to
hold up progress, but here was a valid pretext to wait. On the
other hand, he was increasingly curious about this close-to-land
member of the expedition. If the man were not knowledgeable
about the marine world, why was he needed at all?

But Melanie wasn't knowledgeable either. What was her purpose here? Unless this really was a testing situation, a maze for
average white rats. How would those rats find their way
through? How well would they cooperate with each other? He remembered reading about a test in which a rat could get a pellet of
food by striking a button. Then the button was placed on the opposite side of the chamber from the pellet dispenser. Then two
rats were put in the same chamber. When one punched the button, the other got the pellet. That was testing something other

than wit or mechanical dexterity. Could this be that sort of test?

They cut into the reef. This time Don observed the myriad creatures of this specific locale, and the reef began to align better with his former mental image. The elements were there, just not quite the way he had pictured them. The fish in the open waters had generally stayed clear of the odd bicycle party, probably frightened by the lights and machinery, so that he had ignored them with impunity. But this stony wall was well populated. Yellow-eyed snakes peeped from crevices, teeth showing beneath their nostrils, watching, waiting.

Beside him, Melanie seemed no more at ease. She tried to keep as far from the reef as possible without separating from the human party.

Gaspar saw their glances. "Moray eels," he said. "No danger to us, phased—but if we were diving, I'd never put hand or foot near any of these holes. Most sea creatures are basically shy, or even friendly, and some of the morays are too. But they can be vicious. I've seen one tackle an octopus. The devilfish tried to hide, but the moray got hold of a single tentacle and whirled around until that tentacle twisted right off. Then it ate that one and got hold of another."

"Why didn't you *do* something?" Don asked. He had no love of octopi, which were another group of childhood nightmares, but couldn't bear the thought of such cruelty.

"I did," Gaspar admitted. "I don't like to interfere with nature's ways, but I'm not partial to morays. Actually the thing took off when I came near. Good decision; I would have speared it."

"The-the octopus. Did you have to—kill it? With two arms off—"

"'Course not. Tentacles grow back. They're not like us, that way."

"I guess not," Don agreed, looking again at the morays. They might not be quite in his phase, but he would keep clear of them regardless. Certainly there were prettier sights. He spied zebra-striped fish, yellow and black (juvenile black angelfish, Gaspar said), red fish with blue fins and yellow tails (squirrelfish), purple ones with white speckles (jewelfish), greenish ones with lengthwise yellow striping—or maybe vice versa (blue-striped grunt), and one with a dark head, green tail, with two heavy black stripes between (bluehead wrasse). Plus many others he didn't call to Gaspar's attention, because he tended to resent the man's seemingly encyclopedic nomenclature. Melanie seemed similarly fascinated, now that they had gotten among the pretty fish instead of the ugly eels.

"Good thing you didn't ask me any of the difficult ones," Gaspar said. "There's stuff in these reefs I never heard of, and probably fish no man has seen. New species are discovered every year. I think there are some real monsters hidden down inside."

But the surface of the coral reef was impressive enough. They passed a section that looked like folded ribbon (stinging coral—stay clear), and marveled at its convolutions.

Then the reef rounded away, and they pedaled through. Melanie almost bumped into a large ugly green fish and shied away, still not completely used to the phaseout. But that reminded Don of something.

"We ride on the bottom because that's inanimate," he said. "The living things are phased out. But aren't the coral reefs made by living creatures? How come they are solid to us, then?"

"They're in the phase world," Gaspar said. "They're part of the terrain. They may not be the same reefs we see, but they're just like them. So we have to take them seriously. Otherwise we could have ridden straight through them, and saved ourselves a lot of trouble."

Of course that was true. Don was chagrined for not seeing the obvious.

They climbed into the shallows, passing mounds and ledges and even caves in the living coral. For here it was not rocklike so much as plantlike, with myriad flower-shapes blooming.

Gaspar halted as the ground became too uneven to ride over. "Isn't that a grand sight?" he asked rhetorically. "They're related to the jellyfish, you know. And to the sea anemones."

"What are?" Don asked, perplexed.

"The coral polyps. Their stony skeletons accumulate to form the reef—in time. Temperature has to be around seventy degrees Fahrenheit or better, and they have to have something to build on near the surface, but within these limits they do well enough. They strain plankton from the water with their little tentacles—"

"Oh? I didn't see that," Melanie said, finally speaking. Apparently her revelation of her condition had set her back as much as it had Don, and she had withdrawn for a time. Now she was returning, and maybe it was just as well.

"They do it at night, mostly," Gaspar explained. "We're seeing only a fraction of the fish that live on the reef; night is the time for foraging."

"You certainly seem to know a lot about sea life," Melanie said. "Are you sure you're a geologist?"

Gaspar laughed. "You have to know something about the flora and fauna, if you want to stay out of trouble. Sharks, electric eels, poisonous sponges, stinging jellyfish—this world is beautiful, but it's dangerous too, unless you understand it."

"I believe it," she said.

"And there are practical connections to my specialty," Gaspar continued, gazing on the coral with a kind of bliss. "I could mistake coral for a limestone rock formation, if I didn't study both. Actually it *is* limestone—but you know what I mean. It tells me about historical geology, too. Because of the necessary conditions for the growth of coral. If I spy a coral reef in cold water, and it's five hundred feet below the surface—"

"Say!" Don exclaimed, catching on. "Then you know that water was once seventy degrees warm, and that the land was higher."

"Or the sea lower. Yes. There are hundreds of things like that. Fossils in sediments, for example. They account for an entire time scale extending through many hundreds of millions of years. Check the fossils and you know when that material was laid down and what the conditions were."

"Like pottery shards!" Don said. "Each one typical of a particular culture. Only your shards are bones and shells."

"You're right," Gaspar agreed, smiling. "Now I understand what you do. You're a paleontologist of the recent past."

"Recent past! I wouldn't call several thousand years exactly—"

"Geologically, anything less than a million years—"

"Maybe we'd better make our rendezvous," Melanie suggested.

They moved on, drawing nearer to the surface. The water inside the reef was barren in comparison: pellucid, with a flat sandy bottom. Don did spy a number of swift-moving little silvery fish scooting across the floor, and once something gray and flat flounced away as his front tire interacted with its bones.

Then they hit a field of tall grass—except that it wasn't grass.

Some was green and flat, some was green and round. The stalks offered little effective resistance to the bicycles, but Don still had the impression of forging through by sheer muscle. It was amazing to what extent sight, not knowledge, governed his reactions.

He glanced covertly at Melanie. She looked perfect: still slender and feminine. Had she not shown him her bald head . . .

Finally they came to the "patch" reefs that marked their rendezvous. Between these little reeflets and the shore he knew there was only more grass flat.

"Maybe if someone comes—a boat, I mean," Melanie said, "we could lie down and be hidden by that grass."

Gaspar nodded. "Smart girl. Keep your eye out for suitable cover."

They drew up beside a great mound of coral, one of the patches. All around it the sand was bare. "So much for my smarts," Melanie said ruefully."

This section was as bald as her head, Don thought, and wished he could get that matter out of his mind.

"Grass eaters," Gaspar explained. "They graze, but don't go far from their shelter. So they create this desert ring by overgrazing."

"I would never have thought of that," she said. "But it's obvious now that you've pointed it out. Penned barnyard animals do the same."

"Yes, the absence of life can be evidence of life," Gaspar agreed.

The two were getting along together, Don noted with mixed feelings. He had talked with Gaspar, and he had talked with Melanie, but so far there had not been a lot of interaction between Gaspar and Melanie. Yet why shouldn't there be? It was evident that Gaspar, though surprised by her hairlessness, had not really been put off by it. He had broader horizons than Don did, and greater tolerance. Why should Don be bothered by that?

"Rendezvous is at dusk," Gaspar said. "To let him slip into the water unobserved, probably. We're early, so we can rest a while. Out of sight, if we can. Should be an overhang or maybe a cave."

"Is it safe?" Melanie asked. "We aren't entirely invulnerable."

"Not much danger here, regardless," Gaspar said confidently. "Why would the little fishes use it, otherwise?" He began pedaling slowly around the reeflet. The others, disgruntled, followed.

There were several projecting ledges harboring brightly colored fish who scattered as the bicycles encroached. Then a large crevice developed, and they rode between sheer coral walls. These overhung, and finally closed over the top, and it was a cavern.

The area was too confined for riding, and the floor was irregular. They dismounted and walked on inside, avoiding contact with the sharp fringes. Don was reminded of the cave paintings of Lascaux: the patchwork murals left by Upper Paleolithic man some fifteen thousand years ago, and one of the marvels of the archaeological world. Primitive man had not been as primitive as many today liked to suppose.

But this was a sea-cavern, and its murals were natural. Sponges bedecked its walls: black, brown, blue, green, red, and white, in dabs and bulges and relief-carvings.

There was life here, all right. The smaller fish streaked out as the men moved in, for their eyesight was keen enough to spot the intrusion even though its substance was vacant. One man-sized fish balked, however, hanging motionless in the passage.

"Jewfish," Gaspar remarked—and with the sound of his voice the fish was gone. Sediment formed a cloud as the creature shot past, and Don felt the powerful breeze of its thrust. He appreciated another danger: just as a stiff wind could blow a man down on land, a stiff current could do the same here in the ocean. If his position happened to be precarious, he would have to watch out for big fish. Their bones could tug him if their breeze-current didn't.

"Looks good," Gaspar said. "I'm bushed." He lay down beside his bicycle and seemed to drop instantly to sleep.

Don was tired, but he lacked this talent. He could not let go suddenly; he had to rest and watch, hoping that sleep would steal upon him conveniently. It probably wasn't worth it, for just a couple of hours.

"I envy him his sleep, but it's beyond me," Melanie said, settling down to lean cautiously against a wall.

"Me too," Don agreed, doing the same. The real wall might be jagged, but the phase wall wasn't, fortunately.

"You're not stuttering now."

"Maybe I'm too tired."

"Or maybe you know I'm no threat to you."

"I didn't say that." But it might be true. Before, there had been the frightening prospect of social interaction leading into romance.

"You didn't have to. Now you know why I read books. They don't look at you."

"But people don't—I mean, they don't know—"

"*I* know."

"Well, I read too. Mostly texts, but—"

"I read fiction, mostly. Once I fell asleep during a book, and dreamed the author had come to autograph my copy, but we couldn't find him a pen."

"You like signatures?" he asked, not certain she was serious.

"Oh, yes, I have a whole collection of autographed books, back home." She spoke with modest pride.

"Why? I think it's more important to relate to what the author is trying to say, than to have his mark on a piece of paper."

She was silent.

After a moment he asked, "You want to sleep? I didn't mean to—"

"I heard you. I wasn't answering."

"Wasn't what?"

"Maybe we'd better change the subject."

"Why?"

"You couldn't expect me to agree with you, could you? I mean, I collect autographs, don't I? So what am I supposed to say when you say you don't think they are very much?"

What was this? "You could have said you don't agree."

"I did."

"When?"

"When I didn't say anything. I think that should be obvious."

"Obvious?"

"Well, you seem to use different conversational conventions than I do, and it's unpleasant to talk to someone who doesn't understand your silences."

"Why not just say what you mean? I have no idea what's bothering you."

"No more than I did, when you kept cutting me off."

Oh. "I'm sorry about that. I just had this notion it was all men on this circuit, and I thought something had gone wrong, the way my food did. I would have answered if I had realized."

"Well, then, I'll answer you now. I don't want to be placed in

the position of having to defend something I know you don't like.
I mean, if I answered you there would be all kinds of emotional
overtones in my voice, and that would be embarrassing and painful."

"About *autographs?*" he demanded incredulously.

"Obviously you didn't mean to be offensive," she said, sounding hurt.

"What do you mean, 'mean to be'? I wasn't offensive, was I?"

"Well, I shouldn't have said anything about it."

"Now don't go clamming up on me again. One silence is
enough." He was feeling more confident, oddly.

"I was trying to hint that I didn't agree with you."

"About meaning being worth more than a signature?"

She was silent again.

"Oh come *on!*" he snapped. "What do you expect me to say to
a silence?"

"I've already told you why I don't want to talk about it any
more. You could at least have apologized for mentioning it
again."

"Apologized?"

"What kind of unfeeling barbarian culture did you grow up in,
anyway?"

"Primitive cultures are *not* unfeeling!"

There was no answer.

"You're right," he said with frustration. "We do have different
conversational conventions." Sane and insane, he was tempted to
add.

And so they sat, leaning back against the spongy coral wall,
watching the little fish sidle in again. Don wondered what had
happened.

Chapter 4

●

Eleph

Proxy 5-12-5-16-8: Attention.

Acknowledging.

Status?

Three recruits are in motion, with the fourth incipient. The liability of the third has been established, with what impact is uncertain. The group seems to be melding satisfactorily.

Such melding is a two-edged tool. If they unify against the mission, it will be lost.

I mean to see that they react properly. They will not be advised of the mission until the time is propitious.

And if that time does not manifest?

This group must be abolished and another assembled.

You are prepared to destroy them?

No.

Though the alternative is to lose their world?

I will abolish the group without invoking the mission. The individual members will return to their prior lives.

And if you invoke the mission, and they oppose it?

Then we shall have a problem.

●   ●   ●

"There it is!" Gaspar cried. "Right on time."

Don jolted awake. It was night, and the rendezvous was upon them. He had slept when he hadn't expected to, and it seemed that Melanie had done the same.

They scrambled up and walked their bikes out to catch up with Gaspar, who was standing at the mouth of the cave. Then, together, they advanced on the lone figure beyond.

The third man was Eleph: perhaps fifty, graying hair, forbidding lined face. There was a tic in his right cheek that Don recognized as a stress reaction similar to his own stuttering. Don would have had some sympathy, but for the cold manner of the man.

Gaspar tried to make small talk, but Eleph cut him short. He let it be known that he expected regulations to be scrupulously honored. Obviously he was or had been associated with the military; he would not bend, physically or intellectually. There was an authoritative ring in his voice that made even innocuous comments—of which he made few—seem like commands. Yet he also telegraphed a formidable uncertainty.

Don decided to stay clear of the man as much as possible. Gaspar, undaunted or merely stubborn, used another approach. "Look at that bicycle! How many speeds is that, Eleph?"

Eleph frowned as if resenting the familiarity, though they were on a first name basis by the rules. He must have realized that it was impossible to be completely formal while perched on a bicycle anyway. "Thirty six," he replied gruffly.

Don thought he had misheard, but a closer look at the machine convinced him otherwise. It had a thick rear axle, a rear sprocket cluster, three chainwheels, and a derailleur at each end of the chain. The triple gearshift levers augmented the suggestion of a complex assortment of ratios. The handlebars were turned down, not up or level, and were set with all the devices Don had, plus a speedometer, horn, and others whose functions Don didn't recognize. What paraphernalia!

"Don here's an archaeologist," Gaspar said. "I'm a geologist. Melanie knows the coordinates for our various encounters. How about you?"

Eleph hesitated, oddly. "Physicist."

"Oh—to study the effects of this phaseout field under water?"

"Perhaps." Eleph vouchsafed no more.

It was shaping up to be a long journey, Don realized.

"Melanie, where next?" Gaspar asked.

"Twenty five degrees, forty minutes north latitude," she said. "Eighty degrees, ten minutes west longitude."

"Got it. Let's get deep."

Gaspar led the way through the shallows, pedaling slowly so that there was no danger of the others losing sight of his lights. Eleph came next, then Melanie, and Don last. That put the least experienced riders in the middle, out of trouble.

All four of them would have to douse their lights and halt in place at any near approach of a boat. So far they were lucky; the surface was undisturbed. Once they reached deeper water there would be no problem unless they encountered a submarine. That was hardly likely.

The barren back reef had come alive. Great numbers of heart-shaped brown sea biscuits had appeared. Delicate, translucent sea anemones flowered prettily. Fish patrolled, searching for food; they shied away from the beams of light, but not before betraying their numbers. Some were large; Don recognized a narrow barricuda, one of the few fish he knew by sight.

The outer coral reef had changed too. The polyps were in bloom, flexing rhythmically, combing the water with their tiny tentacles, just as Gaspar had said they would. In one way they were flowers; in another, tiny volcanoes; in yet another, transparent little octopi. What had seemed by day to be forbidding rock was by night a living carpet.

Now Don observed the different kinds of coral in the reef. Some was convoluted but rounded, like the folds of a—yes, this had to be brain coral. From it rose orange-white spirals of fine sticks: yet another kind of flower that Don was sure was neither flower nor even plant. He swerved toward one, reaching to touch it though he knew he couldn't. As his hand passed through its faint resistance, the flower closed and disappeared, withdrawing neatly into a narrow tube-stem.

Yet there were dull parts, too. In some regions the coral featured little or no life. It was as if tenement houses had been built, used, and then deserted. But surely the landlords hadn't raised the rent, here!

"Pollution is killing the reefs," Gaspar remarked sourly. "Also over-fishing, sponge harvesting, unrestrained memento collecting, the whole bit. The sea life here isn't nearly as thick as it used to be, and species are dying out. But the average man doesn't see that, so he figures it's no concern of his."

"They are wiping out species on land, too," Melanie pointed out.

"You think that justifies it?" Gaspar asked sharply.

"No! I think it's horrible. But I don't know how to stop it."

"There are just too many people," he said. "As long as there keep being more people, there'll be fewer animals. It's that simple."

Don gazed at the barren sections of the reefs. Was it that simple? He distrusted simple answers; the interactions of life tended to be complex, with ramifications never fully understood. Still, it was evident that something was going wrong, here.

The moray eels were out foraging. One spied Don and came at him, jaws open. Don shied away despite his lack of real alarm, and it drifted back. Melanie, just ahead of him, was veering similarly.

Then, remembering his own initial reactions, Don looked ahead to see how Eleph was taking it. This was a wise precaution, for Eleph reacted violently. Two eels were investigating him, as if sniffing out the least secure rider.

Both Eleph's hands came off the handle bars to fend off the seeming assault. The bicycle veered to the side and crashed into the sand.

Don and Melanie hurried to help the man, but Eleph was already on his feet. "The phase makes the predators harmless," Don explained reassuringly. "All you can feel is a little interaction in the bones."

"I am well aware of that!" And Eleph righted his machine and remounted, leaving Don and Melanie to exchange a glance.

Angry at the rebuff, Don let him go. For a physicist specializing in this phase-field, Eleph had bad reflexes.

"And they say that pride goeth *before* a fall," Melanie murmured.

Don had to smile. Then he seized the moment. "Melanie, whatever I said before, I'm sorry. I—"

"Another time," she said. But she smiled back at him.

Then they had to follow, orienting on the lights ahead.

Lobsterlike crustaceans were roving the floor, making free

travel difficult. Swimming fish were easy to pass, and living bottom creatures, but inanimate obstructions could be every bit as solid as they looked. When a living creature obscured a rocky projection or hole, and the wheel of the bicycle went through the living thing, it could have trouble with the other. Successful navigation required a kind of doublethink: an object's position and permanence, not its appearance, determined its effect. More or less.

They coasted bumpily down past the outer reef and into deeper water. But more trouble erupted.

A blue-green blob with darker splotches rose up from the sand in the wake of a scuttling crab. Gaspar's light speared it—and suddenly the green became brighter as tentacles waved. It was an octopus, a large one.

Gaspar slowed, no doubt from curiosity. Don caught up, while Melanie remained behind. But Eleph, in the middle, didn't realize what they were doing or what was there. He sped straight on—into the waving nest of mantle and tentacles.

Ink billowed. Eleph screamed and veered out of control again, covering his head. Meanwhile the octopus, who had been traversed and left behind, turned brown and jetted for safer water. Each party seemed as horrified by the encounter as the other.

For a moment Don and Gaspar stared, watching the accidental antagonists flee each other. Then a chuckle started. Don wasn't sure who emitted the first choked peep, but in a moment it grew into uncontrollable laughter. Both men had to put their feet down and lean over the handlebars to vent their mirth. It was a fine release of tension.

When at last they subsided, Don looked up to find Eleph standing nearby, regarding them sourly. Melanie stood behind him, her face straight. Abruptly the matter lost its humor.

Gaspar alleviated the awkwardness by proceeding immediately to business. "We're deep enough now. Eleph, do you have the instructions for our mission? We have been told nothing."

"I do not," Eleph replied. The episode of the octopus had not improved his social inclinations. "Perhaps the next member of the party will have that information."

Don had thought there would be three members, and Gaspar had guessed four. Evidently there were five.

Gaspar looked at Melanie. "How long hence?"

"Sixty hours," she replied. She had evidently known, but had kept silent, as it seemed she was supposed to.

Gaspar grimaced, and Don knew what he was thinking. Another two days and three nights before they caught up to the final member of their party and learned what this was all about. Maybe.

"Well, lets find a comfortable spot to turn in," Gaspar said. "Maybe we'll find a mound of gold ingots to form into a camping site."

"Gold?" Melanie asked.

"From sunken treasure ships. There are a number, here in the channel between Florida and Cuba, and they haven't all been found by a long shot. Whole fleets of Spanish galleons carried the Inca and Aztec treasures to Spain, and storms took a number of them down. That cargo is worth billions, now."

"Maybe that's our mission," Don said. "To explore this region and map the remaining treasure ships."

"I'd be disappointed if so," Gaspar said.

"Yes," Melanie agreed. "We have to hope that something more than greed is responsible for us."

"We can best find out by getting on with the mission," Eleph said. That damped the dialogue.

Gaspar led the way to the more level bottom and located a peaceful hollow in the sand. There was no sign of gold. This time they pitched their tents, which they had not bothered to do before: one for Eleph, one for Melanie, and one formed from Don and Gaspar's combined canvas.

This really was more comfortable than sleeping in the open, though the difference was more apparent than real. There was nothing to harm them in their phased state anyway. But Don liked the feeling of being in a protected, man-made place. Appearances were important to his emotions. Which brought him back to the subject of Melanie. Her appearance—

He shoved that thought aside. The emotions were too complicated and confused. That business about the autographs —where had he gone wrong? Suddenly he had run afoul of her, and he didn't quite understand how it had happened. So it was better to let it lie, for now.

"That wig," Gaspar said.

So much for letting it lie! "You noticed it too," Don said with gentle irony.

"I want to be candid with you, because it might make a difference. Melanie is one attractive woman, and I'd be interested in her. Except for that wig. If she meant to see whom it fazed, she succeeded."

Fazed. A pun, since they were all phased? Evidently not. "But there's more to a woman than hair," Don said, arguing the other side.

"I know that. You know that. Everybody knows that. But I have a thing about hair on a woman. I like it long and flowing and smooth. I like to stroke it as I make love. My first crush was on a long-haired girl, and I never got over it. So when I first saw Melanie I saw a nice figure and a pretty face, but the hair didn't turn me on. Too short and curly. But hair can grow, so if she was otherwise all right, that could come. But then she took off that wig, and I knew that her hair would never grow. A wig won't do it, for me. The hair has to be real, just as the breasts have to be real. I don't claim this makes a lot of sense, but romance doesn't necessarily make sense. Melanie is not on my horizon as anything other than an associate or platonic friend, regardless of the other aspects of our association."

Don was troubled. "Why are you telling me this?"

"Because I can see you are shy with women. You wouldn't want to go after one actively. You sure wouldn't compete with another man for one. Well, maybe you don't have the same hang-up as I do. In that case, I just want you to know that there's no competition. If you can make it with Melanie, I'll be your best man. The field is yours."

"B-but a woman can't just be p-parceled out!" Don protested.

"There's a difference between parceling and non-commitment. I think Melanie needs a man as much as you need a woman. In fact I think you two might be just right for each other. If you were with her, you'd keep her secret, and she'd love you for it, and other men would wonder what she saw in you, and she would never give them the time of day. Ideal for you both, as I see it. I can see already that she's got her quirks, but is one great catch of a woman. But matchmaking's not my business. I'll stay out of it. Just so you know that no way am I going to be with her. She lost me when she lifted that wig, and she knows it. You are in doubt. I mean, she doesn't know whether you can handle the business of the hair. When you decide, that will be it. I won't mention this again."

"Th-thanks," Don said. His emotions remained as confused as ever. He knew that the best thing he could do was to put all this out of his mind and let time show him the way of his feelings and hers. He would just relax.

Yet sleep was slow, again. He told himself it was because of his recent nap in the patch-coral cave, but he knew it was more than that. There was a wrongness about this project, and not just in spoiled rations or breaking bicycle chains or undue secrecy. Gaspar seemed to be the only one qualified to do anything or learn anything here. Don himself was a misfit, as was Melanie—and what was a man like Eleph doing here? Not a geologist, not a biologist, not even an undersea archeologist—but a physicist! His specialty could have little relevance here. A mysterious mission like this was hardly needed to check out the performance of the phase-shift under water—if that were really what Eleph was here to do. The man wasn't young and strong, and certainly not easy to get along with. He could only be a drag on the party. At least Melanie wasn't a drag.

"It's Miami," Gaspar said, startling him.

"Who?"

"Those coordinates. Offshore Miami. Must be another inexperienced man."

Don shook his head ruefully. "I wish I had your talent for identifying places like that! I can't make head or tail of those coordinates."

"It's no talent. Just understanding of the basic principle. The Earth is a globe, and it is tricky to identify places without a global scale of reference. On land you can look for roads and cities, but in the sea there are none. Think of it as an orange, with lines marked. Some are circles going around the globe, passing through the north and south poles. Those are the meridians of longitude, starting with zero at Greenwich, in London, England, as zero, and proceeding east and west from it until they meet as 180 degrees in the middle of the Pacific Ocean at the International Date Line. The others are circles around the globe parallel to the equator; they get smaller as they go north and south, but each is still a perfect circle. Thus we have parallels of latitude. Since we happen to be north of the equator and west of England, our coordinates are in the neighborhood of twenty five degrees north latitude and eighty degrees west longitude. Just keep those figures in mind, and you'll know how far we go from where we are now."

It began to register. "Twenty five and eighty," Don said. "Right here. So Miami is—"

"Actually those particular coordinates would be about ten miles east of Miami, and fifty miles south of it," Gaspar said. "We're on the way there. I meant our neighborhood on a global scale.

"Just as all of man's history and prehistory is recent, on the geologic scale," Don said wryly. "Fifty miles is pinpoint close."

"Yes. Our bicycle meters give us our immediate locations."

"Still, I'll remember those numbers. It will give me a notion how far we are from Miami, and that's a location I can understand. Southern tip of Florida."

"Well—"

"Approximately!" Don said quickly. "In geologic terms."

"Approximately," Gaspar agreed, and Don knew he was smiling.

Don returned to the matter of their next group member, glad to have company in his misgivings. "What do you think he is? An astronomer? An electrician? A—"

"Could be a paleontologist. Because I think I know where we're heading, now. The Bahamas platform."

"What?"

"The Bahamas platform. Geologically, a most significant region. It certainly made trouble for us in the past."

Don would have been less interested, had he not wanted someone to talk to. "How could it make trouble? It is whatever it is, and was what it was, wasn't it, before there were geologists?"

"True, true. But trouble still, and a fascinating place to explore. You see, it's existence was a major obstacle to acceptance of the theory of plate tectonics."

"Of what?"

"Drifting continents."

"I've heard of that," Don said. "They're moving now, aren't they? An inch a century?"

"Faster than that, even," Gaspar agreed wryly.

"But I don't see why those little islands, the Bermudas—"

"*Bahamas*. The thesis was that all the continents were once a super land mass called Pangaea. The convection currents in the mantle of the earth broke up the land, spreading the sea floor and shoving the new continents outward. North and South America drifted—actually, they were *shoved*—to their present location, and the Mid-Atlantic ridge continued to widen as more and more lava was forced up from below. But the Bahamas—"

"You talk as if the world is a bubbling pot of mush!"

"Close enough. The continents themselves float in the lithosphere, and when something shoves, they have to move. But slowly. We could match up the fractures, showing how the fringes of the continental shelves fitted together like pieces in a jigsaw puzzle. All except the Bahamas platform. It was extra. There was no place for it in the original Pangaea—yet there it was."

"So maybe the continents didn't drift, after all," Don said. "They must have stayed in the same place all the time. Makes me feel more secure, I must admit."

"Ah, but they *did* drift. Too many lines of evidence point too firmly to this, believe you me. All but that damned platform. Where did it come from?"

"Where, indeed," Don muttered sleepily.

"They finally concluded that the great breakup of Pangaea started right in this area. The earth split asunder, the land shoved outward in mighty plates—and then the process halted for maybe thirty million years, and the new basin filled in with sediment. When the movement resumed, there was the half-baked mass: the Bahamas platform. Most of it is still under water, of course, but it trailed along with the continent, and here it is. The site of the beginning of the Atlantic Ocean as we know it." The man's voice shook with excitement; this was one of the most important things on Earth, literally, to him.

But Don wasn't a geologist. "Glory be," he mumbled.

"*That's* why I find this such a fascinating region. There are real secrets buried in the platform strata."

But Don was drifting to a continental sleep. He dreamed that he was standing with tremendous feet straddling Pangaea, the Paul Bunyan of archaeologists. But then it cracked, and he couldn't get his balance; the center couldn't hold. The more he tried to bring the land together, the more his very weight shoved it apart, making him do a continental split. "Curse you, Bahama!" he cried.

Chapter 5

●

Pacifa

Proxy 5-12-5-16-8: Attention.
Acknowledging.
Status?
Four members introduced, final one incipient. Progress good. Group is melding. They are as much concerned with interpersonal relations as with the mission, but unified in their perplexity about it. The likelihood of success seems to be increasing.

That is good. We have lost another world via the straightforward approach. If your experiment is effective, we will try it on the remaining worlds.

But the outcome is far from assured. Human reactions are devious and at times surprising.

How well we know!

●　　●　　●

Offshore Miami: the continental shelf was narrow here, but they could not approach the teeming metropolis too closely. The rendezvous was just outside the reefs, thirty fathoms deep and sloping.

Gaspar tooted on his whistle. The answer came immediately. Before they could get on their cycles the fifth member of the party appeared, riding rapidly. Don noted the turned-down handlebars and double derailleur mechanism first: another ten-speed-or-more machine, perhaps an expensive one.

"It's a woman," Gaspar said.

Don and Melanie peered at the figure. It was female, but neither buxom nor young.

She coasted up, turned smartly, and braked, like a skier at the end of a competition run. "Pacifa," she said. Her hair was verging on gray, obviously untinted under the hard helmet.

The others introduced themselves.

"Well," Pacifa said briskly. "If I had known you would be three handsome men and one pretty girl, I'd have sent my daughter. But she's all shape and no mind and this is business not pleasure, so we're stuck with each other for the duration. Any problems with the bikes?"

They assumed that this was small talk, so demurred. Don saw Melanie react at the reference to "pretty girl," but she did not speak. He wasn't sure whether it was the first word or the second that bothered her.

"No, I'm serious," Pacifa said with peppery dispatch. "I'm your mechanic, in a couple of ways, and I can see already that none of you except Gaspar knows the first thing about cycles, and he doesn't know the second thing. Three of you have insufficient and the fourth too much. Can't be helped now, though. Who has the coordinates?"

"Twenty four degrees fifteen minutes latitude," Melanie said. "Eighty four degrees fifty minutes longitute."

"But that's—" Don started, trying to figure it out.

"Right back the way we came," Melanie said. "Eleph was at 24°30′, and this is 24°15′.

"But farther along," Gaspar said. "In fact, offshore northern Cuba."

"We're picking up a Cuban?" she asked.

"Unlikely," Gaspar said. "If there was supposed to be another person, he should have joined us at the same place Eleph did, not close by. Now I think we're complete. A larger party would be unwieldy. So it's more likely the site of our mission—or a supply depot." He sounded disappointed. It seemed they were not going to the Bahamas platform.

"Let's go," Pacifa said. She mounted and moved out with such smoothness that the three were left standing.

Gaspar filled the leadership gap again. "Don, you catch her and make her wait. Eleph, I saw a map in your pack. Let's you and I check it and find out more specifically where we're going, because Cuba just doesn't make sense to me. Maybe there's something in the Gulf of Mexico I'm missing."

Don took off. But Pacifa was already out of sight, lost in the vague dark background wash that was the deep ocean at dawn. There were no tire tracks, of course. It was hopeless.

"Fool woman," he muttered.

"Whistle for her," Melanie called. He hadn't realized that she was following him, and indeed she wasn't very close, but it was a good suggestion. He blew his whistle.

Pacifa answered at once, just a short distance to the side. "Are you lost, young man?" she inquired solicitously as he drew up to her.

"No. You are—were. Wait for the rest of us!"

"Why?"

"W-we have to operate as a p-party," he said, annoyed.

"I'm glad that's settled. Let's get on with it."

They returned to find Gaspar and Eleph poring over the paper held before one headlight. Gaspar lifted his bike and spun a wheel by hand when the headlight began to fade, to keep the light bright. There were a number of sections of the map, each overlapping the boundaries of the next, so that they could travel from one to another without interruption. It looked to Don as if the entire Gulf of Mexico was covered, and perhaps more.

Gaspar looked up. "It's in an American explosives dumping area," he said.

"A what?" Pacifa demanded. "That can't be right."

"It's the location Melanie gave us," Gaspar said evenly. "Got any other?"

"Do I understand correctly?" Eleph demanded. "Must we venture into a munitions dump?"

"I have no knowledge of munitions dumps," Pacifa said. "I don't know anything about undersea coordinates either. It does seem strange, but if they want to keep our ultimate destination secret, this is as good a waystation as any, I suppose."

"That must be it," Don said. "For some reason they don't want us to know our mission any sooner than we have to. But it must be far enough away so we'll have to reload on supplies." He would be glad to get good rations to replace his bad ones; so far there had been plenty for the others to share with him, but it made him feel as if he wasn't carrying his own weight.

"But an explosives dump!" Gaspar said.

"Can't hurt us," Don reminded him. "We're out of phase."

"I'm not so sure about that. Our weight is still real, and if we were to ride over an old live depth bomb—"

"They do not dump that way," Eleph said. "Those weapons are sealed in."

"How do you know?"

Eleph hesitated. "I have had military experience."

So there *was* a military background, Don thought. That explained the man's military bearing and attitude. But it still didn't explain his presence here.

"Probably it was easier to dump supplies on a regular run," Gaspar said after a moment, evidently not wishing to appear unduly negative. "But it's a good three hundred and fifty miles from here. And if that's only half way to our goal—"

"Our goal may be even farther," Don said. "Because we've been riding back and forth with our initial supplies."

"Of which we still have plenty," Melanie said. "Even sharing."

"Sharing?" Pacifa inquired alertly.

"Don's are bad," Melanie explained. "We don't know if it's poor quality control or what."

"Or what?" Pacifa asked.

"Or intentional," Gaspar said.

"Whatever for?" Pacifa demanded.

"We don't know," Don said.

"Regardless, it seems odd to start us far from the site of our mission," Gaspar said. "It's been bad enough, having to ride all around just to assemble our party. Now to have to go farther yet—"

"Maybe it's that crater off South America," Don suggested.

"The one with the dinosaurs."

Gaspar brightened. "Could be. They could start us here, so that no one could guess our destination from our initial motions."

"But what's the point of secrecy?" Don asked. "If that crater is sixty five million years old and has no military value—"

"Never underestimate the secrecy of the military mind," Eleph said.

"Still, that's a thousand miles!" Gaspar said.

"That's why we have our bicycles, isn't it?" Pacifa asked.

"A thousand miles!" Don said, horrified. "That'll take weeks!"

"Days," Pacifa said. "What's wrong with that?"

Eleph regarded her with severity. "Madam, have you any notion how far that is on a bicycle?"

"I ought to," she said, smiling. "I have traveled ten thousand miles in the past year on this bicycle, and I didn't ride much in winter."

The other four stared at her.

"That's my business, after all," she said. "Checking touring paths for bicycle clubs. Terrain, hazards, accommodations available along the way—I earn a few dollars a mile, plus expenses, for doing what I like best. Being independent."

Don didn't comment, and neither did the others. Who wanted to be the first to inform an old lady that she was off her rocker?

Eleph finally broke the silence. "This route takes us in an unexpected direction."

Pacifa shrugged. "So?"

"It's more than we bargained on," Don said. "I thought this mission—well, maybe down off the continental shelf to investigate a sunken ship, not that I wanted to—"

"Or to check the configurations of the terrain beneath the Gulf Stream," Gaspar said. "And the Bahamas platform—"

"To field test the phasing apparatus," Eleph said. "Which requires no great amount of travel, and is not antipathetic to the other—"

"Or to see how well a group of strangers can get along under the sea," Melanie said. "Male, female, young, old, with different—"

"Fiddlesticks!" Pacifa snapped. "This tour will obviously give you all your chances to look at the bottom and search for ships and test your equipment and get along together or quarrel incessantly, whatever direction we go. There must be something special at the end—something more important than any of our separate little specialties. The sooner we get there the sooner we find out what that is."

She was making sense. "But food—water—we can't survive indefinitely under the sea," Don said, feeling the dread of the unknown.

"We certainly can," Eleph said, surprisingly. "These concentrates we carry are pure nourishment. All we need is water—and the recycling system insures the supply. The only really crucial external commodity is oxygen, and the diffusion field takes care of that."

"So there is a field," Gaspar said. "I wondered. We seem to be riding in an alternate realm, where there is ground but no water and perhaps no air. What do you know about it?"

"This is within the province of my specialty," Eleph replied stiffly. "The solid material, animate and inanimate, with which we associate, has been shunted into an alternate framework. That's what that "phase tunnel" is: the shunting device. That material, which includes our living bodies, will remain in that state until reprocessed. But it is not feasible to recycle oxygen, so within each bicycle is a generator supported by batteries that creates a temporary partial phase, permitting a certain interaction between frameworks. In this manner oxygen is diffused in, and carbon dioxide is rediffused out, enabling us to breathe."

That explanation relieved one of Don's main concerns. But only one of them.

"My, my," Pacifa said. "If one of those generators fails—"

"That is unlikely," Eleph said.

"But you said that Don's supplies are bad. Why not some of the equipment too?"

Don found that question painfully on target.

"I am conversant with the mechanism," Eleph said, "and should be able to repair most malfunctions."

Gaspar whistled. "You must be some physicist."

"I'm sure each of us has his particular area of expertise." Eleph's tone discouraged further comment.

Melanie, nevertheless, made one. "So carelessness or poor quality control may have wiped out Don's food, but anything else can be fixed."

"Precisely," Eleph agreed.

"I'll make a note," Don said. He rummaged in his pack and brought out his pad of paper and pen. Melanie smiled and Gaspar laughed. Don appreciated that.

Pacifa was studying the map. "I see where we are and where we are going. Now must we follow the exact route, or do we have some leeway?"

"What difference does it make?" Eleph demanded.

"Now if we start out grouchy, we'll never get along," she snapped back.

Don had to turn away to hide a smile, and he caught Gaspar doing the same. Neither commented directly.

"Because if we do have leeway," Pacifa continued, "and it seems we have to, because we're the ones who have to do the job, whatever it is, and you can't ride a bike from some fat-bottomed swivel chair—it seems to me that we ought to get off the coral shelf and get down under the Gulf Stream—it's going the wrong way for us, isn't it?—and coast down around here into the Gulf of Mexico. We have to get down there anyway, and according to this map it is sixteen hundred fathoms deep at our depot—what's that in real terms, Gaspar?—and the drop-off doesn't get any—"

"About one and three quarter miles deep," Gaspar said.

"Don't interrupt," Pacifa told him. Don exchanged a glance with Melanie. "The drop-off doesn't get any easier down beyond the keys, from the look of this."

"No, it doesn't," Gaspar said. "But don't go thinking of the continental slope as a sheer cliff. It may have cliffs and canyons in it, and overall it represents a more formidable climb than any mountain we know on the surface, but it is a slope. We can manage it on the bicycles, if we watch where we're going."

"You're the geologist," she said dubiously. She had caught on to all their names and specialties astonishingly quickly, but it was evident that she was as ignorant as the others about the nature of the sea floor. "Let's slant down it and be on our way."

Gaspar shrugged, out of arguments. Pacifa suited action to word, evidently being a person of action. This time Don and Melanie fell in behind her, and Eleph followed them. Gaspar, most familiar with the depths, was this time at the rear.

They dropped down to two hundred feet, three hundred, four hundred. The terrain became more even, though it was hardly the smooth slope Don had pictured from Gaspar's description. Of course the man had not claimed it was smooth, only that it was a slope. Only flat beds of sand seemed smooth, and there weren't many of them here. They reached a hundred fathoms, and Don gave up converting to feet. It was easier to go along with his depth meter.

Pacifa abruptly slowed. In a moment Don saw why. A tremendous and weird-looking fish was pacing her. It had a vertical fin like that of a shark, but its head terminated in a horizontal cleaver.

"Hammerhead shark," Gaspar murmured, coming up. "Average size, maybe fifteen feet. The eyes and nostrils are at the edge of the spread, helping it to triangulate on prey. Very efficient."

"A science fiction monster!" Pacifa exclaimed, shaken.

"Nothing to worry about," Eleph said, just as if he had never been frightened by a marine creature. "Only one tenth of one per cent of its mass can affect us, and vice versa."

The hammerhead looped gracefully, circling them. "You know that," Pacifa said. "I know that. But does *it* know—"

The shark charged. All five people leaped for their lives. The wide-flung nostrils and open mouth passed through the party, stirring it further, feeling like a harsh gust of wind. The tail caught Don, and he felt again that disquieting interaction of substance.

They all looked at each other, tumbled unceremoniously. "Well, it *is* a man-eater," Gaspar said, apologizing for them all. "Our conditioned reflexes still govern us. That may be dangerous, because they don't apply in this situation. Maybe I'd better take the lead, now."

Pacifa, momentarily chastened, acquiesced.

Gaspar moved ahead, and Don took the end spot, and travel resumed. Don was privately satisfied to be following Melanie again; his headlight played at intervals across her well proportioned backside. He liked her body and her personality. If only she didn't have that condition with the hair!

At a hundred and fifty fathoms the dawn of the near-surface had become the deepest blue-black of unearthly night. It was cooler, too; the meter said the temperature had dropped almost fifty degrees, and was now approaching what he thought of as the freezing point.

The pace slowed as they navigated a devious stretch, and Don took the opportunity to pull abreast of Eleph. "Should we stop to put on heavier clothing?" he asked.

"The temperature is a function of the heat of the converter, modified by very limited external factors, such as the caloric content of the incoming oxygen," Eleph said curtly.

"Limited, my foot!" Don said. "My meter says—"

"That meter is oriented on the oxygen, as a guide to conditions in the other framework," Eleph said. "Surely you are not cold."

Don was embarrassed to realize that he wasn't. All this time he had been reacting to the meter, instead of reality. Naturally he couldn't expect the bicycle temperature to be controlled by that one-thousandth transfer across the phase.

But it did make him wonder again just what the phase world was. Didn't it have temperature or weather of its own? Why couldn't they see it? They could feel it, because that was what their tires rode across. Invisible mass?

There were fish about, but not many. Increasingly Don felt alone, though Melanie's taillight remained in sight ahead of him, and Eleph's ahead of hers, bumping over the irregularities. Don thought he saw another shark feeding on the bottom, and there were a number of unidentifiable glows. But no vegetation at all, at this depth.

The path turned, until they were going southwest, parallel to the reefs, not away from them. Then Don saw why: the drop-off did become steep. Gaspar was making it easier by descending on the bias.

But it wasn't easier. The roughness of the ground increased. Large sponges, grotesquely shaped, loomed out of the gloom to force detours. The land seemed formed into irregular rocky ridges which had to be portaged across. No erosion here to smooth things. Finally Gaspar stopped, letting the others catch up.

"This is messier than I figured," he said as they clustered together, pooling their lights. "We're riding along an outcropping—Oligocene deposits, I'd say—of rock, and it probably parallels the coast for a hundred miles."

"Why not check the map?" Don asked.

"Map doesn't show it; too general. There are sharp limits to what they can do by echo-sounding, anyway—which is why we need people down here to do the job properly. There's no erosion to speak of at this depth, so every jagged break is as sharp as it ever was. From what I know of this shelf, I'd guess this interruption isn't broad; two or three miles should traverse it, crosswise. Then it's fairly easy coasting on to the foot. But here it's a rough two miles. We're probably better off going straight across it, then riding the trough—but we may have to go mountain style. Who's game?"

Pacifa grinned. "Good idea. We have rope, pitons—"

"Rope and pitons!" Eleph exclaimed. "Madam, these are not the Alps!"

"Nor the Himalayas," Gaspar said. "They're worse, in places. The greatest mountains on Earth are under the sea."

"Now don't exaggerate," Pacifa said.

"No exaggeration. The great mid-ocean ridge runs forty thousand miles around the globe. The largest single mountain of the world, Hawaii, is far larger than Everest, as an entity. Just be thankful we're not trying to navigate a fracture zone. As it is, we'll be seeing moon landscape and Mars landscape before we're through."

"Goody," Pacifa said with almost girlish gusto. "What a marvelous guided tour that would make. Moon and Mars under the sea."

It occurred to Don that he'd like to meet her daughter—the one who was all shape and no mind. Was her personality like this? But of course he would go into a terminal stuttering attack if he did encounter her, so the fancy was pointless. Better to wrestle with the problem of Melanie's hair. Melanie just might be attainable, if—

"Guided tour," Eleph muttered with disgust.

They unlimbered the rope. "Now we'll have to stay on foot while we're tied," Gaspar said. "I don't know what effect a sharp rope-jerk would have on a rider. No sense risking it."

"No sense at all," Pacifa agreed. "We're a long way from the hospital."

"But we have to hold the bicycles," Don pointed out. "How can we climb and hold on to ropes at the same time?"

It turned out to be less of an obstacle than he had supposed. Pacifa looped the rope firmly but not bindingly about each person's waist and knotted it in place with quick competence. This linked them securely without occupying their hands. She connected the bicycles to short offshoots. The hike would have been more convenient without the bikes right at hand, but of course this was out of the question; the oxygen went with the machines.

Cautiously they proceeded on down the continental slope. A pass opened in the projecting ridge, and they made their way through without difficulty. The steepness leveled off into a smooth, steady, undemanding decline. For miles they trekked downward when they could have been riding, their lights spearing into drab mundane waters, reflecting from harmless sponges and innocuous fish.

At last, embarrassed, Gaspar called another halt. "Wouldn't you know there'd be a break right when I geared us up for a real climb!"

"Security before convenience, always," Eleph said with his normal stiffness. Don was beginning to appreciate that the man was fair, if taciturn. Gaspar had erred on the safe side, and that certainly was best.

"Might as well unhitch now and go on down," Gaspar said. "Should be no more trouble. 'Course we don't want to get reckless. There is always the unexpected."

They unhitched. "I'm glad it *wasn't* bad," Melanie confided as Don helped her. He had to agree.

Gaspar led the way southwest, picking up speed—and dropped out of sight.

It was a depression in the ocean floor resembling a sinkhole. A spring of water issued from a hole at its base. Gaspar had held his seat, and the bicycle straddled the hole, making his clothing billow up and out. "Must be a freshwater well," he remarked. "I had forgotten they were here."

No harm had been done, but the episode served as a sharp reminder. This was unknown, largely uncharted terrain; no one had ever mapped it in fine detail. Anything, geologically, could be here, and they would have no more warning than that provided by their scant headlights.

They made it down safely. Hours had passed, and Don's waterproof watch claimed it was afternoon. The depth was 380 fathoms: a scant half mile. It seemed like a hundred miles, with the phenomenal weight of all that water pressing down. The very fact that they could not feel that weight made the experience vaguely surrealistic. This was indeed an alien horizon.

They stopped and ate and rested, but were soon on their way again, because it was cold when they stopped, whatever Eleph might say about imagination. There was something about the depths and gloom that chilled Don from the mind outward.

Gaspar led them another thirty miles in the next four hours, then halted at a partial cave in a hillside. "Let's camp here," he suggested, knowing that no one was about to argue. "We have had a good day."

"We have indeed, considering," Pacifa agreed, though she looked as fresh as when she had started. "Suppose we join our shelter-canvases together and make one big tent and heat it?"

"Sounds good," Don agreed eagerly. "But—"

"Now I won't tolerate any sexual discrimination," she said briskly. "I'm an experienced camper and I know more than the rest of you combined about setting up. I'll prove that right now."

And she did. Her nimble fingers fashioned the tent much more efficiently than the others could have, even working together. She also set up a separate minor tent for sanitary purposes, a refinement the others had not thought of. That eliminated the need to take individual hikes into the gloom. She detached each person's converter from the bicycles and carried them into that tent, since each person's ecological balance depended on that recycling system. This amazed Don, and evidently the others; they had not realized that this could be done. She set four bicycles inside the tent, bracing the walls, and the fifth beside the privy.

"Now you'll have to hold your breath to cross between tents, because there'll be an oxygen shortage," she warned. "But the one bike will provide for one person in the sanitary tent. You will have to carry your own converter with you to use; that can not safely be shared. Don will have to contribute bad food packages to the other converters at the same rate he borrows good food from the others, to keep the approximate balance. Right, Eleph?"

"There is some oxygen in the alternate framework," Eleph said. "But this is insufficient without supplementation by the field, yes. And it is true that the converters must remain virtually sealed systems."

Some oxygen in the other realm. Don wondered about that, but couldn't quite formulate a specific question. What kind of alternate was that? He wished he had a better notion.

Pacifa set the five converters in the main tent on "high." The

heat wafted through the tent as the accelerated chemical compost-
ing proceeded within each unit, processing the wastes of the day.
It became a thoroughly pleasant place, walling out the gloom, almost making this seem like a chamber in some civilized city on
land. Don felt his fatigue and tension melting away.

"But it will be necessary to relocate periodically," Eleph
warned. "The oxygen dissolved in sea water is limited, particularly at this depth, and unless refreshed by current—"

"You're right!" Gaspar said, snapping his fingers. "I should
have thought of that. We could suffocate in our sleep."

"I did think of it," Pacifa said imperturbably. "We are camped
in a slight but steady current that should provide fresh oxygen as
we need it. Now for supper." She took the food packages from
each supply except Don's, squeezed water into them, and set the
result on top of the center converter. It's surface was now burning
hot. In a few minutes she served them a hot meal that seemed
vastly superior to what they had had before, even though it had
to be the same stuff. "Seasoning," she confided with a wink.

Don basked in the warm tent and ate his hot food. Yes, the selection of personnel was starting to make sense. A man did not
live by archaeology alone; he required the minimum comforts of
life. Pacifa had provided them, and at this moment he would not
have traded her for anyone. Not even her shapely daughter, even
if his stutter did not exist.

That reminded him of Melanie. He was sitting beside her in
the tent, hip to hip, but it was as if she were far away. "You've
been quiet. How are you doing?"

She turned her face to him and smiled. "You are interested?"

It became as if the two of them were alone. "Yes."

"I was imagining myself on land. While we were riding, and
now."

"While we were plunging to the dismal depths, risking our
very lives?" he demanded facetiously. One thing her revelation of
her condition had done for him was to distance her enough emotionally to make her approachable socially. This was not a para-
dox so much as an eddy-current; he could talk with a woman
who was not a romantic prospect, just as he could talk with a
man who was not a rival. "What if something had happened?"

Gaspar half-smiled and lay back comfortably. Pacifa had eaten
her serving quickly and was quietly cleaning up. Eleph seemed to

be falling asleep. It was Don's conversation to carry, if he chose.

"What could I have done if it had?" Melanie asked reasonably. "I'd be better off far away."

He played the game, beginning to enjoy it. "Where did you go? To the beach again?"

"No, this time I rode around town."

"Around town!" he exclaimed, evoking a small smile from Pacifa. "In the daytime? Didn't people see you?"

"No. At least, not exactly."

He was beginning to see it himself: her riding her bike as he had at the outset, on land. "This is a secret mission. If you—"

"I couldn't stand being alone anymore!" she cried with the edge of hysteria.

Don felt a wash of sympathy. He saw Gaspar nod, and Pacifa paused for a moment. But still they stayed out of it, letting Don talk to Melanie alone, as it were.

He had never held a dialogue like this before, and was afraid he would muff it. At the same time, he was profoundly grateful for it. He would try to calm her down, not merely because it might help her, but because it felt good to be trying to help her. This was on one level a flight of fancy, an escape from the emotional pressure of this fatigue and mystery in a strange dark, cold place. But on another it was personal truth.

"I can't blame you," he said. "This whole project is weird. What did you see?"

Her eyes were closed now, and she seemed to be truly in her vision or memory. "I rode right along the downtown streets." Now she sounded almost breathless, as if she were active instead of passive. "Beside the cars, through crowds of people, in the middle of the day. I obeyed all the traffic signals and gave pedestrians the right of way. It was all so ordinary I nearly cried."

"Like the beach," he said. "When you walked on the sand and saw the seagulls in the wind. I didn't have the nerve to go out among people. After being phased out, I mean." Or before, really, he realized. He had always been a stranger, as much when in the city as when in his home neighborhood.

"I guess so, pretty much," she agreed. "But then I got so hungry for some kind of interaction I—"

Because she too had always been alone: without family support, and with that stark lack of hair making her a freak—

He brought himself up short. "Yes," he said gently. "It's hard to be alone." He was discovering that no artifice was needed, just identification.

"I started breaking the rules," she confessed. "I'm basically a social creature. I—I rode right through people, to see what they'd do. And—"

This was getting too real. Don was afraid to ask, but afraid not to. Was this truly invention, or had she done this while waiting for the rendezvous? "And—?"

"And they never even noticed. Any more than the sea did. No contact."

"Not even the bones?"

"I—I didn't know about that, then. There was a—but I don't want to talk about that. It's too much like violation. I meant there was no personality contact. They just shrugged and apologized and went on. They—they never realized what it was."

"Never realized they had had a ghost on a bicycle ride through them? How could they miss it?"

"Well, I guess in a crowd you get banged quite a bit anyway, so you don't notice things. Maybe you don't want to. And all the world's a crowd, today. They never really looked at me."

"That's incredible."

"No it isn't," she said sadly. "When I thought about it, just now, I realized that it was no different from the rest of my life. Being alone, no matter how big the crowd, no matter how different I think I am, no one notices. The mind, the personality, I mean. All they notice is the other."

Now Pacifa spoke. "What other?"

For answer, Melanie swept her hands up and dragged off her wig. "Just a little physical interaction," she continued. "Like that gruesome meshing of bones, but no awareness of what's inside, what's beyond the label, beyond the . . ." There were tears now, flowing from the doll's eyes in the doll's bare skull.

"Oh, my," Pacifa murmured.

Melanie seemed oblivious. "It reminds me of a song that was popular before my time. I had it on a record. 'Nobody loves me 'cause nobody knows me.' It was called 'Single Girl.'" She hummed the tune.

She was feeling sorry for herself. But Don could not deny she had reason. Those who blithely disparaged the state tended to be unfeeling louts, he felt. He had not liked his own lonely first section of this mission, and that had been for less than a day. Melanie had been isolated longer, waiting. But for her, as it was for him, this was only an episode in a life of similar isolation.

What could he tell her? Her problem was real, and it would be hypocritical to pretend that it wasn't. Don found himself tongue-tied, when he least wanted to be.

"May I?" Pacifa inquired.

Don looked at her. She came to kneel before Melanie. Melanie's eyes opened. "What?"

"I am one of those who does not know you," Pacifa said. "How could I? I am new to this group. But perhaps I know your type."

"My type?"

"And you do not know me. But this much can be rectified. I can tell you in a few minutes what is relevant."

"N-now wait—" Don started.

Gaspar lifted a hand, signaling peace. Don took the hint and was quiet.

"We are all of us alone, I think," Pacifa said. "That seems to have been a requirement for this mission, which is not the most comfortable thought. It may mean that we're expendable. But it could mean instead that we are fragments capable of uniting into a kind of family. Then none of us would be alone."

Melanie's eyes widened, but she did not speak.

"About me," Pacifa continued. "I oversimplified. I could not have sent my daughter here. I was once part of a reasonably typical family. My husband was fifteen years older than I and a good man. But he did not take care of himself. He smoked—too much, drank—too much, ate fatty foods, did not exercise, and had a high-stress job. He led, in general, the conventional unhealthy life style, and it took him out with a heart attack at age sixty. I had taken a job which absorbed my attention, and somehow had not seen his demise coming. My daughter was beautiful, but she ran off with an alcoholic who finally beat her to death. That I saw coming, but she wouldn't listen. Had I my life to live over, I would address both situations in time and save my family. But I was wise way too late. I disavowed it all, their parts and mine, and focused thereafter on a totally healthy lifestyle, maintaining economic and emotional independence. Yet satisfaction eluded me. I signed up for this mission in the hope that it would offer me not only a challenge but—" She paused.

"I understand," Melanie murmured.

"You are in a way like my daughter. I realize that this is artificial, and there are no quick fixes—"

Melanie lifted her arms. The two embraced, awkwardly but tightly.

Don closed his eyes. Why couldn't he have done something like that?

Chapter 6

•

Mystery

Proxy 5-12-5-16-8: Attention.
Acknowledging.
Status?
Group is complete and melding is proceeding. There should be further progress as they encounter the next group challenge.
When will they learn the mission?
When melding is complete.
Do they know that one of them is an agent of a local government?
The others do not know.
Or that you are a member of their group?
They do not know.
You run the risk of destroying the group and with it the mission, when they learn.
Yes. I hope the risk is less than that of the direct approach.
We hope so too. A world is at stake.

• • •

As they progressed, the differences between bicycles became more obvious. Gaspar was in the best physical condition of the men, being muscular and accustomed to strenuous activity. Yet he seemed to tire the most rapidly. Pacifa, a woman in her fifties, was indefatigable. Don and Eleph and Melanie fell in between, with a slight advantage going to Eleph. It had to be the bicycles.

Don watched, working it out. Gaspar had a one-speed machine without fixtures, apart from those attached for the phase trip. Up hills he panted; down hills he used the coaster brake. When the way was steep, he had to walk because he could not put out his feet to steady himself in emergencies in the way the others could—not without sacrificing his necessary braking power. Thus his muscle was inefficiently employed, and it cost him.

Melanie had three speeds, and they seemed to help her a lot. She was young and trim; her lack of weight surely helped her keep the pace, because it took less work to haul that weight upslope. But she was structured in the fashion of a woman, not a man, and simply lacked the muscle mass to do a lot.

Don himself had five speeds. Ordinarily he remained in third or fourth gear, but on a sustained climb he shifted down to second. A smooth decline allowed him to speed along in fifth. The range seemed quite suitable, and he had no complaints, though he certainly felt a day's travel. He was hardening to it, as they all were, but he did wish the sea floor was both smoother and more level.

Eleph, who was of Pacifa's generation, had all of thirty six speeds. He seemed to use only a few—no more than Don did, perhaps—but he could choose them precisely, and could take advantage of the best ratio for any situation. Those turned-down handlebars looked awkward, but they caused the man to assume an efficient riding position: head down, body hunched so as to reduce wind (water) resistance and allow the most effective use of the leg muscles. The whole body was positioned in line with the thrust of the pedals: therein might lie the real key. Don tried to imitate the position, though his higher handlebars forced his elbows out awkwardly, and it did seem to help.

Pacifa's bicycle had only ten speeds, and the same turned-down handlebars. She was no more muscular than Melanie, and a generation older. Yet she moved effortlessly, it seemed. What advantage did she have over Eleph?

The differences seemed small. Pacifa wore gloves, not the dressy kind or heavy protective ones, but a kind of open webbing with the fingers cut off. They seemed useless, a pointless affectation. Until he noticed how sweaty his hands became on the hard rubber grips. Her gloves removed the palms from the rubber—actually she had black tape wrapped around the bars instead, for some reason—just enough to ensure ventilation, and they also provided friction. That could count for a lot, after eight or ten hours of arm-muscle twitchings. She had loops over her toes, fastening them to the pedals. This looked clumsy and dangerous at first; what if she took an unexpected spill? But Don soon saw that the straps did for her feet what the gloves did for her hands. Furthermore, she could actually pull-up on the pedals as well as push-down, using different muscles while increasing power. As if that weren't enough, her shoes were cleated, and seemed to have metal-reinforced soles to protect her feet from battering. Don's own feet felt as if someone had been hammering on them, the soreness extending right into the bone.

Even so, it didn't seem to account for her stamina. She was in good physical health, but so was Gaspar. She wasn't muscular, yet she seemed to have the endurance of a woman twenty years younger. Don resolved to talk to her about it at the next opportunity.

When that chance came, he was surprised. "Ankling," she said. "Cadence."

"What-ling?"

"Ankling. That's half my secret. You men just push on the balls of your feet; I use my ankles. Like this." She positioned one foot in the stirrup. "At the top of the stroke, my toe points up. As I complete the stroke, it angles down, until at the bottom—"

"But that makes your ankle do all the work of pedaling, instead of the large muscles," Don protested.

"No, the entire body participates. Ankling merely increases the effectiveness of the stroke, letting me use every muscle to advantage. You can't put the whole load on one part of the leg and expect it to stand up."

Don tried it. "Seems awkward."

"For you, the first time, yes. But so is a baby's first meal with a spoon. Here, let me raise your saddle; you can't operate effectively unless your bike is adjusted to your leg-length."

She loosened a bolt with her wrench and raised the seat about an inch and a half.

"I can barely reach the pedals now!" Don protested, trying it.

"Nonsense. Any change feels strange at first, even when it's for the better. In the long run—"

"Maybe so. I'll practice ankling tomorrow, if I don't fall over. But why didn't you tell me about it at the beginning?"

"Why didn't you tell me about hammerhead sharks?"

"That's not the same."

"It will do."

"I suppose we all have to learn by experience. But at least they could have had us standardize on bicycles. Experience won't change our problem of equipment. Poor Gaspar—"

"There will be adaptation equipment at the first supply de-pot," she said with a smile.

"How do you know that?"

"We women are not so amiable as you men about the finicky details. I put conditions on my participation in this venture. I knew someone would foul up on the hardware, as it seems they already have on your food."

"I never realized bicycles were that different," Don said sheep-ishly.

"Oh, they are. Wait till you try a lightweight tourer, instead of that milk wagon you're on now. Ten speeds, rat-trap pedals—"

"Rattletrap pedals!"

"Rat-trap. Like this." She showed one of her pedals. Don was amazed; with all his comparison of the bicycles, he had not picked up on this detail. The thing was empty. There were only two strips of metal paralleling the main bolt. It did look like the jaws of a rat trap.

"Cuts weight, provides a better grip for the foot," she ex-plained. "The true racing pedals have saw-tooth edges for real friction. But I'm not racing."

Don would never want to race her, however. "About those ten gears. Eleph has—"

"Thirty six speeds. Talk about overkill! Trust the military mind to squander resources. But it is a good machine, for all his ignor-ance. Once he learns how to use it, he'll be all right."

"Why is it you have only ten speeds, instead of—"

"Ten's all I need. The point of gearing is not to give you different speeds, in the manner of a car, but to enable you to maintain a suitable cycling rhythm. That's cadence. A steady turning of the crank arm at constant revolutions. Find what's most comfortable for you—say sixty turns a minute—and stick to it. Your forward speed may vary, but not your cadence. That way you'll last longer with less fatigue."

Don shook his head. "If I didn't see you standing there all peppery while I'm beat, I'd figure it was quibbling."

"That's right." She started off to see about camping arrangements.

"Uh, one other thing," he said, suddenly feeling awkward. "Last night—what you did for Melanie—that was a g-generous thing."

"Don't give me credit that isn't due," she snapped. "I did it for me."

"For—?"

"Your turn will come, when you get over this nonsense about appearances." She moved off.

Bemused, Don went about his own business.

• • •

They traveled a hundred miles a day, under the Gulf Stream. However warm the water might be above, it remained cold here, for they were in the region of deep-water circulation. The cold current was opposite to that of the warm one, giving them an effective tailwind. Though only a thousandth of the water temperature affected him, Don was very glad for the protective warmth of the converter unit.

At the end of the first day of full bottom travel the depth was over six hundred fathoms. At the end of the second day it was one thousand fathoms. On the third day they reached fourteen hundred fathoms and encountered the vast sedimentary plains of the Gulf of Mexico. As far as their headlamps would show, which was not any great distance, the sea floor was flat and featureless except for spider-like brittlestars and occasional sea cucumbers. Some few glass sponges stuck up in clusters, and some fanlike sea fans. Ugly two-foot long fish, which Gaspar identified as rattailed grenadiers, scouted here and there, as well as spindly-legged crustaceans. But the overall impression was that of a desert.

A desert under water! Could this be the result of man's pollution? Actually it was a swamp. Don imagined the muck giving way beneath the weight of the bicycles, scant as the effect might be with the phaseout. If they slowed, would the thin tires sink?

The answer was no. The phase world's surface was hard. Don mused again about that, without effect. The full nature of that other realm remained a mystery.

On and on, for hours, unvarying. There was no danger here, merely boredom. Yet this region was tiny compared to the great abyssal plains of the main oceans, according to Gaspar. The Bearing Plain was supposedly about as large as the entire Gulf of Mexico.

"*Abysmal* plains," Pacifa retorted to that statement. "Not much for tourists here."

"You'll just have to bus them over this stretch," Gaspar said with a smile. The seat of his bike was higher now, and the level terrain helped too, so that he was doing better.

"Impossible," Eleph said, taking him seriously. "No motor will operate within the atmospheric conversion field."

"Oh?" Don was interested. "I thought it was just electricity that got fouled up."

"Ignition is required for a motor."

"How about a diesel?"

"That might operate, if allowance is made for continuous oxygenation in the chambers. But the exhaust would foul our limited environment very quickly and asphyxiate us. The same is true for almost any flame. Human usage is the reasonable maximum the infusion of oxygen can sustain."

"But our radios work," Melanie said. She too had her seat higher, and was doing better, but Don thought the bike was only a small part of the reason. For one thing, she was no longer wearing her wig. She had packed it away, and was going openly as she was. That had bothered Don at first, but he discovered that after the first few hours it didn't matter. She was herself.

"The radios are shielded," Eleph said. "The current they use is minor."

"Still, if electricity does—" Don began.

"Of course electricity functions," Eleph said sharply. "I never said it didn't. Our own nervous systems are electrical. But the heavy-duty applications involved in a motor become complex."

"So we use bicycles," Pacifa said. "They always did make more sense than cars, anywhere, and are mighty handy if you want to sneak up on something."

"Sneak up?" Eleph demanded, frowning.

"Cuba is a hostile foreign nation," she said. "Our mission may be to circle it, spying out its secrets. We couldn't do it if we made a lot of noise."

"I hope it's not that," Melanie said. "I don't want to spy on anyone."

Don agreed. Exploration was fine, but not spying.

"We should know, when we are informed of our mission," Eleph said.

"Aren't we getting close to that depot now?" Don asked. "My meter says so."

"Close," Pacifa agreed. "The depot is right in these flats, or we wouldn't be here at all. I've been watching for dud shells, or whatever. How's the ankling?"

"Doesn't seem to help much."

"Oh, come on. Get your toes up, and don't push with the middle of your foot. If you had proper gear, you wouldn't be able to do that. We'll have to lift your saddle a bit more. Lean forward; get your weight where it belongs. You aren't tricycling around the city block, you know."

Indeed he wasn't. The resistive muck had sapped his scant strength, though he knew that resistance was largely in his imagination. Oh for a good long rest.

Melanie cycled close. "Mothers are like that," she said.

They rode on for another half hour. Pacifa pulled up to talk with Gaspar. Then the two called a halt.

"We're past the spot," she announced. "Anybody hear a beacon?"

No one had. "A beacon is a visual indication, not a sonic," Eleph muttered. "You must have misunderstood."

"It's supposed to be the same whistle we use to find each other," Pacifa said. "But mechanically generated. Check it yourself."

"Madam, I shall." Eleph led the way back, watching his locator closely. There was a slight difference between units, so that when Eleph's read exactly 84°50′ west longitude, Don's read 84°49′, and the others varied similarly. That represented a divergence of a mile, and the whistle was limited to about a mile. No one on the surface, a mile and a half above, could pick it up, theoretically. Don questioned the validity of any claim that a sound could be completely damped out by distance, but he wasn't going to question a physicist on that. Perhaps the phase had something to do with it.

They checked the exact coordinates as interpreted by each of their meters, then circled the entire area at one mile and two mile radii. There was no whistle, and no sign of the depot.

"We appear to have inaccurate coordinates," Eleph said gravely.

They knew what that meant. No supplies. It would be impossible for them to find the depot without knowing its precise location, for the Gulf of Mexico was a thousand miles across. An error of as little as twenty miles would reduce their chances to sheerest accident.

"Cuba?" Don asked, remember Pacifa's suspicion. "If they knew—"

"They do not control these waters," Eleph said. "They would have no clue to the location, even if they were aware of the mission."

"Must be a simple mistake, then," Gaspar said. "Melanie, are you sure you remembered the coordinates correctly?

"I'm sure," she said. "I wish I weren't."

"Mistakes of this nature are not made," Eleph insisted, the tic in his cheek beginning to show again.

Pacifa began unpacking the tent sections. "If it isn't a mistake, and no one took away the depot, it must be deliberate. Do you really think we would be set up for nothing?"

"Of course not!" Eleph said. "The depot is here, somewhere. The coordinates must have suffered a change in transmission."

"Hey are you saying I—" Melanie demanded.

"No. I am saying that you must have been given the wrong coordinates. Such information is routinely transferred from one office to another. Someone in the chain must have changed it, to strand us here."

"Who?" Pacifa asked.

"A representative of anyone who wanted this mission to fail."

Gaspar shook his head. "The simplest explanation is most often correct, correct? These government bureaucracies make a living from fouling things up. Some dolt put spoiled food-powder in Don's pack and never checked it, and another dolt must have misquoted the coordinates. No mistake is too idiotic for a bureaucrat to make, especially when lives are at stake. Remember all the boo-boos over the years in the space program! Tying down delicate equipment with baling wire, putting faulty wiring in an oxygen chamber, sending up a manned mission when there were icicles on the rockets—"

"Icicles?" Eleph asked.

"Remember when the Challenger exploded? Because the cold had stiffened the O-rings? That mistake cost seven lives. And the Hubble orbiting telescope—two billion dollars, and then they discovered they'd put in the wrong shaped mirror."

Eleph frowned as if confused, but rallied in a moment. "Those were isolated incidents in an operation of unparalleled complexity. Still, I fear that something of that nature is the case here."

"We shall have to go backward to land—or forward to the mission," Pacifa said. She had been working all along, and now had the tents assembled and was starting on supper. "We do have access to the location of the next depot, fortunately."

"No certainty of that," Eleph muttered.

"For someone who's as pro-government as you are, you're mighty suspicious!" she snapped at him.

The tic was rampaging now. "Madam, I am merely being realistic. We are already short of food, and further complications—"

"If this was an accident," Pacifa said evenly, "the next depot may be all right. But if someone deliberately changed the number, he could just as readily have changed all the numbers. So we had better guess right."

"Maybe if we knew what the mission is, we could tell whether it's an accident," Melanie said. "I mean, who cares if we're just riding around? But if we're spying—"

"I don't see why anyone should try to abort undersea geology," Gaspar said.

"Or archaeology," Don said.

"Or a new kind of tourism," Pacifa said.

"Or a mere testing of equipment," Eleph said. "But—"

"But our specialties may be just a cover for what we're really supposed to do," Pacifa concluded. "So we really don't know and can't guess. But it occurs to me that our smartest move, if this trouble is deliberate, might be to get on with it in a hurry and catch them by surprise. They'll be expecting us to turn back at this point, and if something is going on under the ocean, that re- prieve may be all they need to cover it up."

"Precisely my sentiments," Eleph said.

"If those two agree, they must be right," Gaspar said with a smile.

"B-but if we don't find the s-second depot—"

"Then we'll simply blow the whistle," Pacifa said. "Ride up on the nearest land and make a scene that'll bring our bureaucrats scampering. They may have ignored Melanie, in her vision, but I suspect that if we made a concerted effort, we would not be ig- nored."

Melanie clapped her hands. "How beautifully simple!"

Indeed, Don liked the notion too. No one could hurt them in their phased out state; they would be pedaling ghosts. The fearful hullabaloo would publicize the whole business. A drastic step, and not one to be taken short of necessity—but still a realistic al- ternative that would ensure prompt action. It would have to be prompt, if they ran out of food.

And probably there was no conspiracy anyway. But then he thought of one more thing. "B-but suppose no land is near?"

"Well, let's find out," Pacifa said. "If there's nothing, we'll just have to plan ahead. Save enough food to make it on land. Mela- nie?"

"I'm not supposed to give out the new coordinates until—"

"Until we're at the prior ones," Pacifa finished for her. "As we are now. Satisfied?"

"Yes, I suppose so," Melanie agreed. "Twenty one degrees fif- ty north latitude, eighty nine degrees thirty west longitude."

"The Yucatan," Gaspar said promptly. He showed the relevant map segment. "North coast, about here."

Don stared. "Dzibilchaltun," he breathed.

The others looked at him.

"Dzibilchaltun," he repeated. "Fabulous ancient city of the Mayans, and before. That's the area. I don't know it from the co- ordinates, but I could never forget that spot on the map."

"I thought you were a European archaeologist," Gaspar said, not unkindly.

"I am. I know almost nothing about the new world. But who

hasn't heard of Dzibilchaltun?"

"Who, indeed," Pacifa said wryly. It was obvious that the name meant nothing to the others. "But at least it gives you something to work on."

"Yes!" Don said. "Dzibilchaltun was contemporary with the Minoan culture, though of course there was no connection between them. Certainly I'll want to compare—"

"Maybe we'd better save the exploration for when we get there," Pacifa said. "We have a long hard ride on short supplies. At least it *is* near land—quite near. Right now we'd better sleep." She served up reduced rations, and they turned in.

But Don, as always when under stress, could not get the rest he needed. The entire project had taken on new meaning. He strove to remember what he had picked up about the Mayan culture, but there were only inconsequential fragments. The Mayans had had what some reckoned to be the world's finest calendar, and much fine handiwork in metals and cloth, and superior art—but what of their considerable history? Dzibilchaltun dated from about 3000 B.C., as did the Minoan civilization, but the Mayans hadn't built that city. They had come later. That was all he could remember, if he had ever known more. He had been too narrow a specialist, engrossed in the wonders of his own specialty, poring over the language and script of the ancient Cretans until these seemed almost as familiar to him as his own people. He had neglected the other side of the ancient world almost completely. If only he had known of the opportunity that was coming!

As he wrestled with his uncertainties and frustrations, an unpleasant truth emerged. Pacifa was correct: their specialties were only a cover for their real mission, which had nothing to do with anything they had studied. Otherwise Gaspar would have been sent to the Bahamas platform, and Pacifa would have had a feasible tourist route to clarify. There would have been a Mayan scholar along, instead of a Minoan one. And Eleph—what was he doing, anyway? He said he was a physicist, and that he knew how to repair the breathing field, but probably that would never have to be put to the test.

If Don and Gaspar and Melanie and Pacifa were merely along for appearances, with Eleph doing the dirty work—it *had* to be dirty, with secrecy like this!—why had the government bothered? There *were* no appearances on this mile-deep tour.

The more he thought about it, the less he liked it.

Melanie was lying beside him. "You're not sleeping, Don," she murmured. "And I don't suppose it's because of frustrated passion for me."

He had to laugh, but it was forced. "I'd rather be honest, and just admit that your hair has severely shaken my romantic notions," he said. "But you're a good enough person, Melanie, and—"

"Don't belabor it. What's really on your mind?"

"Do you ever get the feeling that we're penned in a madhouse?"

"All the time," she agreed.

"I mean here/now. The group of us on this mission."

"Oh, you're not mad," she said. "Not really. I've seen much worse."

"Worse than a militaristic physicist or a bike-toting grandma?"

"He's not as bad as all that. And she's not a grandma. Just—I do like her, Don. I do need her."

"Sorry. That business between you two—"

He broke off, but Melanie didn't respond.

"Hey, did I say something to—?" he asked, concerned.

"Oh, no," she said quickly. "I was just thinking. About worse people. I knew some real characters at—at another place. One woman was a farmer, slaughtering and butchering her own hogs—do you have any idea how much blood—?"

"I don't care to," Don said quickly, not from squeamishness, but because it was an oblique way to support her. She was doing him the kindness of talking to him now, and he wanted it to last a little longer.

"And once I met a couple of young men at a John Birch meeting. I wore the wig, of course; they didn't know. One had a gun collection—"

"John Birch?" Don demanded, surprised. "Isn't that the far right group that—*you* went to—?"

"I do try to listen to everyone's viewpoint," she said defensively. "When I get up the nerve to go out among people. Anyway, he collected guns. About twenty rifles, eight pistols, three submachine guns, and two bazookas, with ammunition. He said he was a monarchist. He had a bottle he'd picked up in Turkey, he said—full of enemy eyeballs. Turkish enemies—I don't know where the eyes came from originally, but they were awful. Maybe it was some other country; I don't know whether I can believe him. But those eyeballs certainly looked real. He talked about impaling the Supreme Court justices on the front steps of the Court Building, the slow way."

"Impalement!" Don exclaimed. "I didn't know there were fast and slow ways."

"Neither did I. In fact, I didn't know what impalement *was*. But he explained. In detail. I think I got sick."

"But how—?"

She was silent.

Don decided not to push the question. He was beginning to remember how the Assyrians had done it. The sharp point of a long stout pole was inserted in the subject's posterior, and he was thereby hoisted into the air, his own weight completing the impalement, in the course of agonizing hours. Melanie *had* known worse people!

"I guess we're pretty well off, here, after all," he said.

"Yes. Despite all the doubt, it's sort of nice. In its way. We're together, all of us, perforce. Holding hands, as it were. I haven't felt that sort of thing in a long time."

He pondered briefly, and decided to take a plunge. "M-may I?" he asked.

She laughed. Then her hand came to him in the darkness, and he took it.

Then, holding hands, they slept.

Chapter 7

•

Crevasse

Proxy 5-12-5-16-8: Attention.
Acknowledging.
Status?
The members of the group are coming to terms with their situation. They realize that something is wrong, and that it may be because of external malice, but have resolved to proceed regardless. This is an excellent sign.
Are you sure of them now?
No. There remain too many complex currents. They are for the moment united in a specific effort, but are not melded. They need more time. Progress is being made, and the young woman is forming attachments to two of the other recruits. The outcome looks positive, but cannot be presumed. We need four attachments.
How will you achieve this?
I will continue putting challenges before them, as planned. The next one is natural: a crevasse which will be difficult to pass rapidly.
We hope you know what you're doing.
I hope so too.

•   •   •

"Now we'll have to set up rationing," Pacifa said. "We're already short because of that spoilage. No trouble stretching the food of four between five people; we each have more than enough. But we have five hundred miles to go with no refills, and that's a rough haul. We'll make it because we have to, and because perhaps some other party doesn't think we can—but we aren't going to enjoy it much."

Don felt guilty, because it was the failure of his food supply that intensified the squeeze. He knew it wasn't his fault, yet it bothered him.

"Now I'll ration it out with strict impartiality," Pacifa continued in her brisk way. "You will all carry your own, but we shall do a count now. You'll get suspicious when you get tired and hungry and short of sleep—and believe me, you'll be all three!—and that's natural. So I want you to check the count now, so we all know exactly how many packages there are."

There were sixteen.

"Each package is supposed to be good for one meal," she continued. "At three meals a day for all five of us, that's about one day. At our normal progress, we have five days travel coming up." She paused, making sure they all understood. "So we'll have to speed up. Our limit is food, not strength. We've toughened up the past few days, warming up for this effort. We'll do it in two and a half days. And we'll make the food stretch to cover that. Five meals a day."

"Five meals a day!" Eleph exclaimed. "Madam, we haven't enough for three, let alone—"

"Small ones, Eleph," she said. "Eat often, and you eat less. You never get really hungry, so never have to compensate. And your system processes the small amounts efficiently. Especially when you're exercising."

Gaspar caught on. "We'll split one package between the five of us, each time. Five times a day, two and a half days—and—"

"Almost," she said. "I believe we need more than that; one quarter of a package at a time should be about right. So we shall quarter them, making sixty four quarters in all. We shall eat twenty five quarters a day, for two and a half days, or a total of sixty two and a half quarters. That's nonsense, of course; no one will eat half a quarter. But the point is, we shall have a slight reserve, which we can dispense as necessary. If one of us is required to do heavy work—" she glanced at Gaspar—"he will get an extra ration. We can not safely assume that the way will be completely without challenge."

"That's for sure!" Gaspar agreed. "Well have to climb the continental shelf to reach the Yucatan peninsula, and that in itself will be a formidable task. If there are any obstructions—"

"Precisely," she agreed seriously. "We need that emergency reserve. We all have some fatty reserves; we can put out some energy without killing ourselves. But if we go too slow, we can starve before getting there. Now let me brush you up on riding technique. First, posture. Eleph, you ride like an old woman—and even old women don't do that, if they want to get anywhere. I ought to know."

She went on to give them all the information she had given Don before, while she adjusted saddles and handlebars and checked each bicycle quickly for problems. Eleph and Gaspar were shaking their heads dubiously, but Don knew she was right.

"We must make two hundred miles a day," she continued. "Roughly fourteen miles per hour, average. That may not sound like much, and it isn't—for me. It'll kill *you*, in this terrain. But not quite as dead as hunger will. At least you know what the deep sea is like, and won't stop to gawk at the fish." She smiled briefly. "Are you ready?"

Of course they weren't, but there was no choice.

They rode, paced by Pacifa. Gaspar led, followed by Eleph, then Melanie and Don. Pacifa changed positions, riding parallel to each of the others in turn, making sure they were all right. Her stamina was amazing; she really did have far better ability than any of the others, in this regard.

On the level it wasn't bad; the hunched posture did seem to diminish the watery resistance. But then they crossed low hills rising out of the abyssal sediment, and Don quickly felt his leg muscles stiffen. As time passed, it got worse. From knee to crotch, the great front muscles tightened into dull pain. His breath came fast and sweat ran down his forehead despite the minimum setting on the converter. He shifted from fifth to fourth, and then to third; this eased the immediate strain but increased his rate of pedaling. Just as much energy was being drawn from his body, but in a different manner, and his cadence was being sacrificed.

He saw that Melanie was having similar trouble. Fortunately

she had good legs, and she was keeping the pace. She had a small advantage because her bald head presented less resistance to the current-wind.

Don concentrated on the techniques Pacifa had described, leaning forward to put his weight over the pedals instead of into his posterior, utilizing his torso as well as his legs, and ankling. The higher saddle no longer felt strange. He saw the others doing the same, looking worse off than he felt. That was gratifying. As the grueling pace robbed his leg muscles of their capacity, these other actions did come to fill the power vacuum, and he gained a second wind that was much more durable than the first. He was moving!

But when they clocked 120 miles and stopped for the fourth meal of the day and Don stepped off his bike, his knees buckled and he sprawled ignominiously on the ground. There was no gumption left. Gaspar and Eleph were no better off. Melanie was standing as if both knees were in casts, afraid to bend them at all.

Pacifa remained distressingly spry. "Eat hearty, folk," she said as she divided a package of fish-flavored glop. "We'll be doing some riding, soon."

Don ate, and she was right: it was enough, for his hunger was as small as his fatigue was large.

● ● ●

They struck the continental slope of the Yucatan Peninsula of Central America. In the space of ten miles they climbed a thousand fathoms, and were still deeper than they had been in the straits of Florida. A rise of one part in ten was a killer. When it became steeper than that, they dismounted and trudged, leaning on their machines for support. No fourteen miles per hour here!

The terrible climb went on and on, dragging at the last vestiges of bodily strength. Here even Pacifa suffered, for she was a cyclist, not a hiker. But no one would give up, and when at last the land leveled into the continental shelf, about six hundred fathoms deep, four of them dropped without eating into the troubled collapse of exhaustion. Only Pacifa remained on her feet.

They had not made their mileage quota, but they were well over the hump.

"Here, Gaspar, I'll give you some ease," Pacifa said. She sat and took one of his legs and kneaded the muscle. He sighed with dawning bliss.

"That looks good," Melanie said. "Trade?"

Don sat up and took one of her legs. He watched what Pacifa was doing and tried to do the same to Melanie. She smiled rapturously. His arms were merely tired, not knotted; he was working with the part of his body that had some reserve energy. But even in his fatigue, he noticed how nice her legs were. At any other time, he would not be able to handle them like this without getting seriously distracted. Did hair really matter? He could feel his doubt growing. A wig could emulate hair, but what could emulate flesh like this?

But soon she insisted on taking her turn and doing his legs. Her hands were marvelously healing. It was a wonderful feeling which had nothing to do with sex; his legs started to relax. If he had been bringing this feeling to her, he had been doing right. Did her thoughts drift as his had?

"One thing really impressed me about taking birth control pills," Melanie said as she kneaded. It was her way: to embark on some remote subject that nevertheless related in some manner to whatever was going on in the foreground. It seemed that her thoughts *did* drift. "They impaired my ability to follow abstract arguments. I had been working my way through Henri Bergson's book *Time and Free Will*. I don't know how the pills did it, but the results were too obvious. The most direct was indirect: how much more readily I could follow the arguments after I stopped taking the pills. That kind of thing always brings to my mind the specter of chemical control. A subtle, insidious thing. Control of the higher faculties. Maybe it was all due to a mild induced anemia or some such, but whatever it was, it was most effective. It robbed me of my spark, or inner drive or whatever, which was about all I had going for me."

Don's leg muscles were relaxing, but his mind was not. Melanie was supposed to be a shy single girl. Why was she taking birth control pills?

Why, indeed! Was he hopelessly naive? She had wanted social interaction, and if she didn't remove her wig, a short-term relationship was feasible. Sex could be quite short-term.

"I consider myself more a complete determinist than Bergson is," she continued. "But my final conclusions about free will are

very close to his. To me it has always seemed as if all these arguments are aspects of an inner drive that is trying to assert itself. A
drive toward higher abstraction. Something I consider to be char-
acteristically human."

Don wondered what kind of a drive accounted for talking
about birth control pills while massaging a male companion's
legs. He also wondered irrelevantly why she had shown him and
the others her bald state. The one could almost be taken as an
oblique sexual come-on, while the other was the opposite. He had
never heard of Bergson and had not thought much about free
will.

"Human beings greatly desire to be free," Melanie continued.
"But freedom as experienced by the self is not the absence of
prior determining experiences, but rather the opportunity to act
in accordance with one's innermost drives. So that if one assumes
that physical determinism is all-pervasive—that the combination
of one's past history and one's physical reality completely deter-
mines one's choices—even then there is no absence of freedom.
Because no matter how completely one's choices have been pre-
determined, there always remains complete inner freedom. I can
make any possible choice as long as I am willing to suffer the consequences of my actions. If a person says 'I can't do that' about
anything it is physically possible for him to do, he is saying in effect 'I am unwilling to suffer the consequences of that action.'"

Don wondered morosely whether she thought that taking
birth control pills was an evasion of the consequences of her actions. Here she was talking about freedom, but all he could think
of was what she was planning to *do* with that freedom. Why had
she been thinking about those pills, right now?

Then it came together. Melanie was chained by her circumstance: any man who saw her bald would be turned off. So whatever she might have done while on pills was not relevant, because it could not last. Now she was being open about her
liability, and taking the consequence. But apart from that, she was
a human being, and a lonely one, like him.

He sat up. "I-I'm going to exert *m-my* free will," he said. "And
take the consequence." Then he caught her shoulders, drew her
in, and kissed her. He had been massaging her legs, right up to
the buttocks, and the buttocks too, but that had been a necessary
courtesy without special significance. This was personal, and

therefore more intimate.

She neither returned the kiss nor withdrew. She seemed not quite surprised. "I shall have to think about this," she said. Then she lay down beside him, taking his hand.

Whatever consequence there was was not apparent. Except that it had shut her up. Perhaps that was just as well. He had done what he had done, but he had perhaps surprised himself more than her. In the darkness her baldness had not been apparent. Could he have done it in daylight? Or was he merely testing the waters, as it were, to see whether a romance between them was possible?

If only that hair—

●   ●   ●

Don had forgotten, in the deep-sea interim, how much life teemed in the shallows. He woke to find fish nibbling at him curiously, or trying to, supposing that they had free will in this matter. Starfish were easing through his territory.

But a good distance remained across the wide continental shelf, and Pacifa gave them no time to lie about. She allocated two and a half full food packages, making up for the missed meal. "We'll make it," she said.

Don's muscles seemed to have coagulated during the night, despite the massage. Every motion was agony. Melanie looked drawn. Suddenly her decision made sense: to make no commitment when she was dead tired. He wasn't sure whether he had offered any commitment. The kiss had somehow seemed appropriate after the pseudo-intimacy of their handling of each other's legs. But it might have been a mistake. Certainly it seemed remote, now.

He climbed aboard his bicycle and bore down on the pedals, and lo! the machine moved. Melanie started off similarly, somewhat unsteadily. The other men were no better off. Grimly they followed the ever-sprightly Pacifa across the sandy slopes, working the adhesions out of their sinews.

They had overestimated the total distance by about a hundred miles. The result was that they were slightly ahead of schedule despite the slow climb. But their slowly growing optimism was abruptly squelched.

Less than a hundred miles from the depot—they all maintained the firm fiction that there was a depot—they encountered a crevasse. It was not the scope of the Grand Canyon, but it was quite enough to halt the five cyclists.

They verified the depth only by tying a package of tools to a rope and letting it down until it bumped. The near wall dropped into a plain below. How broad it was they could not know; Gaspar tried for a whistle-echo, but came to no conclusion.

"What," Eleph demanded severely, "is a canyon doing *under the sea?*"

"Mocking us," Melanie said dully.

Pacifa smiled through her frustration. She was tired too, and the extra muscles the males carried were beginning to tell in their favor. Melanie had the advantage of youth. "Obviously there is a river on land. It continues as a freshwater current for some distance over the shelf, cutting away the ground."

"No such luck," Don said. "Fresh water is less dense than salt water, so it would tend to float. It takes a *land* river to cut a canyon. No doubt it was a land river, in the Ice age when so much water was taken up by the glaciers that the sea level dropped several hundred feet. This canyon must have been carved then, then covered up when the sea level rose again."

"I thought Gaspar was the geologist," Pacifa said.

"Well, I run into such things archaeologically," Don said. "Many of the old civilizations were shoreline cultures, and some were buried by the slowly rising waters. In fact, civilization itself had a hard go of it until about 3000 B.C., when the ocean level finally stabilized. How could you maintain an advanced cultural exchange when your leading seaports kept sinking under water? It was no coincidence that the Minoans and Egyptians developed only when—"

"I hate to interrupt," Gaspar said, "but we're talking beside the point. We have to get across this detail of the landscape, and a detour may be too long. Our food is almost gone. Any ideas?"

"What about the map?" Pacifa asked. "Let's assess our handicap. There may be a better place to cross."

"Our general map doesn't show it. Probably there was a detailed map at the first depot, but—" He shrugged.

"Better not gamble, then," she said. "We'll rope it." She unlimbered the long cord. "Now we have a logistical problem. We can get people down, and we can get bicycles down, but both together is tough."

"Not at all," Eleph said. "The problem is physical, not logistical. Merely rig a pully and use one mounted rider as counterweight for another."

"Pulley? Good idea if we had one!"

"Remove the tires from one bicycle. String the cord through the rims."

Pacifa nodded. "Eleph, I hate to admit it, but you do have something resembling a brain on you. We can even hitch a loop to the pedals to serve as a brake. But how do we get that bike down afterwards—and how do we get it up the other side, to haul us *up?*"

"One problem at a time, woman," he said curtly. "We need a suitable location."

"And we'll have to select a bike," she agreed. "Let's see. The multiple-speeders are better constructed, but they all have hand brakes. We need a coaster brake, and good heavy construction."

Gaspar had anticipated her. He was already unloading his machine.

Eleph, meanwhile, scouted the canyon, riding perilously close to the stony brink. "This will do," he called. "An outcropping. We can suspend the bicycle over this, and rig a trip-wire to drop it down afterwards."

"Is that safe?" Melanie asked, gazing at the brink with dismay.

"Safe enough," Eleph replied.

Don had thought of Eleph as a grouchy desk scientist, but now the man was displaying considerable practical finesse. This challenge was evidently bringing out the best in him.

They rigged it. Gaspar's stripped bike was tied to the rock spur by the safety rope, and the rear wheel hung down below. The cord fitted neatly within the bare rim, both ends dropping down into the depths.

Pacifa, the lightest member of their party, went down first, complete with her bicycle. Gaspar and Don paid out the line according to Eleph's terse instructions. Eleph straddled the bike with his foot on one pedal, using the coaster brake to prevent slippage. The whole procedure looked awkward and dangerous, and it was—but it worked. In a surprisingly short time Pacifa reached bottom and the line went slack.

"No trouble," she called after a few minutes. "Smooth and flat. Far wall's two hundred feet off. Little squid, crayfish, sponges, and maybe a sea monster or two. Send down the rest."

Eleph was the next. He and his bicycle were tied to the upper loop, while Pacifa herself, below, served as the counterweight. As Eleph went down, she came up. Braking was hardly necessary, as there was only a twenty pound differential. Don had not realized that Eleph was so light, but part of it could be a difference in the bicycles and other gear.

Then it was Melanie's turn. Pacifa served as the counterweight again, because it had to be lighter than the one who was descending. As it was, it was close; Melanie had the fuller flesh of youth, but nothing more. In her case, it *was* her heavier bicycle that made the difference.

After that Don went down. He mounted his bike and hung on as he dangled over the seeming abyss, slowly rotating. He tilted to the right, and automatically turned his front wheel to compensate, though this was useless in the circumstance. His second reaction was to haul on the suspending rope, and this righted him promptly.

Down he went—and up came Pacifa from the murk, burdened with extra items to increase the mass of the counterweight. "Fancy meeting you here!" she called with a cheery wave as she passed. "If you jump off and let me drop, I'll never speak to you again."

Macabre humor. In a moment she disappeared above.

The descent slowed as he neared bottom. Melanie was waiting for him. Don knew that Pacifa had come into sight above, giving warning, so that Gaspar had applied the brake.

Then he touched down. His line did not go slack, for Pacifa's counterweight maintained tension. "Okay!" he called.

There was a jerk, and then the line did slacken. Pacifa had grabbed hold of the pulley wheel, relieving the rope of most of her weight, and Gaspar had braked hard to hold her there.

Don unhooked quickly. "Off!" he shouted.

Slowly the loop moved up. Slowly Pacifa came down. This was the dangerous part; if Gaspar slipped or if the bicycle chain broke—don't even think it!—she would plummet. She had confidence in her handiwork and in her companions, and she had courage.

"Next time we'll have to use rocks for counterweights," she said, smiling. "Then we can send someone down with every shift."

"We shall," Eleph agreed.

Pacifa gave a short laugh, but the notion made sense to Don. What did she see wrong with it?

The rope slackened. "All right—get off," Gaspar called from above. Pacifa unhooked.

Then the rope jerked upward, halted, and jerked again. Gaspar was handing himself down, using both ropes. No—he was tying the other end, for the doubled strand would reach only half way.

Down he came, handing it along the single rope without his bicycle. Don was amazed. Gaspar had nothing to breathe!

Gaspar dropped the last few feet and jumped into Don's field. He took a tremendous breath. He had been holding it! "Cold out there," he exclaimed.

"Must be nice having muscle and wind like that," Eleph remarked, a bit wistfully.

"Just conditioning," Gaspar said. "A diver has to keep in shape. I'd have been in trouble if I'd had to depend on my worn-out legs! Got a counterweight?"

"Here," Pacifa said with a chuckle, indicating a rock.

"But that's phased out!" Don protested, suddenly realizing why she had found the matter humorous. "I mean, *we* are."

But Eleph was serious. "It still weighs the same," he said. He brought out a tiny cylinder, opened it, and drew forth an almost invisibly fine thread. He strung this around and within the open tire casing that had been removed from Gaspar's bicycle. Then he folded the tire about the rock and tied it in place with the rope.

The others watched silently. Don could make no sense of the procedure. The moment any pull was exerted on the rope, the whole phased tire would slide through the unphased rock without significant effect. Only if the rock also existed in the phase realm could it be used, and they had encountered no loose fragments there.

"Will you two healthy specimens carry this over to the hoist, please?" Eleph asked.

Don looked at Gaspar. Pacifa hummed a merry tune. Melanie looked studiously neutral.

Gaspar shrugged. He walked to the rock, and Don followed.

Gaspar took hold of the rope and yanked, one-handed.

Then he looked down, surprised. "It resists!"

Don tried it. The stone did resist. It was heavy. He poked his finger into it, and found only that whipped-cream semi-solidity. He hauled on the rope again, hard—and the stone budged.

"Let me see that," Pacifa said, no longer laughing. She repeated the experiment, while Gaspar took her place at the hoist-rope so that his bicycle would not crash down. Then: "Eleph, you sphinx—what have you done?"

Melanie was smiling now, appreciating the interplay.

"Merely another facet of the phasing," Eleph said as if it were unimportant. "This thread they gave me has been passed only half way through the phasing tube, so represents a compromise between the two frameworks. It interacts with both, partially. It is a very dense, very strong alloy, I understand, so that it can withstand the double load. See, it does not penetrate the surface of the rock."

"But our own interaction with the sea is only one part in a thousand," Gaspar said. "If this is twice that, or one part in five hundred—"

"It seems the phase does not operate in a linear manner," Eleph explained. "We are standing on another world, not the Earth we know. This one is without an ocean and with very little oxygen in the atmosphere. This half-phase thread, if I may employ an inexact term, seems to occupy both worlds, and to act in each with equivalent effect."

"I see," Gaspar said thoughtfully. "Not one five-hundredth, but one half. So we can use it to lift this rock."

"But the rock itself—" Don began, then reconsidered. The rock was real. His notion that what he could not directly touch was unreal—that was the fallacious concept.

"That thread must drag against you when you're carrying it," Pacifa said shrewdly. "The friction of the water—"

"Normally this is minimal, for the wire is very fine," Eleph said. "I also carry it so that the narrow side of the coil is forward, decreasing the effect. However, I admit the effect can be awkward when I encounter a solid object."

Gaspar's mouth dropped open. "That little octopus—you were knocked out of your saddle, when—"

Don remembered. So Eleph had not been reacting foolishly

when marine creatures approached. They really could strike him, via that little spool of thread.

"Lord grant that I may walk a mile in the other fellow's shoes before I . . ." Gaspar muttered, embarrassed.

They carried the rock and tied it to the dangling hoist rope. They let go. The rock traveled upward at a moderate pace. "If it jams now, we've lost a bike," Gaspar said.

It didn't jam. Gaspar's bicycle, rigged this last time as a counterweight, came down. How the man had anchored it firmly enough for a man's descent, while leaving it free to be lowered like this, Don could not imagine.

Melanie's brow wrinkled. "If the bike is down here, where's the pulley?" she asked.

Don stared up into the gloom. She was right: the bicycle had been the pulley.

"I put a loop over the smoothest projection of the ledge I could find," Gaspar said. "And hoped that the lighter weight of the bike wouldn't cause it to chafe too much. Then I handed myself down. The rock-counterweight allowed us to lower the bike slowly, instead of bringing it crashing down. Thanks to Eleph."

"But Pacifa could have gone up again—"

"Ha!" Pacifa exclaimed.

Then Gaspar jerked hard, so that the rock was pulled up over the ledge. They stood back as it came crashing down. It was expendable; Pacifa wasn't. Now he understood the last of it. They had done a nice job of maneuvering.

Once this mission was over, Don wondered, would he ever be able to swim without feeling as if he were flying? To a swimmer, this entire hoist would have been unnecessary.

But a swimmer would never have been able to traverse the mile-deep bottom, camping out among the living fish. He would know the difference immediately.

Gaspar carried his bicycle across the canyon, not bothering to reassemble it until they knew their next move. Don followed, expecting to find a stream of water down here, until he reminded himself again that the whole atmosphere was water. The hazard of the cliff made it hard to credit, emotionally.

"Here it is," Pacifa said. "Vertical cliff again. How do we string the rope this time?"

"I have been thinking about that," Eleph said. "I hope we can borrow from a principle of flotation. Gaspar—how do divers lift substantial objects from the bottom?"

"Shipboard winch, mostly. Or do you mean balloons?"

"I understood they used canopies similar to parachutes."

"Oh. Yes, the archaeologists have a system."

Don perked up. This was new to him. Of course the entire field of underwater archaeology was new to him. That was one of the incongruities of this assignment. Even had this been near the island of Crete, he would not have been much help in any practical way.

"They fill those little parachutes with waste air from their scuba rigs, and after a while the flotation is enough to lift almost anything," Gaspar said. "Pretty neat system, but tricky, if the chute slips or tilts. A current could make havoc."

"Hey, that's smart," Don said appreciatively. "Using their bubbles to do the hard work. Trust an archaeologist to figure that out."

"But we don't have bubbles," Pacifa said. "Just an oxygenating field that *doesn't* float. How can we use that?"

"By interfering with the carbon dioxide rediffusion, and capturing the resultant accumulation."

Pacifa looked around. "Anybody understand that?"

"Sure," Gaspar said.

"No," Don and Melanie said simultaneously."

"Oxygen filters in for us to breathe," Gaspar said. "Otherwise we would suffocate. The molecules are the same, regardless which world we're in. The problem is getting them across to us. But we have to get rid of the spent air, too. The carbon dioxide. So that moves out while the oxygen moves in, right, Eleph? Like scuba—"

"Self Contained Underwater Breathing Apparatus," Eleph said. "The principle differs, but for the sake of analogy—"

"Fair exchange, no loss," Gaspar said. "Actually, the scuba isn't exactly self-contained either, because the bubbles do go free. But if we can save our own lost air, we might fill balloons."

"Correct in essence," Eleph said. "We are not actually inhaling air as we know it. We are inhaling oxygenated nitrogen. The field—"

"Fill balloons," Pacifa said. "That much I follow. But A Number One, we don't have any balloons. B Number Two, how can we fill them when they're phased out? The bubbles would pass right through, just as we pass through water and fish. C Number Three—"

"Not if the balloons were filled with our air," Gaspar said. "Normal air would pass through, but not matching-phase air."

"C Number Three," Pacifa repeated, "we've got to use non-phased balloons, because only that kind can provide any lifting power in natural water. Obviously our own air won't lift us very high in a gaseous medium—which is what natural water is to us. Mouth-blown balloons don't float in air; only the helium or hydrogen-filled ones do that."

"Precisely, Madam. We have the enormous advantage of being in a liquid medium. Tremendous flotation is available, provided we are able to invoke it. Fortunately we came prepared." He rummaged in his pack. "We do have balloons, half-phased in the manner of the thread. They will proffer similar resistance to water that a normal balloon might to air."

Eleph brought out the balloons and passed them around. Each member of the party began to blow. Soon each had a bobbling sphere a foot or more in diameter.

"This is hard work," Don said. "And it feels funny. As if I'm not really blowing."

"That's the water filling the shell, in the other world," Gaspar explained. "It's passing right through your head to squirt into the non-phase aspect of the balloon, that is a vacuum there."

Don shook his head, not following the reasoning.

"They aren't floating," Pacifa pointed out. "In fact, they're shrinking."

"Naturally. The carbon dioxide is phasing through, while the nitrogen remains. You will observe a bubble of gas trapped in the water of the other world, within the balloon."

"Yes, I see it," Don said, peering through the transparent material.

"Now we shall have to squeeze out the water, that corresponds to our nitrogen. Save only the bubble, and keep the nozzle down, so the gas can't escape."

They did so, intrigued. They were actually witnessing the operation of their breathing fields.

"Now refill the balloon, so that more carbon dioxide can phase through."

Soon the trapped bubbles were larger.

"But what about the oxygen phasing through the other way?" Don asked. "Wouldn't it balance and cancel the effect?"

"No," Eleph said patiently. "Only the transfer of gas from here to there, within the balloons, is significant. For this limited purpose."

Don gave up trying to understand it all. It was hard enough just to keep blowing.

It was a long job. Only a portion of the exhaled breath was carbon dioxide, and only that portion they actually breathed into the balloons could be used. Eleph had calculated that each person should be able to fill a balloon to serviceable dimension in two hours, provided that all his carbon dioxide was utilized This proved to be impossible. The phasing through normally occurred throughout the volume of the breathing spheres, and the rate was adequate for the need. The much smaller volume of the balloon allowed only a portion of the field to operate. Thus it was several hours before the balloons swelled into real instruments of flotation, though each person worked on three simultaneously.

In one way this was good, because they all got needed rest for their legs. But their food supply was diminishing. This balloon device had to work, now, or they would not make it to the depot.

But finally the upward tug became strong, and they knew that success was incipient.

"Keep the lift under control," Gaspar warned. "We don't want to float right to the top. When you're rising too fast—and you'll tend to accelerate, because the balloons will expand as pressure decreases—let a little gas out of one. When you reach the brink, get hold and ease yourself over onto ground." He showed the way by making the first ascent.

It worked. Don was amazed at the hauling power of three medium balloons. He watched Gaspar go up, and then Melanie. He felt guilty for looking up under her skirt, but did so anyway. He had massaged those legs; they were nice ones. But somehow this illicit peek was more evocative than the direct handling had been.

When his turn came he puffed a last burst into his third one and waited while it diffused into full strength. His front wheel came up, then his rear, and he was waterborne.

It seemed precarious, and he decided that he preferred the rope and pulley method. What if a swordfish took a poke at his balloons? They were vulnerable now. Or a shark, taking an experimental bite.

But he had more immediate concerns. His rate of climb, slow at first, was now swift. The balloons were ballooning alarmingly. One atmosphere less pressure for every thirty-three or thirty-four feet, and now he was above the rim, but too far out.

Fortunately his problems had a common solution. Don angled the snout of one balloon and let out a jet. This did not provide the propulsion he had hoped for; the bubbles rose toward the flexing surface of the sea, now so near. But at last his ascent slowed, and he had to cut off the valve lest he commence a descent that would speed up the same way.

The last bubble passed through his hand as he tied off the balloon. Then he breast-stroked his way across to the ledge, tediously. He didn't have much leverage, because it was like paddling in air, but he didn't need much. He landed and deflated his balloons, hating to see that hard-won gas escape. But its job was done.

Eleph, the last to start up, had arrived before Don, having managed his ascent better. The crevasse had been navigated.

"Why didn't you tell us about this before we climbed down?" Pacifa demanded of Eleph. "We could have floated down, or even straight across. Much less effort."

"Horizontal travel is hazardous, because of the time consumed," Eleph said. "A few seconds are reasonably safe, but a few minutes multiply the opportunity for inquisitive sea creatures to come. Descent is not recommended, because of its accelerative nature."

"Hard bump at the bottom," Gaspar agreed. "Can't let out gas to stop it, going down."

Whatever the merits of the case, it had provided them with a needed change of pace. It was now too late to complete the trip to the depot this day, but they proceeded with renewed vigor and optimism.

Chapter 8

•

City

Proxy 5-12-5-16-8: Attention.

Acknowledging.

Status?

The crevasse has been navigated in good order. Melding is proceeding. The next three challenges may complete it.

These are natural or unnatural challenges?

Both. They are works of man, but of unusual nature. I routed the travel to include them. It is not safe to interfere any further with their supplies; they have no remaining food, and will march onto land and give up the mission if further denied.

This seems like unity of purpose.

Yes. That is why I am optimistic. They could have turned back, but did not. This group is integrating, and I think will become what we need.

We hope so. Two more worlds have been lost since we last communed.

This one we shall save, I think.

•   •   •

As they lay in the joint tent at night, Melanie remained uncommunicative, so Don entertained himself by sketching Minoan symbols on his note pad, analyzing them for new meanings. The writing had been largely deciphered, but some obscure aspects remained, and these were his special challenge. It occurred to him that it was a similar case with Melanie; much of her was coming clear, especially when she spoke so freely about her memories and impressions, but some of her was opaque. He had kissed her, perhaps surprising himself more than her, and she was taking time to consider her reaction. The thing was, he had done it while she was bald. His first shock at her state had faded, and increasingly he was becoming aware of her other traits. There was a lot about her that he liked, both physical and mental. Maybe she thought he was teasing her, but he wasn't; he was coming to terms with her. He knew that if he could truly accept her bald, it would be all right if she wore her wig again. But he was not yet sure of his deepest feeling about that. So he focused on symbols, as if their interpretation was also the key to Melanie.

"May I inquire what you are doing?" It was Eleph, also slow this night to sleep. Extreme fatigue did that; the body had to unwind somewhat before it could relax enough for sleep. His tone was carefeully courteous, and Don was flattered to realize that this was the first friendly overture the man had made to any of the rest of them. So Don explained.

"I do not mean to be offensive," Eleph said, and it was evident that he was not used to being inoffensive. It was not because he tried to be offensive, but that he was unschooled in nonmilitary courtesy. "But I had understood that Cretan writing has never been deciphered."

"So how can I read it?" Don asked rhetorically. "That's a good question, and as with most good questions, the answer is not simple."

Eleph actually smiled. "I appreciate a complex answer."

Amazing how simple it was to get along, once the effort was made! Don liked talk about his specialty. "All right. First, you have to understand that what we think of as Cretan writing is fragmentary and inconclusive, and much of it isn't Minoan. It's Greek."

"That's a fair start," Eleph agreed wryly.

"We call this 'Linear B.' It appears to date from the Mycenaean occupation of Knossos, the latter half of the fifteenth century B.C. This has been deciphered, but it turns out to consist entirely of routine palace records. Inventories, receipts, accounts. No chronicles of kings, no literature. Thus it is of limited value to the historian."

"Linear" Eleph said thoughtfully. "Does this mean that it was written along straight lines, like our own script?"

"No. The name is to distinguish it from true hieroglyphic writing, the little stylized pictures such as those used by the Egyptians, where the word for "man" is a stick-figure man, and 'walk' is a pair of legs beside the man. Such pictogramic or ideogramic representation is cumbersome at best. The linear form is much superior, because a few stylized strokes replace the picture, as in the Babylonian cuneiform, done entirely by wedge-shaped imprints on clay. Not only is this faster, it is far more versatile."

"I can see that. But if your linear writing is not Cretan—"

"I'm coming to that. 'Linear B' derives from 'Linear A,' which in turn appears to be the true Minoan writing. But it seems to be restricted to the Phaistos area of Crete, while Linear B appears at Knossos, the capital. Linear A is largely undeciphered; progress is being made, but there is no uniformity of interpretation. So some would say it remains obscure."

"I see. But what, then, do you read?"

"Well, Linear B, of course. But my real interest is in Linear A. A number of characters are common to both, so we do have a starting point. Many scholars have assumed that because Linear B is cumbersome, omitting many middle consonants among other things, that Linear A can be no better. I believe, in contrast, that B was a bastard offshoot used by the barbaric Mycenaean conquerors, therefore representing only a crude fragment of the potential of the original. It is in Linear A that we shall find the real literature of the Minoan culture—and indeed, we are finding it."

"Do you have extensive manuscripts in Linear A?"

Don grimaced. "No. I theorize that the Mycenaeans destroyed Minoan libraries and literature in their vengeful fury. No doubt most of it was on paper or parchment, so it would burn, and King Theseus was a bookburner. Natural calamity was responsible for a great amount of loss, too. But these things can't have eradicated it *all*. Someday we'll excavate some official's private library, and then—"

Eleph smiled. Don relaxed—and was abruptly asleep.

•   •   •

The final miles seemed like nothing. The depot was there, exactly where indicated. The sonic signal was clear.

They pulled up and listened, tangibly relieved. Don had not appreciated how worried he had been until he felt the load depart. They would have food again.

He also felt the fatigue of three hard days' travel, as if it had been stored for this occasion. What a journey they had made, crossing the Gulf of Mexico on short rations! That canyon had wiped out their schedule and their reserve, and they had finished the last food package four hours before.

As they paused, listening, Melanie moved next to him. "I am still thinking," she said. Then she caught his shirt and drew him to her, and kissed him on the mouth. That was all. It was enough.

They resumed their ride toward the depot, their feelings toward each other intensifying with their relief from concern about their supplies. It was as if there was a certain charge of emotion which had to find a new object.

"Hey—isn't this your department, Don?" Gaspar asked suddenly. "Hard to tell, because of the sediment, but aren't these buildings?"

Don looked, startled. He had been paying no attention to his surroundings, just driving onward, and had been distracted by the sonic signal and then by Melanie. But now he saw clearly that they were on the verge of a submerged ruin—perhaps even a sunken city."

"Dizzy Choo-choo," Melanie said.

"Dzibilchaltun," Don corrected her, having to laugh. "Yes, I suppose it has to be. No telling how much of that fabulous city was drowned. The depot must be right in the middle."

Now Eleph and Pacifa exchanged glances "Don, tell us about the city," she said.

"Glad to—what little I know. But first let's get on to the depot. I just want to fill my belly and flop down."

"No, we shall have to wait," Eleph said. "I believe I have read about Dzibilchaltun or some similar Mayan city. Weren't there impressive sacrificial wells?"

"Sacrificial wells?" Melanie asked, frowning.

Gaspar scratched his head. "I'm curious about that too. But I'm with Don: let's nail down the supplies before we gossip about past civilizations. We've missed one depot, remember."

"Gaspar," Pacifa said with motherly gentleness. "Doesn't it seem providential that the depot is right here, inside a famous old city?"

"It was obviously set up this way," Gaspar said. "To give the archaeologist a good crack at it. This must be Don's mission."

"That is plausible," Eleph said. "As is no doubt intended. But if exploration of this city is the object, why did we have to travel underwater from Florida? Why wasn't a Mayan specialist assigned? Why have there been so many problems? They didn't have to route us across that crevasse. I think we need to consider."

"But what is there to consider?" Gaspar asked. "The depot is here, we've found it, and we need it. This is the one time nothing is wrong."

"That's what's odd," Eleph said meaningfully. Now Don realized what the two were driving at.

"Don, is there anything *about* this city?" Pacifa asked.

"Well, as you know, I'm out of my specialty. But I understand that Dzibilchaltun is unique in the western hemisphere. For one thing, it was large—probably the largest city in the ancient world. For another, it's old: continuously inhabited for about four thousand years, until the Spanish Conquistadors destroyed the native culture. It must have been a mighty seaport, and the pinnacle of the old Mayan civilization. That's about all I know. I think the old Mayan script has now been deciphered, but I'm not sure there are texts relating to the history of the city."

"So it may be a mighty good place to visit," Pacifa mused. "Especially underwater, where it presumably hasn't been touched by looters."

"Oh, plenty of looting goes on under the sea," Gaspar said.

"Indeed it does," Don agreed. "The Mediterranean—"

"But why us?" Pacifa continued. "That sticks in my craw. Do you think it's a trap, Eleph?"

"Perhaps. I seem to remember human sacrifices. But there shouldn't be any Mayans here now."

"That was part of their religion," Don said. "But the Mayans were basically peaceful. Mostly they sacrificed precious objects. Golden artifacts, handicrafts, things like that. I think it was the Aztecs who made a wholesale business of human sacrifice. They were comparatively recent and barbarian."

"The city may be a decoy," Eleph said. "It is hard to believe that our real mission concerns the ancient Mayans. Our government is generally more pragmatic."

"There's nothing wrong with surveying a Mayan city," Don said defensively.

"By a Minoan scholar?" Melanie asked. "And the rest of us, who are really ignorant about archaeology?"

Don couldn't answer. It was making less sense.

"Could someone have substituted these coordinates and planted a fake beeper to bring us in?" Pacifa asked.

"After entirely losing the first depot?" Eleph asked in return. "That's unnecessarily circuitous, considering that we surely weren't expected to make it here. And it doesn't account for the selection of this unique spot."

"You're right again," Pacifa said, and it seemed to Don that she had raised the point for the sake of having it refuted. "It's so fouled up it must be the way the bureaucracy planned it. A Minoan scholar sent to an old Mayan city. They both begin with M, don't they?"

Don laughed and the others smiled. "That's reasonable. The bureaucrats didn't know the difference. And I *will* want to look at these ruins closely. I don't mind expanding my horizons. Let's get on to the depot."

The others agreed, though with less enthusiasm. The party rode on—cautiously.

●　　●　　●

The arrival was anticlimactic. The depot was there, almost hidden by a mound of rubble that turned out not to be real—to them. The phased-in supplies could and did occupy the same region inhabited by real-world material. A very neat hiding place for a foreign shore. No local fishermen or incidental looters would have spotted it. Even though they could not touch it, such a discovery could have spread an alarm.

"That bothers me," Pacifa said. "But I don't know why."

"There is no need for us to remain in the vicinity," Eleph said. "We can ferry the supplies out to deeper water and make our own depot, that no one knows about except us."

That they did, quickly, leaving only their surplus waste. There were limits to what the converters could do once the water was recycled, so they had to be emptied periodically. Once safely clear of the city they pitched their joint tent and ate ravenously and slept. The pressure was off, for the time being.

Melanie slept beside Don, and held his hand, but said no more about herself or their relationship. Evidently she was still considering her response. That was just as well, as he was still considering his feeling. If only she had hair!

●   ●   ●

"Okay, Melanie," Gaspar said after breakfast. "How about the next coordinates?"

"Wait a minute!" Don cried before she could answer. "I'm not leaving before I take a good look at this city!"

"You saw it yesterday, didn't you?"

"No. I had a passing glimpse of the cover. Now I want to read the book."

"That city is buried in silt," Pacifa pointed out. "The cover is all you can see, so long as it's phased out."

"What about Eleph's thread and balloons?" Melanie asked.

"These should not be expended spuriously," Eleph said.

Don saw his prize slipping away. The others just did not understand archaeology.

"We don't actually know what our mission is," Gaspar said thoughtfully. "From what Don says, this is a significant location. Maybe we're supposed to investigate, lending our skills to support his skills."

"That's not true," Eleph said.

"How do you know?" Pacifa inquired. "Did Melanie give you the next coordinates?"

Melanie smiled at this teasing.

"No, of course not," Eleph said stiffly. "But the very fact that there are further coordinates—"

"*Are* there?" Gaspar asked.

"You yourself were asking for them a moment ago."

"But I didn't get them—and now I wonder. This place is beginning to make sense to me as a destination, and not just archaeologically."

Now Pacifa was interested. "How do you mean, Gaspar?"

Then, oddly, Gaspar backed off. "I'd rather think about it some more. Why don't we let Don have his look? We're ahead of schedule now, surely, and we can use the rest."

"Why don't we just find out?" Pacifa asked. "Melanie, are there more coordinates?"

"Yes," Melanie said faintly, with an apologetic look at Don.

"How many? You don't have to give the figures. Just tell us how many numbers you have."

"I suppose that's all right," Melanie agreed uncertainly. "Three."

"And are they near or far?"

"I-I think they're far."

"So maybe we'd better get on with it, in case we have more trouble," Pacifa said.

But now it was Eleph who demurred. "We must be fair. I suggest we give Don two days, since we may not return once we go on. Possibly later there will be things important to the rest of us, and the Golden Rule—"

Pacifa threw up her hands, literally. "They talk about *women* changing their minds!"

"But it will be nice to relax," Melanie said. In that she spoke for them all.

●   ●   ●

The city was huge. Don and Gaspar rode for miles along patterns suggesting wide boulevards and rubble-clogged streets though their tires encountered only the rolling sea-floor of the phase world. Everywhere they passed the ruins of what might have been ancient monuments and colossal buildings.

Don shook his head, amazed at the remaining grandeur. "These may seem like mere wreckages to you, but to me they're foundations. I'm beginning to see the structures they supported. They're inherent. I—"

"No, I'm impressed too, Gaspar said. "On a couple of levels."

"You mean you're getting interested in archaeology?"

"No such luck. My interest is geological and practical."

"Geological?" Don asked, surprised. "Look at this: a corbelled arch. See how the columns project sideways, with a capstone across? Not a true arch; I don't think that was known in the New World. What has this to to with geology?"

"Think about it and you'll see."

Don shook his head, suspecting Gaspar of mocking him. "I *am* thinking about it. You can see how this is one of several arches that formed a pattern. See those broken columns there, and the mounds across this court. This silt hides them, but obviously these were entrances to a royal garden or amphitheater. Maybe an outrider to a palace. Can't you visualize it rising around us, perhaps decorated with splendid murals?"

"Oh, some," Gaspar said tolerantly. "But let me show you my vision. We really are riding on a different world, and why we can't see it bothers me more and more. Because if these ruins were in our phase, we'd be able to walk on them and bang into them. We thought only the life was different, because it moves, but the buildings are different too. This proves it. It's the first time we've been able to pass through stone."

"No, there was that counterweight stone in the chasm," Don said. "But I see what you mean. There never was any question, was there? How can there be a city without life, and how can there be life with no real air or water?"

"It wasn't obvious to me until I saw this city," Gaspar said. "These worlds are awfully close. Remember how we rode across the abyssal plain?"

"Sure. But that has nothing to do with—"

"No? How can you form a sedimentary flat—without water? Without erosion and settling? And that canyon—if water didn't cut it in this phase world, what did?"

Don was stunned. "You're right! Our world is water-formed, and the phase world duplicates it. There *has* to be water here. And air. We rode over those coral reefs, and there wouldn't be any coral without—"

"So if there was water in our phase world, what happened to it?" Gaspar asked. "And the life. Things certainly changed, and not very long ago, geologically. That's convenient for us, but alarming."

"Yes." Don tried to visualize how a world might be deprived

of air and water in one quiet operation, with inert nitrogen substituted for both, and could not. "H-how long ago?"

"Within the past hundred thousand years, I'd say. But not within the past six thousand."

"W-why not *one* year ago?"

"Because then this city would be in the phase world too," Gaspar said. "Assuming the history of this world was as similar to our own as it seems. And this city dates from 4000 B.C.—six thousand years ago."

"Y-you're guessing! Y-you're no archaeologist."

"It wasn't built under water, was it?" Gaspar demanded, waiting for Don's reluctant nod. "It was built on land. No earthquake sank it, or it would have been shaken apart, instead of just weathered and buried, right? So the water came in slowly—and that means the end of the ice age. The level didn't stabilize until about five thousand years ago, so this must be older."

There it was: the obvious situation that Don's mind had balked at. A fine city, six thousand years old. "B-but then it c-can't be Dzi-Dzi—"

"No, of course not. This is a good twenty miles out from the present shore, and Dzibilchaltun was onshore or inshore. This city was submerged before the Mayans even appeared in the Yucatan."

And Dzibilchaltun was now inshore, Don remembered. The shoreline had changed, in effect pushing it inland. He had gotten it reversed, thinking the ruins would be out under the sea instead of inland, as the shore silted up. The revelation was so vast that it threw him into a new mental framework, and his stuttering stopped. "You're right! Who could have built it?"

"You're the archaeologist. Pretty nice material for a scholarly paper, eh?"

"But this must predate Egyptian and Sumerian civilization! Nothing in the Old World had this level—"

"So?"

Don shook his head. It was not credible that the American Indians could have built elegant cities before the Mesopotamians. But how could he argue that fine point with a skeptical geologist?

Pacifa had been sure there was something about this region. She had been right. Don had been misled by his blind assumption that this was Dzibilchaltun and his confusion about his assignment, as a Minoan specialist, to a Mayan region. A Mayan specialist would have known instantly that this was not Dzibilchaltun, but would have been no better off. In fact, there might be no archaeologist in the world really qualified to excavate these phenomenal ruins.

Nice material for a scholarly paper, yes. Schliemann had discovered his Troy, Bibby his Dilmun, Mellaart his Catal Huyuk. Would Don Kestle join these illustrious leaders? No, that was a foolish dream. The credit belonged to whoever had come across the city first—or to whoever actually excavated it and unraveled its marvelous secrets. Don was only a visitor, here to look and sigh.

Gaspar was watching him. "What would you give to bring a competent crew here, in the real world?"

"My soul."

Gaspar nodded understandingly and moved on.

The street they were on became narrow and crooked. It was as if they were entering a denser, older inner city. Large structures remained, but they were set much closer together.

"Hey—steps," Gaspar said.

He was right. Their street had become a walkway, with twenty or thirty broad steps, each about thirty feet from side to side, fashioned of—what? Fine marble? He could not tell through the smothering sediment. They led up to the remains of a labyrinthine palace. Don made out the shells of what must have been spacious, shady courts, with elegantly drained lavatories. The few standing columns were tapered downwards, narrower at the base than the apex.

"Typical Minoan architecture," Don murmured professionally.

"What?" Gaspar asked sharply.

"The hygienic sanitary facilities," Don explained. "The Cretans were virtually alone in the ancient world in their fastidious insistence on personal cleanliness. They had the most sophisticated system of water supplies and drainage, with pipes designed on correct hydraulic principles. See, that's the fundament of a flush toilet, I'm sure, even through the silt. The configuration—"

"What kind of architecture?" Gaspar repeated.

"Minoan, of course. I've seen many examples of—" Don stopped. "Minoan! What am I saying? *Mayan!* I mean—"

"You sounded as if you knew, just as clearly as I know metamorphic from igneous."

"Ridiculous! I'm just used to saying—" But he had to stop again. "Damn it, these *are* Minoan configurations, essentially. I don't care how crazy it is. This is my specialty."

"I don't see that it's crazy," Gaspar said. "When did your Minoan civilization develop?"

"About three thousand B.C., or a little later. They appeared suddenly; they must have had a high culture before they came to Crete. But we have no tangible evidence of them before; it's just conjecture."

"So let's say the waters encroached here after 4000 B.C.," Gaspar continued carefully. "It was slow but sure. So wherever they were, they had to move, and they didn't like the barbarian mainland, so they went to Crete and set up shop there."

Don stared at him. "You mean to suggest—they were here? They crossed the Atlantic?" Don shook his head, bemused. "Even if—no, they would have chosen a closer island. Like Cuba."

"Too big. They wanted something the size of Crete."

"Jamaica, then. Why didn't they move to Jamaica?"

Gaspar shrugged. "Got me there. But there must have been some connection. Or could the architecture be coincidental?"

"It must be," Don said. "Crete is six thousand miles from here by water, and even today that's a fair piece. For an Amerind canoe—"

"How about the other way, then? Maybe your Minoans developed earlier than you think. Two thousand years earlier. Maybe *their* main cities were submerged, so most of them set up colonies elsewhere. They had ships, didn't they? They could sail the oceans?"

"They were the leading maritime culture of the ancient world," Don said warmly. "The Phoenicians developed only after the Minoan civilization perished—and the early Phoenicians were afraid to lose sight of land, because they couldn't navigate by the stars. The Minoans were true sea-voyagers."

"Just a moment. If the Minoans were so strong, what brought them down? Maybe *there's* our real city-builder!"

"Two things," Don said. "There was the explosion of the volcanic island of Thera, which devastated Crete, leveled their palaces and probably wiped out their fleet. It was one of the worst eruptions known to man, many times as powerful as Krakatoa. It literally buried Crete in ash. But that was not the end; they did re-build. But they needed an enormous supply of wood, for their ships and buildings, and the rebuilding used it up at a faster rate. Their civilization flourished even more after the eruption than be-fore it, but in the end they ran out of wood and had to leave the island. Lesser cultures, with virgin forests, expanded to take their place."

"Oh. Well, back to the sea. I still think there could have been a connection. Didn't some guy cross from Egypt to America in a reed craft?"

"That was Thor Heyerdahl. Yes, he reconstructed an Egyptian papyrus vessel and crossed the Atlantic in 1970, demonstrating that it could have been done in ancient times. He had a similar venture some years before, crossing from South America to the Polynesian Islands. The Kon-Tiki."

"Right. He discovered new species of fish and had an adven-ture with a whale shark."

"But he knew what he was doing, or thought he knew. Even so, it was an extremely risky business. The Egyptians would hardly have set out voluntarily to cross the Atlantic in a sinking reed craft."

"Maybe they didn't," Gaspar said. "Maybe they set out to reach some port on the western coast of Africa, and were storm-blown toward America. The prevailing winds and currents favor that, you know. If it's possible with a reed craft, it's more than possible with a full-fledged Minoan seaworthy ship."

"In four or five thousand B.C.? The Minoans can't have had such good ships that far back." But Don was wondering, for it could have been the Palace of Knossos he saw here, with its tre-mendous inner court and interminable surrounding walls and passages and cubicles. The court was oblong, about fifty feet across and a hundred long, quite flat and completely walled in. Even through the rubble he could make out the enormous com-plexity of the surrounding corridors, stairs, terraces, and halls, that crisscrossed and dead-ended and right-angled bewildering-ly. A stranger would soon have been lost within the living build-ing."

"What a maze," Gaspar remarked.

"That's the point," Don said. "According to legend, Theseus fought the bull-man, the Minotaur, within just such a labyrinth.

Then he needed help finding his way out. God, I wish I could trench this."

"Do what to what?"

"Dig a trench. Excavate. The vast majority of artifacts are well buried in silt. But if I could cut a trench through the middle—"

"You can't do that," Gaspar said.

"I know. That's the frustrating thing about this phase-out. My inability to interact with the substance of the world when I need to. But if I could dig, I'd mark off the most promising mound here, and excavate a narrow trench across it, very carefully, and note the exact position of every artifact I located. I'd make the sides exactly vertical and smooth them off so I could observe the precise layering, because there are apt to be a number of layers of occupation—"

"You don't understand, Don! You can't do that here. Even phased in. You can't dig a trench underwater. Not the kind you want."

"Why not? Are there laws against it?"

"The law of nature. Start digging, and your trench will immediately fill in from the sides. Silt doesn't pack the way dirt does on land; it's always partly in suspension. Touch it and you stir up a cloud of stuff so that you can't see. You get nowhere."

Don looked at him, appalled. "But how can an archaeologist excavate?"

"Not the way you do it on land. You have to suck up the sludge, then let the water clear, and see what you have."

Don sighed. "It's unnatural."

"But I'll bet we can find you some artifacts right now."

"F-forget it," Don said with disgust. He had glimpsed marvelous visions, but in the end he was impotent.

"I'm not joking. Consider: when you grab a fish, you feel the bones, right? Because they're just a bit more rigid than flesh. Well, what are your artifacts made from?"

"Anything is an artifact. Pottery, statuary—"

"Anything made of gold?"

"Yes, of course. Much of the finest Minoan handiwork—"

"Gold has a density of about twenty-two times that of water. You could almost pick it up through the phase, couldn't you?"

"I suppose I could. But—"

"While this rock must be no more than four or five times as

dense as water. And the silt is little thicker. So—"

"So I could feel the gold under the silt!" Don exclaimed.

"Of course you couldn't actually move it. But you could get a pretty good idea of its shape. That would help, wouldn't it?"

"Yes!" Don cried.

"So why don't we get up a team of five tomorrow and feel through a likely spot? Maybe we'll find something to unriddle Atlantis."

● ● ●

"Why is it so important to explore this city?" Melanie inquired when they got back together. She had spent her day resting, and looked refreshed. "I heard you say it was six thousand years old, but you can't really see it, under all that mud. Or do anything, because of the phase. So it's all sort of pointless, isn't it, holding up the party?"

For a moment Don was irritated. But he realized that it was an honest question. How could she comprehend the drive of archaeological zeal? It was not enough to claim that a mountain had to be climbed merely because it was there; a more rational answer was required. But Don's head was spinning with the irrational notions forced upon him during the day: a city with apparent Minoan affinities that predated the known Minoan culture by a thousand years or more. A mysterious alternate world, Earth's almost perfect duplicate, except that it had lived and then died. Recently. Geologically. His mind still balked at such concepts. And she wanted to know why he had to investigate this city! What answer could he give her?

"Hey, are you doing it to *me*, now?" Melanie asked, smiling. "The silent treatment?"

Don had to laugh, really appreciating for the first time the kind of mood that dictated silence as the best answer. In a year he might explain it all to her, if ever. Had she felt that way about her autographs, that first time she had hit him with a silence? If so, he had been a boor.

"Why do you collect autographs?" he asked.

"Uh-oh. You mean it's that way?"

He didn't answer.

"Well, all right, then. I guess I asked for it." She took a breath.

"As I remember, you said something to the effect that you were more interested in what an author said, and that autographs and such were relatively unimportant. But books are printed by a very mechanical process, and in such a way that one must accept on simple faith that they are written by any one particular person at all. Not that all books are, of course. But we are used to dealing with particular individuals, and it seems somehow proper that a book should have been written by an individual. But if we consider society to be a network of human relations, the believability of the existence of an 'author' back there somewhere becomes rather attenuated. Writing is in some sense a form of sharing. We can all sit at the feet of and listen to whomever we like. Sort of like the university lectures in France. Some of the lecturers have small audiences and some have very large audiences. There the important thing is passing the exams at the end of the four years or so of study, and attendance *per se* is not as important as it is in the system here. But we all long to be recognized for ourselves. To receive some token, however small, of the uniqueness of the relation between ourselves and the author. An autograph is one such token. It all seems to be a striving for affection and attention. For recognition of the uniqueness and value of the individual self. Readers and reviews give recognition to an author, although the relationship is sometimes painful. But authors in their turn give recognition to readers. By writing, of course—but also by standing still for pictures, smiling, saying things and autographing. The relationship between an author and his readers can be very much strained by the very large number of the latter. So—"

"Enough!" Don exclaimed. "You've made your point, I think. And I guess if it could be turned about, you've made mine too. Because the books I read, archaeologically, are the record of an entire culture, and the physical artifacts are like personal autographs that some living hand has shaped and used. When I study a city such as this one, even under the mud, I am relating to living human beings of the past, just as you relate to the author of a novel. That's very important to me. I can never actually come to know them better than this, though I long to. If I could actually *visit* that past—"

"Yes, I understand!" she said warmly. "I suppose it *is* the same. Now I see why you want to find a real artifact tomorrow. And I hope you do. I'll help you look."

Did that mean she had completed her period of considering their relationship? What was his own conclusion about it?

"You know, if you *could* visit the past," she remarked, "well, maybe it wouldn't mean so much."

She had surprised him again. "How can you say that? An actual look at—"

"Because I did visit a writer once. Not settling for just an autograph. If the parallel holds—"

"You you visited the past, in effect?" He was intrigued. They had had a breakthrough in mutual understanding; was another on the way?

Then he thought: was that when she took the pills?

"I had been hinting to Mother now and then that I would like to go on a trip," she said blithely. "Partly to make a pilgrimage to the ocean—that was before I came to Miami on my own—and partly to see something, some place, besides home. I guess I just get the urge to travel a little, every now and then. Maybe expecting to find something better on the other side of the mountain. If I could afford it I would travel around the world a few times, I am sure. But the thing that most immediately precipitated my trip was reading Shirley MacLaine's *Don't Fall Off the Mountain*. Have you—?"

"No, I never heard of it," Don said. Where did she dig up these obscure books?

"Oh. Well, for one thing it made me jealous. For another it is a tribute to the admissibility of a woman wandering around on her own. The voices of conformity sound strongly in my head, and to some extent I live in fear." She paused again. "I shouldn't be saying this."

"I shouldn't be listening," Don said comfortably. "Go on."

"I have always been somewhat of a disappointment to my mother," she continued faintly. "I mean, not just because of the hair. Because she always wanted someone who was level headed. So I try to pretend to be. And quite frankly it is a very painful pretense. Somehow I have learned, rightly or wrongly, to keep silent on many kinds of things."

Was he about to wish that she had kept silent on this? Here he was getting jealous of someone she had visited before he ever met her. But maybe that was a sign: why should he feel that way, unless he cared about her?

"Anyway," she continued after a moment, "I went to visit this writer. He'd published a couple of novels I liked, and there'd been some correspondence. Nothing much—I don't mean to make it sound like more than it is—just some fan letters and a polite acknowledgment. I sent him clippings, too. That sort of thing."

She valued an autograph as a personal touch. How did the things she sent to the writer relate? Did they make the personal touch mutual?

"So when I decided to meet him, one of my reasons was simple curiosity. To see if he looked anything like my mental picture of him. So I glued on my wig and went."

And she took pills, just in case. Damn her!

"And you know, he did," she said. "Close enough."

Don would have hit her with a silence, had he not already been silent.

"Not that it made a great deal of difference. What he looked like, I mean. At least I had a better image to orient on when I thought of him. I have been meeting some people in the flesh always, and some people always through the medium of the written word, and the curiosity is about the similarities or dissonances between the possible views."

"Now you're meeting people under the ocean."

"Yes. I like being with you, Don. I've thought about it, and I like it. Even if it doesn't last." She met his gaze, and smiled.

Suddenly Don regretted his silent objections. She wanted to be with him! Had she brought her pills? But he couldn't say that. "How did your visit go? W-with the writer?"

"Oh, it was nothing, really. That's why I used it as an example. He'd come out with opinions—that's what writers do, you know—and I'd be silent. You know."

"Yes." *Good.* He was still jealous of that writer, and wished the man ill. Yet he remained quite curious about the event.

"I talked with his wife, too. And I played with his little girl. She was about four. She liked to climb. On people. I thought he might invite me to stay to supper, but he didn't. He was locked up in his family. So I took some pictures and went home. It was raining."

So the writer had been married, with a child. Don had visualized a lecherous bachelor. Now he felt ashamed. "I see," he said, because he had to say something. A silence at this point could give him away.

"So that's what I mean," Melanie said. "Really, that writer was just another person, in person. I wouldn't have known he had written those novels, just by meeting him. I can't say it was a disappointment. I mean, people are what they are. But it wasn't exactly a revelation, either."

"So you think that if I traveled into the archaeological past, it might be like that," Don said musingly. "Mundane. I wonder."

Melanie nodded. Then she rummaged in her pack and pulled out her wig. She put it on, working it carefully into place and pressing it down so that it stayed.

"You look strange," Don said.

"Thank you."

Apparently she had made her point, and now was satisfied to resume the illusion.

They settled into sleep.

● ● ●

"I'm no historian or archaeologist," Eleph said as he walked his bicycle through the waist-deep silt of what Don hoped was a temple storeroom. "But I seem to remember something about a unique Indian tribe in North America, racially and linguistically distinct from the norm, with a legend of arrival from the east. Do you suppose they could have—?"

"Oh, yes," Don said, sweeping his hand through the slight resistance of the mud. "I remember now. The Yuchis. They wound up in Oklahoma, I think. From Georgia. But we can hardly rely on such scant evidence as legends. We'd have to believe that some peoples descended from the sun, and others from human miscegenation with animals."

"Well, the sun *is* the ultimate source of our life," Pacifa said. "A legend could reflect this. And man, paleontologically, does derive from the animal."

"That's still a long way from making sense of our expedition," Don said, and they laughed.

Eleph had wandered into another chamber. "Don, would you check this? Possibly a blade."

Don got over there, wading through waist-deep stonework,

and Melanie followed him. She still looked odd in her hair, as if it were a pointless affectation. There was no question now: he could take it or leave it. It was Melanie herself he cared about.

There was a blade: large and curved. It tapered into a narrow stem, then expanded again. There was a swelling in the middle. "That's a double axe!" Don exclaimed, hardly believing it. "A golden decorated double axe!"

Eleph looked pleased. "That is significant, archaeologically?"

Don kept running his fingers through the hidden pattern, his arms elbow-deep in the visible muck. "It's the labrys, the double axe of Minoan Crete. Our word labyrinth derives from it. It's one of the religious symbols."

"So this is a Minoan city," Gaspar said.

Don shook his head. "I told you, the first typical Minoan palace was built after 2000 B.C. This predates it by two millennia."

"But that architectural ability had to come from somewhere," Gaspar said. "It didn't slowly evolve on Crete, you said."

"Yes, it seems to have emerged full-blown on Crete," Don agreed. "But two thousand years—!"

"Perfectly mundane, I'm sure," Melanie murmured.

"Is this city really that old?" Eleph inquired. "Isn't this one of the fracture zones? It could have subsided."

"Not really," Gaspar said. "Continental drift seems to be occurring in six major plates and a few minor ones, with the mid-oceanic ridges and trenches marking the fringes. The Puerto Rico and Cayman trenches represent one such fringe, but it's relatively inactive now. That's several hundred miles from here, anyway."

"But that's not far at all, geologically, is it?" Eleph persisted.

"Far enough." It was a matter of opinion, and Gaspar was not about to give way. But Don recognized it as a reasonable alternative: if subsidence rather than a rising ocean level had submerged this city, the date of its demise could be much more recent. That made a great deal more sense, archaeologically.

Dan and Eleph and Melanie spent some time searching the storeroom for more objects of gold, but found only three small cups. Only? They were fabulous too. They were very thin, but had pictures on the sides in high relief. Don licked his fingers repeatedly to make them tender, trying to pick up every detail by touch. If only he were able to *see!* He was tempted to ask for Eleph's threads and balloons, to haul this up out of the muck and into view. But he didn't want to disturb it; that could ruin it's seeming authenticity when a real archaeological crew came here.

The first cup had people marching in a procession around the sides. One figure seemed to be carrying a lute, another a small calf, and the others unidentifiable objects. The second cup had the figure of a man and a tree and some animals, perhaps cattle. The man seemed to be holding one of the cattle by a rope tied to its back leg.

But it was the third cup that astonished Don. It had two men performing acrobatics with bulls. Could Don's imagination be leading his fingers?

"Melanie, I want you to feel this," he said. He guided her hand to the hidden cup. "Can you make out the embossed picture?"

She concentrated. "One animal, a cow no, bull. A man being thrown from its back. Another man holding on to the bull's horns. Something like that."

Confirmation! Their readings of the illustrations on the cups could be grossly mistaken, but even so, they represented stronger evidence of the city's association with the Minoan culture. The ancient traders of Crete, or of the culture preceding it, *had* crossed the Atlantic!

Chapter 9

•

Glowcloud

Proxy 5-12-5-16-8: Attention.

Acknowledging.

Status?

The group has encountered the evidence of the lost city, and begun to appreciate its nature. This has taken the members a significant step toward melding, though they are not aware of it

What evidence is there for this?

They elected to delay two days to provide time to explore it, though this exploration benefits only one of their specialties. They worked together in harmony, making discoveries cooperatively and discussing them. And they are starting to care for each other on a personal basis.

How so?

The older and younger women are deepening a relationship similar to that of mother and daughter. The young woman and young man are developing a romantic attachment.

They are having an affair?

No. But she put on her hair.

Proxy, you have lost us.

The young woman is bald. She has been rejected in the past when this was discovered, so is introspective and tends to be diffident about commitments beyond the superficial. She removed her wig so as to cause any rejection by this group to occur at the outset. When the group, and particularly the man, accepted her, she restored the wig. It has become cosmetic rather than substantive. She is now ready to make a romantic commitment.

We must defer to your judgment in this respect. When will you reveal the mission?

After the remaining two challenges have been navigated. They are sufficiently remarkable to cause serious reflection by the group. If it melds instead of breaking up, then it will be ready to handle the reality.

We hope you are correct.

● ● ●

"Eighty-eight degrees west, fifteen degrees north, approximately," Melanie said.

Gaspar worked it out. "Gulf of Honduras."

"Closer to the trenches?" Eleph asked.

"Yes. Cayman. It projects southwest right into the Honduras. In fact there's a valley in the corner there on land, probably an extension. If we find any underwater cities *there*, I'll consider subsidence."

A passing reference to a passing difference of opinion. Yet it had a remarkable effect on Don as the party cycled on around the Yucatan peninsula. Gaspar was his friend, and Eleph an annoyance—but it was Eleph who had made the decisive suggestion that had given Don two days in the ruins, and Eleph who had found the *labrys* and cups. Those were perhaps the most significant New World artifacts ever, and they would make Don famous when he finished this mission and led a party to discover the city and them. Now it was Eleph who was pursuing the archaeological probabilities. Eleph was not only doing Don favors, he was demonstrating the more resilient intellect.

No, that wasn't fair. Gaspar had worked out geological prospects that were as significant as the archaeological ones. Gaspar certainly had preoccupations of his own. Both men were more important to Don's interests than he had thought at first.

"Maybe we are after all heading down to that dinosaur crater," Don said.

"Let me tell you, that would give me the same thrill you just got," Gaspar said. "But it's still a long way there, and I won't hope until I see its coordinates."

They decided to skirt the eastern Yucatan close to shore. Gaspar said the typical depth of this region was five hundred fathoms—three thousand feet, over half a mile—extending almost to the brink of land. They could travel this deep water safely, completely hidden from human perception. "But farther out it drops to twenty five hundred fathoms," he cautioned.

"Two and a half miles!" Melanie exclaimed.

"That's nothing compared to the trench," Gaspar said, checking the map. "It reaches a depth of over five miles. But no point going way down, when we'll only have to climb out again. Anyway, the sea floor's irregular. Used to be a land bridge from Cuba to the Yucatan."

The others were glad to agree about keeping to moderate depths. The climb from the abyssal plain to the continental shelf had worn them out, and only the two days exploration of the city had allowed them to recover.

Even so, it wasn't easy. In places the continental slope was so steep it resembled a cliff rising to their right, forcing them not only to walk, but to rope themselves together, just in case. Don knew that if they could only see it clearly, it would be the most impressive mountain any of them had experienced.

"That's the trouble," Pacifa remarked, affecting distress. "Here I'm supposed to survey potential scenic routes—and they aren't scenic. It doesn't do a tourist much good to know that he's passing near the most remarkable view, only it's invisible."

Don had grown accustomed to the continuing night of the deeps, and to the ocean bottom animals. But there were surprises yet. One day they bore down on a giant squid, who was so startled that it emitted a cloud of glowing ink and disappeared. That horrified Don, for some reason that he decided was more instinctive than rational.

"Makes sense," Gaspar said. "Where there's light, darkness conceals, so the inkfish makes it dark. But where it's dark, maybe light conceals."

"Pretty smart," Don agreed, shuddering as that ghostlike nimbus drifted through him. Melanie closed her eyes so that she couldn't see it, which was perhaps a better reaction.

"They are smart," Gaspar said. "Cleverest animals in the ocean."

"Except for the dolphins?" Pacifa asked.

"I wouldn't except the dolphins," Gaspar said, getting that stubborn tone again. It seemed harder than ever to avoid this attitude. "Everybody talks about them, but what are dolphins, really? Friendly mammals. Overrated."

"Don't they help ships?" Pacifa demanded. "Imitate human sounds? Do tricks?"

"So do birds," Gaspar said. "I don't despise the dolphin or the other intelligent cetaceans. But I think we'd profit more by studying the squid. He's more versatile, and as I said, probably smarter."

"Well, we have a good chance now," Pacifa said. "Old Glowcloud is back."

"I'm not surprised," Gaspar said. "They're curious creatures. See, his skin is green. I think that's his curiosity color."

"Don't tell me they're chameleons!" Melanie said, becoming interested.

"A chameleon is unworthy of the name, compared to this. Here, I'll show you." Gaspar rode up to the slowly moving squid and waved his arms violently.

The mollusk turned white and jetted away, backwards. The color shift was so sudden and complete that the other four of them gaped. One moment the squid was green; the next, pale watery white.

"How—?" Melanie asked, amazed.

"There isn't any light down here, normally," Eleph said. "Why should it change color?"

"Squids are versatile," Gaspar said with satisfaction. "They inhabit all levels. Probably this one has fed in surface waters at another season. And of course there are some natural sources of light. Anyway, it has different color pigments in tiny sacs all over its skin. Muscles attach to elastic walls, opening these sacs, pulling them into star shaped patches of color. There are several layers, so the squid can blend colors like paints. Because the effect is muscular, not chemical, it happens instantly, with every change of mood. Hey, he's back again."

The squid was swimming tentacles-first, slowly flapping broad fins near its rear. Don tried to conceal his automatic apprehension. It was hard to tell how long the creature was because Don didn't know where to measure from, but the tentacles seemed to be twelve or fifteen feet from base to tip. The body was now light green.

"Watch," Gaspar cried, and charged it again.

"Don't tease it!" Melanie cried, her fear of the monster becoming sympathy. But she was too late.

This time the squid did not blanch or retreat. Black stripes flickered over its body. Its tentacles reached forward in a mass and grabbed at Gaspar, who was of course untouched.

"Octopi are timid," Gaspar said. "But squid are bold, and the larger they are, the fiercer. The biggest ones will fight small whales. I'd never try this in real life."

It looked none too safe even in phase. Startled at the lack of contact, the squid flashed black spots and grabbed again. It brought one huge eye to bear, trying to comprehend this thing that it could see but could not hold. It moved up and opened its massive, horrible parrot beak to take a bite. When this also failed, it turned reddish brown and waved its tentacles angrily.

"It's furious," Melanie said. "Justifiably."

Gaspar laughed. Then the squid quit. It faded to a neutral gray and jetted away smoothly, its long arms trailing behind.

"See, he learns from experience, and controls his emotions," Gaspar said with a certain pride. He had evidently decided the creature was male. "He won't try to grab me again, you can be sure."

But to Don it was macabre sport. Had they been on the same plane of existence, the monster could have devoured them all.

They rode on, but several hours later Glowcloud was back. He checked each rider over, refusing to be dissuaded by shouts or action. Don was irrationally terrified, and even Pacifa looked quite uncomfortable as the tentacles passed through her. But Eleph had the most reason to take evasive action, because of his half-phased thread and balloons. If the squid discovered these, he would have leverage, and would surely use it.

Perhaps to forestall this, Melanie nerved herself and tried to distract Glowcloud. "Hello, you gorgeous monster," she said, trying to pet a tentacle. "How many colors can you make, when you feel artistic?"

The squid's reactions were extraordinarily rapid, and his manner disquietingly purposeful. He surely wanted to understand the nature of these little intruders, so as to consume them, and he intended to keep after them until he had solved the riddle.

In fact, Glowcloud followed them. He would disappear for hours, but always reappear, no matter how rapidly they moved.

His water-jetting mode of swimming was beautifully effective, and he could—and did—swim rings around them. Perhaps it was imagination, but the squid did seem to prefer the company of Melanie, and she was definitely warming to him. Was it because Glowcloud was hairless?

"Beauty and the beast," Pacifa remarked.

Melanie, flustered, demurred. "I'm no—"

"*He's* the beauty," Pacifa clarified with a smile. "Look at that color."

"B-but you are too," Don added. Melanie seemed not to hear.

"Good thing Glowcloud's not one of the large ones," Gaspar said merrily. "They grow up to over fifty feet, with tentacles over thirty feet, and maybe much larger yet."

"In horror magazines," Eleph muttered, again avoiding the creature's advances.

"There's pretty good evidence," Gaspar insisted. "Sperm whales like to eat squid, and tentacles over forty feet long were found in a whale once. That squid must have weighed over forty tons, alive. But even that's small compared to the ones that get away."

"From the sperm whales?" Eleph demanded. "How can you judge what the whale doesn't catch?"

"Maybe they tell squid stories," Melanie suggested.

"By the sucker marks," Gaspar said. "You see the suckers on Glowcloud, here? All down his arms? Well, when a whale goes after a big squid, that squid fights, and his suckers make imprints on the whale's hide. A fifty footer leaves scars four inches across. But some sperm whales have been caught with scars eighteen inches across."

"Talk of the kraken!" Pacifa exclaimed, awed.

"They *do* tell stories," Melanie said, tittering. "'Hey, Joe, you should have seen the sucker that got away!'"

"If the ratio holds true," Eleph said, "eighteen inch suckers would indicate a squid over two hundred feet long, massing over a thousand tons. That would be the largest creature ever to inhabit our world."

Gaspar shrugged. "The ocean has secrets yet."

All of which did not make them feel easier about Glowcloud. But the squid was gone again, rocketing smoothly into the murk. Any notion any of them might have had about clumsiness of such creatures had been abolished. Octopi might be awkward and slow when traveling, but squid were sleek and fast.

They rode on down a narrowing valley, breathing hard.

"I can't catch my breath," Pacifa complained. "Eleph, will you check the field generator on my bike?"

They stopped, and Eleph checked. Don also felt out of breath, and Gaspar's chest was pumping. Melanie's bosom was heaving in a manner Don would have found interesting at another time.

"The field is in order," Eleph said. "But I must admit—"

"Uh-oh," Gaspar said. "I know. We're in a valley that's low on oxygen. Some of these exist in the ocean, if the water doesn't circulate enough. See—almost no life around here. Turn and go back in a hurry."

They retreated with alacrity, but the breathing did not improve. Even if there were more oxygen in the water, the field would take time to phase it through.

"Up!" Gaspar said. "Got to get out of the trough, into richer water."

"The map shows a steep rise to your west, as I remember," Melanie said, trying to help.

"Thanks!" Gaspar bore west immediately. "The rest of you— keep alert for Glowcloud. Where he is, there's oxygen, sure."

They found the rise, but it was too steep to climb. Pacifa reeled visibly, the first sign of physical weakness she had shown, and Eleph was almost collapsed over his handlebars. Don felt like lying down and sleeping, and knew he dared not.

"Glowcloud—where are you?" Melanie gasped.

Gaspar found a discontinuity in the impassible face of the cliff, and scrambled up, hauling his bicycle along. The others followed, helping each other up. This was mountain climbing, for the path was narrow and the walls bare. Still there was little life.

On they slogged. When Melanie seemed about to fall, just ahead of him, Don simply put the top of his head against her rear and pushed, and she made it to the next ledge. This was no place for niceties. He lost track of the others, concentrating on getting himself and Melanie to the higher ground.

A tentacle passed through his face. Don blinked—then shouted. "Glowcloud! Glowcloud! He's here!" Indeed, it was almost as though the giant squid were trying to pull Melanie upward. They struggled a few more feet, until their heads were buried within the body of the monster, and collapsed. Oxygen!

● ● ●

When they resumed the climb they were roped again. This time there was no question of the necessity; a misstep could mean a fall of hundreds of feet. Where the way became narrow, they anchored front and rear while the middle proceeded. Gaspar was the front, Pacifa the rear, with Eleph, Melanie and Don not ashamed to admit their incompetence in the center.

And it was not so bad. Much of the climb was gentle, and some was downhill, for the continental slope was by no means regular. They were neither rushed nor hungry now, and they had become experienced at this sort of thing. Just so long as there was some current in the water, and some animal life.

"I heard that," Melanie said during one of their pauses for anchorage. "You think I'm beautiful?"

It took Don a moment to orient. She was referring to the "Beauty and the Beast" exchange. "Yes."

"Physically?"

"Th-that too."

She looked startled, but pleased.

Then it was time to move the anchor along.

At the next stop Don looked around. "Where's Glowcloud? Never thought I'd miss the sight of his ugly beak, but—"

"We're changing depth pretty rapidly," Gaspar said. "Few creatures can handle substantial and rapid pressure differentials. We aren't being subjected to them, phased out, or we'd be in real trouble. By the time he adjusts, we'll be gone again."

"Too bad," Melanie said. "But not worth going back down into that deadly valley!"

Near the top—fifty fathoms—Gaspar gave a cry. "Hey! There's a cave."

There was. "We need a safe place to spend the night," Pacifa said. "Let's check it out. I don't want to roll off any ledges in my sleep."

Her given reason was spurious; she had no fear of ledges. She merely liked to explore. But so did the others. They were all adventurers, now that they had the means.

They moved in cautiously, Don staying close to Melanie, or

perhaps the other way around. There was no concern about wild-life, of course, except to make sure that it was present, but a gap in the floor would be every bit as hazardous to them as to land dwellers in a land cave. They remained roped.

The passage wound about, going first up, then down. The floor was irregular, so that they would have to walk. Then the way opened into a large cavern.

"Stalactites!" Don exclaimed. "This was once a land cave!"

"Why not?" Gaspar called back. "You said yourself that the water receded this far during the ice age, and I agree."

"Stalactites," Eleph repeated. "They hang from the top?"

"And stalagmites rise from the floor," Don said. "Remember it mnemonically: C for ceiling, G for ground. Stalac, stalag."

"Strange they have not dissolved away," Eleph said.

"They may, in time. They must have been millions of years in the forming, while the sea has been here for only a few thousand."

"Was the sea level down for millions of years?"

"Well, no, but this cave could have been sealed off with air in it."

"Maybe cave men used it," Pacifa said half facetiously. "They cut this passage in, little dreaming that the sea would return."

"I'm not sure the Amerinds used caves," Don said. "Certainly, they did not paint on the walls the way the Reindeer People did in Europe."

"How do you know?" she asked.

"Well, they—" He stopped. "You know, *I don't* know! Maybe they did, at that."

"If habitable caves were available, they would have been stupid not to utilize them," Eleph said. "Man is not stupid."

"Man's an idiot," Pacifa retorted. "Look at what he's doing to the world!"

"I can only draw a parallel to the European situation," Don said. "Certainly caves were used there, from time to time—but not by all men, and seldom by civilized ones. There is evidence that many of the caves that were used, were not used for residence."

"What else would a cave be used for?" Eleph asked. "Storage?" He seemed to be fascinated by this region, though he evidently knew little about it.

"Religion. Or some similar ceremony. The golden age of stone age man was probably the Magdalenian culture, about fifteen thousand years ago. They hunted reindeer and other animals during the ice age, and used sympathetic magic to help overcome these creatures. They painted pictures of them on the walls and ceilings of deep grottoes, some of the finest naturalistic art ever rendered. But then the glaciers receded, the reindeer migrated north, and the Magdalenians declined."

"The glaciers," Gaspar said. "That was an ice age culture."

"You haven't been paying attention," Pacifa said.

"Very much an ice age culture," Don said sadly. "In some ways man's civilization was shaped by the ice. It gave him a real hurdle to overcome, for it overran his choicest residential areas and reshaped the land. To survive he had to develop clothing—"

"And that killed him," Melanie said. "It stopped the sun from striking his skin, and Neanderthal man was wiped out by rickets, the Vitamin D deficiency disease."

Don stopped short. "Where did you hear that?"

"I read it somewhere. Isn't that what you were saying?"

"No. It may have been Cro-Magnon man who developed civilization as we know it, and he wore clothing too. We can assess its approximate coverage by noting the places where our own bodies lack heavy hair. We have light hair all over our bodies, of course. Possibly his skin was lighter, so that he could adapt better to the scant sunshine of the northern latitudes, but that alone could hardly have wiped out Neanderthal. He lived in the tropics as well, after all."

"Ah, well," she said with cute resignation. "But then what happened to Neanderthal man?"

"We're still not sure. He overlapped modern man by eighty thousand years or so, so it seems unlikely that he was conquered. There is evidence that Neanderthal was truly robust, physically, capable of feats that our champions can't match today. He had the same braincase and tools as Cro-Magnon. But it may have been his diet."

"No Vitamin D enriched milk?"

Don had to laugh. "Vitamin D isn't even a vitamin! No, he seems to have become a vegetarian, perhaps living on fruits and nuts. He may have driven Cro-Magnon man out of the good forests and forced him to become a scavenger, taking the leavings of hunting animals. Finally modern man became a hunter himself, his system adjusting with difficulty to the wholesale consumption of flesh. Then the climate changed and the dense forests shrank—and Neanderthal man was starved out, because he could not eat the foods of the savanna. It may be that he had never developed truly organized hunting techniques, and it was too late for him to change. When modern man did, he started hunting game species of animals to extinction—and perhaps used those same techniques on his longtime rival Neanderthal, exterminating him at last. Cro-Magnon man was better equipped to survive, being less specialized. It's a common theme, paleontologically."

"You mean we're murderers?" Melanie asked, distressed.

"As Cain slew Able, perhaps. It's all conjecture."

"But the glaciers," Gaspar said again. "There's the connection."

"Between Neanderthal and Cro-Magnon man?" Don asked.

"No, between the Minoans and the Mayans. Your finest cave culture was the result of the ice age. Well, the ice age was worldwide. Why couldn't there have been fine cave cultures over here in the Americas, too?"

"And when the world warmed up," Melanie added eagerly, "and the waters rose, those cultures didn't just expire, they went elsewhere. Maybe they kept their civilization alive for thousands of years, building great cities, until—"

"Hunter-gatherer societies do not build cities," Don said, laughing. "How many reindeer do you see roaming the streets of New York?"

"Well, small cities, then, she said. "Villages, maybe. Rome was not built in a—"

"Something strange ahead," Eleph said, and they broke off. This spared Don the onus of debating against more amateur theories of civilization.

Strange it was. A horizontal sheet of something crossed the entire top of the next cavern, cutting it off. The demarcation was so level and regular that it had to be artificial. A sheet of clear plastic?

"That's the surface!" Gaspar cried, laughing.

"At forty five fathoms?" Eleph demanded.

"An air pocket. Come on, we can ride up out of the water for a change."

But they couldn't. The surface was twenty feet above their heads, and the cavern walls were vertical. They could only look.

"Do you suppose there are cave paintings remaining in the dry portion?" Eleph asked.

"I doubt it," Don said. "But I'd sure like to look."

"We're wasting time," Gaspar said. "Let's find a place to set up our tents."

This callousness to archaeological potential irritated Don, but he knew Gaspar was right. The man wasn't really uninterested; he merely wasn't going to worry about reaching an inaccessible spot. He was being practical.

"Perhaps if we used the balloons," Eleph murmured.

"Yes!" Don agreed. It was becoming difficult to dislike the man.

Gaspar and Pacifa set up camp, anchoring the tents to the rising spires of old stalagmites. Don and Melanie and Eleph blew up balloons, waiting for them to achieve sufficient flotation. Working together, they inflated six balloons in somewhat over an hour, and hitched them to Don's bicycle. In time Don lurched to the surface and whipped his lamp around.

There was nothing. The walls were completely natural.

A small blind fish nosed up. "Get out of here!" Don shouted, bashing through it with one fist.

But the disappointment was minor, compared to what had been discovered before. As they settled down for the night, Melanie took his hand again. "But suppose you found a girl with real hair?" she murmured.

"What is hair?" he asked rhetorically. "It's just dead cells. It's superficial. I can take it or leave it, now."

"Can you? I think you should meet such a girl, and see."

He laughed. "Here?"

"Well, after the mission. Then you'll know."

She didn't want to be hurt. He understood that. He knew that if he met a pretty girl in the regular world he would be tongue-tied anyway. Part of the appeal of Melanie was that he had seen her shorn, and gotten to know her without romantic pressure, and now there could be romance, if she wanted it. Evidently she did want it, if she could only be sure of him. He had accepted her without hair, but that was only half way there. He had to show that he would not change his mind when he encountered a woman with body and hair. That he did not see her as a Neanderthal, to be discarded in favor of Modern. So it was necessary to play it through. Once she saw him with anyone else, she would know that hair had nothing to do with it, anymore.

●   ●   ●

In the morning they completed their preparations and moved out, single file. Don hated to leave this cave without exploring it more thoroughly, for the discussion of the evening before had taken hold of his fancy. Suppose man had lived here? This cave was three hundred feet below the present surface of the ocean. Its entrance could have been exposed only when the water was low enough—if, indeed, someone had not cut the passage into it, as Pacifa had suggested. Ludicrous, yet not impossible. Either way, that would have been 15,000 years ago, at the height of the ice age—the same time as the European Reindeer culture. A fantastic notion, but tempting.

Yet hardly more fantastic than the idea of a mighty city off the coast of the Yucatan, dating back perhaps six thousand years and containing Minoan artificats. But with the sea washing off any pictures that might have been on the walls, and the fish consuming any bones, and the sediment covering whatever remained, this quest was hopeless. If only he had the facilities to investigate thoroughly!

Don sighed. That was the nature of archaeology. The breakthroughs were wonderful, but most of it came to nothing significant. Some other man would have to discover the wonders of pre-Mayan cave cultures, if any were to be found.

The trip along the continental shallows was more difficult than Don had anticipated. While the Yucatan was hardly a modern center of commerce, it was populated. Small boats plied its waters, fishing and hauling. Several times the cyclists had to hide, to prevent possible discovery. But the shelf here was so narrow that they had either to remain quite close to shore, or negotiate the descending slope to rejoin Glowcloud and perhaps the valley of death.

It was hot. Maybe the ambient temperature was governed mainly by the converter and the nitrogen atmosphere of the phase world, but when Earth was warm, *Don* was warm. Their terrain was not smooth, and he sweated steadily with the exercise. So did Melanie; her blouse was plastered to her skin. He knew she would not appreciate him staring, so he tried not to. Hair? Who cared about hair!

The problem was that the mountainous inland features were duplicated near the water, forcing repeated gear-shifting and portages, with occasional use of the safety rope. At one point they actually had to cross overland in order to avoid an ocean canyon that would have forced an unreasonably long detour.

But they made it in good order to the third depot. There was plenty of food there, and spare wheels for their bicycles—most of which did not fit, since it had been presumed they would be in the better ten-speed machines that had supposedly been waiting at the first depot.

"Eighteen degrees, thirty minutes north latitude," Melanie said. "Seventy eight degrees, ten minutes west longitude."

"I don't know coordinates, but I know that's toward Cuba," Pacifa snorted.

"Maybe," Gaspar said, sounding disappointed. "It's not toward South America, for sure. Let me work it out. Eighteen, nineteen—no, that's Jamaica. Northern coast, I think."

"Port Royal!" Don exclaimed. "We're going to see Port Royal!"

"That doesn't sound like a stone age culture, or even an old Mayan city," Pacifa said.

"It isn't. Port Royal was an English town of the seventeenth century, notorious for its illicit trade and rich living. It suddenly sank beneath the sea, around 1690 I think. Its enemies thought it was divine retribution. But for my purpose a quick burial is much better than a slow decline, because all the common artifacts of daily existence remain."

"You archaeologists are ghoulish," Melanie said, smiling.

"I remember the story," Gaspar said. "That's a legitimate case of subsidence along the fault. It does happen. But wasn't Port Royal on the south of the island? We're going to the north of it."

"I don't remember," Don said, disappointed. "The New World just isn't my specialty. You're probably right."

"It's as if whoever set this up is teasing you," Melanie remarked. "Sending you close to something really important to you, then turning away."

"What would be the point of teasing us?" Gaspar asked.

"I don't know. I don't understand what's going on at all."

"You and the rest of us," Pacifa agreed.

"The spot is very near the trench, isn't it?" Eleph asked. "It may be several thousand fathoms down. What could be so important there?"

"Maybe an eight thousand year old pre-Minoan city," Gaspar said with half a smile. "Complete with television sets."

Don did not deign to respond.

They proceeded. The great Cayman trench coincided almost exactly with the Honduras shoreline in this region, forcing them to hew to an even narrower margin than before. Here they could not avoid a canyon, so they used rope and balloons in combination and followed it down . . . and down.

"Just how far did the waters recede during the ice age?" Pacifa demanded.

"Three hundred feet," Don said. "Four hundred at the most."

"Do you realize that we are down to two hundred fathoms? Twelve hundred feet, and no sign of the end?"

"I can't explain it," Don said.

"Fortunately I can," Gaspar said. "You were right about the cutaway on the Yucatan shelf. But the really large canyons are below that level. Some go right to the ocean floor, three miles deep."

"How can they be formed, with the water always there?" Pacifa asked.

"Turbidity currents. A function of that same sediment you see all over the ocean floor. The large rivers deposit a lot of silt, and a lot remains suspended in the water. Periodically it builds up to the point where it must come down, especially when the motion of the river is lost within the mass of the sea. So it overturns, and the loaded water drops. That forms some pretty formidable currents—up to forty miles per hour. With that sort of motion, you can cut canyons anywhere. They still have trouble with undersea cables getting snapped that way. Any natural tremor can set off a mud slide, and once it starts, it's like an avalanch. That has a similar effect."

"Ocean currents and mud slides cut this?" Pacifa asked, gesturing about. "This is like the Grand Canyon!"

"Makes you respect mud, doesn't it," Gaspar said, smiling.

"We'd better move on, because even in our phased-out state we could be in trouble if some such action occurred around us."

There was no argument, though Don was sure they would have to wait years for a mudslide. Why take any more of a risk than they had to? And suppose their passage did set off such a slide? He tried to suppress his nervousness.

They rode and hauled and climbed vigorously, searching for safer waters. But it was more than a hundred miles before there was room to diverge freely from the trench's edge. Even then there was not much improvement, because the sea floor became mountainous. Progress was slow.

"Maybe we should just drop down to the center of the trench," Pacifa suggested.

"I wouldn't," Gaspar said. "The trench is not your ordinary innocent sea floor. Remember what I said about the Bahamas platform?"

"No."

"How it filled in at the beginning of the great continental crackup? Well, the Puerto Rico–Cayman trench runs right under it, cutting off the bottom part. That makes it especially interesting for me, of course, but it also means it may be especially hazardous for us."

"You talked about the trench, but not about any platform," Pacifa said.

Melanie broke in. "You weren't there, Pacifa. That was just before you joined the party."

"Now wait a minute," Don protested. "Why should a crack in the platform or under it or wherever—why should that be bad for us? Worse than any other crack, I mean?"

"Because the great trenches of the ocean are not just cracks. They are stress points of the globe. They are where the spreading ocean floor pushes down under the land mass, because it has nowhere else to go. They are in motion, swallowing mountains. Such regions are deep and jagged, and always the raw material for volcanism and earthquakes."

"Volcanoes and earthquakes," Melanie said morosely. "And I thought this trip might be fun."

"I just don't see that," Pacifa argued. "A volcano is an eruption of lava and ash, while an earthquake is a shaking of the ground. This is just some ground going slowly down, you say. Maybe an inch a century?"

"I can't go into the whole of sea-floor spreading right now," Gaspar said, exasperated.

"You don't need to. I know about the magma coming up and pushing apart the sea floor and continents. There is surely some violence there! But why should there be earthquakes and volcanoes here at the other end?"

"Because when the leading edge of one plate collides with another above a certain speed, one plunges under the other to make room. It descends into the asthenosphere—that is, deep down—and is destroyed by pressure and heat. That impact and that action are responsible for both the local quakes and the local volcanoes."

"You are beginning to make sense," Pacifa admitted. "Does that mean we'll get sucked into the crevice if we aren't careful?"

Gaspar smiled. "Unlikely. These are the processes of many millions of years. Sea floor spreading occurs at the rate of a few inches per year, average."

"Inches a year," she said. "That's certainly faster than an inch a century. But you made it sound like a ravening maw."

"It is, geologically. A few inches is plenty, when you consider the masses of the material involved. The Caribbean is a twisted area, and the heart of that twist is that trench, because it is at right angles to the nominal direction of spreading. I think one of the Pacific plates has crossed over the continent and ridden sideways across the Atlantic plate. Now it's coming up against the Bahamas platform, which is a considerable mouthful even for this process. We don't know what we'll find down there."

"You really want to see it, don't you," Melanie said.

"Not as much as I want to see the dinosaur crater. But yes, the whole ocean is interesting, and this especially so."

"Just as Don wants to excavate New Atlantis on the Yucatan," Gaspar agreed. "But I don't want to travel the length of this crevasse. Better to make our next depot, then make forays from there at our convenience."

"So you won't be tempted to stop at every sexy outcropping on the way," Pacifa said. "I know the problem. All right, why not travel the rim to the next depot? Then we'll see."

"You are assuming that simple exploration is our mission," Eleph said. "I remind you that we do not yet know what we are getting into."

Pacifa nodded. "Good, grim point. Well, let's travel."

Easier said than done. The rim of Cayman was knifelike in places, with an overhang on one side and a precipice on the other, and cut into segments by transverse cracks yards or miles across. The rope and pulley were too tedious, so they kept the balloons inflated just under the necessary amount of air needed for full flotation, and added to them when a bad section had to be traversed. This was tedious, as the balloons had to be dragged at other times, making progress extremely slow. But the terrain was so jagged they had to take what precautions they could.

One section was terraced like a contour farm, the individual ridges seeming to continue indefinitely. They deflated the balloons and cycled along the broadest ledge, making better time. Here too there were cracks, but most were less than a yard across, and negotiable. Occasional breaks in the wall gave access to the more regular ocean floor beyond the trench—but that was such a wilderness of crosshatched ridges that they stayed on the terrace. It was somber and impressive and rather peaceful.

That peace was suddenly to end.

Chapter 10

•

Decoy

Proxy 5-12-5-16-8: Attention.

Acknowledging.

Status?

The party is approaching the next challenge. It is integrating well. I believe it will accept the mission.

Why not acquaint it with the mission now, in that case?

Because it will be more certain after the last two challenges. I do not wish to risk loss by premature presentation.

They still are not aware that one of them is a local government spy and another is an agent from another world?

They do not know. I will acquaint them with this information when the challenges are done. Then they should be ready for it.

Yet if they are ready now, and you delay, you risk the interference of some outside factor.

I believe this is a risk that must be taken. It seems slight at the moment.

Even a slight risk is unwise, if it is unnecessary.

I deem the risk of rejection at this point to be greater than the risk of random interference.

That is your assessment to make. Continue.

•　　•　　•

"What's that?" Melanie cried, alarmed.

They all looked. A light was coming through the water, floating over the abyss.

"That couldn't be Glowcloud," Pacifa said.

It was huge and bright, reminding Don of a Cyclops: a giant with a single glowing eye in its forehead. Fantasy, surely—but whatever was coming was surely trouble.

"That's not natural," Gaspar said. "That's—"

"A submarine!" Eleph cried. "Douse the lights!"

In a moment the five bicycle lamps were off. Now they could make out the big machine's outline: a monstrous barrel with small bulging ports and large fins. It was absolutely silent.

"Why no sound of engines?" Pacifa inquired from the darkness.

"Don't talk!" Eleph cried with dismay.

Too late. As they spoke, the great headlight rotated, orienting on the sound. The machine's listening devices were sophisticated, evidently distinguishing their faint noises from the background cacophony.

Don threw himself down and hauled his bicycle after him, seeking the cover of the nearest stone. Where was it? If only he had made a note before turning off his light!

The sub's beam swept near, splashing across the jagged rock and highlighting two stages of the terrace wall. Don saw to his relief that he was sheltered behind an upthrusting ledge, and was hidden from the sub. Melanie was almost behind him, similarly sheltered. Gaspar and Pacifa were not in sight, so must also have found concealment. But Eleph—

Eleph stood frozen, and the beam had already picked him out. Don cursed the man's ineptitude—then saw that Eleph was stranded on a narrow platform. He could not move without falling into the trench. It was the luck of the draw.

"Who are you?" Eleph shouted suddenly. "You're not native to these waters!"

Why was he calling attention to himself? Don was tempted to run over and haul the man back out of the light. But how could he manage it on his bicycle? That pause gave him time to realize the foolishness of such a gesture. He could only expose himself. And the sub could not actually harm Eleph, considering the phase.

"So you have found me!" Eleph continued, doing something with his bicycle. "But I'm going to lose you!" Then he pedaled on.

Now Don saw that Eleph had unhitched the safety rope. He was going off by himself!

That was it, of course. Eleph had been spotted, and knew it. He had nothing to lose, and might find out something that would help the others, while they stayed hidden. He was serving as a decoy, so that the main party could escape undiscovered. He had spoken aloud to cover Pacifa's blunder; the sub oriented on sound, and knew that *someone* was there.

This must be a foreign sub; an American one would not have been sneaking about silently. No—perhaps it was a bathyscaphe, a research diver, checking for life in the trench, quiet so as neither to disturb the fish nor to foul its own auditory receptors with mechanical noise. But Eleph had said it wasn't native, and Don had a feeling the man would not make a mistake about such a thing. Not with his military background.

Whatever the truth, Eleph had demonstrated intelligence and courage in a crisis, and perhaps self-sacrifice. How could they know the intention of that submarine? If it represented a foreign power, it might seek to eliminate anyone who saw it. It would have trouble doing anything directly to a man who was phased out, but if it managed to shove him into the trench, that would do it.

The spotlight followed the moving man, the sub gliding smoothly after, still silent. The decoy was working.

They waited for several minutes. Then Gaspar stood up. Don saw the glow of light from the man's covered lamp, and felt the tug of the rope. That was what Eleph had been doing: detaching himself from the rope, so he could travel alone. Don stood himself, and carefully walked his bike over.

The four of them met by that faint glow. Gaspar pointed back the way they had come, one finger limned against the headlight. Away from the sub.

They moved, quietly. Gaspar seemed to have a good memory for the terrain, for he proceeded with greater confidence in the dark than Don could have.

They diverged from the rim of the canyon at the first opportunity, climbing to the upper levels and thence through a mountain pass. Only when they were well clear of the great trench, concealed by myriad and labyrinthine projecting stones, did they stop to confer.

There were no recriminations. They all understood what Eleph had done. They had let him do it because there was no better choice. The less the enemy sub knew, assuming that it was hostile, the better off they were. They had to preserve their privacy for the sake of their as yet unknown mission. Perhaps it concerned—submarines.

"Suppose we split," Gaspar said. "Each look for him alone, keeping out of sight. He'll slip the sub all right; it can't touch him and can't possibly follow where he can go. But he'll probably lose himself in the process, and we can't use the whistle while the sub is near. So we'll have to locate him visually. Rough job."

"What about the radio?" Don asked. "We're all on the same private circuit—" He stopped, appalled. "The radio! Can the sub intercept it?"

"I don't think so," Gaspar said. "We're transmitting in the phase world, and it shouldn't cross over."

"Light crosses over," Don said. "Sound crosses over. How can we be sure the radio doesn't?"

"Good question," Melanie agreed.

"Eleph's the only one who can answer that," Gaspar said.

"And he's maintaining radio silence," Pacifa said, snapping off her radio. The others jumped to do the same.

Now they were cut off from their missing member. If anything happened to him, such as a fall into the chasm, they might never be able even to verify it. They had not been using the radios much, once all of them were together, but had known that they could not get truly separated as long as the radios were functional. Now Don felt a bit naked.

"What is a foreign sub doing here?" Pacifa asked.

"When we know that," Gaspar replied slowly, "we may know our mission. That's a deep-diver." He paused. "Now suppose we meet here in four hours? We can't afford to get permanently separated."

Don and Pacifa agreed, but Melanie looked doubtful.

Gaspar glanced at her. "No offense, Mel, but maybe you shouldn't go alone. Why don't you go with Don?" She nodded gratefully. The notion of being separated in the deeps evidently appalled her. She might have been emotionally isolated all of her life, but this was a rather special physical isolation. She lacked both the muscle of the men and the expertise of Pacifa, and with radio silence she would be even more alone.

They split up. Gaspar took the trench, because he was most familiar with its hazards. Pacifa took the encircling approach, because she could make the best time. She would be trying to intersect the trench ahead of Eleph, and work back. If Gaspar and Pacifa met, they would know that Eleph was not on the terraces. Don and Melanie took the mazelike periphery.

Four hours deadline: in his present toughened condition, Don might have done eighty miles in that time, on a decent level surface. But he would have to reserve half his time for the return, and the surface was anything but decent. His effective range—the most distant spot he could check—was probably about twenty miles. He would use up much of that winding about the interminable projections. It didn't matter; he wasn't going anywhere, he was searching for a lost man.

But with Melanie along, they could double the width of the search path. They could ride parallel, keeping each other in sight while extending their range. That would help not only in effectiveness, but because they were keeping each other company. Because Don didn't like the notion of being alone in this dangerous murky region either. It was indeed lonely, being alone. He understood the ocean much better than when he had first entered it, but its dark immensity still cowed him when he became aware of it. He was aware now.

" . . .when I was in college," Melanie was saying.

Don realized that she had been speaking, and he hadn't been hearing. She must have started quietly, really talking to herself, when they were at a farther separation, and then he picked it up when they veered closer to each other. So he listened. He doubted that the sub could pick up on this, if it were even in the vicinity; only because he had become accustomed to picking a human voice out of the constant background noises was he able to hear her at all.

"I liked my favorite very much," Melanie continued equably. "Mostly he just listened. Most of the time he just looked as if he were going to sleep. I guess he wanted me to start thinking aloud about some of the important things in my then-current life. He would just prod me now and then. After a while I noticed that he seemed to give quite a number of compliments. Sometimes they were strange. One day he said that I had erected one of the most formidable barriers around myself that he had encountered in all his years of practice. In fact that was my favorite of all his compliments."

"That was no compliment!" Don snorted. "He just wanted to seduce you."

"What?" She seemed confused.

"That dumb writer you visited. Telling you about barriers. That was just his l-line."

She choked and made strangled sounds. It dawned on Don that she was suppressing laughter.

"It's not funny," he said. "A man like that—you didn't tell him about your hair, did you? So—"

"That was my psychiatrist," she said. "Long before I visited the—"

Oops! Don felt his face burning. He had gulped his foot to his knee that time.

"You're jealous," Melanie said.

"I—I—" Damn that stutter! He couldn't get anything out.

"I'm thrilled and flattered," she said, sounding pleased. "I don't think anyone was ever jealous on my account before. You really do care."

"Of *course* I care!" he snapped. "Y-you visiting s-strange men, and taking p-pills, and—"

"Pills? I never—"

"B-birth control pills. You told me—"

She laughed again. "Oh, that. Don, I only took those pills because my mother insisted. Just as she insisted about the psychiatrists. While I was in college. She wanted me to be a normal, extroverted girl. Not to be afraid of foolish little things. Like pregnancy."

"Your mother!"

"She was pretty domineering, in her fashion."

"But that's white slavery. To make you—"

"Oh, Don! I took the pills. That was all. The only thing they ever did for me was to foul up my analytical ability. As soon as I got out on my own, I dropped them. It seemed pointless to waste the money any more. Even with the pills, I could analyze things to that extent."

He had definitely blown it. "I—I'm sorry. I a-apologize."

"Oh, don't be! I'm reveling in the feeling. You know me as I am, Don. Words I never quite know whether to believe, but jealousy I believe."

Then maybe his miscue hadn't been as bad as it could have been. "Okay."

"You know, Don, I've been thinking. It seems to me that I was told that the radio has no crossover. Otherwise we'd be getting Earth broadcasts, interference, and—"

"So the sub can't intercept!" Don said, hugely relieved. "And since we had our radios on before, and the sub didn't seem to know about us until it spied Eleph, probably it wasn't following any radio signal. But why isn't Eleph talking, then? He knows more about the equipment than we do."

"I don't know. Maybe he turned his radio off automatically, as we did, before thinking it through, and then forgot to turn it on again."

"*Him?* He'd be the first to remember it."

"Or he might be hurt."

"Hurt too bad even to talk?"

"I don't want to guess," she said.

"Well, we have to find him. Where do you think he is?"

"Maybe we should think like a fifty year old conservative physicist with a military background," she suggested. "Where would he go?"

Don thought. "Into a cave!" he exclaimed. "He showed real interest in that Yucatan coastal cave. I'll bet it wasn't for the archaeological or geological prospects, but because it served as a secure retreat. Agoraphobia, not claustrophobia—fear of the heights."

"That's acrophobia," she said. "I know, because I've got it too. A little."

"I mean fear of the open spaces," he said.

"Are there caves, here? There can't be any erosion as we know it. How would caves form?"

"Only a geologist knows for sure. Maybe a freshwater spring could do it. I don't know. But if there's one, that's where he'll be, maybe. For one thing, the sub couldn't follow him there."

"We'll just have to look," she agreed. "For cave openings."

"Um."

They rode on, looking for cave openings, but saw none. There were fish here, but not many, and they seemed to be blind. The cousins of the starfish were far more common, and snails and clams were abundant.

This was mountainous country, and the constant steep climbing and fierce coasting were wearing. A man could readily lose himself here, and it would certainly be hazardous for a submarine to maneuver too close to these jagged rocks.

They searched for another twenty minutes, looking carefully into every recess, but it was apparent that they were needles looking for another in a haystack. The ground was too rough; there could be a hundred caves, and they could miss them all unless they dropped a wheel into one. They needed an overview, and even then, the opacity of the water would severely restrict their scope.

"At least we know the sub probably didn't keep him in sight, once he decided to shake it," Melanie said.

A shape loomed near, long and oval and glowing slightly. "Speak of the devil!" Don cried, throwing himself to the ground. Melanie peeped and did the same.

But even as he barked his shins, Don realized that it was a huge squid, some twenty feet long. As if they didn't have troubles enough!

The squid glided up, light green in the beam of light Don angled at it. Its monstrous eye contemplated him. "Go away!" he cried.

The squid jetted in a circle around them.

"It's Glowcloud!" Melanie cried. "He must have been trailing us all the time, and finally homed in." She stood, lifting her hands to the creature. The squid extended a tentacle. That was identification enough; obviously Glowcloud remembered.

"Well, at least it's not the sub."

"What determination," Melanie said, her hands playing a game of touch and dodge with the tentacle. "It must be almost impossible to locate anything in this expanse, as we've been discovering."

"Trust Glowcloud," Don said. "He always did know how to find us, as long as we're in his depth. Hey!"

"What?" She was almost shaking hands with the tentacle. "You're not getting jealous of a squid, now, are you?"

"I just thought, maybe Glowcloud can find Eleph."

"Oh, Don, now you're dreaming! A *mollusk?* He may be cute, but—"

Cute? This twenty foot monster with ten tentacles and a huge hard beak? How her attitude had changed! "Worth a try, anyway. Gaspar said they're the smartest creatures in the sea. Glow-cloud!"

The squid rotated gracefully to bring the eye to bear on him. Probably he was reacting to the sharpness of the sound. "Where's Eleph? Eleph! Take us to Eleph. Eleph!"

"Eleph!" Melanie echoed with less conviction.

The squid circled twice more in a climbing spiral, then shot off at a tangent.

"Do you really think—?" Melanie asked. "I mean, he is a wild creature, and can't be expected to—"

"No. But what better chance do we have?"

"Well, we can't follow where he's going, so we'd better keep looking."

They kept looking, with no better success than before.

Ten minutes later Glowcloud was back. "Hey, did you find Eleph?" Don asked facetiously. Yet he did wonder: the squid certainly seemed responsive. Was it possible that Glowcloud understood their need—or cared?"

The squid jetted slowly north, low enough for them to follow. They did so, knowing that one search pattern was as good as another, in this water wilderness. If . . .

But they didn't find Eleph. Eleph found them. "Don!"

Glowcloud looped around them, then took off after a careless fish.

The bicycles almost collided, for Eleph was riding crookedly. "Eleph!" Don cried. "I thought you were lost."

"How could I be lost, with the coordinates plainly visible on the meter?" Eleph asked sourly. "I was merely doubling back to rejoin the company. Why didn't you wait?"

"Why didn't you call, once you were alone? We assumed—"

Eleph looked embarrassed. "There was a slight mishap in transit." He indicated his radio.

"Small mishap!" Don exclaimed. "The whole thing's stove in! And you—you're—"

"I was in too much of a hurry," Eleph admitted, glancing down at his red-stained shirt. "I took a fall."

Some fall! The man's forbidding front had deceived Don, but only for a moment. Eleph's left arm was tucked inside his shirt, and blood soaked the entire length of it. A bruise showed on his cheek, and his trousers were torn. He must have rolled over, with a jagged spike of rock smashing both arm and radio.

The pain had to be phenomenal. Don was no expert in medicine, but his first-aid briefing had familiarized him with the general nature of a compound fracture. One surely rested inside that shirt. Yet Eleph had roused himself and ridden on, one-handed, actively mastering his destiny. Don had not suspected that the man had that kind of courage. It was a thing he admired tremendously, and it transformed his attitude toward Eleph. Yet nothing in the man's manner suggested that he sought sympathy, so Don didn't proffer it, verbally.

But Melanie did. "You poor man! You're all bruised."

"It happens," Eleph said.

"We broke up to search for you," Don explained. "We agreed to meet again in four hours. More than two to go, still. Pacifa has the—the medication."

"Excellent."

"Are you all right, Eleph?" Melanie asked. "Why is your hand out of sight?" Evidently she hadn't caught on to the extent of it, yet.

"Scratches and bruises," Eleph told her firmly. "Do not concern yourself further, my dear."

Don, to his own surprise, was suddenly overwhelmed. Eleph had such courage in adversity, yet was no more expressive than he had been at the outset. This was another silent person, whose speech and overt actions only partly reflected his true passions. He was familiar in an illuminating, *deja vu* fashion, yet completely strange. Don had wronged him grievously by thinking him to be a stuffed shirt, and now he couldn't even apologize without alerting Melanie to the extent of the problem. If Eleph preferred to keep it private, Don had to honor it. But he had to express himself somehow, because he was really not the silent type, just shy in new situations.

So Don held out his hand. It seemed inane, but his conscience refused to stand aside. One token handshake had to say it all.

Eleph understood. He let go of his handlebar—and the wheel flopped sideways, almost dumping him. Don jumped to support him—and banged the injured arm. Eleph winced, and a small strangled cry escaped him.

White-faced and red-faced, respectively, Eleph and Don shook hands. Then they rode on, Melanie leading the way.

●   ●   ●

Depot #4 was tremendous. "There's enough here to last us a year," Pacifa said. "We must have arrived at our major base of operations."

So it seemed. Another set of coordinates was waiting— 19°30′N, 77°0′W—but that location was so close it was obviously an offshoot from this site.

They repacked their supplies and rested for a day, only scouting the immediate vicinity. "These are bad," Pacifa said, indicating one box of glop packages. "See, the serial number matches that on Don's old supply." She was right. But there were twenty good boxes as well.

They held a business meeting. "This has to be it," Gaspar said. "The next are Melanie's last set of coordinates, and they're close—within sixty miles, as the fish swims. Maybe we should come at the site cautiously. After all, if it is all this secret—"

"And with an enemy craft patrolling the vicinity," Eleph said. "We must consider the possibility that we did not lose that submarine. If it realized that Glowcloud was accompanying us, and oriented on the squid—"

"If it's tracing anybody, it's Eleph," Pacifa said. "The sub never saw the rest of us."

"We *think* it never saw us," Gaspar corrected her.

She sighed. "You have a suspicious mind, but you're right. We can't take the chance. How about this, then: you and Eleph decoy Glowcloud south, while Don and Melanie and I maintain radio silence and sneak a peek at whatever is there? We'll meet back here when we can."

"But that's giving them the risk while we take the prize," Don protested.

"We're not going to steal it, Don," Pacifa said. "We're a group. We'll finish this mission together. But we are learning caution."

"Actually Gaspar and I would be running no risk we haven't run all along," Eleph said. "While you have no idea what awaits you."

Don could not argue with that.

"Also," Gaspar said, "the sides of that trench can be steep, and Eleph can't climb. So he can't go anyway."

Which clinched it. Pacifa had doused Eleph with a pain killer from her supplies and supervised the resetting of his arm, no simple task for the squeamish. She had to rummage in all their packs to obtain material for splint and bandage. Don knew it would be weeks before the member healed, and a fair length of time before the man recovered from his loss of blood. The trench was certainly no place for the wounded. Not until they knew there was a safe route there, and what their mission was.

"Actually, I could go with Eleph," Don said.

"No need," Gaspar said easily. "It isn't as if it's a chore. In fact, I'd like to see Jamaica and Port Royal. We can loop clear around the island, and the sub'll think we have a rendezvous there, if it's tracking Eleph. We'll even take pictures."

For a moment Don was jealous. He, the archaeologist, should be going to Port Royal. But the others all seemed satisfied with the arrangement, so he stifled his ire. He knew it was a device to make it easier for Eleph and keep him out of danger.

Eleph distributed his supply of balloons among them, in case they had an emergency requiring flotation. Don put three in his pack. They would exert some drag, but they just might be his lifeline in a crisis.

Gaspar and Eleph packed up and departed, Gaspar leading the way so as to pick out the easiest route. They moved slowly, for Eleph, stiff though his lip might be, was obviously not up to strenuous activity.

Pacifa made them wait four hours before they set out toward the final coordinates. "Just in case," she said. "We don't know exactly how far toward the surface Glowcloud can come right now, or how far he ranges while we're out of reach. We want to be sure El and Gas pick him up before we go down. We need our decoy in order."

There was a great deal of light rope in stock, and they packed several thousand extra feet, knowing they would need it for the canyons. Don did not feel easy about this trip, but didn't care to admit it. He wished that they could have gone as a full group, instead of fragmented. Odd that he should be so glum, when they were so near their destination.

They moved north, directly into the trench. Almost immediately they had to break out the rope, tying a length to a spur of rock, climbing down it, and leaving it there for the return trip. A submarine might discover it, but that risk seemed small, in this craggy wilderness, and they might have to return in a hurry. Without the ropes, they might have to ride a hundred miles out of their way—if any alternate avenues were even available.

It was a fear-of-heights nightmare. In the first five miles they descended a thousand fathoms. The site wasn't close at all, in terms of their effort! Then the ground evened out somewhat, and they rode down irregular slopes another five hundred fathoms.

The scenery was breathtaking, not pleasantly. Bare rock projected everywhere, forming overhanging cliffs, with rifts packed with boulders. Barnacles studded the surfaces, combing the water with their little nets, and sponges bulged wherever they chose: black unenterprising masses. There was little of the beauty of the coral reef, here.

But, aided by Pacifa's energy and expertise, they covered sixty miles in one day. Sixty horizontally, plus three vertically, and not directly toward their objective. They were now in the center of the Cayman trench proper: as grim a region as Don cared to experience. Fortunately there were steady currents of well oxygenated water, so breathing was no problem.

"About ten miles to go," Pacifa said. "Let's hold it until morning. That spot is about twenty five miles south of the coast of Cuba, and that's too close. We may need our strength."

Don agreed. The closer they got, the less he liked it. Geographically and politically, this was a dangerous region. And what *was* it they were supposed to find? All would soon be known, but he feared that it might better remain unknown. Certainly it wasn't any archaeological structure, this deep.

Melanie smiled at him as they settled for a meal. "I'm worried too," she murmured.

"Melanie—" he started, drawing her hand in toward him.

She shook her head. "Not yet, Don. We must tackle our mission. That's what we're here for."

After a few hours rest, they resumed the quest. Now they were exceedingly careful, watching for anything at all. But there was nothing except the rocky, slanting, evil bottom of the trench.

"Half a mile," Pacifa whispered. She was nervous too, though she contained it well.

Suddenly they were struck by a current of warmth. They stared at one another. "Am I going batty, or are you?" Pacifa inquired.

Don squinted at his temperature gauge. "Eighty degrees!" he exclaimed. "Our converters can't account for that! Where does it come from?"

"Only two reasonable guesses. A hot spring, or a nuclear reactor."

"A nuclear reactor!" Melanie exclaimed, horrified.

Don choked. "H-how do you—I mean, would they send us out like this to investigate a h-hot spring?"

That needed no answer. "This close to Cuba," Pacifa murmured. "A nuclear plant. Thermal pollution—but no one would notice, this far down. But what's it *doing?*"

"Nuclear subs," Don said, working it out. "Like the one we saw. Their port of Cienfuegos is just a decoy. The real stuff is here. Maybe hardened missile sites, too. They're not making the same mistake they made before, putting bases in sight of spy-plane overflights."

"But things are peaceful now!" Melanie protested.

"There are a number of nuclear powers," Don reminded her. "Any one of them could be doing this, secretly."

"Now it all makes sense," Pacifa agreed. "And I wish it didn't."

"Y-yes." Don felt very tired. "B-but we'd b-better make sure. Get p-pictures."

"Afraid so. We're the spy-plane, this time. A group of folk no one would ever suspect of undertaking a mission like this, in a fashion no one would ever dream. Riding bicycles under the sea!" She shook her head. "We have to nail it down with absolute proof."

"But what about radiation?" Melanie asked.

"I think I was trying not to think about that. There's sure to be radioactive wastes. That may affect us. Maybe already have."

"N-not if we s-stay in the c-cold water?" Don asked with wan hope.

"Why should it be restricted to the warm? No need to shield, down here. They could saturate the entire area."

"B-but their own p-personnel! They wouldn't—"

"Probably automated."

"Even the s-subs?"

She considered. "You're right. That doesn't make sense. If they had completely automated submarines, they wouldn't need a base. Not this close, anyway. It's men that need all the attention, not machines or supplies. And if they're manned subs, there's got to be radiation shielding. Actually, they can't let too much escape, because those rays pass through water even more readily than we do, and you bet Uncle Sam has telltales to pick it up. Especially around here! So probably it's all safe. Nothing but thermal pollution."

Don nodded. He wasn't really reassured, but realized that if there was radiation, and if the phase didn't nullify it, the three of them had no way to escape it except to run for home immediately—and might already have received a lethal dose. Unless the phase protected them from this, too. Better to pretend that the threat did not exist, and accomplish the mission regardless.

"Still, I can see why nonentities were selected for this mission," Melanie said. "We're expendable."

"We don't know that there's r-radiation," Don reminded her ineffectively.

"What's it going to do to me anyway—make my hair fall out?"

Neither Don nor Pacifa saw fit to respond to that.

They turned their bikes and pedaled upstream, grimly tracing the moving water to its source. Their mission no longer seemed as intriguing as before.

They did not have far to go. The water issued from a vent in the rock.

They stared at it. "I wish Gaspar were here," Pacifa said. "I just can't tell whether that's natural or manmade."

"Natural," Don said.

"Oh, that's right! You're an archaeologist. You should have had practice. Perhaps they wanted you for that reason: your specialty didn't matter, just your general background. But suppose someone went all-out to make it *seem* natural. could you still call it?"

"N-not outside of a laboratory," Don admitted. "You think they're trying to h-hide the p-plant?"

"Maybe." But then she changed her tack. "Seems like an awful lot of trouble, though. Think of the job of construction! And to make a naturalistic outlet aperture like this, when chances are no one will ever see it—do you suppose we're wrong?"

"No atomic plant?" Melanie asked, brightening.

"It *could* be an artesian well, couldn't it? A hot spring?"

"Then maybe there's weird life around it," Melanie said. "Things that live only in permanent deep hot wells."

Don looked. There were encrustations on the rock, and odd natural tubes clustering around the vent, but he had no idea how to classify them, or whether they were alive or dead.

"It didn't make sense the first time round," Pacifa said. "But my female intuition says that there's something fishy here. Suppose we just look around, and if we don't find anything else, we'll bring in the geologist and the physicist to tell us for sure about hot springs and nuclear outflows. Obviously our full party is equipped for this mission; we just happen to be the wrong part of it."

Don agreed, moderately relieved. Pacifa had a sharp mind, and he preferred not to have to argue anything with her unless it was directly in his area of competence. The other two would certainly be equipped to settle the matter. If only that sub hadn't spotted Eleph, forcing their decoy ploy!

They rode on, and abruptly left the warm water. The near-freezing cold of the normal deeps was a shock even though it was more apparent than real, considering the protective environment of phase and field. But soon they were back in the warmth, in a current that spread across and upward, gradually cooling but remaining much warmer than the normal water.

Three quarters of a mile from the assigned coordinates, on their way back toward their original destination, they saw a fish. That was not in itself unusual; though fish were much less common at this depth than at the surface, they remained present. But this was a strange one.

"It has legs!" Pacifa cried, astonished.

They oriented their lights on it, but the strange fish moved out of sight, stirring up a cloud of silt. "Downward pointing fins, I think, to stilt over the bottom muck," Don said. "We saw that on the abyssal flats."

"Uh-uh! do you think I don't know the difference? I saw real lizard legs."

"There it is again!" Melanie cried, catching the fish with her beam.

"Look," Pacifa said. "You can see the articulation of the bones as it walks. But it's a *fish*, with fishtail and fish gills. Not an amphibian muck-wallower at the edge of land."

Don peered more closely at the elusive creature. He had to agree.

"I'm no naturalist," Pacifa said. "But this is odd."

"Prehistoric," Don agreed, thinking of ancient life. "Premammalian."

"No doubt," she said dryly. "But what I mean, Don, is how can a normal cold water fish survive within hot water, legs or no?"

"And fresh water!" Melanie cried. "It can't be salt, coming from the ground!"

"It could, if it's from a nuclear plant," Pacifa said. "Regular ocean water, run through sluices for cooling the equipment."

"Wouldn't the heat evaporate it?" Don asked. "The salt would solidify and gum the works." But he wasn't sure; they probably had ways to handle that sort of thing. Maybe a series of cooling stages, with special sealed-in fluids for the really hot parts. It was probably elementary, for a nuclear power specialist.

Pacifa wasn't sure of her thesis either. "Fish living in this water would not have evolved here, if it's artificial. They couldn't just move from cold to hot. Not in just a few months or years. Or from salt to fresh. These barriers are very strong to sea life, I understand."

"Gaspar will know," Melanie said.

"You think this fish means the springs are natural?" Don asked, hardly daring to hope. "But maybe they stocked the region with laboratory breeds. To fool us."

"Decoy fish," Melanie suggested.

"If this is f-fresh," Don said, arguing a case he hoped would be refuted, "why doesn't it look different? Without the salt—"

"Salt in solution is transparent, isn't it?" Pacifa asked. "You can't see far in any kind of water, because of the refraction."

Don lacked the information to refute her, though he remained doubtful. "If this is what we're supposed to investigate, why isn't one of our number a biologist? Or chemist?"

"I think someone spotted the thermal flow," she said. "They

must have ways to chart such things. Vaguely, at least. Maybe their echosoundings are affected by the temperature of the water. So they had to send in a team to verify—"

"But that doesn't explain *me*," Melanie said. "I know less than anyone."

"Cover," Pacifa said. "Same as me. They could have trained Gaspar or Eleph how to repair a bike or pitch a tent, after all. But by adding us and extending the route to take in that city of yours—who would suspect the real mission?"

"It's ironic that the least qualified members of our group were the ones to come here," Melanie said.

"Just Eleph's bad luck to be spotted by that sub. But don't forget the two of them will see it; we're just doing the preliminary scouting, and finding a route Eleph can navigate, while they decoy the pursuit, if there is any. But we still aren't quite at the coordinates. Maybe it's something completely different."

Don shrugged. Melanie spread her hands. They went on.

They were not, after all, quite at the base of the trench. A new canyon developed, a mere fifty feet deep where they intersected it but possessed of a strong current that seemed to be seeking deeper recesses. They were so close to the specified location that they could not avoid this gap; their objective well might lie within it.

Another descent placed them on the rough but ridable floor, with an uncomfortably stiff wind-current at their backs. As they progressed, the walls rose higher and drew nearer at either side. The narrow valley curved and recurved like a monster snake, and the breeze accelerated. Don and Melanie no longer pedaled; they coasted, blown along, hands nervously near the brake levers.

They rounded another turn. Here the canyon narrowed into a crevice only a few feet across: treacherous terrain for swift-moving bicycles. But Don abruptly forgot that concern.

Melanie made a sound halfway between awe and disbelief.

Straddling the crevice was an ancient ship. Intact.

Chapter 11

●

Ship

Proxy 5-12-5-16-8: Attention.

Acknowledging.

Status?

Doubtful. Mischance struck, and the success of the mission is now in peril.

Details.

A submarine associated with the final challenge happened to come upon the party, and one member of the party was not in a position to conceal himself. So he acted as decoy, leading it away from the others. This diversion was successful, but in the process he fell and broke his arm, and was unable to continue immediately. As a result the party split into two, and one section proceeded to the next challenge. But that fraction of the party may not be sufficiently competent to handle the challenge appropriately.

There is danger?

Not physical. But with the full group not present, the challenge may have a divisive instead of a unifying effect. Therein is the peril to the mission.

But the mission is not yet lost?

Not yet lost. Indeed, it is possible that melding has proceeded far enough so that this hurdle will be overcome. But the issue is in doubt.

Even a failure can have its benefit. We may learn from it a better way to approach the next world.

But a success could offer more of that benefit, as well as salvaging this world.

True. Handle it as you must, Proxy.

● ● ●

They stared at the ship. Not only was it intact, it seemed to be in perfect condition. And it was ancient.

"But the teredo—" Don protested, his belief unwilling to take hold lest it be dashed. "The destructive worm. There *can't* be—"

"But this is fresh water, isn't it?" Melanie asked. "So the clam can't live here . . ."

"That must be it," Pacifa agreed. "Since we all see it, this can't be a mirage or hallucination, so it must be a genuine wreck. But what a strange one! I never saw a ship like that before."

While they spoke, the larger import was filtering into Don's consciousness. This was no Spanish galleon. This was a beaked craft, curiously high in the prow, about fifteen feet across, with a single mast broken off about ten feet up. That was about all he could make out, for they were approaching it endwise. Even so, his pulses were racing. It might have been Roman, but wasn't; Greek, but wasn't; Phoenician . . .no. certainly not Egyptian. By elimination, it had to be—Minoan.

Minoan. A ship of the isle of Crete, at the time of its greatness. Right in Don's specialty. He could not imagine a brighter dream of discovery.

"Right at the coordinates," Melanie said. "This is our mission. What a relief!"

"No accident," Pacifa said. "Our party has an Old World archaeologist. And this is Old World, isn't it, Don?"

"Yes," he answered absently as they braked.

"But what's it doing *here*?" Melanie asked.

They came to a stop almost under the hulk, where its base formed a crude triangle with the canyon, leaving five or six feet for the water to pass below.

"A storm-blown stray—what else," Pacifa said. "What matters is that it's here—and so are we. No nuclear plot, no radiation. All we have to do is help Don study it."

Don hardly heard them. He was in a private rapture, gazing at the ship. A virtually complete, preserved ship of one of the greatest civilizations of the ancient world. This could be anything up to four thousand years old: a phenomenal bonanza for archaeology. A set-group of functioning Minoan equipment. If the teredo hadn't been able to rifle it, who else could have?

"So now we know what they spotted," Pacifa said. "An old Roman ship."

"Minoan," Don said. "Notice, it is carvel, not clinker built, and the configuration of the—"

"And the fresh water preserved it. How old would you say it is, Don?"

"Between 3,500 and 4,000 years, perhaps even more. We should be able to date it more precisely once we really check it over. And later, with laboratory verification of the wood--" He was talking as if the matter were routine, when actually his mind was partially numb. This was the find of the century!

"How can you check it?" Pacifa asked.

"Why, climb aboard and—uh-oh!" He had forgotten the phase again. He couldn't touch this exquisite ship!

Melanie rode slowly to it and lifted her hand, evidently finding it difficult to believe that so remarkable an object could be a ghost. She was just able to reach the keel. She froze in place, the current blowing out her skirt. "Don!"

"Might as well ride through it, if we can get up there," Don said, disappointed. "Maybe we can see inside the hold. It's certainly not a total loss."

"It certainly isn't," Melanie said. "Don, come here."

This time he picked up on her tone. He pedaled over. The ship loomed above, seeming absolutely solid. He could not resist reaching up to put his hand through its hull, as she had.

His hand banged.

He stared at his fingers, then up at the ship. Unbelievingly he extended one digit to touch the wood. It met a hard surface. "It's *here!*" he exclaimed.

"And it shouldn't be," Pacifa said, coming to test it herself. "Because, according to Gaspar, this phase world was denuded at least six thousand years ago, and this ship isn't that old. According to you. And you should know your business. But here it is."

"But the sunken city wasn't—isn't—here!" Don protested.

"How can—?"

"Makes you suspect something is wrong with our theory," she said.

"Terribly wrong!" Don's head was spinning again. "Unless this ship *is* older. Surely ships preceded the city, or it could not have been built. Unless the Minoan culture originated here. But then the ruins would be solid for us too." Nothing seemed to make sense.

"At any rate," she said, "it does suggest that this warm fresh water is natural. A nuclear plant would date from no more than a generation past, not several thousand years. Unless someone planted this ship to make us think—?"

"In both phases?" Don demanded. "If they could do that, they wouldn't be mucking about in the deep trench! They'd have conquered us long ago."

"Who says they want to conquer us?" Melanie asked. "We don't know anything about them."

"True, we don't," Pacifa said. "We'll have to accept the phase aspect as definitive. Which puts it right back in the archaeological pot. Obviously you're here to check it out. If it is genuine, it's highly significant archaeologically. If it isn't, it's significant scientifically, and politically. And I'll be someone who wants very much to know."

"Well, let's get on with it!" Don cried, his excitement growing as his shock abated. The ship might have been here for thousands of years, but it seemed as if it would vanish in a minute if he didn't get busy.

The tight hull curved up to the deck, about twenty feet above the ground, overhanging the three of them. Pacifa assessed the situation in a fashion only an objective non-archaeologist could. She noted the manner the ship was supported by the impinging crevice walls, checking the contacts with her hands.

"It's secure," she reported. "The this-world and that-world ships are identical. Except that the one in our phase sits a little lower, and its sides are stove in a bit."

"There's no water to support it," Don said. "We're just lucky it was so well jammed in that not even the removal of the water in the phase world could drop it far. I'm surprised it didn't collapse entirely, in those thousands of years."

"That is strange," she said. "Though I suppose with no spoil-

age—even so, steady pressure should have warped the wood."
She paused. "Wood? Don, do you realize that this phase ship *isn't*
wood?"

"Isn't wood?" Don asked absently, still staring upward with
awe as the current tugged at his body.

"Feels like stone. The same stuff we've been riding over."

Don remembered the touch. This had bothered him before,
about the landscape. But *wood?* "That makes no sense at all! This
is a wooden ship; it wouldn't have floated if it was stone."

"It *has* to make sense," she said. "Everything does. We just
haven't unriddled it yet. But it does grow intriguing. I'd like to
know too why we don't see anything in the phase world, though
we're ninety-nine-point-nine percent in it."

"I think that's because it has less in it," Melanie said. "Its rocks
are all bare or absent, while Earth's are covered with silt and life.
So we see that outermost layer. We might see the things of the
other phase if they didn't exist also in the regular world."

"Feel that hull," Pacifa said. "Isn't that a good inch lower than
it looks? The phase hull extends beyond the real hull."

Don felt. "I—I can see it now. I—it must have been psy—
psycho—mental blindness. Not believing—"

"I know what you mean," Melanie said. "We're so used to seeing Earthly things that something completely outside that framework disappears, even if it's in plain sight. Subjective. It's powerful." She tapped her wig. "But I'm going to start looking at phase
objects from now on, even if it gives me a headache."

Meanwhile, Pacifa wheeled her bike a short distance upcur-
rent, propped it solidly, and hitched a rope to its frame. Then she
swung a length up over the projecting bow and pulled it taut.
"I'll haul you up as much as I can, and Melanie can help."

Don was so eager to board the ship that the problem of hur-
dling the hull seemed academic. He tied the other end of the rope
to his own bicycle, balancing the weight as well as he could.

Pacifa hauled on the rope, and so did Melanie. There was no
pulley, so this was inefficient, but the rope did slide, and he went
up.

"Heave!" Pacifa gasped, and the two heaved together, drawing him up another notch. It was hard work, even with the three
of them cooperating, but there was only about fifteen feet of actual rising to do, and he was able to put his feet against the side of

the ship and walk on it, to an extent, as if rappelling. Or at least to brace his feet near the top, while the bicycle banged him. He nudged the prow and caught hold before his strength gave out. Now he could have used Gaspar's muscle! The bike dangled on the rope, jerking up as his weight came off.

Don held his breath and swung his feet up. He scrambled over the edge and landed on the deck. He stretched back far enough to catch the bicycle, bringing it and its atmosphere back to his lungs. He had had much recent practice in similar maneuvers, descending into the Cayman trench. But going up was three times as hard as going down.

The deck was firm, though his feet stood about two inches below the visible level. The settling of the phase ship, obviously. Disconcerting, but a useful reminder that what he saw was not necessarily what he felt. The planks were tight. The support strong. This was a well made ship, in both worlds.

He turned and looked down. He waved at the two women who were looking up. "I'm fine," he said. "But I'll be going into the interior of the ship, so you might as well take a rest. I'll report every so often, if you're interested."

"I want to explore some," Melanie said. "I'll go on down the cleft a way and see where it leads, and how far the fresh water extends. I can't get lost, here. Pacifa can stay in touch with you."

"But to go alone—"

"I've got to learn to do it sometime," she said. She rolled her bicycle under the ship and moved on beyond.

He realized that she was disciplining herself to eliminate her own weaknesses. This was as good a place and time as any, since she had nothing to do. If it built up her confidence, good.

"Get to work," Pacifa told him. "I'll pitch a tent."

Don tried to absorb it all at once, greedy for information. The timbers of the hull were mortised together with precision, and the whole was extremely well insulated with what appeared to be tar. No doubt it had been on the outside too, but the current had washed it away. The Romans, later, had even impregnated their ships with lead, for protection against such things as the teredo; but this ship predated such sophistication. There were portholes along the sides for oars—ten or twelve pairs. Later the Cretans were to distinguish between war galleys and merchant ships, with the former carrying oars and the latter only sails. This partic-

ular ship was evidently a compromise between the two developing types, lacking the cargo space of the fat wind-driven vessels,
but also lacking the sleek power of the warships. Not that the Minoans ever had been much for war; peace was their normal
course.

The hatch to the interior had what seemed to be a watertight
covering, so that storm waves could not swamp this ship unless a
hole had been bashed in. But the hatchcover had been removed; it
lay to the side, and his hand passed though it. Near the stern
stood several cages, built into the deck. Those would have been
for pigeons, those invaluable aids to ancient navigation.

Don took a deep breath. This was Minoan, all right! There
were markings on the base of the mast and on the inside of the
bulwarks: script "Linear A," the writing of the Cretan heyday.
These were mainly cautions about the care of the equipment, as
nearly as he could tell without more careful analysis. Probably
marked by the manufacturers and of course ignored by the illiterate crewmen.

The ship was about seventy five feet long, and fifteen wide
across the mid-deck: in the middle range for seagoing craft of the
period. And it *was* seagoing, despite the oars; in all its appoint-
ments and arrangements it spoke of the long haul.

"What do you see?" Pacifa called from the ground.

Don was jolted out of his preoccupation. He flashed his light
around again, organizing his thoughts for a coherent reply—and
saw a mermaid.

She had just floated up out of the open hatch. Her hair hung
about her in a dark cloud, and her black eyes were piercing in a
pale face. She had two splendid breasts, a narrow waist, and
overlapping scales that gleamed irridescently from naval to
flukes. She carried a small, dim lantern that highlighted her remarkable characteristics.

"S-splendid!" Don breathed idiotically.

"Say, are you all right?" Pacifa called.

The mermaid spun around at that, orienting on the sound of
the voice. But immediately she returned to Don, shielding her
eyes against his bright beam.

She was real! On top of all the other incredible developments,
this fish-girl was alive!

"Don, answer me!" Pacifa called more urgently.

But he couldn't answer. That dazzling female torso, so abruptly phased into piscine anatomy. That fantasy amalgam of woman
and fish. If the mermaid were genuine, what was she doing here,
four miles down, far below normal light and warmth? It was nonsensical.

Which meant that he was having a vision. Too much or too little oxygen must have saturated his field, affecting his brain. He
wasn't sure which way led to hallucination.

"Knock once if you can hear me," Pacifa called.

Numbly, Don knocked his heel against the deck.

The mermaid turned, lithe and sleek as any living fish, and
swam rapidly away from him. Her tail worked powerfully, so
that she used her hands only for course corrections. Her luxuriant
hair streamed behind her as she disappeared over the rail.

Now Don was able to speak. "Splendid!" he repeated.

After a moment Pacifa spoke again, hardly loud enough.
"Don—did you see that?"

"I—I—yes!"

"I declare, I thought for a moment it was my idiotic daughter,
reincarnated as a sylph. Until that tail—"

"I—I thought it was—brain damage," Don admitted, walking
his bike across the deck to peer down at her. He didn't know
whether to be relieved for the state of his brain, or apprehensive
for the state of reality. A live mermaid!

"You realize, of course, that this is ridiculous," Pacifa said mat-
ter-of-factly. "The real mermaids were dugongs—and you'd never find any of those down here! They're air breathers."

"B-but she didn't have g-gills," Don pointed out.

"Yes, of course. She's mammalian. You must have noticed."

Don had noticed.

"Here's my speculation," Pacifa said. "See what you make of
it. A bathyscaphe was photographing this region of the trench,
looking for geological features or stray foreign fusion plants, and
it caught one shot of this preserved sunken ship with a mermaid
on deck. Later the analysts went over the material, and called
their experts, and the archaeologist said 'That's a 1723 B.C. Minoan craft of the Zilch II class from the shipworks of King Tut-
Tut!' and the artist said 'That's a statue of a mermaid by the hand
of Artisan Smut-smut!' and the archaeologist said 'Impossible,
you dolt, the Minoans didn't *make* any statues of mermaids that

year!' and the artist said 'Oh, yeah? Then it must be a *real* mermaid, stupid!' and the psychiatrist said 'Tut, smut, calm down, boys, what you need is another picture.' But the next time the bathyscaphe stopped at that station, the mermaid was gone. And the artist said 'See, it's all your fault! You didn't believe in her!' and the archaeologist slugged him."

"Archaeologists don't slug people!" Don protested, laughing.

"So they packed up a bicycle party with a nonslugging Minoan scholar on board, but they didn't want to prejudice the case by mentioning the mermaid . . ."

Don had to smile. "Must be. We had no idea what to expect! But what do we do now?"

"Maybe it's time to break radio silence."

"Yes. We've found what we were sent for, obviously."

"Then again, we don't *know* that either ship or mermaid are genuine. Maybe we should make quite sure before we say much. If we make a wrong report—"

"Somebody might slug *us!* I'd like nothing better than to stay here and study this ship in detail," Don said fervently. "But we have to rendezvous with the others, or contact them by radio, so they won't—"

"Yes," she said thoughtfully. "But if we'd reported as we went along, we'd have had them depth-bombing the trench for that atomic plant. There are still enough incongruities so that we know we have only part of the story. We've kept our noses clean so far by being cautious; let's hang on a little longer."

"I agree. But still—"

"Look, Don. You're the expert, here. I could prowl around this ship for the rest of the year and never find out anything worth knowing. So I'm expendable, as far as this part goes. I could go back—"

"Alone?"

"Don't look so horrified! I'm no tender violet. I can rejoin the others faster by myself than with company."

Surely that was the truth, Don thought ruefully. "But Melanie—"

Pacifa nodded. "It would be difficult at best to get her up there with you, though you will be able to let yourself down by the rope when you're through. I'd better take her back with me. You should be safe here, and you won't be going anywhere soon."

"That's for sure! I could stay here a year and never notice the time. The things I can learn here—"

"And maybe it's best if she doesn't see that mermaid, right now. All that hair, you know."

Don hadn't thought of that. "It could be awkward, yes. That mermaid is not of our phase; still—"

"All right, we must act with dispatch. Let's compromise: you can turn on your radio and keep company with Melanie that way, while she and I travel back. We'll have quite a climb to make, even with the ropes in place. Just don't give away any details on this situation. There's no danger of Glowcloud zeroing in on you here—not in this hot freshwater. But anything you broadcast just might be intercepted by parties unknown. Not worth the risk of giving away anything of substance. Meanwhile I'll tell Melanie not to mention me, so no one knows where we are, and when we get back we'll acquaint the other two with what we know so far. If Gaspar or Eleph tunes in, you just pretend I'm here with you."

"But—"

"Because we're really not sure that that sub can't pick up our radios. It may know we're here, but it doesn't know what we're doing or where we're going. Best to play it safe."

Don mulled this over. He did not like the deception entailed, but there seemed to be considerable merit in her caution. There was indeed so much they didn't know! Meanwhile, he could study the ship with complete freedom and without distraction, and Melanie on the radio would be a comfortable hedge against the specters of isolation. It would only be for a while, after all, until the entire group returned here, or he returned to the base camp to rejoin them.

Still, he argued. "Yet with the phase—there's been no evidence that there's any other party on our radio circuit."

"Do you think we're the only ones ever to go through the tunnel? They could easily have a man sitting just this side, monitoring everything we say. They'd be fools not to."

"Oh." Ever the practical mind! "But what if the mermaid comes back?"

"For God's sake, don't blab on the radio about that! Gaspar would think you're crazy, and Melanie would be insanely jealous."

"Melanie jealous of a *mermaid*?"

"Imagine Melanie in the husky arms of a handsome triton."

"Triton?"

"Merman. Man with a fish tail. Picture him kissing her and running his slippery hands over her torso—"

"The bastard!"

"See? And *you're* not in love with her."

"W-what?"

"You wanted to know about jealousy, didn't you?"

"N-not that much!"

"Well, if that mermaid comes back, study her too. We have to ascertain the truth, and that's part of it. Just don't talk about it on the air, because another misunderstanding—"

"That sub might fire torpedoes!"

"Or something. All through your nice Minoan artifact. Want to gamble that men like Eleph *aren't* running this show?"

Men like Eleph. How cunningly she planted her barbs. This one was misdirected, for Eleph was a fine man under his crust. But no, Don didn't want to gamble on the militaristic mind, and there was surely one in that mystery submarine. Silence was a mandatory virtue, here.

●　　●　　●

It was done with dispatch. Soon Pacifa and Melanie were on their way back, leaving Don at the ship. They had never pitched their tent; the appearance of the mermaid had given them reason to change plans immediately.

Don explored the ship plank by plank. This was not as easy as he had expected. He could not leave his bicycle; he needed its field to breathe, and its light to see. There was not enough oxygen in the water inside the ship for his purpose. He had to haul himself topside regularly, lest he be asphyxiated. He could not conserve oxygen by sitting still, because the bike had to be in motion for the generator lamp to function more than a few seconds. In addition, he took a surprise tumble over a heavy beam that crossed the hold. It was invisible until he concentrated; it existed only in the phase world. He decided that it had been placed deliberately, to brace the ship against the outside pressure of the canyon walls, and it felt like metal. Which meant that someone had been here, in phase, before him—a lot less than four thousand years ago. Highly significant—but that was one thing he was not going to discuss on the radio.

There were no amphorae, those large two-handled point-bottomed jars used for the transport of grains and liquids in ancient times. Ordinary folk wondered why big jars should be pointed at their bases, so they could not stand up; the reason was that those points were wedged into pegboards, so that they were firmly planted and could not be dislodged by the heaving of the ship. Only a few pottery sherds remained, the kind that were so valuable archaeologically for the identification of cultures—when there was no chance to save the complete urns.

But far in the stern, in a nook in the galley section, stood a greater treasure: two intact *pithoi*, the monstrous ornate wide-mouthed storage jars typical of the Minoan society. Each had eight small handles, hardly large enough for a fingerhold, arranged around the top and near the base. No doubt these eyelets had held rope, so that the jars could be securely anchored as the ship heaved. But the rope itself had long since dissolved away.

Don peered inside, but could not bring his headlamp to bear conveniently. His hand passed through the jars without effect. They existed only in the other world: another frustrating dichotomy.

What had happened to the cargo? A ship this size might have had a capacity of several hundred tons, and carried a thousand amphorae. All the sherds remaining could not account for more than a dozen. They would not have been washed out when the ship sank, for the hull remained tight. In fact, the ship should not have sunk. Yet here it was, with a phase-world beam supporting it.

Was it a plant, after all? A manufactured artifact, placed within the past few years or months? All his experience with Minoan artifacts told him no, that the ship was genuine—but these logical incongruities were weighing heavily.

"You've been quiet too long," Melanie said on the radio. "Don, what are you up to?"

"I'm short of oxygen, I think," he said. This was true enough. As he spoke, he remembered what Pacifa had said of Melanie, indirectly: *And you're not in love with her.* That spoke volumes! But it wasn't necessarily true.

"Well, get yourself into a better current," she said, her concern coming through. Yes, she was perhaps in love with him, but that did not mean that he did not return the feeling. Why had Pacifa suggested otherwise?

He hauled himself up to the main deck again, short of breath. He was glad he had some physical justification for his discomfort, because with every discovery he made, his intellectual certainties took another battering. It was becoming difficult not to blab something on the radio that would give away more than was wise.

On the deck, walking the bike for oxygen and light, Don blinked. The mermaid was back.

Chapter 12

•

Splendid

Proxy 5-12-5-16-8: Attention.
Acknowledging.
Status?
Complicated. Dissension is occurring, and I fear that this is going to be difficult. The mission is in peril. I cannot make a proper report at this time.

• • •

Still dizzy from his interior explorations and the effort of getting himself and the bicycle clear of the hatch, Don nevertheless had the presence of mind to snap off the radio. "Splendid!" he exclaimed. There really seemed to be no better name for her, considering her attributes. That cloud of hair surrounding her head in the water . . .

She retreated with a graceful flexing of torso and tail. Her natural swimming motions only accented the flair of her wide hips. Don realized that she was afraid of him. That gave him confidence. He was as strange to her as she was to him!

The remaining mysteries of the Minoan ship could wait for a bit. Right now there was the living mystery of the mermaid.

He studied her carefully. She was beautiful, from hair to waist; he could imagine no more perfect attributes in the female of the species. Her breasts in particular stood out, being full-bodied and supported by the water so that there was absolutely no sag. "Splendid," he said once more.

Actually, her nether portion was beautiful too. The smooth green scales began as her narrow waist expanded into what would have been a remarkable derriere of a normal woman. From there her body tapered into a strong, sleek tail, with only a suggestion of thighs near the origin.

Why had she returned, if she feared him? Where had she come from, really? She was mammalian, not piscene; there were no gill slits in her neck, and he could see her handsome chest expanding and contracting as she breathed.

Yes, breathed. Through her nose and mouth.

Was she phased?

No, for she swam. She had to be breathing water.

Okay, he thought. *Accept her as she is. And find out* WHAT *she is.*

"Come here, Splendid," he said. "Let's talk."

She heard him. But she seemed not to understand. She hovered off the edge of the deck, beyond his reach, and surveyed him nervously. At least she did not swim away, this time.

"Are you as curious about me as I am about you?" he asked her, pleased to note that he had no stutter. "Is that why you're h-here?" Oops.

She surveyed him a moment longer, then upended attractively and swam swiftly to the ground.

"Don't go away!" he cried. "I won't hurt you. I only want to know—"

But in a moment she was back, carrying something flat. It was a slate, like those once used for school lessons. ENGLISH? she wrote.

"American!" he exclaimed. "You *do* understand!"

Then, again, he wondered whether his mind had been affected. Fresh water under the sea; a preserved Minoan ship; a mermaid—who comprehended his own language. The stuff of dreams!

WHY DO YOU COME? she wrote.

And to her, *he* was the stuff of dreams! "I'm an archaeologist," he said.

Her eyes widened. I, TOO, she wrote.

A mermaid archaeologist? How far could credulity be stretched?

More and more, this reeked of a setup. Someone had been expecting him. Yet the problems of technique and motive remained. Who could do such a thing—and who would bother?

Which suggested again that the principle error lay within his own brain.

National security be damned, if that was what it was! If he was inventing all this, talking about his delusion could not hurt anyone but himself. If it wasn't all in his mind, the others needed to know. He needed to discuss it with someone.

He turned on the radio. "Melanie?"

There was a pause, and he thought she wasn't going to answer, but then she did. "Don, I wish you wouldn't just cut off in the middle—I mean, I'm afraid that you're hurt or—"

"Melanie, something came up."

Abruptly she expressed concern. "Are you all right? Say you're all right, Don!"

"Yes. I hope so. I—" But what could he say now?

RADIO, Splendid wrote. WHO?

"That's Melanie," Don explained. "I—"

"What?" Melanie asked.

"I—I'm all confused." Lame apology for what Melanie could hardly understand. But with the mermaid right here, what was he to do? "I'm not sure I'm quite sane at the moment. Too little oxygen—though I have enough now."

"I knew I shouldn't have left you alone! But you can tide through, Don. As soon as—" Then she evidently realized that she was breaking the rule herself, because she was supposed to pretend that Pacifa was with him.

Her voice was reassuring, because it was so familiar. But Splendid remained before him, observing and listening. It was evident that she understood the nature of the radio, and heard it. Don's headlamp had faded, so he saw her by her own lantern. Of the equipment that required power, the light went first, then the radio, and finally the battery-supported oxygenation field. He lifted the front of the bicycle and spun the wheel with his hand, to keep the radio going.

"Listen, Melanie," he said urgently. "I—when you're alone, do you ever *see* things? That don't make sense?"

"You're hallucinating? Oh, Don—"

WIFE? Splendid inquired on her slate.

"No, I'm single!" Don said. Then, to the radio: "I mean, Melanie, I'm not alone, exactly, and—" But how could he explain, without saying too much? He had made a bad tactical mistake, calling Melanie in the presence of the mermaid. "I'm—I'm just not sure I—I think the sea is—"

"You're seeing things, you mean? And you're not sure whether they're real?"

Splendid things—and they looked completely real. "Well, I— that is—Melanie, suppose I met another archaeologist?"

"In the *sea?*"

"Yes. Right here. In the trench."

"Another archaeologist—under the sea?" She was having understandable trouble with this.

"I'm trying not to say anything, until we—we muddle this through. Let's make it hypothetical. If I met—"

"Would you be seeing things?" she finished. "Not necessarily. There could be another party with the same mission. That makes as much sense as a sub with an eavesdropping radio. More bicycles starting from another point."

"Not on a bicycle," he said, eying Splendid's tail. The mermaid, catching on to the problem, flipped a fluke.

"Well, I suppose they could walk. It would be slower, but the phase would still—"

"Not phased." Fortunately?

"That submarine!" she exclaimed. "You mean it's ours? With archaeologists aboard? And they can't get out to check what's at the coordinates, while you can, so—"

"Not exactly. The sub's not here."

Melanie paused. "What are you trying to tell me, Don?"

"I'm trying *not* to tell you! It's just that I—"

"Oh, forget all the secrecy! I'm not going to blab. Tell me."

"Well, all right. I'm where you left me, only there's a mermaid here."

"A what?"

"A mermaid. A woman with the tail of a fish. She's hovering about fifteen feet away, and she's an archaeologist."

"Don, are you serious?"

"Afraid so," he said dubiously.

"You didn't fall and hit your head or something?"

"That's why I'm talking to you. It seems so crazy I hardly believe it myself, but here she is."

"Right there? Physically?"

"Completely." Splendid laughed silently, her breasts heaving. "Except for the phase, of course."

"Can she talk?"

"No, I don't think so. At least she hasn't, so far."

"Then how do you know she's an archaeologist?"

"She wrote it. With slate and chalk, or the equivalent."

"In English?"

"Yes."

There was a short silence. "Don, I hate to disappoint you. But I do think you're cracking up. Maybe you'd better talk to—to Pacifa." She was trying, belatedly, to pretend that Pacifa was with him.

"I did. She saw Splendid too."

"She *what?*"

"Saw Splendid. The mermaid, I mean. While you were exploring."

"What do you call it?"

"I don't know her real name."

"Splendid?"

"Well, I —"

"What's so splendid about her?" Melanie demanded.

"She—" Don looked nervously around, hesitant to mention breasts and knowing that hair would be disaster. His eye caught that of the mermaid, who was smiling above her splendors, her hair spreading out like a cape. That made it worse. But it gave him the inspiration of desperation. "Maybe you can talk to her!"

"Oh, now she talks!" Melanie said coolly.

"Through me, I mean. I'll read you what she writes."

"Don, this is—" Then she reconsidered. "All right. Ask her how she breathes."

He looked at Splendid, but she was already writing. Obviously she had grasped enough of the situation to participate, and her fear had dissipated. How could anyone be afraid of a man as bumbling as he was proving to be?

OUR LUNGS ARE ADAPTED TO ABSORB OXYGEN FROM

WATER.

Don read it off to Melanie.

She did not sound convinced. "Where did she learn English?"

I STUDIED IT WHEN YOUNG.

"Don," Melanie said. "I can't keep ahead of your subconscious invention. These answers prove nothing."

Splendid frowned. It seemed that she did not appreciate being doubted.

"Melanie, she's really here! I'm not inventing this. I hope. Ask her something I can't answer."

"What color is George Washington's white horse?" she inquired sarcastically. "Look—did she study any other languages? Where is she from, anyhow?"

FROM CHINA. STUDIED SPANISH, GERMAN.

From China! Now he realized that part of what he had taken to be mer-features were actually the oriental cast, especially the eyes. He remembered that the orientals had adapted to the rough climate of their region with slightly different patterns of the distribution of fat, and flatter faces. These might also help in the rigors of the deep sea. They in no way diminished Splendid's beauty.

"Well, now," Melanie said. "It happens I know some German. Do you, Don?"

"No. Nothing except nein."

"And that's probably a number to you."

"No, I—"

Melanie fired off a paragraph in what sounded to Don's untrained ear like German. He was amazed; he had had no idea she knew any foreign language.

Splendid blushed. Splendidly. Then she looked angry.

"What did you say to her?" Don demanded.

Melanie sounded smug. "If I told you, you'd know. I want her answer, not yours."

"She's blushing. I didn't know mermaids could blush."

"They're female, aren't they?" Melanie inquired with satisfaction.

Now Splendid was writing furiously.

"I can't read her answer to you," Don said. "It's German, I think."

"That's all right," Melanie said. "Just spell it out. I'll copy down the letters and read it here. Then we'll know."

"Know what she says? Or that I'm not imagining—?"

"Yes."

Don sighed and began spelling out letters. "D-A-S M-Ä-D-C-H-E-N . . ." When he had spelled out the slateful, Splendid erased the tablet and started over. The transcription seemed interminable, because Don wasn't familiar with the alphabet, which had some funny squiggles, and had to read or describe each letter with extraordinary care. For example, there were two dots over the A in MÄDCHEN. The nipples of breasts? " . . .D-E-M A-B-O-R-T. H-A-B-E-N S-I-E V-E-R-S-T-A-N D-E-N?"

"You bitch!" Melanie exclaimed.

"What?" Don asked, startled.

"Not you, dope. Her. With the splendid bosom."

"You mean you b-believe in her now?"

For an answer, Melanie let out another torrent of German. Her fury was manifest. This was an aspect of her Don had not encountered before. But this time Splendid merely turned her back, not deigning to respond. Don noticed that she had buttocks shaped under her scales, and there was a stronger suggestion of bifurcation, rear-view.

And he realized something else: the mermaid resembled a Cretan court lady, with her terraced skirts (scales) and generously open bodice. That was one reason she had been so appealing to him at first glance. A Minoan ship, with a Minoan lady? That sense of visiting the past . . .

"Well, what does she say?" Melanie demanded. There was a sharpness in her voice that he had not heard before, in all their long conversations. It did not become her.

"Nothing. She's just facing away. I think she's ignoring you"

"Of all the nerve!" Melanie cried, and clicked off.

Now Splendid turned to face him. There was a new look of confidence on her face. She had evidently had the best of it, despite the initial setback. It no longer seemed so strange to be talking to a mermaid on an ancient ship, in the depths of the deepest trench in the Atlantic Ocean. "What were you two *saying?*"

WOMAN TALK, she wrote noncommittally. HOW DID YOU COME HERE?

How much could he afford to tell her? He hardly knew her! On the other hand, how could he learn about her, if he didn't exchange information? She was a tough bargainer. "I rode my bicycle. How about you?"

She looked at his bike, and her eyebrow lifted as she noted the way the tires sank beneath the visible deck when he rode it, picking up oxygen and recharging his headlamp. Then she looked at his feet as he stopped, for they also sank. Some of her confidence dissipated. She had to admit he resembled a ghost in this respect.

WE ARE AN EXPERIMENTAL COLONY, ADAPTED TO LIVE UNDER PRESSURE IN WATER. HOW DO YOU SURVIVE THIS?

So she was willing to trade information. "I'm phased into another framework," Don said, making sure his radio was off. "I'm not subject to pressure, and the water's like air. You say you're adapted. You mean you were born on land? With--with legs?"

YES. I STILL HAVE LEG BONES, FUSED AT THE BASE ONLY. FOR FLEXIBILITY. She rotated her nether portion, switching her tail. It was remarkably supple, and the motion reminded him vaguely of a hula dance. It certainly accentuated her anatomy provocatively. HOW CAN I PERCEIVE YOU, IF YOU ARE NOT HERE?

"Well, I am here—in a way. I am of this world. But I'm not very solid, as far as this world goes, right now. Here, I'll show you." He walked his bicycle toward her.

Splendid backed off, then reconsidered and propelled herself forward by means of little swimming motions that accentuated her various attributes intriguingly. She put out a hand to touch his.

The two hands passed through each other with that odd temporary meshing of bones. Splendid's mouth opened, and she catapulted herself backward with a grand flip of her tail.

"It's just the phase," Don said reassuringly. "I'm not a ghost." Then he remembered to ask his question. "If you're Chinese, why are you here? In the Western hemisphere?"

WE NEED TO MATCH THE PRESSURE OF JUPITER'S ATMOSPHERE. THIS IS ONE STAGE. BUT FIRST WE MUST HAVE WARMTH AND FRESH WATER, AND THERE IS NONE THIS DEEP NEAR CHINA. CAN YOU SURVIVE ANYWHERE?

Jupiter's atmosphere! Were the Chinese planning a colony there? Don had no idea whether the pressure of four miles of water on Earth came anywhere near approximating that of the atmosphere on monster Jupiter; it probably depended on how deep in that atmosphere they went. It did seem reasonable that what could be adapted to survive in the one medium, could also be adapted to survive in the other. A fish tail here; wings, there?

"Pretty much," he said, answering her question. "But it has its limitations. I can't do anything much in the real world, and I can't leave my bicycle. And I have to keep moving around, to pick up oxygen, unless there's a good current." Was this too much information? American relations with China varied through the years, and changed as the administrations of either country changed. No, she couldn't use the information against him, because she couldn't touch him. He had told her nothing that wouldn't be evident if she watched him for any length of time. "And are you studying this ship?"

It turned out that she was. She was part of a mer-colony whose main object was mere survival at this depth. Pressure *per se* was not the greatest hurdle to overcome, for anyone could live at any depth provided there was a life support system and no sudden or extreme pressure flux. But it was a convenient starting place, and much had to be learned about the long-term complications of such existence before the sophisticated aspects of alternate-medium colonization could be explored. Later there would be other adaptations, to compensate for the cold, and the methane atmosphere, and turbulence of liquid Jupiter. Meanwhile, the hot fresh water enabled the human beings to survive naked without osmotic dehydration—and also preserved remarkable artifacts, such as this ship. That was an unplanned bonanza! So Splendid, an amateur archaeologist, had expected, before being selected for this experimental mer-colony, to specialize in one of the pre-Columbian American Indian cultures and to trace the connections between it and the prehistoric Mongolian cultures from which the Amerinds derived. She had given up her first dream to realize the second: mankind's exploration of a really new world. Now she was making herself useful by returning to her first specialty, recording the ship's anomalies to the best of her abilities. She knew little of Minoan culture, to her regret, but did recognize this as an Old World vessel of considerable antiquity. She had cleaned up much of the interior and had taken all but two of the unbroken *pithoi* jars to her village for transshipment to China by submarine.

"But that's plundering!" Don protested. "The relic should be preserved intact!"

WE DID NOT EXPECT ANY OTHER PARTY TO HAVE AC-
CESS TO IT, she explained contritely. WE DARE NOT REMOVE
THE WOOD, FOR IT MIGHT DISINTEGRATE ON LAND. BUT
THE AMPHORAE ARE GOING TO OUR BEST ARCHAEOLOG-
ICAL MUSEUMS. THERE ALL THE PEOPLE WILL SEE AND
LEARN AND BENEFIT, INSTEAD OF ONLY THOSE FEW
WHO DWELL IN THE DEPTH OF THE SEA.

What could he say? The Chinese were perhaps the most cultu-
rally aware people in the world; they would not be hawking invaluable ancient relics on the streets. The deep reaches of international waters were open to any party for salvage—anyone who
could manage to reach them. It would be a criminal waste not to
recover as much of the ship and its contents as possible.

"I'm sorry," Don said after a bit. "You're right. Except about
the amphorae. They're *pithoi*—wide-mouthed, flat-bottomed jars.
But I don't think it's fair to remove everything before I have a
chance to study it. This entire ship represents an artifact of my
specialty, Minoan Crete."

Splendid drifted toward him excitedly. She opened her mouth
as if to speak, but no sound came. Obviously she had once talked,
and still tried to do it when she forgot herself. Probably her vocal
cords had been exchanged for some liquid filtering device. But he
needed no words to grasp what was on her mind.

"Yes. That's why I'm here. I—"

But it wasn't that simple. Splendid tried to take his hand, and
failed. But this time she did not recoil. She beckoned to him as
she swam across the deck.

Perplexed, Don followed, walking his bicycle. She dived down
into the hold, but he balked at the access hole, fearing that there
was not yet enough oxygen. The water changed slowly, here. But
he did crank up his light and shine it down inside so that he
could watch her.

She passed through the cross-timber as if it did not exist,
which was true for her, then drew up to the two remaining *pithoi*,
and reached inside one. There was something there. She lifted it
and carried it back, breathing rapidly.

Don realized as she angled up through the hatch that she, too,
suffered from the lack of oxygen. Her chest was heaving strenu-
ously. This was impressive for an irrelevant reason, as he tried to

remind himself.

As she recovered her breath in the fresh water topside, she offered him the object she had taken from the jar. It seemed to be a flake of stone, rectangular and flat.

"Sorry—the phase won't let me touch it," Don said regretfully. He passed his hand through it by way of illustration.

Disappointed, she held it up so that he could see the face of it. It was a tablet of some sort: clay, not stone. At least it had a ceramic coating. He cranked up his light again and flashed the beam across the surface.

There was writing on it! Don recognized the typical configuration of Minoan Linear A or B: the lines, boxes, and slashes. It was an ancient manuscript!

He had thought that the discovery of the ship was the ultimate in his career desire. Now he knew he had been too conservative. A document relating to the ship and its business, perhaps dated, putting things into context— it was probably the A script, considering the age of the ship. Ideal!

Smiling, Splendid turned the tablet away.

"Wait!" Don cried. "I can read it!"

She wrote on her own tablet. BUT I CAN'T.

"You don't understand! I can read some of the Minoan signs— but you have to hold it up, because I can't touch the tablet myself. I need your cooperation!"

She nodded affirmatively, her hair flaring in the trace currents the action made, but did not expose the face of the tablet.

"What do you want?" he demanded, frustrated.

She wrote: IT MUST BE SHARED.

"You mean you want to know what it says? I certainly don't object to that."

TRANSLATE ALOUD.

"But that's a long, tedious task! Nobody can decipher such a document at a mere glance! When I said I could read it, I meant— given time. A day, a week, perhaps more, depending on the clarity and dialect. There'll probably be many symbols I can't make out at all, so the narrative will be fragmentary."

She nodded as she wrote. BOTH JARS ARE FILLED WITH SIMILAR TABLETS—ALL DIFFERENT.

It was like being informed of victory in a million dollar sweepstakes. A sizable cache of narrative Minoan Linear A! His single glance had told him that this was no list of accounts; he could recognize numbers instantly, and this contained few. It was text!

But she had a stiff price. "That will take months," he exclaimed with mixed concern, intrigue, and greed. It didn't seem feasible to commit himself to such a long period of shared labor, that would certainly be complicated by involved explanations of nuances. He didn't know when Pacifa and the others would return to cut it short.

On the other hand, this might be his only chance to really study the tablets. That was an opportunity it was inconceivable to squander. He did need her assistance, and it would not be exactly boring, considering her body and exposure. Too bad he couldn't touch her.

Touch her? What was he thinking of? What of Melanie, with whom he was developing a significant relationship. Why should he be distracted by a creature who was both out of phase and of a different, if newly-created, species? It was nonsensical.

Yet those breasts, that hair . . .

So he was a voyeur. As was any man who watched what was paraded on television or motion pictures. Just so long as he didn't confuse the vision with the reality. Meanwhile, he had a vital job to do, that he might never be able to do at another time.

"All right," he said at last. "I've got to see those tablets. You handle the hardware; I'll translate. Aloud."

She clapped her hands noiselessly and dived down the hatch with marvelous grace. Her tail now seemed to be a natural part of a lovely creature.

Splendid had not exaggerated about the number of tablets. It took some time to bring them all up, and she was breathless and tired. She had been holding her breath while working in the hold, to avoid the oxygen-depleted water there, but that hardly added to her comfort. Don became concerned, watching her game struggle. She was doing her part, certainly.

How fortunate that the tablets had been in the last remaining *pithoi*. No, not fortune, but design, for the huge jars were normally used for liquids and grains, not ceramics. Splendid must have found the tablets elsewhere in the ship, and hidden them. Why? Surely not in the hope that a phased-out American archaeologist would ride up on a bicycle.

Now the tablets were all present, and minor reservations were forgotten in the excitement of incipient discovery. Already he could see that there were numerical designations in the corners of each tablet, probably representing dates and order. That suggested a single coherent narrative spanning the tablets as if they were pages of a book. Nothing like this had been found on Crete itself, as far as he knew.

Splendid put her hands over the nearest, warningly.

"Okay, okay!" Don said. "Aloud. I was just getting organized. See those symbols in the corners? The simplest ones are in the upper left, here. These are numbers. These four little lines | | | | stand for the number four. The Minoans didn't have separate signs for each, as we do, but they did use the decimal system. This has to be a serious document, and this is page four. The first thing to do is put them in order."

Comprehension lighted her face, and he was reassured that she really did have serious archaeological interest. She soon located the little sun-circle ° that stood for number one, then the stacked circles °₀ that were two, and the ¯_¯ that was three. The first four pages were intact.

Their luck could not hold forever. Tablet number 5 was missing, as was number 11, of an original total of twelve or more. Even so, Don was gratified that the all-important opening tablet was present, because he saw that it contained some truly remarkable material: lines of symbols in different scripts.

"Another Rosetta Stone!" he exclaimed. "Column One is Linear A; Two looks like Ugaritic, and Three is Sumerian cuneiform!"

DO YOU READ THEM ALL? Splendid inquired, amazed.

Don laughed. "N-not really. But I have studied many ancient forms of writing in the course of my attempts to decipher Minoan, so I am familiar with a number of the common symbols. See, here's a column of Egyptian hieroglyphs, too, but they aren't as important as the Linear A here. See this insect-form? We can trace it right along . . ."

Because the text was extensive, consistent, and straightforward, and because he was aided immeasurably by the key-code of parallel languages, Don found the text much easier to decipher than he had feared. There were still a number of terms he didn't recognize, as the tabulation was representative rather than comprehensive, but the context made many of them clear, and his own knowledge of Minoan culture offered hints for the remainder. This was a narrative like none other known of this culture. He could not vouch for place names, but was sure his general rendition was reasonably accurate. Splendid turned out to be far more help than hindrance, industriously running down word-repetitions and offering alert conjectures for unintelligible symbols.

They had a story—and what a story it was!

Chapter 13

●

Minos

Proxy 5-12-5-16-8: Attention.
Acknowledging.
Status?
Remains difficult. Two members of the group have developed
a suspicion, and are trying to verify it. One is holding me captive,
and I am unable to tell of the mission for fear it will only be mis-
understood. I must wait for the assembly of the remainder of the
group, and hope I can then persuade it. The final two challenges
have become passe.
Then it will be better to abort the mission. We can recover you—
No! There remains some hope. I will remain with it. I am con-
vinced this method can be effective. I must see it through.
Your insistence may cost you your life.
And it may salvage this world!
It remains your prerogative. Signal us at need.

● ● ●

You who peruse this printed clay, I charge you by the name of the Great Earth Mother, and by the Sacred Leaf of the Tree of Life, and most particularly by our common bond of scholarship: honor the foible of a kindred spirit. Grant to me the favor I ask herein, or relegate this manuscript unread to that place from which you recovered it, that one after you may honor it instead.

Don exchanged glances with Splendid as they shared this opening injunction. "Can we be bound by that?"

She thought for a moment, then wrote: BY EARTH MOTHER, NO. BY TREE OF LIFE, NO.

"But by 'our common bond of scholarship'? He really covers everything!"

WHAT IS HIS SPECIFIC REQUEST?

Don glanced ahead at the partly blocked out text. "He doesn't seem to say, here. Maybe he's saving it for the end." He moved toward the final tablet, but Splendid swam to block him. Their bodies passed through each other with a complete meshing of skeletons: hip against hip, rib against rib, skull against skull. His open eyes stared through the fog of her brain. It was as close as he would ever be to a woman, but he did not find the experience exhilarating.

Splendid emerged from his back with a startled expression, but quickly recovered and flashed around him to the tablets. She covered the last with her tail, so that he could not see the script.

"But you asked—" Don said, still assimilating impressions from their momentary merger. Had he actually felt her living heart beating?

She shook her head, recovering her slate, and explained: HE WANTS US TO DECIDE FIRST.

"Yes, certainly. But we *can't* commit ourselves blindly, whatever his conventions may have been. Maybe he wants us to commit ritual suicide so we can't pass on the secret. Considering how long he's been dead himself—"

NO. HE WANTS IT KNOWN. ONLY A SCHOLAR COULD READ EVEN ENOUGH TO RETURN THE TABLETS TO THE SEA.

"That's the point! An illiterate is not bound. He can do anything he wants with the manuscript, but he'll never know what it says. A scholar must either return it unread, or bind himself to an unspecified commitment. Which may be to forget that he ever read it."

AN UNSCRUPULOUS SCHOLAR WOULD IGNORE THE STIPULATION. HE IS ADDRESSING THE PERSON OF INTEGRITY. WHY SHOULD HE COMMIT ONLY THAT ONE TO SILENCE OR DEATH?

Don began to see it. "Only a really honest man would—" He paused as she wrote emphatically on the slate.

PERSON.

Oh. She objected to usage which seemed to exclude her. Melanie would have approved that sentiment! "Only a really honest person would comprehend certain niceties. Would understand the necessity of doing—whatever is requested. And he'd have to read the full manuscript first, to get the background. But maybe the thing is difficult, so he has to be committed first, and not depend on his own first reactions."

Splendid nodded agreement.

"I really don't care what the price is," Don said. "I must find out what this manuscript says. Now more than ever."

I AGREE IF YOU DO.

Don sighed. "I agree to our Minoan's terms. I hope I don't regret it."

I am Pi-ja-se-me, appraiser for Minos by vocation, antiquarian by avocation. To me it has fallen to record the termination of civilization.

Surely no parchment can survive the eons until mankind recovers the cultural level of the Thalassocracy, even were that document not to reside beneath the restless turbulence of this phenomenal and distant ocean. Therefore I have fashioned this stylus and this tablet of clay, and I shall fire it well in the hearth of the ship's galley until it has the permanence of fine pottery. A tedious task, but I have nothing if not time, until the wine runs out.

I append here a glossary of signs, that my manuscript may be intelligible for the eye of whatever national who at length recovers it. I regret I can do no more, but I am not expert in all the myriad written variants of the world, even had I the space to render them here. Perhaps even this token is wasted, for who but the gods can say what shall arise from the depths of the unknowable future. Yet must I essay it.

Our merchant fleet of five fine ships was bearing south after engaging in profitable trading with the Megalithic cities of the far west as we knew it. We exchanged pithoi of fine Cretan olive oil for equal measure of their special stone pigments. Our sophisticated gold ornaments for their rare ores. The Megalithics seem less cultured than we, but this is deceptive; their knowledge is confined largely to their priesthood, and they are unexcelled builders and astronomers. In fact, I suspect their culture goes back farther than ours, for some of their most impressive monuments are ancient by our standards, and we still could learn from them were their priestly hierarchy less canny about the disposition of their arts. But I diverge; it is the wine. Yet must I imbibe what offers, or thirst interminably. This salty sea . . .

It was at [indecipherable place name—north coast of Iberia?] that Admiral Su-ri-mo and I first had word. We had been at sea five months, and I was eager to return to villa and concubine. My villa: none quite like it on all [Thera], though never was I a wealthy man. Situated high on the side of the holy mountain, provided with fiercely hot water by duct from the sacred spring: few in all our empire possess rights to such overflow, but I, as royal antiquarian/appraiser was favored by the priesthood. I do not mean to exalt my own importance, which is not great; I seek only to explain in part the kindly favoritism extended to me by a monarch who values cultural studies. All about my residence perched the artifacts of my life's collection: ancient identification seals of baked clay from [Anatolia—Turkey]; faience from the orient, distinct from ours; a fine flint dagger from a burial mound in [Arabia]; and of course many varieties of decorative pottery, each representative of a vanished culture. For years my concubine, otherwise a very fine woman if a trifle tight about the waist-ring, was jealous of the attentions I paid these objects, not understanding how a man could see as much value in a discolored sherd as in a living woman. In truth, I was at times grateful for that jealousy, for it prompted her to ever-greater imagination in her calling.

Don could not restrain a smile at this point. Splendid, after due consideration, decided to smile too. How little some things changed!

This amount of translation had taken two days. But it was time well spent, and the remainder promised to move more rapidly as the last difficult symbols yielded their meanings.

It seems I cannot hew precisely to my theme; my mind insists upon revisiting those things that were dear to me. Must I then ramble, however pointlessly, and hope to cover the essence in whatever fashion I can manage.

The omens were ill. The sky turned drab, and the sunset was like a stifled inferno. A hideous odor suffused the air. Yet there was no storm. We put into a local port and made inquiries, and received a story brought by runners, of a disaster unlike any known.

Neither admiral Su-ri-mo nor I believed it at first. We supposed Greek enemies had spread the foul story in an effort to dismay us and force us to divulge our technical secrets. But within a few days one of our own ships hailed us and confirmed the disaster in all its awfulness.

Terrible fire and storm had ravaged all Crete. Our cities had been destroyed by waves taller than the mast of this ship, our crops buried under a thick mass of choking hot dust. Of our mighty fleet, the finest ever to rule the [Mediterranean] sea, only that fraction at sea and far from home escaped. The land itself, buried in noxious mud, was unlivable.

Now those far-flung ships were summoned home. Our people needed them for migration to unspoiled lands, lest our power be dissipated entirely. Vain hope! The strength of our civilization lies not in our ships, but in the extreme fertility of our land, the density of our great timber forests, and the unexcelled craftsmanship of our artisans. We must rebuild our palaces, as we have in the past, if we are to maintain any portion of our national well-being.

"But what of our own fair city?" I cried. "Our isle is not Crete, our homeland is not Knossos. Surely we, at least escaped the holocaust?"

"Your city is no more," our informant said. "We sailed by it, checking all our cities. The fire consumed [Thera] utterly. Not even the island remains, merely a burnt shell."

Still we could not believe. But if we went home to verify
this horror directly, and it were true, we would become subject to this makeshift government and have to give over our
fine ships to the transport of women and cattle, and our
treasures to usurping tyrants. No way to salvage our culture, this! Yet if we did not go back, and this report were
false, what then of our loyalty?

The Admiral and I discussed the matter at length, the
crushing hand of calamity gripping us both. We professed
not to believe, we reassured each other repeatedly, but at
the root we withered. At length we decided to detach two
ships, who would return to ascertain the truth, while the remainder stayed clear. One ship at least would come back to
us to make report. This was a cumbersome procedure, but
it seemed the best strategy, given our divided belief.

I remained aboard one of the three. I would have gone
home, but Su-ri-mo chose to keep me with the bulk of the
merchandise, for only I knew its precise value and the details of its inventory.

For a time we continued to travel the coast of the [Atlan-
tic] ocean as if seeking more trade, though we had little remaining for barter. At night we found safe anchorage and
sent the men ashore to gather driftwood and make a fire to
cook the main meal. The crewmen would grind grain and
bake the morrow's bread over the embers, and the wine
would circulate. They slept on the sand, the smoke from
banked fires driving off the nocturnal pests. The Admiral
and I had to remain aboard our respective ships, guarding
the cargo, for not all the impressed hands were trustworthy.
I made do with the ship's galley, learning by scorching my
fingers on the inadequate hearth. How I envied the landed
crew, and how I cursed my isolation here! Yet it would seem
that the Great Earth Mother destined this, for now I have
need of this hearth.

Time hung heavy as we awaited confirmation of the fate
of our land. The men shaved each other with the few precious iron blades available, with much cursing and scraping
of skin. Perhaps not all of the cuts were accidental. They
wagered interminably. I completed the inventory of cargo of
all three ships, and started it over, for want of other diversion.

Winter came, harsh in these hinterlands, and it was impossible to continue at sea in the treacherous weather and waters. We docked at [another Megalithic city?], paying an exorbitant harbor tax. Now at last I could depart ship, for our wares were secure. But it was scant improvement. This was no Knossos.

Knossos! I had visited there often, in my official capacities, and though I would not have cared to reside in that crush, it was a splendor. Four and five stories high, with the magnificent reception hall on the second girt by the massive, artful pillars—would you believe it, I have seen pillars elsewhere that actually contract toward the apex, making the entire structure appear inverted. Any refined eye must readily perceive that a decorative column must expand toward the apex—which shows little aesthetic hope, for example, for the [Mycenaeans—Greeks].

But this Megalithic port: the houses were all separate, none possessing even a second story, and all without proper sanitary facilities. These people hardly believed in bathing, and the odor inside became appalling. Their men were thick-bodied, wearing waist-clasps only to support their rude garments. They even had the effrontery to remark on our own style, calling our narrow waists unnatural. Unnatural! How could I ever forget my pride when I donned the metal belt of adulthood at the age of ten, wearing it to preserve that aesthetic slenderness of torso that so befits the physically fit. I wear it to this day, and no man of this expedition can lay claim to a smaller or more manlier waist than I, despite the fact that my gaming days are long past. To watch Island-born Cretans laying aside their clasps of honor and allowing their bodies to grow gross with dissipation—that is unnatural!

Yet I must admit they had some cause. The semi-savage women of this town were alluring in their very primitiveness. If a man must put aside his belt in order to enjoy the favors of such—well, I would not do it myself, but I can not entirely blame the younger males who never had relations with a competent concubine. It was a long, bitter winter, and the women were warm-bodied.

I did find some solace. Not far distant was one of their great monuments, not of stone, unfortunately, but still impressive in wood. Impressive architecturally, that is to say; to my way of thinking, the man is far more important than any monument, and needs no wood or stone to bolster his glory. He is the ideal. Hence we have few actual monuments in [Keftiu] or any of the islands. For foreigners seldom comprehend. There, again, is the distinction between the civilized and the pseudo-civilized. Consider, if you will, the extremes of the [Egyptians]. Yet, in fairness, I must say that the Megalithics do put their edifices to marvelous uses, and I understand their astronomical data are the most precise in the world. It is always a folly to take too narrow a view. Even clumsy cultures have their points.

I found a number of significant artifacts about the premises. Enough to satisfy me that the Megalithics have, indeed, had a long history, and may even have declined from prior greatness. Of course I have no absolute way to date any given sherd of pottery, but I believe it is safe to assume that those excavated from deep in the ground are of greater antiquity than those near the surface. I was extremely fortunate in discovering a clay seal in good condition that I suspect is several hundred years old. That is especially gratifying, because of the symbolism of my own seal. As a matter of information, I shall imprint it here. [Imprint of an oval scene, a representation of a pottery sherd, on which is a mazelike pattern.] Note the design on the sherd: it is a precise duplicate of an actual decoration on a sherd I recovered from a cave on the [Syrian] coast. But the linkage between seal and design is more than this. I have reason to believe that this particular pottery design is itself emulative of the pattern on a fabric, perhaps a hanging tapestry. And that, in turn, the design was imprinted on the fabric by a large clay seal. So the complete symbolism on my own seal, of which I am justly proud, is that it completes the circle. It is a seal bearing a representation of a design copied from a tapestry imprinted by a similar seal! I suspect that this was, in fact, the original purpose of seals, and that only later did they evolve into personal signatures. Whatever the truth, I believe my own seal captures a portion of it. Alas, no one else appreciates this meaning, yet is sustains me in times of gloom, as it sustains me now. I speculate endlessly: in my collection is a seal recovered from a mound in [Anatolia], that I once toured with a [Hittite] scholar. Our own Cretan origins, according to legend, are there. Certainly there are similar bulls there, and similar plants, and I saw the ruin of an ancient city there that was very like one of our own. Foreigners consider our palaces to be mazes in their complexity—and there in [Anatolia] are maze patterns. Yet in opposition I must say that our legends also speak of a seafaring tradition extending very far back and covering an even wider scope than at present, so that our ancestors could have traveled by ship from much farther ports than [Anatolia]. How dearly would I like to know the answer!

Don pushed away the tablets, and naturally his hands passed through them instead. "I like that man!" he exclaimed. "He's a real archaeologist!"

Splendid looked thoughtful. HE IS MUCH LIKE YOU, she wrote.

Flattered and embarrassed, Don changed the subject. "I've hardly been aware of time! Do you realize we've used up two more days? But at the rate this is accelerating, we'll finish it tomorrow. This is obviously the mission for which I was sent, and it's the greatest experience of my life. And you are making it possible, you gorgeous creature."

She smiled, touched her hand to her lips, and put it to his mouth.

Don, fatigued from his strenuous intellectual labors and intoxicated by the combination of Minoan revelation and lack of sleep, was moved. Splendid had kissed him! He had spoken to her with the camaraderie of their intense recent intellectual association, without stuttering, and she had responded. How things had changed! "Watch that," he told her facetiously. "Old Pi-ja-se-me relaxed with his jealous concubine after a hard stint of business."

Splendid smiled again and opened her arms invitingly to him.

"God, no!" he exclaimed, shocked now. "You're—I'm—I was joking. I mean, the phase—"

She drifted up to him and put her arms about him, barely touching. He could feel that fringe contact of flesh through flesh, and it was very like the feather-gentle caress of a real woman. Her face came up to his, and he could not resist meeting her lips. It was like kissing a wisp of fog, yet it had considerable impact on him.

Don backed away, guiltily. "What are you trying to do?"

She only shook her head, still smiling.

Don turned away. What would she be doing, except playing with a man she knew could not touch her? Both because of the phase, and because she was a mermaid. Was that why mermaids had such fascination for men, mythologically? Because, anatomically, they were genuinely unobtainable?

Still, he was tired and he did envy Pi-ja his jealous concubine. Who could say what he might do, given the ability actually to touch a female like Splendid?

When he turned again, she was gone. Nothing exceptional about that; she departed regularly to fetch food and take care of natural calls. However she performed them. She would return, as decorative and helpful as ever. She had left the remaining tablets face down on the deck, so he could not cheat; this remained a business association, with safeguards.

Jealous concubine. That reminded him of Melanie, perhaps unkindly. He had been severely distracted these past few days, but down below his consciousness he had not forgotten her, or Pacifa's remark about her. Melanie loved him? How would he feel about Melanie in the arms of a virile merman, or even merely alone with one for several days, unchaperoned?

It was time to check in with her. He turned on the radio. "How are you doing, Melanie?" he inquired, not sure her set was even on. It had been off the other times he had tried calling her.

She was waiting for him this time, however, her hand evidently on a figurative detonator. "Why don't you go make out with your paramour, instead of wasting my time?"

Taken aback because this so baldly reflected the lascivious thoughts he had just entertained, Don could only stutter. "I—I—"

"I, by God, am a human being," Melanie informed him wrathfully. "A female only to the extent I choose to be."

She couldn't know about Splendid's seeming invitation! The radio had not been on for any dialogue for four days. What had set her off, aside from that tiff with the mermaid?

What else but jealously! Hell had no fury. Yet it was baseless, because Splendid simply was not obtainable, and he understood that on both the intellectual and emotional levels. What good was the most impressive body known—and Splendid had that—when it might as well have been an untouchable hologram? Melanie, in contrast, was real for him, and not merely physically. He had to reassure her about that.

"Melanie, you don't un-understand—" he started lamely.

"I am quite certain that you have conscious control over the specifically male aspect of your life—sexual intercourse —but I am much less certain that you have much conscious awareness of your internal myths concerning sexual roles."

She certainly wasn't tongue-tied! But what was this about having sex? She knew the phase made that impossible. "I d-don't know what you're t-talking about," he said, nevertheless feeling guilty. Suppose it *had* been possible? What would he have gotten into—bad choice of words—then?

"You mean you haven't tried the balloons yet? How considerate of you?" Her tone was cutting.

"B-balloons?"

"Oh, you're impossible!" She clicked off.

Don shook his head. She was furious, all right. But what was responsible? This seemed like more than mere irritation because of his necessary association with another woman.

Then he began to see. The balloons were about the only way the phase world could interact with the real world, since they were half-phased. Gas trapped in the balloons made them rigid in both frameworks. If they were put on the fingers like gloves, they would make it possible to handle something, and to feel it fairly firmly. Even human flesh. A balloon was a lot like a condom.

In his naivete he had never thought of this in connection with Splendid. Obviously Melanie had. Maybe she did have grounds for jealousy.

Yet that could not be the whole of it. Even if Melanie assumed that he, as a man, would take whatever offered—why should she think that Splendid would offer? The mermaid had a community of her own kind. Her interest here was archaeological, and it was genuine, as was his.

Don had a question for Splendid when she returned: "What did you tell Melanie, that made her so mad?"

The mermaid shook her head negatively. She wasn't telling.

"Uh-uh," Don said. "Y-you tell me, or I'll s-stop translating!" It was a bluff, for he knew nothing could keep him away from the tablets after he'd had a few hours of sleep. But it was important to unravel this personal matter too.

Splendid elected to yield to the threat, though he doubted that she took it seriously. She took up her slate. ONLY WHAT SHE

ASKED.

"Then what did she ask?"

There was just a hint of that blush. HOW WE DO IT.

Um, yes. How *did* mermaids reproduce, etc.? There simply seemed to be no apparatus in the nether section of her body. "And what did you t-tell her?"

THAT I WOULD SHOW YOU.

Brother! Every day of his radio silence must have been new evidence to Melanie that Splendid was, well, showing. And that he was using the balloons in a new way.

"I—I wish you would apologize to her. She's furious!"

Now Splendid looked stubborn, with a heightening of the blush. I HAVE NOT YET SHOWN.

"You don't *need* to show!" he yelled. "Melanie's jealous because she thinks—never mind. Just tell her what we've really been doing. She refuses to believe *me*."

SHE WOULD NOT BELIEVE ME EITHER.

Probably true. But it was necessary to make the effort. "Look, Splendid, this—she—I—it's important."

The mermaid cocked her head, evidently catching on. YOU LOVE HER?

"I—I—yes, I guess I do."

SHE KNOWS WE CANNOT TOUCH?

"There might be a way."

She nodded. I WILL TELL HER.

Don felt a wash of relief. "Thank you! I—" He gave up trying to express himself, and turned on the radio.

It was no use. Melanie's radio remained off. It might remain that way for some time.

He sighed. She would just have to stay mad for as long as it took. At worst, until they got together again, and communication between them could not be cut off.

Right now he had to sleep.

● ● ●

Our two vessels never returned. By spring we were assured the story was accurate, and we had a fair notion what had occurred. I have seen volcanic action upon occasion, and know how devastating such blasts from the deep earth can be. I also know that the fumeroles and hot springs that made our islet warm and fertile had to stem from similar forces. It was surely a volcanic eruption near or at [Thera], and the fire and stone from it, and the waves it made in the sea, and the dust and gases of its murderous exhalations, that ravaged our world and brought our very civilization to its knees.

But that is the lesser of two *mysteries*. The greater is not how, but *why*. Surely our priests were well aware of the propensities of the mighty Bull of the Earth, and surely they propitiated it regularly and generously. Every sacrifice, every spectacle of bull-leaping, every intoned prayer—all these tokens, and indeed our cultural outlook, have been dedicated to the pacification of that shuddering Power. Had we been remiss in our worship, then might such retribution have been justified. But I am certain that we were not; the rites were maintained faithfully right up until the moment of the holocaust. Why, then, did the monster turn on us?

I have no answer. I must instead face the reality, as Admiral Su-ri-mo and I faced it then. What should we do with our treasures, so laboriously acquired? They became meaningless when our homeland ended. Our king was dead, our homes destroyed. The barbarians who had seized titular power in our misfortune were not worthy of our allegiance. We should not, could not, go home. But neither could we endure another winter in a pagan city. It was necessary to get our men away from such influences, lest we lose our identity along with our culture and our wealth.

After much consideration we plotted course for [Africa]. Because many of our men on all three ships had become corrupted by the life among the Megalithics, and were almost openly rebellious, we were forced to voyage far out to sea, planning to make landfall only in the direst emergency. For this reason we loaded our holds with a tremendous volume of supplies, though we had to sacrifice the goods for which we had already traded. What use were ores and pigments, now?

Yet even to me, the sheer volume of wine and grain seemed excessive. I tried to caution Su-ri-mo, but he assured me that [Africa] was farther distant than I realized, and that we needed a good margin in case of delays. We would be traveling shorthanded, for we could not hope to recruit enough oarsmen to fill the seats of the defectors. But with good winds it would not matter as much. One sail is worth all the oarsmen, when the wind is right.

Thus I bowed to his judgment, for he was much experienced on the sea and the responsibility was his. Certainly I had little cause for misgiving on this score, since too much food is far less burdensome than too little.

For a month we journeyed south, impeded by adverse winds and contrary currents. It seemed that our store of misfortune had not yet been expended. Discipline among the men, never good since the disaster, became ragged, for they sought surcease from the toil of rowing through still seas and wished to return to the pleasures of the city. Also, they did not like such a long period out of sight of any land. But the Admiral held firm, and after several troublemakers had been quartered the noise subsided somewhat. I was glad that harsh measures had not been required. We remained far out to sea, however, for fear of mutiny should the men catch sight of land and know their bearings.

Still, I knew that navigation entirely by sunstone was precarious, and I feared the Admiral himself lacked precise knowledge of our whereabouts. Yet he seemed assured, even confident. First I supposed this was a false front, so as not to show weakness before the crew; then I suspected that he was deluded. But in no wise did he play the role of delusion, apart from this foolhardy westward drifting. I am a fair judge of men, necessarily, and I knew the Admiral well. Gradually it came upon me that he had a destination—and that it was not [Africa]. I braced him one day when I caught him privately during a routine inspection of my ship.

"Admiral, I must know the truth if I am to function effectively," I said with some asperity.

He attempted to evade. "Do you doubt my bearings?"

"Not at all, except as they pertain to [Africa]. Our homeland is gone; what use are secrets now?"

He understood my reference. "Yes," he said slowly. "There is no proper home for us in [Africa]. It is the far port we voyage to."

"It is forbidden!" I cried, shocked by this bald confirmation of my dark suspicion.

He was unmoved. "As you have so eloquently pointed out: what are secrets, what are prohibitions, when we have no one to answer to? It is for us to carry the news, and to make a new life for ourselves. Surely we can not do so among the savage Greeks or land-hugging Canaanites."

"[Atlantis]!" I breathed, uttering the forbidden name.

"Atlantis!" Don repeated, as amazed and excited as ancient Pi-ja-se-me had been. The fabulous continent introduced to historic mythology by Plato, who had it from Solon, who had it from an Egyptian priest. The story had been that Atlantis, a rich and powerful and happy island continent, had suddenly sunk in a day and a night. It had been most generally supposed by scholars that Atlantis had in fact been Minoan Crete, ravaged by the phenomenal eruption of Thera in the fifteenth century B.C. The ignorant had spun grandiose stories of a continent in the Atlantic Ocean, for which no justification was offered. Of course Plato had said that Atlantis perished nine thousand years before his time, and was ten times the size of any ruins found at Thera, but this was readily explained by postulating an error in translation of one decimal place. That brought the capital city of Atlantis right down to the size of the settlement on Thera—Pi-ja's home city— and the time lapse to nine hundred years, which was a close match to the geological record of the eruption. Thus Don had hardly concerned himself with the legend of Atlantis, knowing it to be extrapolation from a clerical error. True, Plato had placed it beyond the Pillars of Hercules. But that was standard practice for the Greeks, who were too familiar with the Aegean to accept such mysteries there.

Now it seemed that the Atlantis legend predated Thera. Don went over the symbol on the tablet again and again, trying to discover whether he had misinterpreted, but it stood firm as the best guess. If the concept were not Atlantis, it was similar. To Pi-ja, as with the later Plato, Atlantis was a tremendous island across the great ocean.

Yet who would know the source of the legend better than the Minoans, the foremost seafaring people of the ancient world? If they had had a legend of Atlantis, that land must have existed!

Actually the eruption of Thera had not ended Minoan civilization. They had suffered terribly, but soon enough had reasserted themselves and driven off the marauding Greeks and gone on to greater heights. Their power had not faded until they depleted the natural resources of their island, and had to shift their bases elsewhere. But the eruption had been remembered. Thera had been something like four times as great an explosion as the later Krakatoa. Surely the gods had never spoken with greater authority than that! So the Cretan captain, far distant, had misjudged the situation, understandably. Many others had done the same.

Abruptly a new conjecture opened like a fragrant flower. It had not been Atlantis that sank, but Thera—the major European contact. The Minoans had kept the secret, and only their limited reports at their home base had leaked out. So the legend had funneled through that blasted aperture and emerged distorted, for the Greeks and Egyptians had not known the whole truth. Their contact with the news and goods of Atlantis had been shut off, so they assumed that it was dead. All the civilized world had accepted that.

Atlantis still existed—and now Don knew where it was.

Chapter 14

•

Atlantis

Proxy 5-12-5-16-8: Attention.

Acknowledging.

Status?

Dismal. I dare not tell the truth for fear of sacrificing the mission, yet I cannot prevail otherwise. I think I can accomplish it only by the intercession of one member of the party, and I am unable to contact that one. I must bide my time, and hope.

Then terminate it.

No. Not until all hope is gone. Sufficient time must come for the one to be ready. Then if I can manage contact, I can still succeed.

In view of the risk, we feel that greater judgment than yours should be invoked. Obtain our acquiescence before presenting the mission to your group.

I will do so.

• • •

"Atlantis," Su-ri-mo agreed. "It is at least a civilized port.

A few days later a terrible storm formed, and for two days we rode before it, and two more within it, hardly knowing day from night. All our hatches and oar-ports were sealed, lest we be swamped; we rode blindly.

Just when the winds were worst, they abruptly abated, and we sailed serene in sunshine. But the Admiral allowed no relaxation, and drove us all on all three ships to batten down even more firmly than before, with no sail and every oar-port closed. The men thought him moonstruck, and even I had my doubts—but suddenly a frightening wall of cloud swept over the horizon, and almost before we could fetch down our heads and cling to the beams the wind struck again, fully as fiercely as before. It was another storm—blowing from the other direction!

Surely this ocean was cursed by the gods, to have such incredible storms. How was it that the first storm had not crashed headlong into the second, and so dissipated both? But the gods are not limited by such considerations; they do as pleases them, and it was evident that our presence here did not please them. For three more days we cowered before the awful wind, the huge waves striking our ship as if to sunder it in twain. The crewmen prayed valiantly to one god or another, but the elements seemed almost beyond the control of divinity.

When at last the weather eased, we were alone and completely lost. Our sail was in useless shreds, our mast stripped bare. The admiral's ship was gone, as was the third vessel; we could not ascertain their fate. We ourselves were helpless before the currents of the sea, for our oars had all been broken off.

The ship's captain supervised repairs, but there was no new tackle to mount and no new sail. Our hull at least was tight, for our own guild of shipwrights at Thera was ever the finest, and after bailing out the bilge and the wash from the storm waves we floated as high as we had before. We had a fair supply of food and wine, because of the staples the Admiral had laid in for the voyage to Atlantis, though we seemed unlikely to arrive there now. And of course we fished.

Now fish is fit for kings, but seawater is not. As for imbibing the discolored juices of crushed fish in lieu of water, and drinking bilge salvaged from rain—well, then we really appreciated the hardships of existing on a derelict. I suspect that had we had good Cretan wine we might have endured even so without complaint, but what filled our supply jars was Megalithic Mash, as the cynical crewmen put it.

The captain of our ship consulted with me, as I was now the ranking remaining officer of the fleet, but I could tell him nothing. It was not that I chose to preserve the secret of our destination from him; it was that it was pointless to tantalize him with it when we had no hope of achieving it. Even had I said it, no one had the bearing of Atlantis. Only the Admiral had that.

On we drifted, ever farther from our homeland, for the seas were moving west. Illness broke out among the crewmen, and we had no proper physician to attend to it. I suffered pains in my own bones, at times so pervasive that I lay in my cabin unable to move, seeking to alleviate my discomfort by consuming bad wine and dreaming of diversions of the past. I saw in my mind a gallery of our sprightly island ladies, with their long gaily colored skirts tiered with five and six bands of flouncing, bright bracelets on their wrists and ankles, their puffed sleeves and lush breasts standing behind thin gauze, their elaborate jeweled headdresses over curly black hair, a snakolike strand bobbing in front of each ear, large dark-etched eyes—ah, ah! Who can lay claim to knowledge of beauty, who has not gazed on such as these!

At other times it seemed I was traveling down a street in my palanquin, passing well-kept houses flush with the edge of the pavement, their windows filled with taut oiled parchment panes. I would enter one, my slaves waiting outside. The sweet smell of cooking-smoke tantalized my nostrils, and I knew that a fine repast was in the making. I would sit on a red cushion on a fine stone bench in the pale blue chamber, awaiting invitation to the central patio. I do not know whose house it was; not my own. Just an average domicile in a better neighborhood. Perhaps that was the point of this vision: its reassuring suggestion that such houses and such neighborhoods still existed, when I feared they did not. The life I had known lingered wistfully within me.

Sometimes I recovered enough to sit on the open deck, and then my gaze fixed on the steady waves and I dreamed of the sea-ancestry of our culture. If our origins lay in Anatolia, yet we had been sea-faring before achieving fair Crete and fairer Thera—could these legends be reconciled? As I now analyzed them, two thousand years ago we were part of an empire of all the seas, whose ports touched on every shore. But slowly the waters rose and those fabulous ancient cities were drowned, and lacking the means to hold back the waters the empire fragmented, leaving pieces of itself scattered across the world like broken pottery sherds. One fragment became the Megalithics, another the Kingdom of Meluhha, yet others Egypt, Makan, Ubaid, and Dilmun. Even farther spread were the enclaves in southern Africa and eastward beyond the farthest reaches of the Sumerian trade routes—and of course Atlantis. Crete was only a minor refuge, then. Or so I conjecture, making allowance for the inflation of our own importance in our legends.

I myself have visited a number of the old sites that produced such material as obsidian, that volcanic glass once so valuable for tools and weapons. Now we prefer bronze, of course, and iron when we can obtain it. But still the extent of that old empire is suggested by the ores it mined and the technologies it disseminated. If I could but go back to learn the full history of that golden age of . . .

At this point the first missing tablet manifested. Damn! Any loss from the narrative was painful, but when the discussion was on ancient history as seen by an ancient scholar, what a loss!

Disgruntled by the insuperable interruption of the story, Don took a break. Splendid was glad to relax, too; she had been making notes on small waterproof sheets, recording this for her community.

Don turned on the radio by force of habit, but Melanie still would not answer. Splendid noticing, smiled.

Don's frustration at the double balking by tablet and woman abruptly focused on what was available. "What are you laughing at?" he demanded.

The mermaid was unperturbed. WHY NOT LET ME SHOW YOU, she wrote. WHILE THE MINOAN DRIFTS AND FRETS.

"Show me what?" Then he remembered: how mermaids reproduced. She was teasing him, secure in the barrier of phase. Or was she trying to tempt him into some sexual attempt, that had to fail embarrassingly? Revenge for what Melanie had said to her?

That reminded him of what Melanie had said about the balloons. All this time, he could have handled the Minoan tablets himself! Instead he had had to bargain with the mermaid, and compromise, translating only in her presence. That had not been a bad experience, actually, but he cursed himself for not thinking of the balloons before. Now she was cocksure, and his frustration found a way of expression.

He brought out one of the balloons. It was very fine and flexible, and felt as if he were moving it through the resistance of water. As he was, now that it was no longer balled up. He stretched it carefully over his clumped and stiffened fingers, clamping it in place with his thumb. Hardly a perfect glove, but serviceable.

"Come here, Splendid," he said.

She swam forward with enticing undulations, ready to play the futile game. She expected him to make a pass, literally: a sweep of his hand through her body without contact.

He poked her left breast with the gloved fingers. Her flesh was firm and resilient, a genuine delight to poke. Splendid was laughing silently, enjoying her invulnerability.

Then she realized that the touch was real. With one phenomenal thrust of her flukes she shot straight up a good two fathoms.

Don's *pique* dissipated, but he maintained a straight face. "Please *do* show me how," he suggested as she leveled out and peered down.

She touched her breast herself as if verifying what had happened. Now it seemed she was not so eager. She looked at the sheath on his hand, realizing that it did not have to be restricted to a finger. Her bluff had been called.

"While the Minoan drifts and frets," Don added encouragingly.

Splendid glanced westward, as if debating whether to flee back to her village. He would not be able to pursue swiftly enough to keep her in sight, because of the difficulty of getting off the ship with his bicycle or out of the chasm the ship was in. Even on the level she could lose him, merely by swimming upward until gone.

"If you go home, I shall continue translating on my own," he said.

That got to her. She was as eager as he to read that manuscript.

Now he had possession.

Then she dived purposefully for the tablets. She was going to carry them away!

"No you don't!" he cried, diving for them himself.

They collided. This time flesh and bone passed through flesh and bone as before, but the balloon-glove got hung up against her torso just where flesh merged into scales. Don tried to yank back his hand, but his arm actually passed through her abdomen, leaving the hand at her rear, and he goosed her royally. Her mouth opened in an outraged O as she jackknifed, inadvertently showing him a bottom that resolved the long-standing question of "how." It was all there in normal human order when the legs folded clear and the scales parted.

Don had to roll away, finally managing to disengage, and go back to his bicycle for a breath of air. Splendid used the opportunity to pick up two of the tablets. Don, now aware of her liability, charged back balloon-first and tickled her under one raised arm, just where the breast began.

She shrieked silently, squirming away, and dropped the tablets to the deck. One cracked apart.

Appalled, they both broke off hostilities and stared. The damage was not total, as the tablet had split into two major portions rather than shattering. But had it not been buoyed by the water it would have been another matter. The look on Splendid's face showed that she was as chagrined about the accident as he.

She recovered her slate and wrote. I WILL NOT GO. I WILL MAKE IT RIGHT WITH YOUR FRIEND.

Don merely nodded, putting away his balloon. Too bad it had taken this near disaster to straighten them both out. Yet now he realized that this was the first time he had had an interaction like this with a woman; his shyness had not gotten in the way. Ordinarily the mere thought of poking, grabbing, or goosing a woman would have made him flee, stutter-bound.

Splendid wrote a treatise in German, and Don spelled it out over the unresponsive radio. He didn't inquire what it said, and he had no evidence Melanie was listening, but it was the best he could do. He planned to broadcast it again in a few hours, and then yet again, until she picked it up.

They returned to the manuscript, picking up the text after the missing tablet.

. . . snake. Certainly we have many legends, and the serpent, as an aspect of the earth, is commonly worshiped in Crete. I use that term advisedly. Actually we worship no animals, as that is a practice for barbarians. We merely use them as adjuncts of the ritual in the worship of that divinity we may not approach directly. Yet this is difficult to justify to foreigners, and I have fallen out of the habit of trying. I myself have offered incense before the altar of the lovely Snake Goddess. And our regard for the bull as another aspect of that same Earth Spirit is too well established to warrant repetition here. Yet there are elements that do not entirely jibe, and the legend is in many ways alien to our comprehension. I shall present it here only in summary:

Three thousand years ago—they are specific, as they possess a marvelously accurate calendar, but I round it off for convenience—there was an upright priest king who was identified with the Bull God for his strength and determination. No woman could resist him, and thus he attracted the romantic attention even of his sister, identified with the Bird God. She it was who nursed him when he was stricken ill as his penance for neglecting the Snake God, and in this case the Bird prevailed and she cured him. He was so joyous to be well again that he celebrated for forty days—some say four hundred. A ritual figure, subject to interpretation. She then tempted him with wine, making him intoxicated, and disguised herself so that he did not know her, and thereby seduced him. When he recovered equilibrium and realized what he had done, he built a great pyre and threw himself on it, ascending to the Heaven of the Bulls. But she endured alone and in due course gave birth to the Feathered Bull: a creature at once ferocious in animal aspect while well-favored in human aspect. He was both beast and god, but at the same time a man, with mannish appetites. This entity in due course became king, and set out to rule all the world of men. He discovered how to grow plants, how to sail a ship, and how to work with metal. His reign was long and glorious, extending over all the islands of the world and all the lands bordering on the sea. But in his old age, when he was five hundred years old—perhaps fifty, allowing for the rituality of figures—he became savage, for he was simultaneously a child of incest and miscegenation. He attempted to destroy what he had wrought, and at last his subjects had to confine him in a massive temple. For many years they fed him sacrifices of living flesh, but then they neglected him, and slowly he weakened. When he expired, the earth shuddered and groaned with the rage of a bull, and the sky whipped itself into a tremendous storm signifying the rage of the birds, and the sea came up in the rage of the Snake of the Water and inundated all the great cities of that kingdom, which was the original Atlantis. It fell apart and was no more.

That, at any rate, is the legend. I have heard it in many variants, but all agree in essence. How strikingly it concurs with ours of the ancient sea-empire! Elements do seem contradictory, such as the father of the Feathered Bull becoming intoxicated by wine, when plant cultivation—surely including that of the vine—was discovered only later by his son. And I question the capacity of his subjects to imprison this powerful, god-imbued, man-bull-bird, however old he became. But as I noted before, legends of this nature must be taken allegorically, and the seeming errors analyzed for the more subtle truths they hint. What intrigues me primarily is the presence of the bull, for I have found no evidence of this animal existing in contemporary Atlantis.

"So they made it to Atlantis after all!" Don said, satisfied. "I rather thought they would."

BUT THEY WERE ADRIFT AND LOST, Splendid protested.

"Haven't you figured out where Atlantis is? The winds and currents naturally carried the ship there—which has to be the way the Minoans discovered it in the first place."

Her face lighted. AMERICA!

"Certainly. It meets all the criteria. It is far across the sea to the west, beyond the Pillars of Hercules; it is larger than all of the Mediterranean lands combined—as far as they could tell, anyway, since they could not get around it either to the north or south; and it possessed great wealth and high civilization. Probably it was the major remnant of that worldwide maritime culture both legends speak of—a culture in its prime about 4000 B.C., before the celebrated Flood. But by 1500 B.C. only the Minoans maintained contact, as far as we or they knew. The Megalithics had declined and were no longer a significant maritime empire, despite their residence all along the European Atlantic coast. The several highly advanced cultures around the Arabian peninsula and India—Dilmun, Makan, and Meluhha, of which we have archaeological record—were blocked from it by the huge mass of Africa. The Chinese—your civilization—were balked by the sheer immensity of the Pacific. When the Cretan contact was severed by the eruption of Thera, it didn't destroy the Minoan culture, but did end that contact with Atlantis. Atlantis became a myth."

BUT WHAT REALLY DESTROYED THE ORIGINAL MARITIME EMPIRE? she was writing.

"The rising of the seas, of course. The melting ice of the glaciers of the ice age caused the water to cover much of the prior shoreline. The worldwide legends of the great flood may derive from "

THIS SHOULD NOT HAVE DESTROYED CIVILIZATION. IT WAS VERY SLOW IN TERMS OF MAN'S HISTORY.

Don hesitated. "I suppose not. Certainly we owe much more to the ice age than it can ever have cost us, for the Magdelanean cave art culture derived from ice-age conditions. In fact, I'm sure those reindeer people migrated to the Near-East when conditions changed, building cities in Anatolia like Catal Huyuk of 6500 B.C. in which the cave motifs were transferred to house walls and ceramics, and metalworking first developed. But remember, two and a half thousand years elapsed between that civilization of 4000 B.C. and Pi-ja's time. It could have atrophied, as all civilizations have well within that span, and the rising waters then covered up most of its architecture, leaving little evidence but legends. After all, consider how knowledge of the Minoan culture itself was lost for milennia, surviving only in that passing reference to Atlantis and such things as the Theseus legend."

She considered. YES, I SEE IT NOW. AND THE MAYAN LEGEND OF QUETZALCOATL, THE FEATHERED SERPENT.

Don was electrified. "The feathered *serpent?* In American legend?"

She looked askance. YOU ARE NOT FAMILIAR WITH THIS FAMOUS STORY?

"I—I've concentrated pretty much on Crete," Don admitted. "I guess I have heard of it, but I'm hazy on the details."

She provided them, and his wonder grew. The American Indian legend, common in many languages and variants in both north and south continents, told how the goddess Coatlicue gath-

ered white feathers, placing them in her bosom; but she swal-
lowed one and thereby became pregnant. She gave birth to Quetzalcoatl, whose name was a combination of *Quetzal*, a special
green-feathered bird; *Co*, a snake; and *Atl*, water. Thus he represented air, earth, and water, and was a complex symbol of man's
condition and possibilities. He was the Feathered Serpent.

Quetzalcoatl grew up tall, robust, handsome, and bearded. He
loved all living things, and would not kill a bear or pick a flower.
Then an enemy showed him his image in a distorting mirror, and
he saw himself as wasted away. He was shocked, and went into
seclusion so that his people would not see him. But then his enemy dressed him well, painted his face, and gave him a fine tur-
quoise mask, making him appear so handsome that he had to cel-
ebrate. He was then tempted with wine: first just a sip, then more,
until he became intoxicated. His sister Quetzalpetlatl was similarly tempted into inebriation, and in this carefree state the two in-
dulged in an act of incest. Later, in remorse, Quetzalcoatl immo-
lated himself on his own funeral pyre.

"That derives from this legend on the tablet!" Don exclaimed.
"The symbolism, the elements of illness and incest—only the bull
has been eliminated!"

Splendid nodded, eyes bright.

"And the bull—that carried on through the Minoan culture,"
Don continued, seeing whole sections of the puzzle fall into place.
"The Greek legend of Theseus—it derives from the same source!
According to it, King Minos controlled the seas, but his wife became enamored of a bull, and finally concealed herself inside a
wooden cow in order to couple with the bull. Then she gave birth
to the Minotaur, a man with the head of a bull, who fed on human flesh. He was confined to the Labyrinth—the Greeks' notion
of the complex Minoan palace, in whose center court the bull-
leapers performed. But the Greeks transferred his hero-properties
to their prince Theseus, who slew him. The mythic lineage is
plain, now. A forbidden sexual act that spawns a man-creature
with godlike properties who finally dies ignominiously, in both
the Mayan and Minoan/Greek versions."

AND SO WE VERIFY ATLANTIS, she wrote.

"*And* the ancient sea empire," Don agreed. "It explains so
much. Like that fabulous sunken Yucatan city, that Pi-ja apparently didn't know about—and the later Dzibilchaltun, whose

source of culture was such a mystery."

Then he had to explain about that, for of course Splendid hadn't known of the submerged city. She knew about Dzibilchaltun, though, and was fascinated by the apparent connection.

At last they returned to the manuscript. New horizons had opened, and Don was in a hurry to assimilate the remainder, for the rest of his group was overdue to return. He would have been more concerned about what was delaying them, had he not been so distracted by the Minoan manuscript.

I conjecture this: our bull and snake honoring ancestors of many thousands of years past emerged from the coastline of Anatolia, becoming a great seafaring nation. Soon they spread even to Atlantis, perhaps under some great king whose birth was clouded: illegitimate, possibly, the result of covert incest. Thus his identification as the anomaly of the feathered bull. The wealth to be derived from widespread trade would account for this basic initiative, and there would be a powerful civilizing effect wherever this trade touched, as there has been in the case of our own missions about the Aegean and other islands and peninsulas. The case of the Greek tribes may seem hopeless, but even there there are signs of promise. But under poor kings even the soundest empire becomes weak, and there may have been extensive natural catastrophes. Again, as we know from bitter experience. So the empire that spawned all the present cultures of the world at length passed, and was almost forgotten.

But I could discourse interminably on the ways and legends of these people. It must suffice to establish that they differ in many ways from our own culture, but not so completely that we could not accommodate. And that is the problem. For if we adapt too amicably to their customs, and marry their women, and become absorbed in their culture— then we shall surely lose our own identity. We were not spared the holocaust of our island, we did not survive the ferocity of the ocean storm, we did not endure the mutiny of the hungry crew merely for this!

So I did what I had learned with such difficulty when the captain died at sea, and I assumed once more the leadership of our remaining group. There was some strenuous resistance, but I performed as necessary, even to distasteful

bloodshed, and we won free and set sail by night. North-
ward across the round sea, bearing toward the place we understood there was a colony of kinsmen. If we could join
these, our situation would be better.

"Don! Don!"

Don jumped, startled. It was as if Pi-ja-se-me had called to him
directly! But it was the radio, which he had left on in the hope
that Melanie would respond to one of the Germanic spelling
broadcasts.

"I'm h-here," he said, reorienting. "What—?"

"Don, return instantly! And be careful! I cannot—"

There was a click, and Don was unable to get further response.
The other radio was off.

Splendid was evidently annoyed by this abrupt interruption of
the Minoan narrative. HER VOICE HAS CHANGED.

"That's not Melanie! It's Eleph! And something's wrong. He's
not one to play games—" He paused. "He doesn't even have a radio, now. He must have been using Gaspar's, or one of the others.
And someone must have stopped him. Why?"

THERE MUST BE TROUBLE IN YOUR PARTY.

"Yes! I should have been suspicious about this long radio silence. I have to get back. When Eleph cries for help--" But again
he paused. "The translation! I may never have another chance. I
can't go without finishing that!"

I CANNOT GO WITH YOU, Splendid wrote. THE COLD
AND THE SALT AND THE PREDATORS OF THE MARINE—

"And Pi-ja's request! I agreed to honor it—but I don't know
what it is. But if I keep Eleph waiting—I know I can't afford to
waste any time!" Don was not a man of decisive action in a crisis;
he felt himself falling apart. What should he do?

Splendid looked at him compassionately while her hand print-
ed her message. COMPROMISE. PROMISE TO SPEAK WELL OF
US TO YOUR PEOPLE, AND I WILL HELP YOU RETURN
SWIFTLY.

"You can't help me! The phase—"

But she was still writing. THE OLD WOMAN TOOK AWAY
YOUR ROPES. WE CAN SHOW YOU A BETTER ROUTE.

Don was aghast. "Pacifa wouldn't take away the lines! I need
them to climb out of this trench! The cliffs—"

"She did, you know," Melanie said suddenly on the radio. "She told me we might need the rope, and it seemed to make sense at the time. I never thought—"

"Melanie! Where have you—?"

"Something *is* wrong," she said. "Nobody else has used the radio since we split into two parties. Except you and me. And now Eleph. I—"

"You refused to t-talk to me!"

"I was in a jealous snit. Because—well, never mind. I thought the radio silence was just to keep from alerting the sub to the locations of the others. But Eleph wasn't fooling. I can tell."

"Why didn't you say something before? I never realized—"

"And interrupt your charming relationship with that fishwife? You can go to hell for all I care! But not Eleph. You've got to go back!"

Don caught a movement, and turned to see Splendid swimming swiftly away. "Wait!" he cried. "I agree to your compromise! I—"

Then he saw that her tablet was filled with writing. He moved over to read it.

"*What* compromise?" Melanie demanded.

"The mer-people will show me a fast route back to the depot, if I agree to speak for them when I get back. I really don't know much about them—"

"*Don't* you?"

"I think they're afraid of the U.S. reaction to their presence here. You know, the depth-bomb psychology. They mean no harm; they're practicing for colonization of Jupiter. But Splendid just took off. She left a message—"

"Well, read it!"

Don read aloud: IT WILL TAKE ABOUT AN HOUR TO GET THE INFORMATION FROM OUR PERIMETER GUARD. I WILL RETURN WITH A MAP YOU CAN COPY. MEANWHILE, TRANSLATE THE END OF THE NARRATIVE. YOU CAN KEEP BOTH PROMISES.

"*Two* promises?"

"Melanie, the author of the tablets made a condition for anyone who reads them. Splendid and I have been translating the whole time. Didn't she explain that in the German?"

"Yes," Melanie admitted. "She also said you goosed her."

"Well, she deserved it! And if you don't stop being so cynical, I'll goose *you*, first chance. I tell you, we never—"

"That's three promises," Melanie muttered.

"So you know you don't have reason to—"

"Well—"

"Melanie, I love you! I—"

She was evidently startled. "But—"

"But Splendid has a glorious head of hair. So I've been exposed to that, now. And I know. So if you—"

"If you repeat that when we get together again, I'll say it too. But that's personal. Right now you have to get on that translation."

"Yes. I—I'll see you soon, Melanie. I hope. Then—"

"Then," she agreed. She clicked off. He knew this was to guarantee him the undistracted time he needed.

Don pored over the remaining tablets, picking out those symbols he could read easily so as to get a rough gist before settling down to the final one. He was pegging in meanings with a facility that amazed him. He could almost read the text straight, now!

Pi-ja, it seemed, had directed the ship north toward the American Gulf coast, searching for the settlement whose descendants would be known as the Yuchi Indians. But another storm, or perhaps an arm of the Gulf Stream, carried them east and south, at last brushing the north shore of Cuba. There his men jumped overboard and swam for shore, for what reason Don wasn't clear. But Pi-ja-se-me seemed to be an extraordinarily capable and hard-nosed leader, despite his literary background. He had invented magic to cow the superstitious, and perhaps had overdone it. But he was suffering again from debilitating illness, possibly nutritional deficiency symptoms.

At any rate, only one loyal slave remained. The two attempted to sail the ship, but lacked the ability to do more than keep it clear of the shoals. It was in poor condition, with its repairs haphazard after the hurricane that had sunk the other two ships, and a tattered partial sail on the stripped mast was all they could muster. Mostly it drifted, while Pi-ja wrote his long memoirs, baking each finished tablet in the galley hearth. Apparently the ship passed all around Cuba and between it and the island of Haiti, losing its mast in another storm, and was progressing back toward the Yucatan when Pi-ja called a halt. His augurs had identified this particular spot as most propitious for his purpose. He had his slave bail water *into* the ship, already half swamped by the storm, until it sank. The implication was that ship and passengers went down together.

Then the final passage:

I have considered carefully the destruction of my own world. We were a prosperous, carefree people, much given to pleasure, but we knew our gods and took them seriously. I remain satisfied that in no way did we renege on our rituals prior to the calamity. In fact our religious exercises had become more detailed as our wealth and power waxed, and many more youths of either sex were sacrificed in the bull-leapings than had been done in prior centuries. Almost every year we had a champion who performed so well as to complete the leap uninjured and in perfect form. Had the Earth Mother chosen to rebuke us, she should have done it long ago, before our faith and technique were perfect. Almost, it seems, our very closeness to our subject was our undoing, for the farther away any given city was from Thera, the less it suffered.

So I am forced to a conclusion that counters the faith of my lifetime: *Our Gods do not care.* Our worship was vain, not because the object was false, as it demonstrably was not, but because of our conceit that anything we might offer could have any conceivable ameliorating effect on that arrogant Power. We are as ants before the hoof of the bull: neither our love nor our hate can mitigate the weight and placement of that deadly tread. We were fools ever to think otherwise, and we have paid the ultimate price.

Oh, scholar, honor then my charge: Build not on the flank of the Bull. Delude not yourself about the propensities of the Beast, by whatever guise it manifests. Imagine not that you can propitiate it by dances or offerings or prayer, lest that monster heave without reason or warning and destroy all that you have wrought.

Chapter 15

•

Crisis

Proxy 5-12-5-16-8: Attention.
[No answer.]
Status?
[No answer.]

●   ●   ●

Don looked up. Splendid was back. He had continued translating aloud, from habit and for Melanie's benefit (if she tuned in), and knew that the mermaid had heard enough.

"Do you know," Melanie said after a moment, "we have already built on the flank of the bull. We call it the Bomb."

Don nodded, though she could not see him. "It's a bigger bull than that. Nuclear power has enormous advantages and equivalent liabilities. But it's only one facet of the danger to our species and world. We are overrunning the planet, enslaving or destroying all other species. The climate is changing, deserts are being made, the sea is dying. Maybe we are the bull, this time. The world is too small for us. But we have no way to get off. Nowhere to go."

EXCEPT TO GO TO JUPITER, Splendid wrote.

"Maybe so," Don agreed after reading her words to Melanie. "I'll do what I can—for Eleph and Jupiter." Yet he suffered a background doubt. Could this be all of it? Just to come here and read the Minoan warning? Meet the mermaid? These things somehow seemed incidental to whatever mission might have been set up. Who had set it up? And what had gone wrong? Why had Pacifa seemingly arranged to isolate him here, by taking the ropes and not returning? Where was Gaspar, and why was he maintaining radio silence in the face of this situation?

Pi-ja's story might be over, but Don's wasn't. And it might not have any happier ending. Key pieces were missing.

Splendid swam to the edge of the deck, then hovered, waiting for him to let himself down. By the time he was ready to ride from the ship, she had another message:

ONE STRANGE THING. WE FOUND TRACES IN THE SHIP. NO BONES, BUT METAL BELTS AND JEWELRY. IT SEEMED TO US THAT THE ARTIFACTS NEAR THE CACHE OF TAB-LETS WERE FEMALE.

For a moment Don was stunned. Then he shook it off. "That narrative was written by a man."

She paused to write again. THERE IS TROUBLE IN YOUR CAMP. WE DON'T KNOW THE MOTIVES OF THE OTHERS, BUT TRUST YOU.

"Well, thanks, Splendid. But I have no idea what's going on."

YES, YOU ARE INNOCENT.

That, it seemed, was his prime recommendation.

Splendid swam ahead, and he followed, riding rapidly across the rocky floor of the sea. She led him down the trench below the ship, then up out of the canyon by a winding path and onto a broad plain. In a surprisingly short time they arrived at the mer-colony.

The artifacts were not impressive. A cluster of cylindrical tanks evidently deposited by submarine and camouflaged so as to be difficult to spot from above. Several vertical nets, perhaps intended to strain fish out of the moving current—or possibly a kind of defense, as there weren't many fish in this freshwater enclave. And the mer-people themselves: seven or eight women and about a dozen men. All were well proportioned, the women running to large breasts, the men to powerful chests. Don realized that this might not be a matter of mammary or muscle. They probably needed extraordinary lung capacity to make use of the meager oxygen in the water, and a padding of fat to protect their vital organs, accounting for their notable attributes. The men had no visible genitals, but did have a kind of codpiece effect in the arrangement of their scales. Streamlining, of course.

Then he saw the submarine. Similar to the one they had encountered before. Don felt an apprehensive chill. It was coming clear how the mer-people had known about the status of the ropes. The sub had indeed kept track of the party. Had it found a way to mess up the other members, perhaps taking them captive one my one? Was this a trap for one more? "They have a sub," he murmured to Melanie.

Splendid tried to reassure him. WE KNOW YOU SAW ONE OF OUR PERIMETER GUARDS. THE MACHINE IS HERE TO HELP YOU. ONLY IT CAN LEAD THE WAY OUT OF THE TRENCH. TRUST US AS WE TRUST YOU.

Well put! Of course they had submarines; how else could this colony be supplied? It was now to the interest of the Chinese to assist him—or to kill him. If Gaspar or Pacifa had gotten away and could not be stopped, then only Don or Melanie could speak in favor of this mer-project. But his intuition told him that these folk were not hostile to his mission; they were coincidental to it. Splendid seemed like a fine creature. He had to trust them. They only wanted to be left alone to complete their project. He hoped.

Then he realized what Splendid meant. "Oh—to hitch a ride!" For the submarine could go where the mer-peoople couldn't, into the cold salt water. The cliffs of the trench would be no barrier to it.

Splendid laughed in her silent way, then looked thoughtful. The other mer-people did not understand English; at least they did not react. Had Splendid told them about the phase?

THE GLOVE—Splendid wrote.

"The balloons. Of course. If I can have a handhold, and carry my bike too—"

"Is that safe?" Melanie asked. "I was always warned against hitching rides on trucks—with a bike, I mean."

"Safer than climbing those cliffs without anchored ropes! The sub could cut my time in half!"

"But if it dropped you—"

"I'd smash. I wish you hadn't brought that up, Melanie. But I have to trust them. And I do. Just from knowing Splendid, I'm convinced they're—"

"Oh?" Melanie interjected with a certain emphasis. He'd have to stop mentioning the mermaid!

"I wish I could stay and really study their c-culture," he said a bit lamely. "There are mer*men* here too, you know. Tritons. It's a whole v-village."

"So I gather." She seemed mollified.

HERE ARE CHARTS, Splendid wrote. THEY WILL HELP YOU. CAN YOU CARRY THEM? COPYING WOULD TAKE A LONG TIME.

"Can you fold them tight and put them in a small packet? I could carry that wrapped in a balloon."

"So you *did* use a balloon," Melanie said accusingly.

"N-not the way you th-think!"

"N-no?" she mimicked. "Just how do you think I *think*? And you were being so upset about my being on the pill!"

Splendid, meanwhile, went to one of the mermen to explain, using sign language Don could not follow. The man's face was expressive. First he nodded agreeably. Then his brow furrowed. Then he looked angry.

"Uh-oh," Don murmured to Melanie. "I think that triton she's talking to is her mate, and now he has a notion about the balloon too."

"Serves you right," Melanie said gleefully. "Hey, merman! Let me tell you about—"

Don hastily snapped off the radio. As if he didn't have problems enough! Melanie might be teasing him, since Splendid had already explained things, but such words could be dangerous.

Soon the job was done, despite the glower of the muscular triton. Don was glad to see the sub lift, so that he could tie on firmly to the rail at its base.

Splendid waved good-bye, one breast heaving in unison with her arm, as sub, bike, and man rose into the sea. Don didn't wave back, as he had to hang on and the triton still looked extremely ugly.

The journey itself was almost disappointing. The submarine lifted high, so that the opacity of sea water closed in and fogged out sight of land. Don soon lost his bearings, and had to depend on the changing coordinates on his meter. His head brushed the bottom of the sub, and passed through it, reminding him distressingly how slight his support was. If even one balloon gave way—

but of course it wouldn't.

He looked ahead, but there was only the great light spearing out, now and then impaling stray fish. That made Don wonder where Glowcloud was. He missed the giant mollusk.

He had underestimated the capacity of the sub. It plowed through the water at phenomenal velocity, though with almost no sound. It felt like fifty miles an hour, but was probably closer to twenty five. The Chinese had to know more about the construction of such machines than the other nations suspected. He was glad that he saw no evidence of missile or torpedo ports. He wanted to believe this was a peaceful project.

In just two hours they glided to land in the shallows just north of Jamaica. They had agreed to stand by for two days in case he needed more help. A slate was provided for messages. It turned out that the sub had not been able to tune in on the phase radio; their communications had been private all along. But it could pick up the sounds of their travel, so had known their whereabouts. It was amazing the cooperation Splendid had been able to arrange. "An apple a day keeps the depth bombs away," Don muttered a bit cynically.

He disengaged, took down his balloons, used them to tie the charts low on the bike frame, and pedaled through the base of the sub. His fully-phased upper section encountered only trace resistance, and the balloons and charts were now below the sub, experiencing only the drag of the water. He was curious about something. Yes! Regular human beings were manning the sub, not tritons. Their faces turned to him in amazement as he waved and coasted out the far side.

Now, abruptly, he was nervous. What *had* happened to Eleph? What *were* Gaspar and/or Pacifa up to?

He stopped after a couple of miles, waiting silently to see whether the sub was trailing him. Meanwhile he used the balloon-gloves to fumble open the package of charts. It made an uncomfortable resistance as he rode, because the charts were of the same phase as the water. But they were remarkable detailed, much better than the maps they had been using. The colony must have supervised a really thorough survey.

Two routes were marked through the complex trench terrain, calculated to avoid cliffs of more than six foot elevation. Either would have cut many hours off his journey.

As it was, he would arrive less than four hours after Eleph's terse call, instead of fifty. That was very good.

The sub did not seem to be following. Reassured, Don resumed his ride, centering on the depot coordinates. He slowed again when within a mile. Eleph must have had good reason for advising caution, before that abrupt cutoff. Yet Gaspar and Pacifa were nice people, under their sometimes crusty exteriors. Why should either make trouble?

But when he moved quietly to the depot, there was only one figure there. "Melanie!"

"Don! How—?"

"The mer-folk gave me a lift, so I'm back much sooner."

She waited for him to draw close, then stepped into his embrace. "I'm sorry I was so bitchy," she said. "This business—"

"That mermaid—there really wasn't—"

"I know. I was so lonely for you, and then when I had you on the radio, all I did was quarrel with you. I've never been in—I mean, I don't know how to handle emotion like—"

"I have a notion," he said. He hugged her tight.

Then they kissed. Maybe it was the excitement of his fast, unusual trip back, or maybe the heightened emotions of their argument, or maybe just her. It was like the discovery of the Minoan Manuscript.

But there was pressing business. "What's been happening? Where are the others?"

"I don't know. I don't think Gaspar and Eleph ever came back here, and Pacifa must have gone to join them. She told me to wait here while she checked around, and then she was gone. I've been going crazy, worrying."

"Do you think their radio silence means anything?"

"It must. But what?"

"I don't think it has anything much to do with the mer-colony," he said. "They seem innocent."

"How would you know?" she asked sharply.

He spread his hands. "I guess I don't."

"Well, I believe it. They helped you return here in record time, and that's a monstrous relief to me. And your splendid fishwife—with nerve like hers, why should she bother lying to an innocent like you?"

"But if it's something else—some other crisis—why the radio

silence? I mean, if someone got hurt, they'd call for help."

"I don't know," Melanie said, frustrated. "But there certainly is something, and it has to involve Pacifa, because she deliberately stranded you there at the ship, she thought. Maybe Gaspar is in on it too. So Eleph tried to warn us."

"But Pacifa is a good person! She wouldn't—"

She laughed somewhat bitterly. "Men of any age aren't very smart about women of any age. *Women* aren't dumb about women. Though how I managed to fall for that business about taking up the ropes—"

"But if all of you were planning to come back, then the ropes would have been placed again."

"Only that evidently wasn't the plan. I'd have had to do it alone, and I'm not competent. I was isolated too, except for the radio, and I didn't dare blab my suspicions there."

"So what do you think—?"

"I think Pacifa had a mission from the start, and separating us had something to do with it, and now she's completing it—and we'd better find out what it is and stop her, before—"

He nodded. "All we can do is look for them—carefully."

She looked at his bicycle. "What is that?"

"Oh, the mer-folk gave me some charts of the area, so I can find my way around. They were going to show me the best routes, but then they gave me the lift on their sub, but I took the charts anyway, because they know something's wrong and want to help. They said I would need them I—I made a deal. They're just testing how adaption works under pressure, so they can adapt people for colonizing Jupiter. Now that their presence here is known, they just want America to know that's all there is to it. I promised to do my best to—"

"Yes, of course. Let's take a look."

He used the balloon-gloves and opened the charts again. They were indeed detailed; they were contour maps with special sites marked, such as the mer-colony, the Minoan ship, and the extent of the freshwater region. Also the supply depot.

"They didn't need to follow us," Don said. "They knew where we were going, all the time."

"And they didn't interfere," Melanie said. "Unless that other depot—?"

"We didn't see any evidence that anything had ever been

there," he reminded her. "I think that was our own foulup—I mean, whoever set up this mission."

"Yes. We still don't know who hired us, or for what." She peered more closely. "What's that?" She poked her finger through the chart without touching it.

He looked. "Two dots. Not far from here, by bike. Another supply depot?"

"That's not the depot symbol."

Now he saw something else. "Look—there's one dot at the ship. And one here. Where we have been."

"Those dots are *people!* One for you. One for me. And two others."

"Where's the fifth?" he asked.

They looked, but could not find a fifth dot. "They marked every member of our party by location, and kept it right up to date," she said. "But one of us is missing."

"Eleph?"

"He couldn't have been alone, because he didn't have a good radio. And someone cut him off. So he must be one of the two."

"Then that's where I have to go. Since I'm two days faster than anyone expects, my arrival may be a surprise. Maybe I can learn from him just what's going on."

"I'm coming too!" she said.

"But there may be danger."

"What safety is there in being alone? I've had more than enough of it, these past two days."

"Glad to have you with me," he agreed.

They set off for the two dots, radios remaining off. Don wasn't sure whether to be glad for the murky water; it prevented him from seeing far ahead, but also shielded him from the view of others. He took care to make no noise as they approached the place marked, and hooded his light. But he had to have some light to see, as the site was low enough to be dark.

He gestured to Melanie to stay back. Then he moved directly to the dots.

A tent was there, pitched onto a slope as if to allow for drainage. Don felt about himself—then realized with a shock that he was actually searching for some kind of weapon! What would he do with a weapon? If he had a gun, he wouldn't know at whom to point it, and wouldn't have the nerve to shoot it. He was just here to find out what was going on.

Still, if Gaspar were in on it—the man was powerful and stubborn, and experienced under the water. Don was very poorly equipped to tangle—

This was ridiculous! Don nerved himself and hailed the tent. "Hello!"

There was no response. But he saw the wheel of a bicycle. Eleph's, by the look of it.

"Eleph!" he cried, going in.

Eleph was there—but he was unconscious. Don tried to shake the man awake, but had no success. Apparently he had been drugged.

There was no sign of the other person. Who had done this? Had Eleph been left here to die? No, the tent had been carefully pitched, open on both ends to channel the gentle current through, providing oxygen. Food packages and water were in easy reach. When Eleph woke, he would have no trouble getting along. He had merely been put out of the way for a few hours. Just as Pacifa had tried to isolate Don and Melanie.

Don cast about for an antidote, but realized that without specific knowledge of the drug used, it would be dangerous for him to tamper. Pacifa had had something that lasted for about four hours; she had used it to put Eleph out, so that they could set his arm. This was probably the same. The man seemed to be resting comfortably.

Don went out and signaled Melanie in. He explained the situation. "One of them must have drugged him, after he called me. That was about five hours ago, so the drug should be wearing off soon."

"They never expected you back this fast," she said. "Or that you'd have a chart that gave you this location. So he must have been drugged to prevent him from taking off while the other person went on some errand. This is our chance to do something."

"Yes, but do what? By the time he wakes, the other will be back."

"Unless we wake him sooner." She knelt by Eleph and patted his face.

"That won't work. I shook him, and—"

"He's coming to!" she exclaimed. "Come on, get him up on his feet. Time is critical."

Don obeyed. He hauled on Eleph, forgetting about the man's arm, while Melanie helped from the other side. They got him into a sitting position. Eleph groaned and opened his eyes.

Slowly he recognized Don. He smiled. "Get me to my feet," he said with difficulty. "That will make it wear off more rapidly. My head is spinning—it seems like only hours since I called you."

"It was," Melanie said. "What happened, Eleph?"

But the man was holding his breath to keep from crying out with pain as they struggled to get him up. It was complicated because of the confined space and the three bikes and the man's injury. But soon they were tramping back and forth between parked bicycles.

"Who drugged you?" Don asked.

"Gaspar. But do not blame him. He was trying to give Pacifa time.

"What did I tell you!" Melanie exclaimed. "What's she up to? Is it the mer-colony?"

"He doesn't know about that yet," Don reminded her.

Eleph winced, but not from physical pain. "I am sorry, Don. I *do* know. I have not been candid with you."

"'That is the understatement of the mission," Gaspar said behind them.

Don whirled around, inadvertently yanking Eleph. If he had had any notion of catching anyone unawares, the initiative had now been reversed. Gaspar was unencumbered, while Don and Melanie had to support Eleph. Not that either would have been any match for the man, physically, under any circumstances.

"What are you talking about?" Melanie demanded.

"Why did you drug this man?" Don asked almost at the same time. "Why have you been keeping radio silence, when the sub couldn't intercept it?"

"We had reason," Gaspar said, maintaining a distance of about six feet. "Pacifa and I knew something was up. Both of you were straight, obviously. But we suspected that Eleph wasn't what he seemed. So we arranged to isolate him."

"So Pacifa *is* in on it," Melanie said. "And she's fooled Gaspar."

"Why did Pacifa remove my return ropes?" Don demanded. "The two of you have been acting a lot more suspiciously than Eleph ever did!"

"She had to be sure you stayed put, until we had a chance to work this thing out," Gaspar said evenly. "We would have preferred to have Melanie stay with you at the ship, but the mermaid complicated that, so Pacifa brought her back."

"Work *what* thing out?" Don was getting angry now.

"The fact that Eleph represents a foreign universe."

"*What?*" Don and Melanie said together. Don wasn't sure which of them was more vehement.

"Not exactly foreign," Eleph said. "And not inimical."

"Will you tell the truth now?" Gaspar asked him.

"I must have appropriate clearance. Give me my communicator."

Gaspar shook his head. "And let you call in an alien strike? No way."

Don could hardly believe this. Eleph was some kind of agent?

"Where's Pacifa?" Melanie inquired urgently.

Don realized that this was relevant. Pacifa had every reason to be here, and her absence was as ominous as Eleph's admission.

"I know," Eleph said, looking at his watch. "She departed twelve hours ago for your home base on land. We have to stop her!"

"You can't stop her," Gaspar said. "You could never keep up with her, let alone make up that hundred mile head start. None of us could."

Don thought of the waiting Chinese submarine. He could catch her—if he had to. But he was hardly going to advertise that to Gaspar now! "Why is she doing that?"

"Because someone has to notify our government that our world is being infiltrated by alien agents."

Don would have laughed had he not been so concerned. "You sound the way I thought Eleph did, once! And Pacifa was the one always talking about Cuba. But now you're both accusing Eleph! What evidence do you have—for anything?"

"This," Gaspar said. He brought out a small object. "Do you recognize it?"

"A locket," Melanie said. "Eleph's; he wears it on a chain around his neck."

"But it's phased," Gaspar finished. "Otherwise I could hardly handle it like this, could I! He has had it all along."

"A phased locket," Melanie said. "Of course it is; it went

through the tunnel with him. What's wrong with that?"

"Watch." Gaspar touched a finger to the little locket, and it sprang open. "Merely a ruse, you see. A tiny transceiver, not the kind we carry. Do you know what it is tuned to?"

No one answered. Gaspar turned it on.

"*No, I'm afraid that won't work,*" a woman's voice was saying faintly. "*They have electronic guards. If I try to phase through, the alarm will sound.*"

"*But there is a world at stake!*" a gruff man's voice responded. "*You have to get through!*"

"*There are a million worlds at stake,*" she retorted. "*Do you mean to risk them all for the sake of this one?*"

There was a pause. "*Sorry, I'm overtired. Near the end of my shift, and we lost three more during it. Very well, you're on the spot. Better your way. Off.*"

There was another pause. Then: "*Proxy 5-12-5-16-12: Attention.*"

"*Acknowledging.*"

"*Status?*"

"*Extreme doubt. They have sought to imprison me.*"

"*But your mission was going well!*"

"*This was illusory. I now realize that they were playing me along, hoping to capture my technology. They refuse to heed my message.*"

"*Then we must terminate your mission.*"

"*I'm afraid this is the case. I regret my failure.*"

"*Stand by for recovery.*"

There was another pause. Then another call for a proxy, by a different number.

Gaspar clicked it off "That goes on continuously," he said. "That's the net that Eleph is on. Always different, always the same. Crisis to crisis. Worlds blowing up. A real alien invasion. If they don't subvert a world, they destroy it."

"No!" Eleph cried. "That's not it at all!"

Don looked at him, appalled. "The city! The ship! You set this all up! Why—?"

"Something we'd all like to know," Gaspar said. "But he won't talk."

"Now, wait, give Eleph a chance," Melanie protested. "He said he would explain, if he gets clearance."

"Tell me how you make contact," Gaspar said.

"Let me sit down," Eleph said. "I am not in good form at the moment."

"Of course," Melanie said solicitously. She and Don helped him get comfortable.

"I am of Earth," Eleph said. "I am human, and of this culture. You can verify this by the language: it is the same on my communicator. But not *this* Earth. I have come to save your world. That is all I can tell you, without clearance."

"You are not getting your hands on this radio!" Gaspar said.

"Maybe you can answer for him," Melanie suggested. "For the clearance."

Gaspar was surprised. "Eleph?"

Eleph nodded. "It will have to do. It is difficult to distinguish individual voices on this curcuit. Turn it on, and when you hear this world's number, acknowledge."

"Number?"

"Proxy 5-12-5-16-8. I am the proxy for this alternate world, which is one of twenty in this frame."

"What's that number again?"

"Perhaps the mnemonic will help. If you number the alphabet, with the letter A being the number one, and B number two, and so on, it spells out E L E P H. 5-12-5-16-8."

"Got it," Gaspar said. "And how do I report?"

"You will be asked for your status. Then simply say that you request permission to clarify the mission for the locals. It will be granted. Then I can tell you."

"If you know it will be granted," Melanie asked, "why not simply tell us now?"

"We have to coordinate. Central must know the status of each mission constantly, especially when one is in trouble."

Gaspar shrugged and turned on the special radio.

" . . . *political situation here is deteorating, and I'll need central guidance, if I haven't blown it already. The president will not be moved on this issue, and unless I reveal myself—*"

"*No! You know that is out of the question, in this situation.*"

"*But there is a diminishing chance that—*"

"*OVERRIDE!*" a man's voice cut in. "*I have failed. The alternate faction has launched a full strike.*"

"*Phase out!*"

"*No. It was my miscalculation. I must remain. Just put a prohibition for all remaining—"*

There was a ghastly sound that abruptly cut off. Eleph winced.

In a moment the first man's voice resumed. *"GENERAL OVERRIDE: Option fifty twenty one demonstrated ineffective. Proxy lost. Prohibition for that course for all alternates within—"* Unintelligible gabble followed. Then the man resumed normal transmission. *"Attention, 16-19. Word from Central: appeal to his vanity. Do you require detail?"*

"Not yet. Off."

Gaspar looked at the others. "This can continue forever!"

"No; they check each proxy frequently," Eleph said.

Sure enough, a few minutes later the number came.

Proxy 5-12-5-16-8: Attention.

Gaspar jumped. "Acknowledging."

Status?

"Permission to inform locals of mission."

"16-8, why have you not acknowledged recent calls?"

"The locals made me captive," Gaspar said with a straight face. "Now I must explain the mission if I am to have further access to this radio."

Do so. We shall call again. Off.

Gaspar looked at Eleph, who nodded. "The essence is simple," he said. "There are a seemingly infinite number of alternate worlds, the adjacent ones very similar to each other. But a considerable number of them face a life-destroying threat. It is a particular type of meteor that—"

"A calcium meteor?" Gaspar asked.

"Why yes. It—"

"It grazes the atmosphere and fragments, interacting with the water of the planet, forming calcium oxide. Not too much damage to the physical features, if it powders thinly enough, other than crusting them. But most or even all of the water could be gone."

"What are you talking about?" Don asked.

"The phase world," Gaspar said. "I've thought about that quite a bit. It's just like ours, only without water, therefore without life. If a meteor with a dark shell came, the telescopes could miss it until too late, and we couldn't stop it anyway. We don't have the technology to intercept something that massive and fast. But there's one thing I can't figure. That world should be buried in ash, especially in the ocean basins. Miles deep, perhaps. That's obviously not the case here. Calcium oxide is fierce stuff. Touch it and you're burned."

"The ash is there," Eleph said. "The phase takes care of that, too. The ashes are phased out, leaving only the stripped world for us to relate to."

"The phase," Gaspar agreed. "Of course. And the weight of that ash prevents the sea-floor from rebounding, so it still matches our world almost exactly."

"I thought you were against him," Melanie said to Gaspar.

"I just want to know the truth," Gaspar replied evenly. "He brought us on this wild chase. There has to be a reason."

"You mean you're the one who set this up?" Don asked, surprised.

"I am," Eleph said. "This is another world facing the disaster of the comet. But this is not the normal type of collision, such as generated the waves of extinctions including those of the dinosaurs. This is a fluke that will extinguish all life on Earth. Indeed it has done so, on countless worlds, and is proceeding to others."

"Wait," Don said. "If it has already happened, where it's going to, then we're out of danger, right?"

"Not so. The worlds differ slightly in time as well as substance. The meteor has already struck some, is striking others, and will strike the rest, in this sector of the spread. We know this, because we are seeing it happen. It is my mission to warn your world of this threat, so that it can expend its effort and resources to save itself."

"Why not just tell our leaders?" Gaspar asked. "Why go through this convoluted business of exploring under the ocean? We aren't significant people! We can't do anything about it."

"That is the crux," Eleph said. "We have been trying, literally, to save worlds, with a poor record for success. The true leaders of the world are generally inaccessible, both physically and intellectually. In America, a man cannot simply walk into the president's office and tell him to change his policies to save the world. The same is true in other parts of the world. Since considerable short-term sacrifice is required, even if the politician understood the need, he would be unlikely to act, because his first concern is the security of his office. We did try this route, and got nowhere, as our ongoing reports from other worlds demonstrates."

"Well, then, why not be more direct?" Melanie asked. "I mean, if you have the technology, land in the capital city in a shining space ship, or something."

"I can answer that," Gaspar said, smiling. "Such a ship would get blasted out of the air before it landed."

"It has happened," Eleph said. "We have also tried sending messages to key figures. So far these have either been ineffective, or have destablized the political situation so that mischief results."

"Such as nuclear warfare!" Don exclaimed, remembering part of the radio sequence of reports.

"Precisely," Eleph said. "While such events are not the disasters they may seem, in view of the coming total destruction by another cause, they do represent failures of our policy. It is our purpose to save worlds, not to hasten their destruction. So I am trying a completely different route. I am attempting to demonstrate the reality of the alternate world framework to a select group of ordinary residents of this world. If I can convince them, then they may be able to convince their world. That is, you can convince yours. Your world may listen to you, when it would not listen to me."

"But what has archaeology to do with this?" Don demanded.

"You, as an archaeologist, are able to appreciate the reality of the knowledge I was able to draw on, from my contact with the larger framework of worlds. I routed the party to the Yucatan ruins, and then to the Minoan ship. You know know how the phase works, and that the information it provides is genuine, not cobbled together. You believe. Also, you are in a better position to understand the cultures of other worlds that are not virtually identical to this one."

"But I have no power to influence anyone!" Don protested.

"Yes you do. You can convince Gaspar."

"But Gaspar can't influence anyone either!"

"Yes he can," Eleph said. "He is an agent of your government. They will give his report credence. Especially when he shows them the ruins and the ship, and you publicize your interpretation of the manuscript. When the four of you together speak in a way that I could not. They will see that the government takes my message seriously. In that may be the salvation of your world."

Melanie was aghast. "What a roundabout route!"

"Yes," Eleph said. "I knew you would reject it if you didn't learn much of it yourselves. So I specified the coordinates, and arranged other challenges whose purpose was to make you interact and learn to rely on each other and to trust each other. This process we call melding. It seemed to be working—until it abruptly went wrong."

"It was working," Melanie murmured, glancing sidelong at Don.

"But there are holes in it," Gaspar said.

"Holes?" Don asked. "You didn't see that ship!"

"I didn't need to. Consider this, Don: if the calcium meteor destroyed all the water and wiped out all life and in the process even leveled those ruins off Yucatan so that we could walk right through them—why did it leave your ship? That wooden vessel would have been completely destroyed, and certainly no documents would have survived."

Don was stricken. That was true!

"The ruins were not destroyed by the meteor," Eleph said. "That world was further advanced archaelogically than this one. Both ruins and ship were excavated. But for this purpose, we arranged to have a similar ship phased back in from a third world, complete, to match the one here. The ship is genuine—but the one in the phase world is not from *this* world. It is merely a prop to enable you to explore the real one. The manuscript is genuine too, as you can tell."

Eleph paused, looking tired. "Now if you can satisfy Gaspar of that, we may yet recover this mission and save your world. You are the key, Don; it depends on you."

Don looked around. He was convinced. But how could he satisfy the others?

Chapter 16

•

Mission

Gaspar frowned. "If what you say is true, we must cooperate with you to save our world."

Eleph nodded. "This is the case."

Now Don remembered how Eleph had hesitated when they had discussed governmental foul-ups, including the exploding shuttle and the wrong-shaped mirrors on the telescope. Eleph had not known of these episodes—because he was not from this world! His world would have had different episodes.

"But first we have to believe you," Gaspar said. "And I'm not sure I do. There are too many oddities. Such as the mermaid Pacifa described."

"Splendid," Don said. "She helped me translate the tablets."

"And he goosed her," Melanie said.

"What's a mermaid doing there?"

"They are Chinese," Don said. "Learning how to colonize Jupiter. The sub is theirs—bringing supplies, protecting them. They mean no harm to us, and should be left alone."

"How do you know?" Gaspar asked.

Don shrugged. "I have no reason to doubt. They helped me get here quickly. They could have dropped me and killed me, if they wanted to stop me. I did get to know Splendid somewhat, and I believe she's sincere."

"But the chances of their being right there by that ship—"

"That was not coincidence," Eleph said. "The freshwater outflow is ideal for both the colony and the ship, and they were interested in the ship anyway. And Jupiter is part of the answer."

"Answer?"

"The mer-colony was to be the last challenge for this group, before you learned of the mission. Once you saw that it is possible for man to adapt for residence on another planet, and understood how much can be done when there is dedication. Then, I believed, you would be ready to grasp the greatest of all: the saving of your world."

"How can it be saved?" Melanie asked.

"Any living things that are to be saved will have to depart Earth, and it is not possible to build enough spaceships for the whole population of human beings, animals, and plants. But Jupiter could serve as a substantial base for adapted creatures. Ordinary ocean denizens could be adapted more readily. They could be ferried there by the shipful."

"Couldn't everyone be put through the phase tunnel to a safe alternate?" Melanie asked.

"No. The phasing is an extremely limited resource, to be used only for those who are trying to save worlds. I was the only one to cross to this world, with my equipment for the recruits."

"Why not simply blow up the meteor?" Gaspar asked.

"That is another possibility. But it would require a phenomenal unified effort, because your technology is barely at the necessary level. It would be better to transfer as many people, animals, and plants to other sites as possible, in case that is not effective." Eleph took a breath. "The point is, your world can surely be saved—if it makes a concerted effort. But first your leaders must believe in the necessity, and organize the effort."

"And other worlds have not made that effort?" Gaspar asked.

"They have not. So the worlds are being lost."

"Because they don't believe," Don said.

"Or don't choose to," Melanie said. "I read about a girl, once. She was grabbed in a shopping center and hauled into a car, and no one objected. Later she managed to get away, and ran screaming down the highway, half naked, and no one stopped to help. Two days later they found her raped and strangled body in a ditch. She was ten years old."

There was a silence. What better comment was there on the nature of man? Knowledge of trouble was not enough. There had to be leadership. *Would I have stopped to help?* Don asked himself, and did not know the answer.

"Nobody will stop to save a world," Melanie said.

"How much time—before the meteor?" Gaspar asked.

"For this world, ten years."

"It couldn't be done in that time, even if everybody believed and acted," Gaspar said.

"It could—with technological advice from more advanced worlds. But it will be extremely close."

Gaspar shook his head. "I can't say I believe you, Eleph. But I don't think I can take the chance. Will you talk to my superiors if I take you to them? Will you open your communications to them? Show your technology to our experts?

"Yes, if the rest of this party will speak for my sincerity and tell what you have seen."

"Then we'd better intercept Pacifa before she reaches Florida and makes a report that brings a force to arrest or destroy us," Gaspar said. "We thought that you were working with the Chinese subs to establish a base here to compromise American interests. You won't be able to persuade anybody of your mission, once she reports that and they send a military force to take out the colony."

"No!" Don cried. "That's what the mer-folk are afraid of. I promised them—"

"How well I know," Eleph said. "My whole effort was to persuade the four of you first, so that you would help me to persuade your world. Other approaches are failing, but I hoped that this personal approach would provide me that necessary channel. I need exactly the right key to alert the right people in the right way. Then it becomes possible."

"It's an odd device," Gaspar said. "I agree with your radio contacts there."

"Well, it worked for me," Melanie said. "I believe Eleph, because I've come to know him. If you hadn't been so paranoid—"

Gaspar smiled. "I was infiltrated into this mission because my superiors were paranoid."

"I can intercept Pacifa," Don said. "The sub will help me, and I can get to the tunnel she used before she does, and stop her." Then he hesitated. "It is still there?"

"Yes," Eleph said. "It is a single unit, left there for our return."

Melanie was perplexed. "Now wait. I can see how you handled the interviews and all, with your fuzzed-up voice. You could have taken your tunnel-generating unit to Don and then to Gaspar and then to me. But you were the fourth person through. How did you get it to Pacifa?"

Eleph smiled. "I wished to conceal my nature, in case of suspicion, until the group had proper chance to meld. That was evidently ineffective, as my present situation demonstrates. So I went to Pacifa and sent her through with instructions to practice her phase technique, until the designated time for rendezvous several days later. Then I went through myself and rode down the highway to my own coordinates. It was a simple ploy."

"Which Pacifa saw through, when she reflected on it," Gaspar said. "So she knew the tunnel was still there."

Eleph nodded. "She is an intelligent woman. I deeply regret—" He did not finish.

Gaspar smiled. "She likes you too, Eleph. She was sorry to learn of your alien involvement. But her first loyalty is to her own world."

"Which I am trying to save."

"I'll have to load up on supplies, though," Don said. "I don't want to be caught hungry."

They went as a group to the depot. "Your direct route is to cut east of Cuba, while Pacifa circles it to the west," Gaspar said. "She won't go to the Yucatan, but will ride up into the Cuban coastal water if she has to. Once she intersects our prior route north of Cuba, she'll be sure of her destination. Unless that sub takes you to the Bahamas platform, you'll still have trouble beating her there."

"I'll do what I can," Don said.

"And your bike may fail. Your rear wheel is warped."

"Yours is no better," Don said.

"Mine is available," Eleph said. "It should not be difficult to adjust it to you."

Don considered the offer. "I'd feel more comfortable on my own bike. Thirty six speeds would just confuse me."

"Now *you're* being stubborn," Melanie said. "I'll bet Eleph's bicycle weighs half yours, and so does Pacifa's. You're an idiot if you race her using your old rattletrap."

Don had to concede the merit of the case. "Okay. Eleph's bike."

Eleph instructed Don on the proper use of the various mechanisms, while Gaspar selected and loaded suppplies. They set the seat and handlebars and adjusted the pedal straps. The taped metal in lieu of handgrips was disquieting, as was the narrow saddle, and it all felt ludicrously off-center, forcing him to hunch way over. The toe straps made him fear for his equilibrium should he need to put out a foot suddenly, and the reversed handles seemed impossible to use effectively. The entire machine felt strange, with everything not quite where it should be and with a different feel to the action. How was he going to steer this thing, let alone ride it? He regretted allowing himself to be brow-beaten into the change.

But before he could formulate an effective resistance, he was on his way. Once the bike was in motion, it seemed to make much more sense. He *was* able to ride, and that was what counted. He concentrated on cadence and ankling and shifting gears and guiding it with his hands set in near the stem, so he wouldn't have to lean over quite so far. He practiced pulling up on the pedals as well as pushing down, a trick impossible without these toe-straps.

It seemed he had only started, but he looked up to find himself already at the submarine. He slid two fingers over each brake lever and coasted to a beautiful stop, even remembering to disengage his feet from the straps in time. He was becoming a pro! The feel of this bicycle was growing on him.

There was a language difficulty, compounded by the phase. Don tried to explain that he needed a ride across the trench and as far around the island of Cuba as possible. They did pick him up and move—only to deliver him instead to the mer-colony.

Don simmered while the tritons stared at him contemptuously. He was trying to save the colony too, as well as to save the world, if only they would comprehend.

In due course Splendid appeared, swimming in from elsewhere. She must have been at the ship, making further notes from the tablets. She had been picking up on the Minoan Linear A, evidently having a ready mind for interpretation. He had been wrong to see her as mainly a creature of myth and sex appeal.

Don explained the present-day situation to her, stressing the need for speed. Pacifa had a one day start on him, and she could travel faster, but his route would cut the distance almost in half.

If Pacifa averaged two hundred miles per day, she would reach the base in nine or ten days. If Don averaged a hundred and fifty a day, he could do it in seven or eight, and just catch her. If the trench didn't stop him.

OUR MACHINES ARE NOT PERMITTED BEYOND THE ENVIRONS OF THE TRENCHES, she wrote. ESPECIALLY NOT NORTH OF CUBA, WHERE AMERICAN PATROLS ARE HEAVY.

This made sense. Relations between America and China were chronically mixed, with minor thaws and re-freezes occurring periodically. A Chinese submarine there would be asking for an Incident.

Yet his need was urgent. "If I don't catch that woman, the Americans will learn about your colony, which she thinks is part of a conspiracy to build a military base of some bad sort within ready range of the continent. My situation turns out to have only coincidental connection to yours, and I hope to avoid mention of your presence here, or to clarify its beneficial nature if it must be told. I know she will be persuaded, but I must catch her before she reaches the base in Florida and gives an alarm that could be very bad for you."

Splendid conferred with the mers. Don reminded himself that these were carefully selected and modified and trained people, but somehow his errant eyes kept centering on the women, with their phenomenal breasts and clouds of hair around their heads. Superficial characteristics, perhaps the largess of the same surgery that had formed their tails and modified their lungs and metabolism, but impressive regardless. The eye of the human male was fashioned to lock onto such things, and it was hard to resist this imperative. In all the time he had worked closely with Splendid, he had never become inured to the sight of her. Melanie's jealousy had been justified to that extent.

But a woman was more than body, and a man's interest was in the long run governed by more than that. Splendid had in her fashion proved to Don that such a body, even had it been fully human through to the feet, was not what he sought for a permanent association. It wasn't that Splendid's mind was bad, for it was excellent; it was that the peculiarities of Melanie's personality were a better match for the peculiarities of Don's own.

So why hadn't he said that to Melanie? Well, he would do so, the first chance he had. He had his good radio installed on Eleph's bicycle, and it was a private circuit.

Splendid swam toward him. YOU ARE CORRECT, she wrote. WE MUST ASSIST YOU DESPITE THE DANGER. THE SUB WILL TAKE YOU TO THE THOUSAND FATHOM DEPTH IN THE OLD BAHAMAS CHANNEL, HERE.

She showed him on the map. It was well around Cuba, about a third of the way along his route, and beyond the trench. From there the channel was comparatively level all the way up to Florida. That might well cut his time in half, and provide him an ample margin.

"Yes!" he exclaimed, giving her a misty kiss that made the jealous triton clench his fist. "That'll do it."

So the sub-lift resumed, though the mers were uneasy. It seemed that the danger from foreign military patrols was formidable, there in the Windward Passage between Cuba and Haiti. But the colony's supply route came through there, along the entire length of the Puerto Rico trench, so Don suspected that their apprehension was exaggerated. Splendid might trust him, but the others did not.

For an hour he passed through the nebulous reaches of the middle ocean levels. It was dull and hypnotic, and he was tired, and he nodded off to sleep astride his bicycle.

Melanie stood before him, trim and pretty. She removed her blouse, showing her bra, and then opened the bra to reveal her breasts. "How do these compare to the fishwife's?" she asked.

"Not as large," he said. "But that's not the point. I—"

"Then how does this compare?" she asked, drawing down her skirt and stepping out of it.

"Well, her, uh, she—the scales of her tail cover—but the point is—"

"She can't exactly spread her legs."

"The body doesn't matter!" he exclaimed. "I mean, not that much. She has hair, you have legs. The point is, you have all your hang-ups, and I have mine, and they make a good fit. The—the bodies—any two bodies fit, when you come down to it, but any two personalities don't mesh. I like you when you're sweet, and I like you when you're angry, and if we were two hands of cards, I think we'd make a winning combination. Maybe that's not exactly commitment, but it's a solid base for it, and if you agree I'd like to try it."

"Well, here is my body. Try it."

"That too. But I mean love. Marriage. The long term. Whatever I'm doing, I want you with me. Your body—oh, yes, I'll take it with or without the wig, and it'll be great. But your convoluted, elliptical, deviously logical mind—that's what I love."

"Is that a proposal, Don?"

"Yes! Marry, me, Melanie, after we save the world."

"After we save the world," she agreed.

"Is that an elliptical yes?" he asked, excited.

"An elliptical yes," she agreed.

That shocked him awake. He was still riding beneath the submarine. "Damn it! I was dreaming!"

"No you weren't," she retorted.

He glanced down. His radio was on! He must have done that in his sleep. "You mean I was talking in my sleep?"

"You mean you didn't mean it?"

"I meant it! If I said what I dreamed I said."

"You said the mesh of personalities was more important than the mesh of bodies. I gather there was some body-meshing going on."

"Not yet. But if you care to repeat what you did there, outside my dream—"

She laughed. "With or without the wig?"

"Yes!"

"Then it seems we have a date."

"Date, hell! We have an engagement."

"That, too," she agreed.

His radio was fading. It lasted only a few minutes when he wasn't riding. He reached down to spin the wheel, cranking it up again. "Oh, Melanie, why couldn't we have had this dialogue when we were together?"

"My, you *are* eager to mesh!"

"That, too." They laughed together, and it was great. Maybe their physical separation had enabled him to be bolder. He hadn't stuttered at all. The luck of his dream, and of the radio being on—

No, they had to be linked. He had unconsciously turned it on, and gone into his fancy—and she had joined it and accepted. He had been able to do in partial reality what had balked him in reality, and then it had turned real, and now it was wonderful.

He was jolted by a sudden change of course. He grabbed onto his bike and fought to maintain equilibrium. "Hoo!" he exclaimed.

"What's happening?" Melanie cried faintly, for he was no longer spinning the wheel.

He grabbed it and turned it vigorously. "The sub is maneuvering wildly! It's going down. I'm straining at my balloon-moorings."

"But why?"

"Wish I knew!"

But in a moment he figured it out: the sub had passed close to the American navel base at Guantanamo, an action which begged for trouble. There had been no choice, because the trench passed that region. So an American sub had fired first, asking no questions.

Then a shark-shape swam in from behind, following the sub unerringly, and he understood. A homing torpedo. The threat of this region had not been exaggerated!

A smaller fish shot out of one of the sub's ports and moved to intercept the torpedo. There was an immense explosion.

Don was not directly affected, because of the phase. But the sound was deafening, and the bucking of the sub seemed about to tear him and his bicycle loose. It seemed that the sub was not defenseless.

"Don! Don!" Melanie cried desperately.

"I'm here," he gasped. "Torpedo—they stopped it—but we're going down."

Now the vibration of the sub's motor was gone, and the machine was drifting as if dead. Don wondered why, since it hadn't been hit. Then he realized that this was part of its defensive strategy. Whoever had fired that torpedo would record the blast, spot the descending hulk, and maybe assume that the job had been done and move on. If they were tuning in on the faint motor, that was gone, with the obvious implication.

Don hoped the ruse worked. What would happen to *him* if the sub were blown up? He was attached to it, and even with the phase he doubted that he could survive that kind of shock. This whole business was his fault, too; the sub was trying to do him a favor, and had gotten into real trouble.

No other torpedo came. The sub kept dropping. The radio was

silent, and he didn't dare spin the wheel for fear that the motion or the sound of the radio would be picked up by the enemy. He hated to have Melanie worry, but stillness was necessary now.

Down, down. This was a deep-diver; it could handle the depths of the trench, as perhaps the attacking sub could not. Probably it would go all the way to the bottom and lie there until it seemed safe to resume. Hours later, or even days.

In which case Don's mission was doomed.

But there was a much more immediate and personal danger. His bike was firmly tied to the bottom rails. If the sub struck the ocean floor, the balloon fastenings would transmit its entire weight to the bike beneath, crushingly. Don himself could walk through the sub and escape, but what good would that be without his bike?

Feverishly Don tried to untie the knotted balloons. But they were under the stress of his own weight and that of the bicycle, and would not budge. Two loose balloons were in his hands, so that he could also hold on directly, but he could free those hands only by putting his full weight on the bike.

Then he had a second and worse realization: the sub was sinking at moderate speed, its fall restrained by the resistance of the water and its own calculated buoyancy. If he let go, he would fall at his own rate, as if through air, and smash to death below. He couldn't afford to desert the submarine!

He was trapped. His choice was between dooms: crushing or smashing. And he had no idea how soon. The murk blocked any sight of what was below.

He put his hand to the wheel to recharge the radio, so that he could tell Melanie. She might have a clearer head in this emergency, and figure out his best course. But the enemy sub might still be watching, with sonar or radar or whatever sophisticated devices it possessed, and his activity could still bring ruin. He had to remain silent, so that he wouldn't inadvertently endanger the friendly sub more than he already had.

Don knew he was on his own, for this crisis.

Then, as if his brain clicked into a new mode, he knew what to do. He took out his pencil and pried at the balloon anchoring the front of his bicycle to the rail. The graphite snapped off, but slowly he worked the taut knot loose, until it gave way and snapped free. The front wheel sagged, forcing him to support it by hand, with his other balloon-gloved hand clenched over the rail. Now he really appreciated the extreme lightness of the bike; it was no trouble to hold.

The second bike balloon was too much for him to untie this way, so he got out his penknife, hooked his elbow over the rail with balloon-padding, and hooked both feet into the chassis of the bike. Then, laboriously he cut the balloon. It parted with extreme reluctance, because of its half-phased condition, but finally the rear wheel also hung loose.

Now he carried the entire bicycle on his legs, hanging onto the rail with left hand and right elbow. But he could not rest. He let go with his left hand and brought it down to his mouth. He used his teeth to wrench off the glove. His small packet of maps was tucked inside that same balloon; he hoped they would be legible after taking this beating. He cupped both balloons under his elbow, his sole support, and got ready to tackle the last connection, his right hand still gloved. The sub might be drifting relatively slowly through water, but his own weight was excruciating, because his full weight was hanging by that one arm.

The ocean floor came into view. Don snapped at his right hand with his teeth. He bit painfully into his own fingers, cursing the awkwardness of his position, but the balloon refused to come.

There was no time! Don let go, dropped the last eight feet, hauled the bike up over his head as a kind of counterbalance to break his fall, and landed running.

The sub came down on top of him. Its substance could not touch him or the bike, but it caught his balloon-hand with a glancing blow and shoved it down irresistibly. Don was felled as if clubbed, but momentum carried him forward. He spun free of the bike and rolled.

In a moment the world settled. All was still.

Don took stock. He was lying under and within the resting sub, but his outstretched gloved hand lay just outside. He had made it.

He got up, pulled off the glove, dropped the balloons to the ground and walked back through the sub to carry out his bike. "Thanks for the lift," he told the crew. "I know you did the best you could, and risked your lives on my account. Now I'll do the best I can. So long." He felt a bit like a carefree hero, dismissing severe wounds with cheer.

But maybe the others saw him that way too. A couple of them waved back as he walked on.

Three balloons and the maps were lost, pinned somewhere under the sub. He picked up the fourth, rolled it into a tight ball, attached a length of string, and pocketed it. If he had any further trouble with the real world, he would dangle the balloon behind him. Better that than getting himself crushed or knocked around.

He checked his position. North latitude 20°30´; west longitude 73° even, approximately. Now he could have used the maps! But his recollection showed his position as north of Haiti and east of his projected route. The sub had gone far astray during its evasive action, not that he blamed it. The Chinese were lucky to have survived.

Now he had a doubt about his prior conjecture. Who had really fired that torpedo? An American submarine—or some other? He hoped American, because that would be less of a threat to him.

The depth was twenty two hundred fathoms, or about two and a half miles. He wished the sub hadn't sunk so far; he would be exhausted long before he made it to the shallows, but there was no choice.

Fortunately he had a fair notion of his route, even without the maps. All he had to do was follow the Puerto Rico trench west until it branched into the Old Bahama Channel, then bear north along the Santaren Channel until he reached the vicinity of Florida. Most of that would be between 250 and 450 fathoms—deep enough to keep well out of sight, shallow enough to keep him out of serious trouble with the terrain. He hoped. If he had to surmount a cliff, he would inflate the balloon. It would take a long time to fill it full enough, and he hoped it wouldn't burst, but it was better than nothing.

Time, time! That was his constant enemy, now. The sub had helped him on his way, but not enough. His easy interception of Pacifa had become chancy.

He rode on. He was learning to respect this bicycle. The narrow seat had grown uncomfortable for sitting upright during the sub ride, but for serious pedaling it was superior, because it did not interfere with his thighs the way a broad seat would have. He was making better time with less effort than normal. There was a gear ratio to accommodate his slightest whim, and this did save

him energy. And it was a much lighter machine; even fully loaded, it moved along more readily than his old one ever had. No
wonder Eleph had kept up so well, even after his injury.

Where could Eleph have gotten it? Not from a regular shop!
Perhaps not from Earth at all. From another alternate?

Was he riding a machine from another universe?

That intrigued Don deviously. His mind seemed to be racing
right along with his pedals, and he moved at quite respectable velocity. What would it be like to visit an alternate world?

"Don."

He jumped. His radio had recharged, and Melanie was paging
him. How could he have forgotten her?

"Here, Mel. Sorry I damped out. Someone fired a torpedo at
the sub, and it had to drop and play dead. I lost the maps, but I'm
on my way now. It'll be close, but I think I can still intercept Pacifa."

"Oh, Don, I'm so relieved! I was afraid—"

"So was I, for some moments there. But I squeaked through.
It's wonderful to have your company!"

"I'll stay with you all the way. Maybe I can help you by checking our maps, if you get lost."

"That will be nice."

Then he saw light. How could that be, this deep? Was it a
beam from a sub, and if so, which one?

Then he saw it more clearly. "Glowcloud!" he cried.

But it was not Glowcloud. It was a monster, so large that he
could see only a small section of any given tentacle at one time in
the haze of water. The thing had to be a hundred feet long!

"Are you sure?" Melanie asked. "You're a long way from
here."

Don snapped off his headlamp and swerved aside, hoping the
squid had not noticed him. Glowcloud he knew and could get
along with, he was even company of a sort. "You're right; it's another squid, a huge one. I'm steering clear."

But the giant mollusk's curiosity had been aroused. It changed
colors in rapid sequence and put forth the great tentacles to investigate. Don could see them because they glowed in the gloom. He
pedaled desperately, trying to avoid their snakelike approach. If
one snagged on the balloon—

The bicycle dropped into a hole, and Don took a spill as he

came to a stop. His arms bashed into rock, and he pulled up his legs to disengage them from the bicycle. He pushed off, as he had from the dropping sub—and plummeted into the blackness, finding no ground.

He flung out his arms, catching hold of a smooth rim of rock, breaking his fall. But the slope was convex, providing no purchase, and his hands slid down. He dropped upright into an aperture like a well.

He landed hard. It had felt like a drop of ten feet, his hands scraping all the way, and his right foot had twisted as he landed. Now the pain was starting. He was in real trouble.

Actually, the squid had been no threat. He should not have reacted so precipitously. Had the balloon snagged on a tentacle, it might have alarmed the squid as much as Don. Now, through his folly of riding blind, he had gotten himself into a hole, literally.

He tried to climb out, but the sides were almost slick. He felt the breeze of flowing water; this was another small freshwater spring, and the constant current had worn off all the rough edges, reaming out the vertical tunnel. Below him, by the feel, it curved and continued on down. No escape that way!

"Don! What's happening?" Melanie called from above.

Don looked up to see the faint glow of the passing squid, obscured by something over the hole. The bicycle! It must have straddled the aperture—about six feet out of reach. The rope was on it, looped and securely fastened. He could not haul himself up.

"I'm in a hole!" he called back. "I can't reach the bike. The radio will fade out in a moment."

"Oh, Don!" she cried despairingly. Her voice was already fading.

A tentacle reached down, searching for him. Don ducked away, avoiding it—and ran out of breath. He was standing at the fringe of the oxygenation field, and had to count himself lucky that the straight section of the hole had been no deeper. He could have suffocated immediately.

He swept his hand through the groping tentacle. "It's your fault, sucker!" he said angrily.

He tried to climb again, this time bracing his feet against the opposite wall. Pain flared in his right ankle, forcing him to desist. That injury was worse than he had thought.

The balloon tugged at its string, borne upward by the current.

Of course! he could blow up the balloon and let it haul him up out of here. It would take time, but it was sure. And if the squid annoyed him thereafter, he could let the balloon go as a decoy, leading the monster in a futile chase upward.

He hauled the package in and opened it. He exhaled with vigor, inflating the balloon. Of course there was no real lift yet, as his breath was mere water in the real world. He had to wait for the carbon dioxide to phase through.

Gradually the balloon shrank—but no bubble formed. He gave it another lungful, and another. Still nothing. The gas was going somewhere, but not into the balloon of the other phase. Was there a leak?

But he should be able to feel little bubbles escaping, in that case. There were none. What was wrong?

"I'm a fool!" he exclaimed as another tentacle felt through him. "Carbon dioxide is compressible! At this pressure, it must liquefy!"

His emergency lifting balloon was useless in deep water. He couldn't even use it as a decoy.

Don swept his hand through the tentacle again, furiously. This time the member withdrew.

Then the weight of despair bore down on him. Don sank down—but gasped for air and had to stand again, his ankle hurting. He couldn't even give up gracefully!

The squid was gone and his radio was dead and he was alone. He felt dizzy; the steady current was washing his oxygen up and away, even as that current renewed the supply.

It wasn't only his mission that was drifting away while he languished here; it was his own life. He had no food or water on him. It was on the bicycle. In time he would grow too tired or sleepy to stand, and then he would suffocate. unless he chose to end it sooner by diving down into the airless lower tunnel.

He thought of Melanie. They had been on the verge of such joy, having discovered each other. Now their love would be lost, along with the world. Damn!

And the story of the Minoan ship—would that be told, now? Splendid knew it, but Pacifa's report might get the mer-colony wiped out too. Everything he cared about—and he did care about Splendid and her people—was doomed. Somehow these things seemed almost worse than the destruction of the world, because they were more immediate.

He woke, and realized after the fact that he could sleep standing up. But his ankle was swollen and hurting, and he was increasingly thirsty.

What was one ankle, compared to life? All he had to do was grit his teeth and brake against that wall and shove himself up and out.

He tried it. Pain overwhelmed him, and he fell hard. He gasped again for oxygen, struggling upright on one foot.

He could not do it. Perhaps eventually he would have what it took. Eleph certainly did. The kind of physical determination that took no note of pain or frailty. Don admired it enormously, but he was made of different and inferior stuff. He could not just walk into that amount of agony, though his world hung in the balance. He would pass out from the pain first, and be lost. And with him, the world. When the meteor came, and the world was not ready.

Build not on the flank of the bull . . .

Good advice! But add this to it: trust not in a weakling, lest he fall in a hole and not climb out.

Eleph had done everything he could. He had phased through to this world with his limited equipment, and set up the mission and almost made it work. But for the bad break of Gaspar's suspicion, he would have persuaded them, and they would be on the way to saving the world. Now he depended on Don, and Don was failing him.

For that matter, the Minoan scholar Pi-ja-se-me had done everything he could, and also failed because of the inadequacy of others. So at last he had resigned himself to his fate and left his message for the future.

If only he could get out of this hole and ride to intercept Pacifa! Yet at this stage, even that was a lost hope. He had lost hours here, and it had already been a close thing; he was probably already too late. Even if not, how could he ride well, with his right ankle unable to sustain any significant weight? And if he could ride, by maybe fixing some kind of splint to brace his ankle and staying on a level route—how could he find that route, without his maps?

Well, maybe he had a map, in the form of his depth meter. The thousand fathom contour was a reasonably straight line passing north of the entire Greater Antilles chain, only recurving well up the channel. He could cut due south to intercept it, then stay right on it, and his route would be level all the way, by definition. Any mindless lout could follow that route, ankle or no.

Maybe it wasn't lost quite yet. Pacifa, expecting no pursuit, might not be rushing; she didn't want to blunder carelessly into any holes either. So he might yet catch her at his slower pace. Certainly it was worth trying. If she turned on her radio to check with Gaspar, he might tell her to wait for Don. So it remained possible to save the world, barely. Except for one thing.

Don Kestle, genius world saver, who couldn't lift his posterior from a hole in the ground to save his life, let alone the world.

He drifted into a daze. Insufficient oxygen, or maybe nitrogen narcosis, because it was almost pleasant. He really didn't know anything about either condition. This was what it felt like to die.

"So it has come to this at last for you too," Pi-ja-se-me said.

Don was not surprised to find the Cretan scholar with him, or to hear him speaking intelligibly. "Yes. But I am neither as bold nor resourceful as you. I simply fell in a hole."

"We all fall, eventually. Are you hallucinating? I did, at the end."

"I must be. But I can think of no person I would rather meet in a hallucination than you."

"Thank you, Don-kes-tle. Have you prayed to your God?"

"No. I don't believe in that sort of miracle. If I can't figure out how to save myself, then maybe I deserve to die."

"I agree. The Gods care nothing for our convenience. But is there a way to save yourself?"

"Well, if the sides of this hole weren't so smooth, I could climb out. Or if I had something to stand on, so I could reach or jump to catch hold of my bike. Or if someone found me, and let down a rope I could use. It is really a simple thing, getting out."

"That glove you used to handle the mermaid—could that help?"

Don brought out the balloon. "If I had something to grab with it, yes. But I don't." He jammed it back into his pocket.

"I am sorry, my friend. I would help you if I could, but words are all I have."

"I would help you too, Pi-ja, if I could. Let me shake your hand."

The man looked confused. "Do what?"

"It is a simple clasping of right hands. By this we signal our appreciation of each other, and our agreement."

Pi-ja nodded. He extended his hand. Don took it.

Then Don thought of something else. "There were female things by your tablets, jewelry, but you mentioned no woman on the ship."

"Of course. They were mementos of my lovely concubine. She had her odd ways, and was jealous, but I loved her, and I kept the things she gave me always close. They were a comfort in my time alone."

Such an obvious explanation! Why hadn't he thought of it himself?

He was awakened again by a tentacle passing through his face. He had lost another two hours, according to the glowing hands of his watch. Not that it mattered, since he couldn't go anywhere anyway. Old long-arms was back again, making a second round investigation after several hours. Damned mollusk curiosity!

The tip of the tentacle hung up momentarily on the useless balloon wadded into Don's pocket.

Don-kes! The glove!

Don snatched the limp rubber out and cupped it in the palm of his hand. Then he clapped that hand to the dangling tentacle, squeezing tightly. He put his other hand over the first, locking it in place.

The squid felt it. The giant limb yanked up—and Don hung on, coming up with it.

His head cracked into the bicycle. Involuntarily he let go—and grabbed the crossbar of the bike. His feet dropped, but he had hold of what he needed.

He saw the startled squid jetting high and away, flashing colors. "Get lost, monster!" he called after it. "Thanks for the lift!"

He heaved up his feet, getting them onto the bike. He fought his way to the side, crawling to land. Then he pulled the bike after him.

He mounted it and pushed off. His right foot hurt, but he could pedal with his left. Inertia kept him moving. So it was possible. But it would be better with a splint, so he could use both feet.

But you are free. Perhaps your concubine can help.

"Melanie," he said, as the radio recharged. "I'm out."

"Oh, Don! I was so worried! All this time with no word from you—"

"But my right ankle is hurt. I have to fix that before I can go on. I don't suppose Pacifa has opened radio contact?"

"No, nothing from her."

He came to a stop and dismounted. Pacifa would have been expert at this, but he was clumsy. How was a splint made? Or could he just somehow fasten something to his knee, to push at the pedal? He had to be quick about it, whatever it was.

There was another light. "Go away, squid," he said.

What is that? There was never a ship like that!

Then he realized that it wasn't squid glow. It was artificial light. A submarine!

Ah, now I have the concept from your mind. What a strange world you have, Don-kes-tle!

Had the Chinese sub come to take him the rest of the way? In that case, the mission had been saved.

But as the thing loomed closer, he saw the markings on its tower. It was American!

Ordinarily this would have been good news, but right now it was bad news. The Chinese sub understood his situation, but the American sub did not. It might think he was some kind of enemy agent. Better to let it pass without noticing him. It had no reason to suspect his presence here; it was only the luck of his fall into the hole that had prevented him from being far away.

Your friend may be your enemy?

"What's happening, Don?" Melanie asked.

A beam of light speared out from the sub, orienting on the sound. It must have heard his prior dialogue, and come to investigate; now it had him pinpointed. In a moment the light illuminated him, making him avert his gaze from its brilliance. Beyond, the sub settled slowly to the ground, and into it, as nearly as he could tell. The sea-floor here was evidently a bit lower than in the phase world, or mushier because of the sediment. He hadn't noticed, but since he automatically attuned to what was in the phase world, now, that wasn't surprising.

Pointless to try to hide, now. "American sub," he said. "Probably the one that fired the torpedo. It must be casting around for the other, to be sure it's dead."

"But they mustn't fight!" Melanie exclaimed.

"I'll try to talk to it." He waved into the blinding light. "Hi! My name is Don Kestle and I'm American!"

The light dropped to cover his feet. There was a metallic squawk. Then a bubble formed on the front deck and something poked out of it. Don couldn't make out any further detail because of the light.

Beware!

Something shot through the water at him. It was past him before he realized what it was: a harpoon. A spear with a line attached. This was evidently a duel-purpose sub, with torpedoes and fish-spearing equipment. It would normally be used to nab specimens for study: when the fired spear lodged, the line pulled it and the fish back.

"They're firing spears at me!" he told Melanie.

Either the sub wasn't equipped to receive and interpret his words, or it didn't believe him. It thought him a hallucination or strange creature, and it was going to spear him, pull him in, and examine him. That shoot-first mentality was in evidence again.

"What's the matter with them?" she demanded.

"I guess they don't understand men riding bicycles on the floor of the ocean."

He could not be hurt by the spears, but this wasn't helping him communicate. How could he get the sub to stop and listen, as the Chinese sub did?

You must surprise it.

Don threw himself to the side as a second harpoon was fired. He wasn't quite fast enough, and it passed through his shoulder.

"That does it!" he said. He picked up his bike, got on it, winced as his right foot hit the pedal, and started moving. He got up speed, then turned to charge the submarine. He rode right into it.

Then he was passing through its nether portion. Because it was sitting several feet lower than his phase surface, he was passing through its second level of compartments. In fact he seemed to be traversing the crew's quarters.

Amazing! Can you talk to them?

Maybe this was what he needed! He turned off his radio, so that there would not be confusion. "Hey, fellows!" he cried, stopping his bike and gesturing.

There were several crewmen there. Their eyes bugged as they saw him among them. "What the hell is this?" one burly sailor demanded, jumping off his bunk.

"I'm Don Kestle," Don said quickly. "I'm sort of like a—a hologram. You can't touch me. But I need your help."

"Get the Officer of the Day!" the man said over his shoulder. Then he came to lay his hand on Don's shoulder. It passed through. "You're a damned ghost!"

Then what am I?

"A hologram," Don repeated. "I'm not really here. But listen to me! I need a lift to Florida, or—" But he knew it would be no good trying to tell them about the end of the world. He got off the bike, waiting.

In what must have been record time, an officer appeared. "It's the same manifestation that was outside!" he exclaimed.

This is the man you want. Address him forthrightly. Show no doubt, Don-kes-tle. Take the initiative.

"I hailed you and you fired harpoons at me!" Don retorted angrily. "What kind of trigger-happy idiots are you? Now listen to me: I have a vital mission. I must get to Florida immediately. You can help me."

The officer looked as if he wanted to freak out, but could not afford to do so in front of the men. "Identify yourself!" he snapped.

"I'm Don Kestle, archaeologist. I—"

"Prove it."

He is recovering the initiative. Do not let him!

Don realized that he could hardly expect to be taken on faith. Any papers he had might be forged, and they couldn't be handled by the officer anyway. But he had a bright idea.

He dived into his pack and pulled out his notepad and pen. "Photograph this and fax it to the American Archaeological Association," he said, quickly printing out the equivalent of a sentence in Minoan Linear A. It incorporated some of the new signs whose meaning he had had to glean from the context. "Tell them to contact Dr. Evans Green immediately. He's the leading contemporary Minoan scholar. This is a matter of life and death."

The officer looked as if he would have preferred to throw Don in the brig. But he elected to play it cool. "Camera," he snapped.

Got him.

By the time they had the camera set up, Don had written enough of a message in Linear A to make any competent Minoan scholar's jaw drop. If such a scholar was reached in time. If he believed. It was a gamble, but the best he could think of at the moment.

They photographed the pages of the notepad. Then they waited while the picture was sent to Naval headquarters, and that office attempted to contact the archaeological association. If this failed, Don knew that he would have no chance to intercept Pacifa; he had lost too much time, and still couldn't move well with his injured ankle. The fate of the world really did lie in the balance.

But the officer was concerned with something more immediate. "What is your connection to the Chinese submarine?"

Trouble! Should he tell, or refuse? The one could result in torpedoes in the mer-colony; the other torpedoing his mission.

Demur. He can not make you say what you do not wish.

"I am not free to say."

The officer frowned. But since it was evident that Don could depart the same way he had come—through the hull—he did not push the matter.

Suddenly the word came back: "Can you contact Gaspar Brown?" the officer asked, after reading the message.

Who was a government agent! "Yes!" They had checked far enough to verify that they had a man on the job.

Don turned on the radio; there would power enough for a few sentences. "Melanie, I'm in the sub. Is Gaspar there?"

"Here," Gaspar's voice came back immediately.

"Talk to the man here." Then Don lifted his bicycle and spun the wheel by hand, so as to keep the radio going.

Gaspar's identification was evidently good, because soon the officer turned his attention back to Don. "We will take you back to your base near Jamaica."

"But I have to go to Florida!" Don protested.

"No. That has been taken care of."

Then Don realized that he had missed the obvious. The moment Gaspar had gotten in touch, Pacifa's message had become inoperative. Whatever Gaspar had decided, the government was acting on.

You have won the day, Don-kes-tle.

But Don wasn't clear what Gaspar had decided. The dialogue had not gone that far.

● ● ●

They let Don tie onto the sub with his remaining balloon. It was a precarious perch, but it held, and in due course he was back with Gaspar, Eleph, and Melanie.

"Oh, Don!" Melanie cried, hugging him. "You got through!"

Your concubine is lovely.

"Yes, in a way. But what did Gaspar—?"

"Eleph kept talking to him, and now he's satisfied that this needs a formal investigation. We will all have to testify, but I think they are going to take Eleph seriously."

"So his mission to save Earth is a success," Don said, starting to be relieved.

"It probably is. And the mer-colony is safe. We're going to need that adaptation technique to get our own people to Jupiter. We'll be cooperating with China."

"I'm glad."

"In fact, it looks as if we've done about as much as we can, here," she continued. "After we testify, we'll be free to go."

"To go?"

"On our honeymoon. Where would you most like to visit?"

Remember our agreement, Don-kes-tle. We squeezed hands, and I helped you as I was able.

Don laughed. "To Minoan Crete!"

"That's what I thought. Eleph says it's possible, if we join the mission."

"The mission?"

"To save other planets. Now that we're melded. A close-knit group. Pacifa's part of it. She didn't like having to blow the whistle on Eleph; she likes him, and she loves exploring. So we know she'll be with us. We were supposed to convince each other that the threat to our world was real, and go as a unit to convince the authorities. That was Eleph's notion, and maybe it seems far-fetched, but they're going to try it on other worlds now. Eleph has talked with the proxies on his radio. But Gaspar is shortcutting that, so we won't need to spend much time here. There are a lot of worlds still in doubt, and more knowledgeable folk are needed to phase into them and convince them of the danger. Gaspar has decided to go, and I want to, if you—"

"Yes!" The thrill of the notion was second only to that of his rapport with Melanie. "But what's this about—"

"The worlds are separated in time as well as phase, but their cultures are similar. The languages. So there are futuristic ones, and ancient ones, and there is one where the Minoans—where your fabulous underwater city is above water and thriving—it's a lot like what your tablets described—"

And I am there, my friend. The culture of those who are now saving worlds derives from mine, and from that of Atlantis. From a world where the ships were not lost, and the broader empire was restored, and grew to dominate nature in much the way I see yours has. Those people never forgot to be wary of the Bull! Help me as you are able. I desperately want to return to my concubine.

Don intended to. He hoped he wasn't merely suffering from a lingering hallucination. But it was too much to assimilate all at once. So he cut it short. He kissed Melanie.

She was ardent. Then she drew back, as if uncertain whether to laugh or snap. "Concubine?"

Author's Note

I wrote this novel in 1971 and couldn't sell it. It was one of eight unsold novels I had at one time, and the only one that I concluded was actually not good enough to sell. One publisher did make an offer on it, but when I commented on the inadequacies of that publisher's standard contract the offer abruptly turned out to be an error in communication and the novel was returned. This is the way publishers treat writers, and one reason why that publisher does not publish Anthony today, though it would like to; writers, too, remember. Another editor, rejecting this and my collaboration with a Cuban, *Dead Morn*, inquired snidely of my agent whether I had a hang-up about Cuba. Editors don't strike me as the most enlightened type. But of course if they had the talent to write salable novels, they'd be doing it instead of editing.

All the other seven Unsolds eventually found publishers. Editors claim that they reject only what is not good enough to publish, but the other seven were taken essentially unchanged. What changed was my reputation, as I became famous for light fantasy. But I didn't even try to remarket *Mer-Cycle*, because I wasn't satisfied with it. It just didn't seem to come properly alive.

So when I got time in edgewise, I did a full revision of the novel, revamping both the characters and the plot. In the process I added 25,000 words. So though this started as an old novel, it's a new one now. My agent placed it, and here it is for you, twenty years later. I hope you enjoyed it.

I did have some credits to give for help on this novel, in 1971. I am long out of touch with those folk, but their contributions remain real, so I shall credit them here and hope that they happen to see it. One is Phyrne (I love that spelling!) Bacon who is responsible for much of the way Melanie thinks. Another is Harry

M. Piper, who has done underwater exploration. He had been written up in a newspaper article, and I got in touch and asked for his advice, and he gave it, making my water scenes more authentic than they would have been. Another is Joanne Burger, who helped with advice on the technical end: density of water at different depths, chemistry, and such.

You may be wondering just what changes I made in the original novel. Well, Melanie was then named Melody, but I had subsequently used that name in *Chaining the Lady*, so had to modify it. She never appeared physically in the novel; she was a radio contact only. The story developed slowly, then suddenly everything broke loose with so many complications that it was difficult to follow. So this time I added heavy foreshadowing, in the form of Eleph's reports to his frame supervisor, so that that element did not seem to come from nowhere. And I simplified the ending, trying to give it more clarity and force. Some things I wasn't sure about, so I let them be, such as the reference to the Yuchi Indians. I was later to do a whole lot more research on American Indians, when writing *Tatham Mound*, but did not verify any strange origin for this tribe. But who knows? I must have had a reference, when I first wrote this novel. It was as if I were collaborating with a promising writer who couldn't quite get it all together; I saw what was necessary and did it. It's the first time I've collaborated with myself, and it was about as difficult as collaborating with another writer. Which is to say, not too bad, when I have the last word.